THE FLASHMAN PAPERS
(in chronological order)

*

Also by George MacDonald Fraser

Mr American
The Pyrates
The Candlemass Road

*

SHORT STORIES

The General Danced at Dawn
McAuslan in the Rough
The Sheikh and the Dustbin

HISTORY

The Steel Bonnets:
*The Story of the Anglo-Scottish
Border Reivers*

*

AUTOBIOGRAPHY

Quartered Safe out Here

*

The Hollywood History of the World

Flashman
& *the* Angel
of the Lord

Flashman
& *the* Angel
of the Lord

from The Flashman Papers, 1858–59

EDITED AND ARRANGED BY

George MacDonald Fraser

Alfred A. Knopf   New York   1995

Maps drawn by Leslie Robinson, with
illustrations by Ken Lewis.

Library of Congress Cataloging-in-Publication Data
Fraser, George MacDonald.
Flashman & the angel of the lord: from the Flashman
papers, 1858–59 / edited and arranged by
George MacDonald Fraser. — 1st ed.
p. cm.
"Originally published in Great Britain by
Harvill, London, in 1994"—T.p. verso.
ISBN 0-679-44172-7
1. Harpers Ferry (W. Va.)—History—John Brown's
Raid, 1859—Fiction. 2. Flashman, Harry Paget (Ficti-
tious character)—Fiction. 3. Brown, John, 1800–
1859—Fiction. I. Title. II. Title: Flashman and
the angel of the lord.
PR6056.R287F58   1995
823'.914—dc20   94-47219
CIP

Manufactured in the United States of America
FIRST AMERICAN EDITION

For Kath,
ten times over

Explanatory Note

Of all the roles played by Sir Harry Flashman, V.C., in the course of his distinguished and deplorable career, that of crusader must seem the least likely. The nine volumes of his Papers which have been presented to the public since their discovery in a Midlands saleroom in 1966, make a scandalous catalogue in which there is little trace of decent feeling, let alone altruism. From the day of his expulsion from Rugby School in the late 1830s (memorably described in *Tom Brown's Schooldays*), Flashman the man fulfilled the disgraceful promise of Flashman the boy; the toadying bounder and bully matured into the cowardly profligate and scoundrel who, by chance and shameless opportunism, became one of the most renowned heroes of the Victorian age, unwilling leader of the Light Brigade, fleeing survivor of Afghanistan and Little Big Horn, tarnished paladin of Crimea and the Mutiny, and cringing chronicler of many another conflict, disaster, and intrigue in which he bore an inglorious but seldom unprofitable part.

So it is with initial disbelief that one finds him, in this tenth volume of his memoirs, not only involved but taking a lead in an enterprise which, if hopeless and misguided, still shines with the lustre of heroic self-sacrifice and occupies an honoured niche in the pantheon of freedom. John Brown's raid on Harper's Ferry was a dreadful folly which ended in bloody and inevitable failure and helped to bring on the most catastrophic of all civil wars, yet its aim was a great and worthy one; the road to hell was never paved with nobler intentions. Needless to say, they were not Flashman's. He came to Harper's Ferry with the utmost reluctance, through the malice of old enemies and the delusions of old friends, and behaved with characteristic perfidy in

6

every way but one: his eye for events and people was as clear and scrupulous as ever, and it may be that his narrative casts a new and unexpected light on a critical moment in American history, and on notable figures of the ante-bellum years – among them the President Who Never Was, a legendary detective and secret agent, and the strange, terrible, simple visionary, known to the world only by a name and a song, who set out to destroy slavery with twenty men and forty rounds apiece.

It is an amazing story, even for Flashman, but my confidence in that honesty which he brought to his writing (if to nothing else) seems to be justified by the exactness with which his account fits the known facts. As with previous packets of the Papers, I have observed the wishes of their custodian, Mr Paget Morrison, and confined myself to amending the author's spelling and providing footnotes and appendices.

G.M.F.

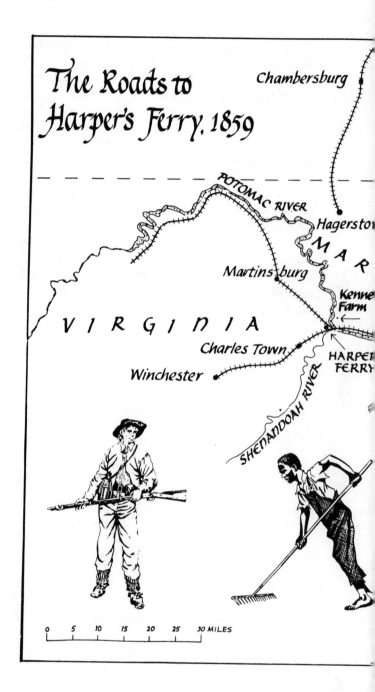

The Roads to Harper's Ferry, 1859

Chambersburg

POTOMAC RIVER

Hagersto

MAR

Martinsburg

VIRGINIA

Charles Town

Winchester

Kenne Farm

HARPE FERR

SHENANDOAH RIVER

0   5   10   15   20   25   30 MILES

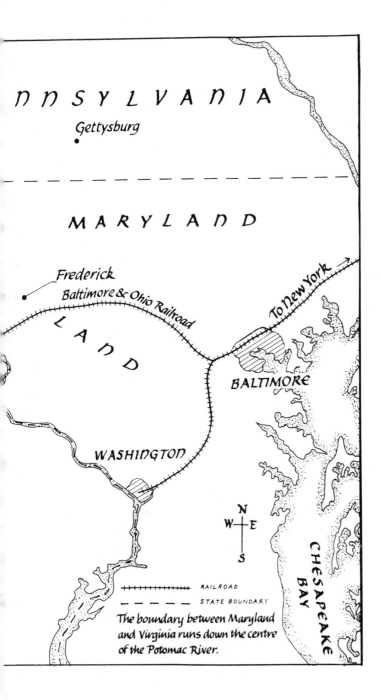

nnSYLVANIA

Gettysburg

MARYLAND

Frederick

Baltimore & Ohio Railroad

To New York →

LAND

BALTIMORE

WASHINGTON

N
W—E
S

++++++++++ RAILROAD

— — — — — STATE BOUNDARY

The boundary between Maryland
and Virginia runs down the centre
of the Potomac River.

CHESAPEAKE BAY

Flashman
& *the* Angel
of the Lord

As I sat by the lake at Gandamack t'other day, sipping my late afternoon brandy in the sun, damning the great-grandchildren for pestering the ducks, and reflecting on the wigging I'd get from Elspeth when I took them in to tea covered in dirt and toffee, there was a brass band playing on a gramophone up at the house, a distant drowsy thumping that drifted down the lawn and under the trees. I guess I must have hummed along or waved my flask to the old familiar march, for presently the villain Augustus (a frightful handle to fix on a decent enough urchin, but no work of mine) detached himself from the waterweed and came to stand snottering before me with his head on one side, thoughtful-like.

"I say, Great-gran'papa," says he, "that's Gory Halooyah."

"So it is, young gallows," says I, "and Gory Halooyah is what you'll catch when Great-grandmama sees the state of you. Where the devil's your other shoe?"

"Sunk," says he, and gave tongue: "'Jombrown's body lies a-moulderin' inna grave, Jombrown's body lies –'"

"Oh! Gweat-gwampapa said a wicked word!" squeals virtuous Jemima, a true Flashman, as beautiful as she is obnoxious. "I heard him! He said 'd—l'!" She pronounced it "d'l". "Gweat-gwanmama says people who say such fings go to the bad fire!" Bad fire, indeed – my genteel Elspeth has never forgotten the more nauseating euphemisms of her native Paisley.

"He shan't, so there!" cries my loyal little Alice, another twig off the old tree, being both flirt and toady. She jumped on the bench and clung to my arm. "'Cos I shan't let him

11

go to bad fires, shall I, Great-grampapa?" Yearning at me with those great forget-me-not eyes, four years old and innocent as Cleopatra.

"'Fraid you won't have a vote on the matter, m'dear."

"'Devil' ain't a bad word, anyway," says John, rising seven and leader of the pack. "The Dean said it in his sermon last Sunday – devil! He said it twice – devil!" he repeated, with satisfaction. "So bad scran to you, Jemima!" Hear, hear. Stout lad, John.

"That was in church!" retorts Jemima, who has the makings of a fine sea-lawyer, bar her habit of sticking out her tongue. "It's all wight in church, but if you say it outside it's vewwy dweadful, an' God will punish you!" Little Baptist.

"What's moulderin' mean, Great-gran'papa?" asks Augustus.

"All rotten an' stinkin'," says John. "It's what happens when you get buried. You go all squelchy, an' the worms eat you –"

"Eeesh!" Words cannot describe the ecstasy of Alice's exclamation. "Was Jombrown like that, Great-grampapa, all rottish –"

"Not as I recall, no. His toes stuck out of the ends of his boots sometimes, though."

This produced hysterics of mirth, as I'd known it would, except in John, who's a serious infant, given to searching cross-examination.

"I say! Did you know him, Great-grandpapa – John Brown in the song?"

"Why, yes, John, I knew him . . . long time ago, though. Who told you about him?"

"Miss Prentice, in Sunday School," says he, idly striking his cousin, who was trying to detach Alice from me by biting her leg. "She says he was the Angel of the Lord who got hung for freeing all the niggers in America."

"You oughtn't to say 'niggers'." Jemima again, absolutely, removing her teeth from Alice and climbing across to possess my other arm. "It's not nice. You should say 'negwoes', shouldn't you, Gweat-gwampapa? I *always* say 'negwoes'," she added, oozing piety.

12

"What should you call them, Great-grandpapa?" asks John.

"Call 'em what you like, my son. It's nothing to what they'll call you."

"I *always* say 'negwoes' –"

"Great-gran'papa says 'niggers'," observes confounded Augustus. "Lots an' lots of times." He pointed a filthy accusing finger. "You said that dam' nigger, Jonkins, the boxer-man –"

"Johnson, child, Jack Johnson."

"– you said he wanted takin' down a peg or two."

"Did I, though? Yes, Jemima dearest, I know Gus has said another wicked word, but ladies shouldn't notice, you know –"

"What's a peggatoo?" asks Alice, twining my whiskers.

"A measure of diminution of self-esteem, precious . . . yes, Jemima, I've no doubt you're going to peach to Great-grandmama about Gus saying 'damn', but if you do you'll be saying it yourself, mind . . . What, Gus? Yes, very well, if I said that about the boxer-man, you may be sure I meant it. But you know, old fellow, when you call people names, it depends who you're talking about . . ." It does, too. Flash coons like Johnson[1] and the riff-raff of the levees and most of our Aryan brethren are one thing – but if you've seen Ketshwayo's Nokenke regiment stamping up the dust and the assegais drumming on the ox-hide shields, " 'Suthu, 'suthu! 's-jee, 's-jee!" as they sweep up the slope to Little Hand . . . well, that's black of a different colour, and you find another word for those fellows. And God forbid I should offend Miss Prentice, so . . .

"I think it best you should say 'negroes', children. That's the polite word, you see –"

"What about nigger minstrels?" asks Alice, excavating my collar.

"That's all right 'cos they're white underneath," says John impatiently. "Shut your potato-trap, Alice – I want to hear about John Brown, and how he freed all the . . . the negro slaves in America, didn't he, Great-grandpapa?"

"Well, now, John . . . no, not exactly . . ." And then I stopped, and took a pull at my flask, and thought about it.

13

After all, who am I to say he didn't? It was coming anyway, but if it hadn't been for old J.B. and his crack-brained dreams, who can tell how things might have panned out? Little nails hold the hinge of history, as Bismarck remarked (he would!) the night we set out for Tarlenheim . . . and didn't Lincoln himself say that Mrs Stowe was the little lady who started the great war, with *Uncle Tom's Cabin*? Well, Ossawatomie Brown, mad and murderous old horse-thief that he was, played just as big a part in setting the darkies free as she did – aye, or Lincoln or Garrison or any of them, I reckon. I did my bit myself – not willingly, you may be sure, and cursing Seward and Pinkerton every step of the way that ghastly night . . . and as I pondered it, staring across the lake to the big oak casting its first evening shadow, the shrill voices of the grandlings seemed to fade away, and in their place came the harsh yells and crash of gunshots in the dark, and instead of the scent of roses there was the reek of black powder smoke filling the engine-house, the militia's shots shattering timber and whining about our ears . . . young Oliver bleeding his life out on the straw . . . the gaunt scarecrow with his grizzled beard and burning eyes, thumbing back the hammer of his carbine . . . "Stand firm, men! Sell your lives dearly! Don't give in now!" . . . and Jeb Stuart's eyes on mine, willing me (I'll swear) to pull the trigger . . .

"Wake up, Great-grandpapa – do!" "Tell us about Jombrown!" "Yes, wiv his toes stickin' out, all stinky!" "Tell us, tell us. . . !"

I came back from the dark storm of Harper's Ferry to the peaceful sunshine of Leicestershire, and the four small faces regarding me with that affectionate impatience that is the crowning reward of great-grandfatherhood: John, handsome and grave and listening; Jemima a year younger, prim ivory perfection with her long raven hair and lashes designed for sweeping hearts (Selina's inevitable daughter); little golden Alice, Elspeth all over again; and the babe Augustus bursting with sin beneath the mud, a Border Ruffian in a sodden sailor suit . . . and the only pang is that at ninety-one[2] you can't hope to see 'em grown . . .

14

"John Brown, eh? Well, it's a long story, you know – and Great-grandmama will be calling us for tea presently . . . no, Alice, he didn't have wings, although Miss Prentice is quite right, they did call him the Angel of the Lord . . . and the Avenging Angel, too . . ."

"What's 'venging?"

"Getting your own back . . . no, John, he was quite an ordinary chap, really, rather thin and bony and shabby, with a straggly beard and very bright grey eyes that lit up when he was angry, ever so fierce and grim! But he was quite a kindly old gentleman, too –"

"Was he as old as you?"

"Heavens, child, no one's that old! He was old*ish*, but pretty spry and full of beans . . . let's see, what else? He was a capital cook, why, he could make ham and eggs, and brown fried potatoes to make your mouth water –"

"Did he make kedgewee? I hate howwid old kedgewee, ugh!"

"What about the slaves, and him killing lots of people, and getting hung?" John shook my knee in his impatience.

"Well, John, I suppose he did kill quite a few people . . . How, Gus? Why, with his pistols – he had two, just like the cowboys, and he could pull them in a twinkling, ever so quickly." And dam' near blew your Great-grandpapa's head off, one second asleep and the next blasting lead all over the shop, curse him. "And with his sword . . . although that was before I knew him. Mind you, he had another sword, in our last fight – and you'll never guess who it had once belonged to. Frederick the Great! What d'you think of that?"

"Who's Frederick the Great?"

"German king, John. Bit of a tick, I believe; used scent and played the flute."

"I think Jombrown was *howwid*!" announced Jemima. "Killing people is *wrong*!"

"Not always, dearest. Sometimes you have to, or they'll kill you."

"Great-gran'papa used to kill people, lots of times," protests sturdy Augustus. "Great-gran'mama told me,

15

when he was a soldier, weren't you? Choppin' 'em up, heaps of – "

"That's quite *diffewent*," says Jemima, with an approving smile which may well lead me to revise my will in her favour. "It's *pwoper* for soldiers to kill people." And pat on her words came an echo from half a century ago, the deep level voice of J.B. himself, recalling the slaughter of Pottawatomie . . . "They had a *right* to be killed." It was a warm afternoon, but I found myself shivering.

"Great-grandpapa's tired," whispers John. "Let's go in for tea."

"What – tired? Not a bit of it!" You can't have grandlings taking pity on you, even at ninety-one. "But tea, what? Capital idea! Who's for a bellyful of gingerbread, eh? Tell you what, pups – you make yourselves decent, straighten your hair, find Gus's other shoe, put your socks on, Alice – yes, Jemima, you look positively queenly – and we'll *march* up to tea, shall we? At least, you lot will, while I call the step and look after remounts. Won't that be jolly? And we'll sing his song as we go – "

"Jombrown's body? Gory Halooyah?"

"The very same, Gus! Now, then, fall in, tallest on the right, shortest on the left – heels together, John, eyes front, Jemima, pull in your guts, Augustus, stop giggling, Alice – and I'll teach you some capital verses you never heard before! Ready?"

I don't suppose there's a soul speaks English in the world who couldn't sing the chorus today, but of course it hadn't been written when we went down to Harper's Ferry – J.B.'s army of ragamuffins, adventurers, escaped slaves, rustlers and lunatics. "God's crusaders", some enthusiast called us – but then again, I've read that we were "swaggering, swearing bullies and infidels" (well, thank'ee, sir). We were twenty-one strong, fifteen white (one with pure terror, I can tell you), six black, and all set to conquer Dixie, if you please! We didn't make it at the time, quite – but we did in the end, by God, didn't we just, with Sherman's bugles blowing thirty miles in latitude three hundred to the main . . .

Not that I gave a two-cent dam for that, you understand,

16

and still don't. They could have kept their idiotic Civil War for me, for (my own skin's safety apart) it was the foulest, most useless conflict in history, the mass suicide of the flower of the British-American race – and for what? Black freedom, which would have come in a few years anyway, as sure as sunrise. And all those boys could have been sitting in the twilight, watching *their* Johns and Jemimas.

Still, I've got a soft spot for the old song – and for J.B., for that matter. Aye, that song which, the historian says, was sung by every Union regiment because "it dealt not with John Brown's feeble sword, but with his soul." His soul, my eye – as often as not the poor old maniac wasn't even mentioned, and it would be:

> Wild Bill Sherman's got a rope around his neck,
> An' we'll all catch hold an' give-it-one-hell-of-a-pull!
> Glory, glory, hallelujah, etc. . . . .

Or it might be "our sergeant-major", or Jeff Davis hanging from a sour apple tree, or any of the unprintable choruses that inspired the pious Mrs Howe to write "Mine eyes have seen the glory".[3] But all that's another story, for another day . . . in the meantime, I taught my small descendants some versions which were entirely to their liking, and we trooped up to the house, the infants in a column of twos and the venerable patriarch hobbling painfully behind, flask at the high port, and all waking the echoes with:

> John Brown's donkey's got an india-rubber tail,
> An' he rubbed it with camphorated oil!

followed by:

> Our Great-grandpa saved the Viceroy
> In the – good – old – Khyber – Pass!

and concluding with:

> Flashy had an army of a hundred Bashi-bazouks
> An' the whole dam' lot got shot!
> Glory, glory, hallelujah . . .

17

Spirited stuff, and it was just sheer bad luck that the Bishop and other visiting Pecksniffs should already be taking tea with Elspeth and Miss Prentice when we rolled in through the french windows, the damp and dirty grandlings in full voice and myself measuring my ancient length across the threshold, flask and all. Very well, the grandlings were raucous and dishevelled, and I ain't at my best sprawled supine on the carpet leaking brandy, but to judge from his lordship's disgusted aspect and Miss Prentice's frozen pince-nez you'd have thought I'd been teaching them to smoke opium and sing "One-eyed Riley".

The upshot was that the infants were packed off in disgrace to a defaulters' tea of dry bread and milk, Gus was sent to bed early – oh, aye, Jemima ratted on him – and when the guests had departed in an odour of sanctity, withdrawing the hems of their garments from me and making commiserating murmurs to Elspeth, she loosed her wrath on me for an Evil Influence, corrupting young innocence with my barrack-room ribaldry, letting them get their feet wet, and did I know what shoes cost nowadays, and she was Black Affronted, and how was she ever going to look the Bishop in the face again, would I tell her?

Contrition not being my style, and useless anyway, I let the storm blow itself out, and later, having ensured that La Prentice was snug in her lair – polishing her knout and supping gin on the sly, I daresay – I raided the pantry and smuggled gingerbread and lemonade to the grandlings' bedroom, where at their insistence I regaled them with the story of John Brown (suitably edited for tender ears). They fell asleep in the middle of it, and so did I, among the broken meats on John's coverlet, and woke at last to the touch of soft lips on my aged brow to find Elspeth shaking her head in fond despair.

Well, the old girl knows I'm past reforming now, and that Jemima's right: I'll certainly go to the bad fire. I know one who won't though, and that's old Ossawatomie John Brown, "that new saint, than whom nothing purer or more brave was ever led by love of men into conflict and death", and who made "the gallows glorious like the Cross". That's

18

Ralph Waldo Emerson on J.B. "A saint, noble, brave, trusting in God", "honest, truthful, conscientious", comparable with William Wallace, Washington, and William Tell – those are the words of Parker and Garrison, who knew him, and they ain't the half of his worshippers; talk about a mixture of Jesus, Apollo, Goliath and Julius Caesar! On the other hand . . . "a faker, shifty, crafty, vain, selfish, intolerant, brutal", "an unscrupulous soldier of fortune, a horse-thief, a hypocrite" who didn't care about freeing slaves and would have been happy to use slave labour himself, a liar, a criminal, and a murderer – that's his most recent biographer talking. Interesting chap, Brown, wouldn't you say?

A good deal of it's true, both sides, and you may take my word for it; scoundrel I may be, but I've no axe to grind about J.B.'s reputation. I helped to make it, though, by *not* shooting him in the back when I had the chance. Didn't want to, and wouldn't have had the nerve, anyway.

You might even say that I, all unwitting, launched him on the path to immortal glory. Aye, if there's a company of saints up yonder, they'll be dressing by the right on J.B., for when the Recording Angel has racked up all his crimes and lies and thefts and follies and deceits and cold-blooded killings, he'll still be saved when better men are damned. Why? 'Cos if he wasn't, there'd be such an almighty roar of indignation from the Heavenly Host it would bust the firmament; God would never live it down. That's the beauty of a martyr's crown, you see; it outshines everything, and they don't come any brighter than old J.B.'s. I'm not saying he deserves it; I only know, perhaps better than anyone, how he came by it.

You will wonder, if you're familiar with my inglorious record, how I came to take part with John Brown at all. Old Flashy, the bully and poltroon, cad and turncoat, lecher and toady – bearing Freedom's banner aloft in the noblest cause of all, the liberation of the enslaved and downtrodden? Striking off the shackles at the risk of death and dishonour? Gad, I wish Arnold could have seen me. That's the irony of it – if I'd bitten the dust at the Ferry, I'd have had a martyr's crown, too, on top of all the honours and glory I'd already won in Her Majesty's service (by turning tail and lying and posturing and pinching other chaps' credit, but nobody knew that, not even wily old Colin Campbell who'd pinned the V.C. on my coat only a few months before). Oh, the Ferry fiasco could have been my finest hour, with the Queen in mourning, Yankee politicos declaiming three-hour tributes full of ten-dollar words and Latin misquotations (not Lincoln, though; he knew me too well), a memorial service in the Rugby chapel, the Haymarket brothels closed in respect, old comrades looking stern and noble . . . "Can't believe he's gone . . . dear old Flash . . . height of his fame . . . glorious career before him . . . goes off to free the niggers . . . not for gold or guerdon . . . aye, so like him . . . quixotic, chivalrous, helpin' lame dogs . . . ah, one in ten thousand . . . I say, seen his widow, have you? Gad, look at 'em bounce! Rich as Croesus, too, they tell me . . ."

There'd have been no talk of roasted fags or expulsion for sottish behaviour, either. Die in a good cause and they'll forgive you anything.

But I didn't, thank God, and as any of you who have

20

read my other memoirs will have guessed, I'd not have been within three thousand miles of Harper's Ferry, or blasted Brown, but for the ghastliest series of mischances: three hellish coincidences – three, mark you! – that even Dickens wouldn't have used for fear of being hooted at in the street. But they happened, with that damned Nemesis logic that has haunted me all my life, and landed me in more horrors than I can count. Mustn't complain, though; I'm still here, cash in hand, the grandlings upstairs asleep, and Elspeth in her boudoir reading the Countess of Cardigan's *Recollections* (in which, little does my dear one suspect, I appear under the name of "Baldwin", and a wild night that was, but no mention, thank heaven, of the time I was locked in the frenzied embrace of Fanny Paget, Cardigan himself knocked on the door, I dived trouserless beneath the sofa, found a private detective already *in situ*, and had to lie beside the brute while Cardigan and Fanny galloped the night away two feet above our heads. Dammit, we were still there when her husband came home and blacked her eye. Serve her right; Cardigan, I ask you! Some women have no taste).

However, that's a far cry from the Shenandoah, but before I tell you about J.B. I must make one thing clear, for my own credit and good name's sake, and it's this: I care not one tuppenny hoot about slavery, and never did. I can't say it's none of my biznai, because it was once: in my time, I've raided blacks from the Dahomey Coast, shipped 'em across the Middle Passage, driven them on a plantation – and run them to freedom on the Underground Railroad and across the Ohio ice-floes with a bullet in my rump, to say nothing of abetting J.B.'s lunatic scheme of establishing a black republic – in Virginia, of all places. Set up an Orange Lodge in the Vatican, why don't you?

The point is that I was forced into all these things against my will – by gad, you could say I was "enslaved" into them. For that matter, I've *been* a slave in earnest – at least, they put me up for sale in Madagascar, and 'twasn't my fault nobody bid; Queen Ranavalona got me without paying a penny, and piling into that lust-maddened monster *was* slavery, if you like, with the prospect of being flayed alive

21

if I failed to give satisfaction.* I've been a fag at Rugby, too.

So when I say I don't mind about slavery, I mean I'm easy about the institution, so long as it don't affect *me*; whenever it did, I was agin it. Selfish, callous, and immoral, says you, and I agree; unprincipled, too – unlike the Holy Joe abolitionist who used to beat his breast about his black brother while drawing his dividend from the mill that was killing his white sister – aye, and in such squalor as no Dixie planter would have tolerated for *his* slaves. (Don't mistake me; I hold no rank in the Salvation Army, and I've never lifted a finger for our working poor except to flip 'em a tip, and employ them as necessary. I just know there's more than one kind of slavery.)

Anyway, if life has taught me anything, it's that the wealth and comfort of the fortunate few (who include our contented middle classes as well as the nobility) will always depend on the sweat and poverty of the unfortunate many, whether they're toiling on plantations or licking labels in sweatshops at a penny a thousand. It's the way of the world, and until Utopia comes, which it shows no sign of doing, thank God, I'll just rub along with the few, minding my own business.

So you understand, I hope, that they could have kept every nigger in Dixie in bondage for all I cared – or freed them. I was indifferent, spiritually, and only wish I could have been so, corporally. And before you start thundering at me from your pulpit, just remember the chap who said that if the union of the United States could only be preserved by maintaining slavery, that was all right with him. What's his name again? Ah, yes – Abraham Lincoln.

And now for old John Brown and the Path to Glory, not the worst of my many adventures, but just about the unlikeliest. It had no right to happen, truly, or so it strikes me when I look back. God knows I haven't led a tranquil life, but in review there seems to have been some form and order to it – Afghanistan, Borneo, Madagascar, Punjab, Germany, Slave Coast and Mississippi, Russia and the back o' beyond, India in the Mutiny, China, American war,

* See *Flashman's Lady*.

Mexico . . . and there, you see, I've missed out J.B. altogether, because he don't fit the pattern, somehow. He's there, though, whiskers, six-guns, texts, and all, between India and China – and nought to do with either, right out o' the mainstream, as though some malevolent djinn had plucked me from my course, dipped me into Harper's Ferry, and then whisked me back to the Army again.

It began (it usually does) with a wanton nymph in Calcutta at the back-end of '58. But for her, it would never have happened. Plunkett, her name was, the sporty young wife of an elderly pantaloon who was a High Court judge or something of that order. I was homeward bound from the Mutiny, into which I'd been thrust by the evil offices of my Lord Palmerston, who'd despatched me to India on secret work two years before;* thanks to dear old Pam, I'd been through the thick of that hellish rebellion, from the Meerut massacre to the battle of Gwalior, fleeing for my life from Thugs and pandies, spending months as a sowar of native cavalry, blazing away at the Cawnpore barricade, sneaking disguised out of Lucknow with a demented Irishman in tow, and coming within an ace of being eaten by crocodiles, torn asunder on the rack, and blown from a gun as a condemned mutineer – oh, aye, the diplomatic's the life for a lad of metal, I can tell you. True, there had been compensations in the delectable shape of Lakshmibai, Rani of Jhansi, and a Victoria Cross and knighthood at the end of the day, and the only fly in the ointment as I rolled down to Calcutta had been the discovery that during my absence from England some scribbling swine had published his reminiscences of Rugby School, with me as the villain of the piece. A vile volume entitled *Tom Brown's Schooldays*, on every page of which the disgusting Flashy was to be found torturing fags, shirking, toadying, lying, whining for mercy, and boozing himself to disgraceful expulsion – every word of it true, and all the worse for that.

It was with relief that I learned, by eavesdropping in Calcutta's messes and hotels, that no one seemed to have

---

* See *Flashman in the Great Game.*

heard of the damned book, or weren't letting on if they had. It's been the same ever since, I'm happy to say; not a word of reproach or a covert snigger, even, although the thing must have been read in every corner of the civilised world by now. Why, when President Grant discovered that I was the Flashman of *Tom Brown* he just looked baffled and had another drink.

The fact is, some truths don't matter. I've been seventy years an admired hero, the Hector of Afghanistan, the chap who led the Light Brigade, daredevil survivor of countless stricken fields, honoured by Queen and Country, V.C. and Medal of Honour – folk simply don't want to know that such a paladin was a rotter and bully in childhood, and if he was, they don't care. They put it from their minds, never suspecting that boy and man are one, and that all my fame and glory has been earned by accident, false pretence, cowardice, doing the dirty, and blind luck. Only I know that. So my shining reputation's safe, which is how the public want it, bless 'em.

It's always been the same. Suppose some learned scholar were to discover a Fifth Gospel which proved beyond doubt that Our Lord survived the Cross and became a bandit or a slave-trader, or a politician, even – d'you think it would disturb the Christian faith one little bit? Of course not; 'twouldn't even be denied, likely, just ignored. Hang it, I've seen the evidence, in black and white in our secret files, that Benjamin Franklin was a British spy right through the American Revolution, selling out the patriots for all he was worth – but would any Yankee believe that, if 'twas published? Never, because it's not what they *want* to believe.[4]

I reached Calcutta, then, to find myself feted on all sides – and there was no shortage of heroes to be worshipped after the Mutiny, you may be sure. But no other had the V.C. *and* a knighthood (for word of the latter had leaked out, thanks to Billy Russell, I daresay), or stood six feet two with black whiskers and Handsome Harry's style. I'd had my fill of fame in the past, of course, and was all for it, but I knew how to carry it off, modest and manly, not too bluff, and with a pinch of salt.

I'd supposed it would be straight aboard and hey for Merry England, but I was wrong. P. and O. hadn't a berth for months, for the furloughs had started, and every civilian in India seemed to be leaving for home, to say nothing of ten thousand troops to be shipped out; John Company was hauling down his flag at last, India was passing under the rule of the Crown, everything was topsy-turvy, and even heroes had to wait their turn for a passage to Suez and the overland route – at a pinch you could get a ship to the Cape, but that was a deuce of a long haul. So I made myself pleasant around the P. and O. office, squeezed the buttocks of a Bengali charmer who wrote letters for the head clerk and had her dainty hands on his booking lists, tempted her with costly trinkets, and sealed the bargain by rattling her across his desk while he was out at tiffin ("Oh, sair, you are ay naughtee mann!"). And, lo, ben Flashy's name led all the rest on a vessel sailing two weeks hence.

I was dripping with blunt, having disposed of my Lucknow loot and banked the proceeds, but there wasn't a bed to be had at the Auckland. Outram pressed me to stay with him – nothing too good for the man who'd smuggled his message through the pandy lines to Campbell – but I shied; only the fast set stayed up after ten in "Cal" in those days, and I guessed that *chez* Outram it would be prayers at nine and gunfire and a cold tub at six, and I didn't fancy above half scrambling out in the dark to seek vicious diversion. I played it modest, saying I knew his place would be full of Army and wives, and I'd rather keep out o' the way, don't you know, sir, and he looked noble and patted my shoulder, saying he understood, my boy, but I'd dine at least?

I put up at Spence's, a "furnished apartment" shop with a table d'hôte but no bearers even to clean your room, so bring your own servant or live like a pig. It served, though, and I could haunt the Auckland of an evening, seeking what I might devour.

I'd been two years without Elspeth, you see, and while they hadn't been celibate quite, what with Lakshmi and various dusky houris here and there, and only the buxom Mrs Leslie at Meerut by way of variety, I was beginning

25

to itch for something English again, blonde and milky for preference, and not reeking of musk and garlic. So the moment I saw Lady Plunkett (for her husband had a title) on the Auckland veranda, I knew I'd struck gold, which was the colour of her hair, with complexion to match. Beside Elspeth you'd not have noticed her, but she was tall and plump enough, with a pudding face and a big mouth, drooping with boredom, and once I'd caught her eye it was plain sailing. Believe it or not as you like, she dropped her handkerchief by my chair as she sailed out of the dining-room that evening (a thing I thought they did only in comic skits on the halls), so I told a bearer to take it after the mem-sahib, satisfied myself that her husband was improving his gout with port in company with other dodderers, and sauntered up to her rooms on the first floor.

To cut a long story short, we got along splendidly, and I had slipped her gown to her hips and was warming her up, so to speak, when the door opened at my back, her eager whimpers ended in a terrified squeak, and I glanced round to see her lord and master, who shouldn't have been up for hours, tottering across the threshold, apparently on the verge of apoplexy. Well, I'd been there before, but seldom in more fortunate circumstances, for I was still fully clad, we were both standing up, and she was half-hidden from his gooseberry gaze. I hastily surrendered her tits, and glared at him.

"What the devil d'ye mean by this intrusion, sir?" cries I. "Begone this instant!" And to my paralysed beauty I continued: "There is only the slightest congestion, marm, I'm happy to say; nothing to occasion alarm. You may resume your clothing now. I shall have a prescription sent round directly . . . Sir, did you not hear me? How dare you interrupt my examination? Upon my word, sir, have you no delicacy – out, I say, at once!"

He could only gobble in purple outrage while I chivvied her behind a screen. "That's my wife!" he bawls.

"Then you should take better care of her," says I, whipping out a dhobi-list and scribbling professionally. "Fortunately my room is close at hand, and when I was summoned your lady was suffering an acute palpitation. Not uncommon – close city climate – nothing serious, but unpleasant enough . . . h'm, three grains should do it, I think . . . Has she had these fits before?"

"I . . . I don't know!" cries he, wattling. "What? What? Maud, what does this mean? Who – why – are you a doctor, sir?"

"MacNab, surgeon, 92nd," says I, mighty brisk, ignoring the mewlings from behind the screen and his own choking noises. "Complete rest for a day or two, you understand; no undue exertion. I shall send this note to the apothecary." I pocketed my paper, and sniffed, looking stern. "Port, sir? Well, it's no concern of mine if you choose to drink yourself under ground, but I'd say one invalid in the family is enough, hey?" I addressed the screen. "To bed at once, marm! Two teaspoonfuls when the boy brings the medicine, mind. I shall call in the morning and look to find you much improved. Good-night – and to you, sir."

Never let 'em get a word in, you see. I was out and downstairs before he knew it, reflecting virtuously that that was another marriage I'd saved by quick thinking – if he believed her, which I'd not have done myself. But, stay . . . even if he did, he'd find out soon enough that there was no Dr MacNab of the 92nd, and start baying for the blood of the strapping chap with black whiskers, and Calcutta society being as small as it was, he was sure to run me down – and then, scandal, which would certainly tarnish my newly-won laurels . . . my God, if Plunkett roared loud enough it might even reach the Queen's ears, and where would my promised knighthood be then? But if I could slide out *now*, undetected – well, you can't identify a man who ain't there, can you?

All of a sudden, Westward ho! without delay seemed the ticket – and scandal wasn't the only reason. Some of these ancients with young high-stepping consorts can be vicious bastards, as witness the old roué who'd sicked his bullies after me for romping Letty Lade in the cricket season of '45 – and he hadn't even been married to her.

So now you see Flashy at the Howrah docks in the misty morning, with his dunnage on a hand-cart, dickering for a passage to the Cape with a Down-east skinflint in a tile hat who should have been flying the Jolly Roger, the price he demanded for putting into Table Bay. But he was sailing that day, and since tea for New York was his cargo it would be a fast run, so I stumped up with a fair grace; after all, I hadn't put cash down for the passage arranged by the Bengali bint, and I didn't grudge her the trinkets; my one regret was that I hadn't boarded the Plunkett wench . . . I hope he believed her.

*　　*　　*

It was about a month to the Cape, with the taffrail under most of the way, but not too bad until we neared Algoa Bay, when it began to blow fit to sicken Magellan. I've never seen so much green water; even less cheering was the sight of a big steamer lying wrecked on a reef off Port Elizabeth,[5] and I was a happy man when we'd rounded the Cape and opened up that glorious prospect which is one of the wonders of the seas – the great bay glittering in the sunlight with a score or more of windjammers and coasters and a few steamers at anchor, and beyond them the "table-cloth" of cloud rolling down the flank of the Mountain to Signal Hill, and guns booming from the Castle to salute a man-of-war putting out, with crowds fluttering hats and scarves from Green Point.

Once ashore I engaged a berth on the Union mail steamer sailing the following week, put up at the Masonic, and took a slant at the town. It was busy enough, for the Australian gold rush of a few years back, and the Mutiny, had set the port booming, but the town itself was a damned Dutch-looking place with its stoeps and stolid stucco houses, most of which are gone now, I believe, and the great church clock tower which looks as though it should have an Oom Paul beard round its face. It had been a wild place in the earlies, the "tavern of the seas", but now it was respectable and dull, and the high jinks were to be had at Grahamstown, far away up the coast, where the more sensible Britons lived and the Army was quartered – what there was of them, for the Governor, George Grey, had stripped the Colony of men, guns, and stores for the Mutiny, and the old Africa hands in the hotel were full of foreboding over their pipes and stingo, with the country arse-naked, as one of them put it, and the usual trouble brewing to the north.

"We'll have the Kaffirs at our throats again ere long, see if we don't," says one pessimist. "Know how many wars they've given us, colonel, thanks to the damned missionaries? Eight – or is it nine? Blessed if you don't lose count! To say nothin' o' the Dutch – not that they haven't got their hands full, by all accounts, an' serve the miserable beggars right! They'll be howlin' for you redcoats presently, mark my words!"

"You never saw a Boer ask help from a Briton yet!" scoffs another. "Nor they needn't – they'll give the Basutos the same pepper they gave John Zulu, if Moshesh don't mind his manners."

"You never know," laughs a third, "maybe the dear Basutos'll do the decent thing an' starve themselves to death, what?"

"Not old Moshesh – that's a Bantu who's too smart by half, as we'll find out to our cost one o' these days."

"Oh, Grey'll see to him, never fear – an' the Boers, if only London will let him alone. Any more word of his goin'?"

"You may bet on it – if the Colonial Office don't ship him home, the doctor will. I don't like his colour; the man's played out."

"Well, he can go for me. We bade good riddance to Brother Boer years ago – why should we want him back?"

These are just scraps of talk that I remember, and no doubt they're as Greek to you as they were to me, but being a curious child I listened, and learned a little, for these fellows – English civilians and merchants mostly, a Cape Rifleman or two, and a couple of trader-hunters down from the frontiers – knew their country, which was a closed book to me, then, bar my brief visit to the Slave Coast, and that was years ago and a world away from the Cape. Truth to tell, Africa's never been my patch, much; I've soldiered on veldt and desert, and seen more of its jungle than I cared for, but like our statesmen I've always thought it a dam' nuisance. Perhaps Dahomey inoculated me against the African bug which has bitten so many, to their cost, for it breeds grand dreams which often as not turn into nightmares.

It was biting hard at this time, not least on Grey, the Governor, and since he was to play a small but crucial part in my present story, I must tell you something of him – but I can't do that without first telling you about South Africa, as briefly as may be. It won't explain the place to you (God Himself couldn't do that), but it may lead you to wonder if two damned dirty and costly wars mightn't have been avoided (and who knows what hellish work in the future?) if only those Reform Club buffoons hadn't thought they knew better than the man on the spot.

You have to understand that in '59 Africa was the last great prize and mystery, an unmapped hinterland twice the size of Europe where anything was possible: lost civilis-ations, hidden cities, strange white tribes – they were no joke then. Real exploration of the dark heart of the continent had just begun; Livingstone had blazed his trails up and down it and across, farther north Dick Burton was making an ass of himself by *not* finding the source of the Nile, but the broad steady inroad was from the south, where we'd established ourselves. The Dutch settlers, not caring for us much, had trekked north to found their own Boer republics in lands where they met hordes of persevering black gentlemen coming t'other way; they fought the Zulus and Basutos (and each other) while we fought the Kaffirs to the east, and everything was dam' confused, chiefly because our rulers at home couldn't make up their minds, annexing territories and then letting 'em go, interfering with the Boers one minute and recognising their independence the next, trying to hold the ring between black and white and whining at the expense, and then sending out Grey, who brought the first touch of common sense – and, if you ask me, the last.

His great gift, I was told, was that he got on splendidly with savages – even the Boers. He'd been a soldier, explored in Australia, governed there and in New Zealand, and saw at once that the only hope for southern Africa was to reunite Briton and Boer and civilise the blacks within our borders,

30

which he'd begun to do with schools and hospitals and teaching them trades. In this he'd been helped by one of those lunatic starts which happen among primitive folk: in '57 a troublesome warrior tribe, the 'Zozas, had got the notion that if they destroyed all their crops and cattle, the gods would send them bumper harvests and even fatter herds, and all the white men in Africa would obligingly drown themselves; accordingly, the demented blighters starved themselves to death, which left more space for white settlement, and the surviving 'Zozas were in a fit state to be civilised.[6] Meanwhile Grey was using his persuasive arts to charm the Boers back under the Union Jack, and since our Dutch friends were beginning to feel the pinch of independence – isolated up yonder, cut off from the sea, worn out with their own internal feuding, and fighting a running war against the Basutos (whose wily chief, Moshesh, had egged on the 'Zozas's suicide for his own ends) – they were only too ready to return to Britannia's fold.

That was the stuff of Grey's dream, as I gathered from my fellow-guests at the hotel – a united South Africa of Briton, Boer, and black. Most of my informants were all for it, but one or two were dead against the Boers, which put one grizzled old hunter out of all patience.

"I don't like the Hollanders any better'n you do," says he, "but if whites won't stand together, they'll fall separately. Besides, if we don't have the Boers under our wing, they'll go on practisin' their creed that the only good Bantu's a dead one – or a slave, an' we know where that leads – bloody strife till Kingdom Come."

"And what's Grey's style?" asks a fat civilian. "Teach 'em ploughing and the Lord's Prayer and make 'em wear trowsers? Try that with the Matabele, why don't you? Or the Zulu, or the Masai."

"You've never seen the Masai!" snaps the old chap. "Anyway, sufficient unto the day. I'm talkin' about settlin' the Bantu inside our own borders –"

"We should never ha' given 'em the vote," says a Cape Rifleman. "What happens when they outnumber us, tell me that?" This was an eye-opener to me, I can tell you, but it's true – every man-jack born on Cape soil had the vote then, whatever his colour; more than could be said for Old England.[7]

"Oh, by then all the Zulu and Mashona will be in tight collars, talking political economy," sneers the fat chap. He jabbed his pipe at the hunter. "You know it's humbug! They ain't like us, they don't like us, and they'll pay us out when they can. Hang it all, you were at Blood River, weren't you? Well, then!"

"Aye, an' I back Grey 'cos I don't want Blood River o'er again!" cries the hunter. "An' that's what you'll get, my boy, if the Boers ain't reined up tight inside *our* laager! As for the tribes . . . look here, I don't say you can civilise a Masai Elmoran *now* . . . but they're a long way off. Given time, an' peaceful persuasion when we come to 'em – oh, backed up by a few field pieces, if you like – things can be settled with good will. So I reckon Grey's way is worth a try. It's that or fight 'em to the death – an' there's a hell of a lot o' black men in Africa."

There were murmurs of agreement, but my sympathies were all with the fat chap. I don't trust enlightened pro-consuls, I'd heard no good of the Boers, and fresh from India as I was, the notion of voting niggers was too rich for me. Can't say my views have changed, either – still, when I look back on the bloody turmoil of southern Africa in my lifetime, which has left Boer and Briton more at loggerheads than ever, the blacks hating us both, and their precious Union fifty years too late, I reckon the old hunter was right: Grey's scheme was worth a try; God knows it couldn't have made things worse.

But of course it never got a try, because the home government had the conniptions at the thought of another vast territory being added to the Empire, which they figured was too big already – odd, ain't it, that the world should be one-fifth British today, when back in the '50s our statesmen were dead set against expansion – Palmerston, Derby, Carnarvon, Gladstone, aye, even D'Israeli, who called South Africa a millstone.

While I was at the Cape, though, the ball was still in the

32

air; they hadn't yet scotched Grey's scheme of union and called him home, and he was fighting tooth and nail to get his way. Which was why, believe it or not, I found myself bidden to dine with his excellency a few days later – and that led to the first coincidence that set me on the road to Harper's Ferry.

When I got the summons, aha, thinks I, he wants to trot the Mutiny hero up and down before Cape society, to raise their spirits and remind 'em how well the Army's been doing lately. Sure enough, he had invited the local quality to meet me at a reception after dinner, but that wasn't his reason, just his excuse.

We dined at the Castle, which had been the Governor's residence in the days of the old Dutch East India Company, and was still used occasionally for social assemblies, since it had a fine hall overlooked at one end by a curious balcony called the Kat, from which I gather his Dutch excellency had been wont to address the burghers. I duly admired it before we went to dinner in an ante-room; it was a small party at table, Flashy in full Lancer fig with V.C. and assorted tinware, two young aides pop-eyed with worship, and Grey himself. He was a slim, poetic-looking chap with saintly eyes, not yet fifty, and might have been a muff if you hadn't known that he'd walked over half Australia, dying of thirst most of the time, and his slight limp was a legacy of an Aborigine's spear in his leg. The first thing that struck you was that he was far from well: the skin of his handsome face was tight and pallid, and you felt sometimes that he was straining to keep hold, and be pleasant and easy. The second thing, which came out later, was his cocksure confidence in G. Grey; I've seldom known the like – and I've been in a room with Wellington and Macaulay together, remember.

He was quiet enough at dinner, though, being content to watch me thoughtful-like while his aides pumped me about my Mutiny exploits, which I treated pretty offhand, for if I'm to be bongered* let it be by seniors or adoring females. I found Grey's silent scrutiny unsettling, too, and tried to

* Flattered (Zulu).

turn the talk to home topics, but the lads didn't care for the great crusade against smoking, or the state of the Thames, or the Jews in Parliament;[8] they wanted the blood of Cawnpore and the thunder of Lucknow, and it was a relief when Grey sent them packing, and suggested we take our cigars on the veranda.

"Forgive my young men," says he. "They see few heroes at the Cape." The sort of remark that is a sniff as often as not, but his wasn't; he went on to speak in complimentary terms of my Indian service, about which he seemed to know a great deal, and then led the way down into the garden, walking slowly along in the twilight, breathing in the air with deep content, saying even New Zealand had nothing to touch it, and had I ever known anything to compare? Well, it was balmy enough with the scent of some blossom or other, and just the spot to stroll with one of the crinolines I could see driving in under the belfry arch and descending at the Castle doorway beyond the trees, but it was evidently heady incense to Grey, for he suddenly launched into the most infernal prose about Africa, and how he was just the chap to set it in order.

You may guess the gist of it from what I've told you already, and you know what these lyrical buggers are like when they get on their hobby-horses, on and on like the never-wearied rook. He didn't so much talk as preach, with the quiet intensity of your true fanatic, and what with the wine at dinner and the languorous warmth of the garden, it's as well there wasn't a hammock handy. But he was the Governor, and had just fed me, so I nodded attentively and said "I never knew that, sir," and "Ye don't say!", though I might as well have hollered "Whelks for sale!" for all he heard. It was the most fearful missionary dross, too, about the brotherhood of the races, and how a mighty empire must be built in harmony, for there was no other way, save to chaos, and now the golden key was in his hand, ready to be turned.[9]

"You've heard that the Orange Volksraad has voted for union with us?" says he, taking me unawares, for until then he'd apparently been talking to the nearest tree. Not

34

knowing what the Orange Volksraad was, I cried yes, and not before time, and he said this was the moment, and brooded a bit, à la Byron, stern but gleaming, before turning on me and demanding:

"How well do you know Lord Palmerston?"

Too dam' well, was the answer to that, but I said I'd met him twice in the line of duty, no more.

"He sent you to India on secret political work," says he, and now he was all business, no visionary nonsense. "He must think highly of you – and so he should. Afghanistan, Punjab, Central Asia, Jhansi . . . oh, yes, Flashman, news travels, and we diplomatics take more note of work in the intelligence line than we do of . . ." He indicated my Cross, with a little smile. "I have no doubt that his lordship values your opinion more than that of many general officers. Much more." He was looking keen, and my innards froze, for I'd heard this kind of talk before. You ain't getting me up yonder disguised as a Zulu, you bastard, thinks I, but his next words quieted my fears.

"I am not persona grata at home, colonel. To be blunt, they think me a dangerous dreamer, and there is talk of my recall – you've heard it bruited in the town, I don't doubt. Well, sir," and he raised his chin, eye to eye, "I hope I have convinced you that I must *not* be recalled, for the sake of our country's service – and for the sake of Africa. Now, Lord Palmerston will not be out of office long, I believe.[10] Will you do me the signal favour, when you reach home, of seeking him out and impressing on him the necessity – the imperative necessity – of my remaining here to do the work that only I can do?"

I've had some astonishing requests in my time – from women, mostly – but this beat all. If he thought the unsought opinion of a lowly cavalry colonel, however supposedly heroic and versed in political ruffianing, would weigh a jot with Pam, he was in the wrong street altogether. Why, the thought of my buttonholing that paint-whiskered old fox with "Hold on, my lord, while I set you right about Africa" was stuff for *Punch*. I said so, politely, and he fixed me with that steely gazelle eye and sighed.

"I am well aware that a word from you may carry little weight – all I ask is that . . . little. His lordship has not inclined to accept my advice in the past, and I must use every means to persuade him now, do you not see?" He stared hard at me, impatient; there was a bead of sweat on his brow – and suddenly it came to me that the man was desperate, ready to snatch at anything, even me. He was furious at having to plead with a mutton-headed soldier (he, Sir George Grey, who alone could save Africa!), but he was in that state where he'd have tried to come round Palmerston's cook. He tried to smile, but it was a wry grimace on the pale, strained face. "Decisions, you know, are not always swayed by senators; a word from the slave in the conqueror's chariot may turn the scale." Gad, he could pay a compliment, though. "Well, Colonel Flashman, may I count on you? Believe me, you will be doing a service to your country quite as great as any you may have done in the past."

I should have spat in his eye and told him I didn't run errands for civil servants, but it's not every day you're toadied by a lofty pro-consul, patronising jackanapes though he may be. So I accepted his hand-clasp, which was hard (but damp, I noted with amusement), marvelling at the spectacle of a proud man humbling himself for the sake of his pride, and ambition. All wasted, too, for they *did* recall him – and then Pam reinstated him, not at my prompting, you may be sure. But his great African dream came to nothing.

That's by the way, and if I've told you of Grey and Africa at some length, well, I'm bound to record these things, and it was a queer start altogether, and he was an odd bird – but the point is that if he hadn't thought he could use me, he'd never have dined me that night, or shown me off to Cape society . . . and I'd never have heard of Harper's Ferry.

The last carriages had arrived while we talked, so now it was Flashy on parade in the hall before society assembled. Grey made me known from the Kat balcony, to polite applause, and led me down the little staircase to be admired and gushed over; there must have been thirty or forty under

36

the chandeliers, and Grey steered me among them; I gave my bluff manly smile, with a click of the heels or an elegant inclination, depending on their sex, but when we came to a group by the piano, I thought, hollo, this is far enough.

She was seated at the keyboard, playing the last bars of a waltz, tra-la-ing gaily and swaying her shoulders to the music; they were the colour of old ivory, flaunting themselves from a silvery-white dress which clung to her top hamper in desperation. She laughed as she struck the final flourish, and as those nearest patted their palms she bowed and turned swiftly on the stool, smiling boldly up at me and extending a slim gloved hand as though she had timed the action precisely to Grey's introduction. I didn't hear the name, being intent on taking stock: bright black eyes alight with mischief, that dark cream complexion (touch o' the tar brush, I fancied), glossy black hair that swung behind her in a great fan – a shade too wide in the mouth for true beauty, and with heavy brows that almost met above a slim aquiline nose, but she was young and gay and full of sauce, and in that pale, staid assembly she was as exotic as an orchid in a bed of lettuce, with a shape to rival Montez as she sat erect, sweeping her skirt clear of the piano stool.

"Oah, I should have played a march in your honour, Sir Harree – nott a waltz!" cries she. Chi-chi, beyond doubt, with that shrill lilt to her voice, and mighty pert for a colonial miss. I said gallantly 'twas all one, since in her presence I was bound to look, not listen – and I knew from the way she fluttered her lids, smiling, and then raised them, wide and insolent, that we were two of a mind. Her hand tightened, too, when I pressed it, nor did she withdraw it as Grey made another introduction, and I saw she was glancing with amusement at the chap who'd been turning her music, whom I hadn't noticed. "My father," says she, and as I faced him I realised with an icy shock where I'd seen her dark brows and arched nose before, for I was staring into the pale terrible eyes of John Charity Spring.

It's a shame those books on etiquette don't have a chapter to cover encounters with murderous lunatics whom you'd hoped never to meet again. I could have used one then, and if you've met J. C. Spring, M.A., in my memoirs, you'll know why. This was the mad villain who'd kidnapped me to the Slave Coast on his hell-ship in '48 (on my own father-in-law's orders, too), and perforce I'd run black ivory with him, and fled from she-devil Amazons, and been hunted the length of the Mississippi, and lied truth out of Louisiana to keep both our necks out of a noose.* The last time I'd seen him he'd been face down in a bowl of trifle in a New Orleans brothel, drugged senseless so that he could be hauled away and shanghaied – to Cape Town, bigod! Had he been here ever since – how long was it? Ten years almost, and here he was, brooding malevolently at me from those soulless eyes, while I gaped dumbstruck. The trim beard and hair were white now, but he was as burly as ever, the same homicidal pirate whom I'd loathed and dreaded; the weal on his forehead, which darkened whenever he was preparing to spill blood or talk about Oriel College, was glowing pink, and he spoke in the old familiar growl.

"*Colonel* and *sir*, now, eh? You've risen in rank since I saw you last – and in distinction, too, it seems." He glowered at my medals. "Bravely earned, I dare say. Ha!"

Grey wasn't a diplomat for nothing. "You are acquainted?" says he, and Spring bared his fangs in his notion of a smile.

"Old shipmates, sir!" barks he, glaring as though I were a focsle rat. "Reunited after many years, eh, Flashman? Aye,

* See *Flash for Freedom!* and *Flashman and the Redskins.*

38

*gratis superveniet quae non sperabitur hora!"** He wheeled on his daughter – Spring with a daughter, my God! – and I dropped her hand like a hot rivet. "My dear, will you not play your new Scarlatti piece for his excellency, while the Colonel and I renew old acquaintance – charming, sir, I assure you! Such delicacy of touch!" And in an aside to me: "Outside, you!"

He had my arm in a grip like a steel trap, and I knew better than to argue. Maniacs like Spring don't stand on ceremony for mere governors – four quick strides and he had me on the veranda, and as he almost threw me down the steps to the shadowy garden my one thought was that he was going to set about me in one of his berserk rages – I could guess why, too, so I wrenched clear, babbling.

"I'd nothing to do with your being shanghaied! It was Susie Willinck – I didn't even know she was going to –"

"Shut your gob!" Oriel manners still, I could see. He shoved me against a tree and planted himself four-square, hands thrust into pockets, quarter-deck style. "You needn't protest innocence to me! You'd never have the spine to slip me a queer draught – aye, but you'd sit by and see it done, you mangy tyke! Well, *nulla pallescere culpa*,† my decorated hero, for it doesn't matter a dam, d'ye see? *Fuit Ilium*,‡ if you know your Virgil, which you never did, blast you!"

So he was still larding his conversation with Latin tags – he'd been a mighty scholar, you see, before they rode him out of Oxford on a rail, for garrotting the Vice-chancellor or running guns into Wadham, likely, tho' he always claimed it was academic jealousy.

"Well, what the devil are you blackguarding a chap for, then?" The horror of meeting him, and being rushed out headlong, had quite unmanned me – but this was civilisation, dammit, and even he daren't offer violence, much. "By God, Spring!" cries I, courage returning, "you'd best mind your manners! This ain't Dahomey, or your bloody slave-deck, and I'm not your supercargo, either –"

* The happy hour will come, the more gratifying for being unexpected.
† Not to turn pale on an imputation of guilt – Horace.
‡ Troy has been (i.e., the reason for dispute no longer exists).

"Hold your infernal tongue!" He thrust his face into mine, pale eyes glittering, and his scar pulsing like a snake. "Take that tone with me and, by God, you'll wish you hadn't! Bah! Think you're safe, don't you, because *mortuo leoni et lepores insultant,** is that it?"

"How the hell do I know? Can't you speak English?"

"Well, the lion may be old, mister, but he ain't dead, and he can still take you by your dirty neck and scrag you like the rat you are!" He gripped my collar, leaning closer and speaking soft. "I don't know what ill wind blew you here, nor I don't care, and I've no quarrel with you – yet – because you're not worth it, d'ye see?" He began to shake me, gritting his teeth. "But I'm telling you, for the good o' your health, that while you continue to foul the Cape with your scabrous presence – you'll steer clear of my daughter, d'ye hear me? Oh, I saw you leering yonder, like the rutting hog you are! I know you –"

"Damn your eyes, I only said 'How-de-do' –"

"And I'm saying 'How-de-don't'! I know it means nothing to vermin like you that she's seventeen and convent-reared and pure!" That was what *he* thought; I'd seen the look in her eye. "So you can spare me your indignant vapourings, ye hear? Aye, *fronti nulla fides*† might ha' been coined for you, you lecherous offal! Didn't I see you tup your way from Whydah to the Gulf?" His scar was warming up again, and his voice rising to its customary bawl. "And that fat slut in Orleans – did you have the gall to marry her?"

"Hush, can't you? Certainly not!" In fact, I had; my second bigamy – but he'd opposed the match, being a Bible-thumper like so many blackguards, and I knew if I admitted it I'd have his teeth in my throat.

"I'll wager! Bah, who's to believe you – lie by nature, don't you!" He stepped back, snarling. "So . . . you're warned! Steer clear of my girl, because if you don't . . . by the Holy, I'll kill you!"

I believed him. I remembered Omohundro with two feet

* The lion being dead, even hares can insult him.
† There is no faith to be placed in the countenance.

40

of steel through his innards – and Spring had only just met him. Now, my carnal thoughts had vanished like the morning dew before the warmth of the fond father's admonition, and it was with relief and true sincerity that I drew myself up, straightened my tunic, and spoke with quiet dignity.

"Captain Spring, I assure you that my regard for your daughter is merely that of a gentleman for a charming lady." Hearing his jaws grate at what he took for sarcasm, I added hastily: "By the way, how is Mrs Spring – in excellent health, I trust?"

"Mrs Spring is dead!" snaps he – and, d'ye know, I was quite put out, for she'd been a harmless old biddy, played the harmonium at sea-burials, used to chivvy her diabolic spouse to wear his muffler when he went a-slaving, mad as a hatter. "And that is not her daughter. Miranda's mother was a Coast Arab." His glare dared me to so much as blink. I'd been right, though: half-caste.

"Miranda, eh? Delightful name . . . from a play, ain't it?"

"Jesus wept!" says he softly. "Arnold must ha' been proud of you!" He considered me, cocking his white head. "Aye . . . perhaps he would've been, at that . . . you've done well – by appearances, anyway." His voice was almost mild – but he was like that, raging storm and then flat calm, and both terrifying. I'd seen him lash a man almost to death, and then go down to afternoon tea and a prose about Ovid, with the victim's blood on his sleeve. The hairy heel was never absent long, though. "Aye," says he sourly, looking me up and down, "I wish I'd a guinea for every poor bastard whose bones must ha' gone to the making of your glorious pedestal. *Gaudetque viam fecisse ruina,** I'll lay!"

Seeing he was out to charm, I said that he seemed to have done pretty well himself – for he was looking mighty prosperous, suitings of the finest and diamonds on his daughter, and I was curious. He scratched his beard, sneering.

"Well enough. That fat strumpet of yours did me a good turn, trepanning me to profit and position, 'though she didn't know it. Yes, my bucko, I'm warm – and I draw enough

---

* He rejoices to have made his way by ruin – Lucan.

41

water in this colony, as you'll find if you cross me. *Felicitas habet multos amicos,** you know!"

I didn't, but couldn't resist a gibe of my own. "Not in black ivory these days, though, I'll bet!" For a second the wild spark flickered in the empty eyes, and I prepared to dodge.

"You'll open that trap o' yours once too often!" growls he. "You're sailing on the next mail, I take it? You'd better – and until then, keep your distance, d'ye hear? Good-night, and be damned to you!"

Shipmate o' mine, thinks I, as he stamped back to the house; I was wet with sweat, and it was with profound relief that I saw his carriage leave a few moments later, my half-caste charmer trilling with laughter and the Scourge of the Seas with his hat jammed down and snarling at the coachee. I ventured in again, but it was a half-hearted hero who acknowledged the compliments of the assembly, I can tell you; the coming of Spring is something you don't get over quickly, and Grey eyed me curiously when I took my leave.

"Interesting man – I had no notion you knew him in his trading days. Oh, he farms now, owns great acres about Grahamstown, and is quite the nabob – must be one of the wealthiest men in the colony, I daresay, has his own yacht to bring him down from Port Elizabeth. His daughter is charming, is she not?" An instant's hesitation, then: "Captain Spring is a considerable classic, too; his lectures on the *latifundia* were widely attended last year. He is on the board of public examiners, you know, and is forever pressing us to found a university here."

I decided to do J.C. a bit of good, in return for the scare he'd given me. "Ah, he misses the cloisters I suppose – you know they unfrocked him, or whatever they do, at Oxford? Never got over it, poor old chap, named his ship the *Balliol College* – slaver, she was, and a pirate, they say. He's wanted for murder in Louisiana, too."

He didn't even stir a patrician brow. "Indeed . . . ah, well. A very good-night to you, colonel . . . and my warmest regards to Lord Palmerston."

---

* Happiness has many friends.

That was how much I shocked *him*. The fact was, you see, that so many chaps who'd been little better than brigands in the earlies – fellows like Brooke and the Taipans and the South Sea crowd – had become upstanding pillars of society in their mellow years, that no one would care a fig if Spring had founded his fortune shipping niggers – not if he was going to apply it to good works like a new university, and went to morning service regular. As old Peacock says, respectable means rich – look at that slippery diamond-slinger Rhodes. What price the Spring Chair of Practical Philosophy? I'd give the inaugural lecture myself, on how he tried to drop blacks overboard before the patrollers boarded him.

That he was filthy rich was confirmed by gossip in the town. "He could write a draft for a million," I was told, and "I'd hate to be the man that bilked him of a fiver, though," says another, from which I gathered that my beloved old commander's belaying-pin reputation still stuck to him, however loud he hollered in church. So it was a relief when I heard he'd gone back to Grahamstown, out of harm's way, leaving the lovely Miranda to queen it at his fine house by the sea, where she was wont to entertain the younger set – of whom I was *not* going to be one, I may tell you. Delectable she might be, but even Helen of Troy would lose her allure if the price of her favours was liable to be a dip in the bay with a bag of coal on your feet. No, I was not tempted . . .

. . . until the day before I was due to sail, when a note was delivered at the hotel. It read:

> My dear Sir Harry – altho' I believe I should not style you so *just yet*, still everyone *knows*, and I have not so many Gallant Knights of my acquaintance that I can forego the *pleasure* of addressing you again as –
> Dear Sir Harry!
> Our meeting was cut so short by Papa that I shall feel myself altogether neglected if you do not call before you leave for Home, which I believe you do on tomorrow's mail. We intend a "Sea-picnic" today, and 'twill not be complete without the handsomest colonel in the Army! There! I have no shame at all,

43

you see! *Do* come, and gratify your *admirer*, and
soon to be, I hope, your friend,
　Miranda Spring
　P.S. Papa continues at Grahamstown, but we have
the *Ariel* for our picnic. I shall send a carriage at
noon – please, let it not return empty!

Well, this was a free and easy miss, if you like, for no
Mama of Simla or Belgravia would have permitted a *billet*
as warm as this one; she might as well have added "P.P.S.
Bed at ten sharp". But then, she had no Mama – and Papa
was seven hundred miles away, bless his black heart . . .
he'd warned her off, that was plain, but this was a filly who'd
delight in defiance, from what I'd seen of her . . . and she
wanted the "handsomest colonel in the Army" to "gratify"
her, the saucy little spanker, and who could blame her? I
tingled at the thought of those soft shoulders and the wanton
glint in the black eyes – aye, but what about the bale-fire
glint in dear Papa's? For a second I quailed . . . but no, I
couldn't let this one slip by.

Don't mistake me – I'm not one of those who count danger
an added spice, least of all in houghmagandie, as Elspeth
used to call it whenever I got her tipsy. But here, while there
was no risk at all, there would be a special zest to romping
Spring's daughter – the pity was that he'd never know . . .
unless I wrote him a line when I was safe in England . . .
"Dear Prospero, have rogered Miranda. O, brave new
world! The weather continues fine. Yours ever, Caliban."
He'd absolutely die of rage. Better still, she might present
him with a little supercargo nine months hence . . . gad, that
would be an interesting infant, Flash-Spring with a dash of
fellaheen. Oh, merry thoughts!

I made my packages then and there, whistling, and settled
up, for the best plan would be to outstay the other guests,
gallop the night away, kiss her a tearful farewell, and tool
straight down to the mail tender. I'd be halfway home before
the swine was back from Grahamstown – oh, I must let him
know, somehow! He'd never dare come back to England to
seek revenge . . . would he? I had another qualm at the

44

memory of those glaring eyes and murderous fury . . . well, we'd see.

The carriage was there sharp on twelve, Malay coachman and all, and I was in prime fettle as we bowled through the suburbs, which were a great contrast to the shabby port, being very grand even in those days, with shady avenues of oak and clumps of silver-trees, and fine houses among the green; it was Cape summer, and the whole countryside was ablaze with garden blossoms and the famous wild flowers. Chateau Spring, which stood by the sea, was even more splendid than I'd imagined, a lofty white colonial mansion in wide grounds fit to rival Kew, with a marble bathing pool[11] secluded among rhododendrons, and as I waited in the airy hall, admiring the circular sweep of the double staircase and inhaling the blissful aroma of money, I reflected that there's no gain like the ill-gotten; it beats honest accumulation hands down.

I'd expected the place to be alive with company, but there wasn't a soul except the ancient black butler who'd gone to announce me – and I found myself wondering about that capital "H" she'd put on "home" in her note. She was half-caste, you see, and they put far more stock in being "English" than we who take it for granted . . . so she'd spelled it "Home" – where she'd never been, and likely never would be. Not that being "coloured", as they call it down yonder, mattered much in those days, not with a white father who could have bought Natal and would have kicked the life out of anyone who didn't treat his daughter like a duchess . . . still, I wondered how many Mamas with eligible sons regretted previous engagements. And I was just concluding hornily that I was probably the only guest, when:

"Sir Harree!" Here she was, sailing down the staircase, and I took in breath at the sight of her. She was wearing a dress of pale muslin, sari-style, that clung like a gauzy skin but flounced out below the knee above thonged sandals; one ivory shoulder and both arms were bare, and as she swept towards me with a swift graceful stride the flimsy material outlined her figure – gad, it was all there. She carried a long scarf of black silk over one arm – and then to my

45

astonishment I saw it was her *hair*, gathered in from behind.

"Sir Harree!" again, with a glowing smile and her free hand extended, and since we were alone and I was bursting with buck I pressed my lips to her fingers – and nuzzled swiftly up her naked arm in Flashy's flank attack, across shoulder and neck to her cheek and fastened on her full red lips. She didn't even gasp; after a second her mouth opened wide, and when I drew her in with a hand on her rump she clung like a good 'un while I kneaded avidly and breathed in her heavy perfume . . . and then the blasted butler's step sounded at the stairhead, and she broke away, flushed and laughing, and quickly drew herself up, mock demure.

"How-de-do, Sir Harree?" says she, bobbing a curtsey. "So kind of you to coll! May I offer you some . . . refreshment?"

"Another o' the same, marm, if you please," says I, and she burst out laughing and drew me out onto a shady veranda commanding a splendid view of the sunlit Bay. There was a low table with liquor and tidbits (for two, I noticed), and cushioned rattan swing-chairs, and when the butler had poured us iced slings and tottered away, she made pretty work of seating herself, shrugging this way and that to display her shape, and sweeping that wondrously long hair over the back of her seat – I'd known at first sight that she was a great show-off, and now she raised her glass with a flourish in smiling salute.

"Thatt is iced brandy and orange, Sir Harree! Your favourite in New Orleans, so Papa told me . . . among other things, oah yess!"

"Did he, now? Observant chap, Papa." How the blazes had he come to tell her that? "But you mustn't believe all he tells you, you know."

"Oah, but I want to!" cries she, quite the rogue. "*Such* a shocking character he gave you, you can nott imagine!" She sat erect, counting on slim fingers. "Lett me see . . . *oll* your naughtee ways, drinking, and smoking and . . . that you are a verree shameless rake – but he would give no particulars, was that nott mean of him? . . . oah, and that you were a scoundrel, and told stretchers – and he said you were most cowardlee – which I did *nott* believe, you are so famous –"

"But you believed the rest, eh?"

"Butt of *carse*, Sir Harree!" Her voice had the native sing-song that can be delightful in a woman, but in her excitement the chi-chi vowels slipped out hot and strong, and for an instant the ivory skin seemed a shade darker, and the sharp nose and heavy brows more pronounced, as she gestured and prattled – and I admired the stirring curves of breast and hip under the flimsy muslin: never mind the pasture it comes from, it's the meat that matters.

"Papa said, of oll the bad men he had known, you were *quite* the worst!" She shook her head, wide-eyed. "So of carse I must see for myself, you knoaw? Are you so verree wicked . . . Harree?"

"Here, I'll show you!" says I, and lunged at her, but she drew back, with a pretty little comical flutter towards the hall, where I supposed the butler was lurking, and pressed me to try the tidbits, especially a great sticky bowl of creamed chocolate – in summer! – which she spooned into herself with gluttonous delicacy, between sips at her sling, teasing me with sidelong smiles and assuring me that the mixture was "quite heavenlee".

Well, women flirt all ways to bed: there are the kittens who like to be tickled, and the cats who must be coaxed while they pretend to claw, and the tigresses who have only one end in mind, so to speak. I'd marked Miranda Spring as a *novice* tigress at our first meeting, and our grapple in the hall had shown her a willing one; if it amused her to play the wanton puss, well, she was seventeen, and a chi-chi, and they're a theatrical breed, so I didn't mind – so long as she didn't prove a mouse, as some of these brazen chits do at the first pop of a button. She seemed nervous and randy together – yet was there a gleam of triumph in the eager smile? Aye, probably couldn't believe her luck.

"So Papa warned you off, did he? And did he tell you he'd sworn to kill me if I came near you?"

"Oah, yess! Jollee exciting! He is *so* jealous, you know, it is a great bore, for he has kept away oll *sarts* of boys –

47

men, I mean – *ollways* thee ones I like best, too! Nott saying he would *kill* them, you understand," she giggled, "but you know how he can be."

"M'mh . . . just an inkling. Cramps your style, does he?"

She tossed her head and dabbed cream from her lips with a fold of her dress. "*Nott* when he is in Grahamstown!"

"When the cat's away, eh? Finished your pudding, have you? Very good, let's play!" I made another lunge, and got home this time, seizing her bosom and stopping her mouth, and the lustful slut lay there revelling in it, thrusting her tongue between my teeth, with never a thought for the butler, and I was wondering how we were going to perform the capital act on a cane swing only four feet long, when she purred in my ear: "Once upon a time, the cat came home . . ."

Fortunately the swing was anchored, or we'd have been over.

"What! D'you mean –"

"Oah, not from Grahamstown, sillee! Papa was here, in town, but not expected. It was two years ago, when I was onlee fifteen, and quite stupid, you knoaw – and there was a French gentleman from Mauritius, much older, but whom I liked ever so . . . And Papa flew into a great rage, and forbade him to see me – but then Papa was absent, and Michel came to the house . . . to my room, quite late . . . and Papa came home from the club, quite early . . ."

"Jesus! What then?"

"Nothing, then . . . Papa looked at him, in that way he has, and said 'You're receipted and filed, mister', and Michel laughed at him, and went away." You're a better man than I am, Michel, thinks I. "And a little time after, they found poor Michel on Robben Island. He had been flogged to death with a *sjambok*."

Just what a fellow needs to hear when he's coming to the boil, you'll agree – but I'm the lad who bulled a Malay charmer in the midst of a battle on the Batang Lupar, regardless of shot and steel – and now the wicked bitch was halfway down my throat, and rummaging below-stairs with an expert hand. And while I didn't doubt her story, knowing her fiend

48

of a father, I knew she'd told it only to plague me. And Spring *was* in Grahamstown – I'd inquired.

"I'll give you *sjambok*, my lady!" growls I, and lifted her bodily out of the swing, but even as I cast about for galloping room, she left off gnawing at me and panted: "Wait . . . let me show you!" I set her down, and she seized my hand, hurrying me down to the garden and through a screen of shrubs to a small stone jetty beyond, and there was the smartest little steam yacht moored, all brass and varnish shining in the sun, and not a soul aboard that I could see.

"For our picnic," says she, and her voice was shrill with excitement. She led the way up the swaying plank, and I followed, slavering at the plump stern bobbing under the muslin, and down into the cool shadows of a spacious cabin. I seized her, fore and aft, but she slipped from my lustful grasp, whispering "A moment!" and slammed a door in my face.

While I tore off my clobber, I had time to look about me, and note that J. C. Spring, M.A., did himself as well afloat as he did ashore. There was polished walnut and brocade, velvet curtains on the ports, fine carpet and leather furniture, and even a fireplace with a painting of some Greek idiots in beards – it was a bigger craft than I'd realised, and rivalled the one in which Suleiman Usman had carried us to Singapore; through an open door I could see a lavatory in marble and glass, with a patent showerbath, which for some reason made me randier than ever, and I pounded on her door, roaring endearments; it swung open under my fist, and there she was, on t'other side of the bed, posed with her back to the bulkhead. For a moment I stood staring, and Spring and old Arnold would have been proud of me, for my first thought was "Andromeda on her rock, awaiting the monster, ha-ha!" which proves the benefit of a grounding in the classics.

She was stark naked – and yet entirely clad, for she had cinched in her long hair with a white ribbon round her neck, so that it framed her face like a cowl, while beneath the ribbon it hung in a shimmering black curtain that covered her

49

almost to her ankles. Her arms were spread out, desperate-like, on the panelling, and as I goggled she pushed one knee through the silky tresses and pouted at me.

We never went near the bed, for it would have been a shame to disturb her *tableau vivant*, much; I just heaved her up and piled in against the panels, grunting for joy, and I'll swear the boat rocked at its moorings, for she teased no longer when it came to serious work, and I wasn't for linger-ing myself. It was splendid fun while it lasted, which was until she began to shudder and scream and tried to throttle me with her hair, so I romped her up and down all the way to the lavatory, where we finished the business under the patent showerbath, once I'd got the knack of the dam' thing, which ain't easy with a mad nymph clinging to your manly chest. Most refreshing it was, though, and brought back memories of Sonsee-Array, my Apache princess, who was partial to coupling under waterfalls – which is deuced cold, by the way, and the pebbles don't help.

Miranda Spring knew a trick worth two of that, for when we'd come to our senses and towelled each other dry, with much coy snickering on her part, she showed me to a little alcove off the main cabin where an excellent collation was laid out under covers, with bubbly in a bucket. We recruited our energies with lobster and chicken, but when I proposed that we finish off the wine on deck, she came all over languid and said we would be "ever so comfee" on the bed – and if you'd seen that exquisite young body artfully swathed in her hair, with those fine ivory poonts thrusting impudently through it, you'd have agreed.

But she must finish her dessert, too – like all chi-chis she had a passion for sugary confections – so she brought it to bed, if you please, and gorged herself on eclairs and cream slices while I fondled her, well content to play restfully for a change. Not so madam; being a greedy little animal, she must satisfy both her appetites at once, and call me conserva-tive if you will, I hold that a woman who gallops you while consuming a bowl of blancmange is wanting in respect. I left off nibbling her tits to rebuke her bad form, but the saucy little gannet stuck out her tongue and went on eating and

50

cantering in a most leisurely fashion. Right, my lass, thinks I, and waited until she'd downed the last cherry and licked the spoon, settled herself for a rousing finish, and was beginning to moan and squeal in ecstatic frenzy – at which point I gave an elaborate yawn, hoisted her gently from the saddle, and announced that I was going on deck for a swim.

She squawked like a staggered hen, eyes still rolling. "Sweem? Wha' . . . now? But . . . but . . . oah, no, no, nott yett –"

"Why not? Better than all this boring frowsting in bed, what? Come along, a dip'll do you no end of good." I gave them a playful flip. "Keep you in trim, you know."

"*Boreeng*?" If you can imagine Andersen's Mermaid moved from dazed bewilderment to screaming passion in an instant, you have Miranda. "Boreeng? *Me*? Aieee, you . . . you –" But even as I prepared to parry a clawing attack, to my amazement her rage gave way to sudden consternation, and then her arms were round my neck and she was pleading frantically with me to stay, kissing and fondling and exerting her small strength to pull me down.

"Oah, no, no, please, Harree, please don't go – please, I am ever so sorree! Oah, I was wicked to tease – you mustn't go up, nott yett! Please, stay . . . love me, Harree, oah please, don't go!"

"Changeable chit, ain't you? No, no, miss, I'm going topsides for a swim, and some sunshine –"

"No, no!" It was a squeal of real alarm. "Please, please, you must stay here!" She fairly writhed on to me, gasping. Well, I've known 'em eager, but this was flattery of the most persuasive kind. "Please, please, Harree . . . love me *now*, oah do!"

"Wel-ll . . . no, later! If you're a good little girl, after my swim –"

"No, now! Oah, I shall be a badd *big* girl!" She gave a whimper of entreaty. "Stay with me, and I will be *verree* badd! Don' go, and I will . . ." She put her lips to my ear, giggling, and whispered. I was so taken aback I may well have blushed.

"Good God, I never heard the like! Why, you abandoned

51

brat! Where on earth did you hear of such . . . ? At *school!* I don't believe it!" She nodded gleefully, eyes shining, and I was speechless. Depraved women I've known, thank heaven, but this one was barely out of dancing class, and here she was, proposing debauchery that would have scandalised a Cairo pimp. Heavens, it was new to me, even, and I told her so. She smiled and bared her teeth.

"Oah, then you will certainlee nott go on deck just yett!" whispers she. "You will stay with wicked Miranda, yess?"

Well, a gentleman should always indulge the whims of the frail sex, even if it does mean foregoing a refreshing swim, but I confess that if I hadn't been a degenerate swine myself, her behaviour thereafter would have shocked me. I'd have thought, at thirty-six and having enjoyed the attentions of Lola Montez, Susie Willinck, my darling Elspeth, and other inventive amorists too numerous to mention, that I'd nothing to learn about dalliance, but by the time young Miranda (seventeen, I mean to say!) had had her girlish will of me, and I was lying more dead than alive in the showerbath, I could barely gasp one of Spring's Latin tags: "*Ex Africa semper aliquid novi,** by gum!"

I must have managed to crawl back to the bed, for when I woke it was growing dusk, and Miranda was dressed and wearing an apron, humming merrily as she cooked omelettes in the galley for our supper, while I lay reflecting on the lack of supervision in colonial finishing schools, and wondering if I'd be fit for more jollity before the mail tender left in the morning. I ate my omelette with a trembling hand, but when she teased me into sharing asparagus with her, nibbling towards each other along the spear until our mouths met, I began to revive, and was all for it when she said we should spend the night aboard, and her butler would see my traps taken down to the wharf in good time.

"But I shall be quite *desolate* at parting, for I have never knoawn anyone as jollee as you, Harree!" cries she, stroking my whiskers. "You are ever so excessivelee wicked – far worse than Papa said!"

* Out of Africa there is always something new.

52

"Then we're a pair. Tell you what – let's take a turn on deck, and then we'll play picquet – and if you cheat, I'll tie you up in that Raphunzel hair of yours, and show you what wickedness is."

"But I am thee *greatest* cheat!" laughs she, so we went on deck, and I had to tell her the story of Raphunzel, which she'd never heard, while she nestled against me by the rail in the warm darkness, with the water chuckling against the hull and the last amber glow dying above the western rim. It was the place to linger with a girl, but presently it grew chilly, so we went down to our hand of picquet. She was no cheat at all, though, so I had to teach her, but once or twice I wondered if her mind was on the game at all, for she kept glancing at the clock, and when it struck she started, and fumbled her cards, and apologised, laughing like a schoolgirl – "clumsee Clara!"

The nursery exclamation reminded me what a child she was – Lord love us, I'd been married before she was born. Aye, and a damned odd child, behind the vivacious chatter and mischievous smile, with her Babylonian bedroom manners. Peculiar lusts are supposed to be a male prerogative (well, look at me), but the truth is we ain't in it with the likes of the Empress Tzu-hsi or Lola of the Hairbrush or that Russian aunt I knew who went in for flogging in steambaths . . . or Miranda Spring, not yet of age, smiling brightly to cover a little yawn. Jaded from her mattress exertions, no doubt; we'll brisk you up presently, thinks I, with a few of those Hindu gymnastics that Mrs Leslie of Meerut was so partial to . . .

There was a vague sound from somewhere outside, and then a heavy footfall on the deck over our heads. The butler from the house, was my first thought – and Miranda dropped a card in shuffling, retrieved it, and offered me the pack to cut.

"Who is it?" says I, and she glanced at the clock. Suddenly I realised she was trembling, but it was excitement, not fear, and the smile in the black eyes was one of pure triumph.

"That will be Papa at last," says she.

53

There is, as that sound chap Ecclesiastes says, a time to get, and if I've reached the age of ninety-one it's because I've always been able to recognise it. I was afoot on the word "Papa" and streaking for the bed-cabin, where I knew there was a window; I wrenched the door open and raced through – into the bloody lavatory, and by the time I was out again it was too late: the biggest Malay I've ever seen, a huge yellow villain clad only in duck trowsers and with arms like hawsers, was at the foot of the companion, making way for John Charity Spring in full war-paint – reefer jacket, pilot cap, and a face like an Old Testament prophet. He took in the scene, hands thrust into pockets, and growled to the Malay.

"On deck, Jumbo, and if he sticks his neck out, break it!" He turned his glare on Miranda, who was still seated, the pack in her hands, and barked at her: "Did this thing molest you?"

She riffled the cards, cool as you like, while my bowels dissolved. "No, Papa. He did nott."

"He tried though, I'll lay! I know the villain!" His voice rose to its accustomed roar. "Did he lay his vile hands on you? Answer me!"

Oh, Christ, I thought, it's the finish – but she simply glanced at me with infinite scorn, shrugged her slim shoulders, and made an inelegant spitting noise. Spring stood breathing like a bellows, his wild eyes moving from one to the other of us; I knew better than to utter a denial – and I didn't laugh, either, like rash Michel.

"Aye, I'll swear he did, though! Didn't you, you lousy lecher!" He strode to confront me, jerking his fists from his

54

pockets, his jaw working in fury. "Didn't you? By God –"

"Oh, Papa! Of course he tried to kiss mee! Do you think he is the first? I am nearly eighteen, you knoaw!" If ever a voice stamped its foot, hers did; she sounded like an impatient governess. "I am nott a child! What were you expecting, after oll?" She tossed her head. "But he is just a great bullee . . . and a great coward, as you said."

His breath was rasping on my face, and his eyes were like a mad dog's, but suddenly he wheeled about, stared at her, and then strode to a cupboard on the bulkhead and dragged out a large volume which I recognised in amazement as a Bible. He slammed it down on the table beside her.

"Miranda," says he, and his voice was hoarse, either with rage or fatherly concern. "My child, it grieves me to do this, but I must! Swear to me on this Book that no . . . no unworthiness, no impropriety, passed between you and this creature –"

"Oh, Papa, what a fuss! Oll about notheeng! This is so sillee –"

"Silly be damned!" bawls paterfamilias. "Put your hand on the blasted Book, girl!" He seized her wrist and slapped her palm on the Bible. "Now, make your oath – and take care . . . aye, *quid de quoque viro, et cui dicas, saepe caveto,** mind – even with a rat like him! Swear!"

I braced myself to leap for the ladder, resolved to kick the appalling Jumbo in the crotch, God willing, for while the dear child had lied splendidly thus far, I knew she was convent-reared on all that hellfire and mortal sin bilge, and wouldn't dare perjure – and I stopped in the nick of time, for she was giving an angry little shrug, looking Papa sulkily in the eye, and swearing by Almightee Godd that she had repelled my clumsy advances with ease and it would take a better man than Flashy to drag her into the long grass, or words to that effect. Spring ground his teeth in relief, and then spoke two words I'll wager he'd never uttered in his life before.

* Take special care what you say of any man, and to whom it is said – Horace.

55

"Forgive me, my child. I never doubted you – but I know this scoundrel, d'ye see . . . ?" He turned his dreadful face to me, and if hair and claws had sprouted from his hands, I'd not have wondered. "It would break my heart," snarls he, "if I thought . . . but there! God bless you, child." He bussed her resoundingly on the forehead, and the little trollop gave him a smile of radiant purity. "You are the bravest of girls and the dearest of daughters, *quem te Deus esse jussit.** Now, go along to bed, and give thanks to Him who has guarded you this day."

"Good-night, dear Papa," says she, and kissed the brute. She walked to the companion – and God help us, as she passed me she pursed her lips in a silent kiss, and winked. Then she was gone, and Spring hurled the Bible into its cupboard and glared at me.

"And you, if you ever pray, which I'm damned sure you don't, can give thanks for the innocence of a good woman! A novelty in your filthy experience, is she not?" Well, novelty was the word for Miranda, no error, if not innocence. "Aye, she's as pure as you are vile, as straight as you are warped, as brave as you are . . . bah! And she don't lie, either!" He gave his barking laugh. "So you needn't stand quaking, my hero! Sit down!"

Now, I'd stood mum and paralysed through the astonishing scene I've just described, because that's what you do when J. C. Spring is on the rampage. Why the devil he wasn't in Grahamstown hadn't crossed my mind – I'd been too busy thanking God that his daughter was a complete hand, and that the old monster had swallowed her tale whole – but since he had, why, all was well, surely, and I could depart without a stain on my character. I recalled my wits and met his eye, two damned difficult things to do, I can tell you.

"Thank'ee, but I think I'll take my leave, if –"

"You'll do no such thing!" bawls he. "Now that you're here, you'll stay awhile, and give me the pleasure of your blasted company! Sit, damn you!"

* What God commanded you to be.

I sat, believe me, and he gave a great white-whiskered grin, chuckling, and poured two stiff tots from the decanter on the buffet. "No orange this time, I think," sneers he. "Ye'll want it straight, if I'm a judge. Cigar? Or cheroot? You Far Easters like 'em black, I believe . . . go on, man – *utrum horum mavis accipe*,* and take your ease! Your health – while you've got it!"

I downed the brandy as if it was water, for I'd seen Spring jovial before, and knew what could come of it. He seated himself opposite me at the table, sipped and wiped his whiskers, and eyed me with genial malevolence. I'd as soon be smiled at by a cobra.

"So ye didn't heed me," says he. "Well, ye've more bottom than ever I gave you credit for. And if you were half the man you look, instead of the toad I know you to be . . . I'd not blame you. Miranda is a maid to bewitch any man. I'm proud o' that girl, Flashman, with good cause . . . and if I thought ye'd laid a finger on her . . ." suddenly the hellish glare was back in his eyes, and his scar was pulsing "– I'd serve you as I served another reptile that tried to defile her, by God, I would!" He smashed his fist on the table. "I found her fighting for her chastity – aye, in her own chamber, by heaven – with a foul seducing frog-eating son-of-a-bitch who sought to have his vile way with her when my back was turned! My daughter, the bastard!" There was spittle on his beard. "What d'ye say to that, hey?"

When a maniac inquires – answer. "Damnable! French, was he? Well, there you are –"

"D'ye know what I did to him?" His voice was soft now, but the empty eyes weren't. "I stripped him stark, and cut the life out of him – sixty-one strokes, and you wouldn't have known he was human. Murder, you'll say –"

"No, no, not at all – quite the –"

"– but the fact is, Flashman, I was beside myself!" cries this raving ogre. "Aye, *homo extra est corpus suum cum irascitur*,† you remember . . ."

* Take whichever you prefer.
† An angry man is beside himself.

57

"Absolutely! May I trouble you for the brandy, captain – "

"There were those suspected me – d'ye think I gave a dam? It was just, I tell you! Condign punishment, as the articles say . . . and that lass of mine, that young heroine – I'll never forget it, never! Fighting like a tigress against that beast's base passion . . . but not a tear or a tremor . . . thank God I came in time!"

You should have seen *her* base passion a few hours ago, thinks I, and quailed at the memory . . . God, if ever he found out! He sipped brandy, growling, came out of his reverie of Miranda-worship, and realised he'd been confiding in the scum of the earth.

"But you were no threat to her!" He curled his lip. "No, not you – ye see, Flashman, I could trust her virtue to be stronger even than your depravity, else I'd never ha' let you within a mile of her, let alone permit her to beguile you here! Aye, that jars you! Oh, you've been had, my son!" For an instant the pale eyes were alight with triumph, then he was scowling again. "But I've been through hell this day, knowing she was within your reach; my skin crawls yet at the thought of it . . . but she's my daughter, steel true, blade straight, and too much for you or a dozen like you!"

It hit me like a blow. I'd known there was something horribly amiss when he'd arrived unexpected, but then Miranda had quieted him, and he'd been civil (for him), and only now was it plain that I'd been trapped, most artfully and damnably, by this murderous pirate and his slut of a daughter – but why? It made no sense; he had no quarrel with me – he'd said so, in those very words.

"What d'ye mean? What d'ye want of me? I've done nothing, you heard her – "

"Nothing, you say? Oh, you've done nothing *today*, I know that – or you'd not be alive this moment! But think back ten years, Flashman, to the night when you and your conniving whore Willinck crimped me out of Orleans – "

"I'd no hand in that, I swear! And you told me – "

" – that I bore no grudge?" His laugh was a jeering snarl. "More fool you for believing me – but your wit's all in your

58

loins and belly, isn't it? You can't conceive what it meant for a man of my breeding – my eminence, damn your eyes! – a scholar, a philosopher, honoured and respected, a man of refinement, a master and commander even in the degraded depths of a slave-ship – a man born to have rule – aye, better to reign in hell than serve in heaven!" roars he, spraying me with his incoherent rage, so consumed by it that for once Latin quotation failed him. "To be hounded before the mast by scum who wouldn't have pulley-haulied on my ship, herded with filthy packet rats, fed on slop and glad to get it, threatened with the cat, by Jesus – aye, stare, rot you! I, John Charity Spring, Fellow of Oriel . . . damn them all to hell, thieves, trimmers and academic vermin . . ." His voice sank to a hoarse whisper, for he was back on the Oxford tack again, contemplating his ruined career, his berserk fit over, thank God, for I'd never seen him worse. He took a huge breath, filled his glass, and brooded at me.

"I cleaned the heads on that ship, Flashman – all the way to the Cape." His tone was almost normal now. "Thanks to you. And d'ye think a day has passed in ten years when I haven't remembered what I owe you? And now . . . here you are, at last. We may agree with Horace, I think – *Raro antecedentem scelestum deseruit pede poena claudo.* I see from your vacant gape that you're no better acquainted with his works than you were on the *College*, damn your ignorance! – so I'll tell you it means that Justice, though moving slowly, seldom fails to overhaul the fleeing villain." He shoved the bottle at me. "Have some more brandy, why don't you? Your flight's over, bucko!"

This was desperate – but terrified as I was, I could see something that he had overlooked, and it spurred me now to unwonted defiance, though I came to my feet and backed away before I voiced it.

"Keep your bloody brandy – and your threats, 'cos they don't scare me, Spring! I don't know what your game is, but you'd best take care – because you've forgotten something! I'm not a friendless nobody nowadays – and I ain't some poor French pimp, neither! You think *you* draw water? Well, you ain't the only one!" A heaven-sent thought struck

59

me. "Your governor, Grey, has charged me – *Sir* Harry Flashman, V.C., K.B., and be damned to you! – with a personal message to Lord Palmerston, d'ye hear? So you can come off your blasted quarter-deck, because you daren't touch me!" I cast a quick glance at the companion, ready to run like hell.

The pale hypnotic eyes never blinked, but his mouth twisted in a grin. "My, what a dunghill rooster we've grown, to be sure! *Vox et prœterea nihil!** But you've forgotten something, too. No one saw you come aboard here. It was a hired rig that brought you to my house – and my servants are safe folk. So if the distinguished Flashman, with all his trumpery titles, were to disappear . . . why, he sailed on the mail for home! And if, by chance, word came months from now that you never boarded the mail . . . a mystery! And who more baffled than your old shipmate, John Charity Spring? What, silent, are we? Stricken speechless?"

He pushed back his chair and reached a flask from the buffet. "You'd better try some schnapps, I think. There . . . don't bite the glass, you fool! Drink it! Christ, what a craven thing you are! Sit down, man, before you fall – *vitiant artus ægrœ contagia mentis,*† as Ovid would say if he could see you. And rest easy – I'm not going to harm a hair of your precious head!"

That was no comfort at all, from him; I knew that diseased mind too well – he meant me some hideous mischief, but I could only wait shuddering until he told me what it was, which he was preparing to do with sadistic relish, brimming my glass and resuming his seat before he spoke.

"When I heard you'd landed, it was a prayer answered. But I couldn't see how to come at you, until Miranda showed the way – oh, she has all my confidence, the only creature on earth in whom I put trust. 'Let me beckon him,' says she – and didn't she just, on that first night at Government House! It was gall to my soul to see it – my girl . . . and you, you dirty satyr! A dozen times I would ha' cried it off,

---

* [You are] a voice and nothing more.
† When the mind is ill at ease, the body is somewhat affected.

for fear of what harm might come to her, but she laughed away my doubts. 'Trust me, Papa!' My girl! D'ye wonder I worship the earth she treads on? Would you believe," he leaned forward, gloating, "'twas she advised I should warn you off! 'He'll come all the faster, to spite you . . . if he thinks it safe', says she. She *knew* you, d'ye hear – oh, yes, Flashman, she knows all my story, from Oxford to the Middle Passage – and she's as bent on settling her father's scores as he is himself! We have no secrets, you see, my girl and I."

I could think of one. Oh, she'd tricked me into his clutches, right enough – but she'd humbugged him, too, whoring away like a demented succubus while he was biting his nails over her supposed virtue. And the doting old lunatic believed her. God knew how many she'd been in the bushes with, his stainless virgin . . . if only I'd dared to tell him! Suddenly I felt sick, and not only with fear; something was wrong with my innards . . .

"And you came to the bait, like the lustful swine you are," says Spring. "And it's time to cast our accounts and pay, eh, Flashman?"

You know me. With any other of the monsters I'd known, I'd have pleaded and whined and tried to buy off – but he was mad, and my mind seemed to be growing numb. Another wave of nausea came over me, my head swam, and I took a stiff gulp of schnapps to steady myself.

"Belay that!" growls Spring, and snatched the glass from me. "I don't want you dead to the world before I've done." He seized my wrist. "Sit still, damn you . . . ha! pulse sluggish. Very good." He dropped my hand and sat back, and as the sick fit shook me again, I saw that he was smiling.

"Now you know what a crimped sailorman feels like," says he. "Yes, the schnapps is loaded – just like the mixture that fat tart slipped to me in Orleans. I believe in eye for eye, you see – no more, no less. You shipped me out, drugged and helpless, and now you're going the same way – *you* can live on skilly and hard-tack, *you* can try your V.C. and K.B. on a bucko mate, *you* can have your arse kicked from here to Baltimore, and see how you like it, damn your blood!" His voice was rising again, but he checked himself and leaned forward to thumb up my eyelid – and I couldn't raise a hand to stop him.

"That's right," says he. "Baltimore, with a skipper of my acquaintance. If I were a vindictive man, it would ha' been Orleans, but I'm giving you an even chance, d'ye see? Baltimore's about right, I reckon. You've been there before – so you know what's waiting for you, eh?"

He stood up, and I tried to follow, but my legs wouldn't answer. I heaved – and couldn't move a muscle, but the horror of it was that I could see and hear and feel the sweat pouring over my skin. God knows what poison he'd fed me, but it had gripped me all in an instant; I tried to speak, but only a croak came out. Spring laughed aloud, and stooped to me, the demonic pale eyes gleaming, and began to shout at me.

"Hear this, damn you! You'll go ashore, derelict and penniless – as I did! And word will go ahead of you, to the police, and the federal people, not only in Baltimore, but in Washington and Orleans! You'll find they have fine long memories, Flashman – they'll remember *Beauchamp Millward Comber*! The U.S. Navy have their file on him, I daresay – perjury, impersonation, and slave-trading . . . but that's nothing, is it? You're wanted for slave-*stealing*, too, as I recall, which is a capital offence – and they're a dam' sight hotter on it now than they were ten years ago, even! And then there's the small matter of complicity in the murder of one Peter Omohundro – oh, it's quite a score, and I don't doubt there's more that I don't know about!"

He stood straight, and now he seemed to have swollen into a ghastly giant, white-bearded and hideous, who struck at me, but I couldn't feel the slaps, although they were jarring my head right and left.

"See how much good your medals and honours and the brave name of *Sir* Harry Flashman does you when the Yankee law has you by the neck! Aye, *olim meminisse juvabit*, rot you . . . !" His bellowings were growing fainter. "Crawl or run or worm your way out of that! If you can – good luck to you! Bon voyage, you son-of-a-bitch . . . !"

The pounding in my ears blotted out all other sounds, and my sight was going, for I could no longer make out his form, and the cabin lights were dwindling to pin-points. The nausea had passed, my senses were going – but I remember clear as day my last thought before I went under, and 'twasn't about Spring or Miranda or the hellish pickle awaiting me. No; for once I'd recognised his quotation – it had been framed on the wall of the hospital at Rugby, where I'd sobered up on that distant day when Arnold kicked me out . . . "*Olim meminisse juvabit*",* and dooced appropriate, too. Seneca, if memory serves.

* It will be pleasant to remember former troubles – Virgil (not Seneca).

Three times in my life I've been shang-haied, and each time there was a woman in the case – Miranda Spring, Phoebe Carpenter, and Fanny Duberly, although I acquit pretty little Fan of any ill intent, and the occasion in which she was concerned saw me trepanned with my eyes open; on the two others it was Flashy outward bound with a bellyful of puggle from which I didn't awake until we were well out to sea, and there's no worse place to come to than below deck on a windjammer when the skipper's in a hurry.

This one was an American with a broken nose and a beard like a scarf beneath his rock of a chin; my heart sank at the sight of him, for he had Down-easter[12] written all over him. I'd hoped, when I crawled out of the stuffy hole in which I found myself and puked my heart out on a deck that seemed to be near perpendicular, that I'd find a good corruptible Frog or Dago on the poop, but Spring had chosen his man well, damn him. This one had eyes like flint and whined through his nose.

"Spew over the side, cain't ye!" was his greeting as I staggered up out of the scuppers and held on for my life; he stood braced without support in a gale that was bringing green sea over the rail in icy showers, soaking me in an instant, but at least it washed my tiffin and supper away. "Do that in a calm an' ye'll swab it up yourself, mister! Now, git back below till ye can stand straight, an' keep out o' the way, d'ye hear?"

It's not easy to conduct negotiations on a spray-lashed deck during a howling tempest, but I was wasting no time.

"A hundred pounds if you'll take me to Port Nolloth or

64

Walfish Bay!" I'd no notion where we were in the South Atlantic, but I doubted if we were far out as yet, and any port would do so long as it wasn't Baltimore – or the Cape, with Spring infesting the place. "Five hundred if you'll carry me to England!"

"Got it on ye?" shouts he. I hadn't; I'd been stripped clean of cash, papers, even my cheroot-case.

"You'll have it the moment we drop anchor! Look, a thousand if you set me down anywhere between Brest and London – it don't have to be English waters, even!"

That was when he knocked me down, grabbed me by the belt, and heaved me aft; I'm over thirteen stone, but I might have been his gunny-sack. He threw me into his cabin, kicked the door to, and watched me crawl to my feet.

"That's the short way of tellin' you I ain't for sale," says he. "Least of all to a lousy Limey slave-stealer."

Even in my distempered state, that sounded damned odd. "You ain't a Southerner! You're a Yankee, dammit!"

"That I am," says he. "An' I make my livin' 'tween Benin an' Brazil, mostly – that satisfy ye?" A slaver, in other words, if not this voyage. Trust Spring. So I tried another tack.

"You'll hang for this, d'ye know that? You're a kidnapper, and I'm Sir Harry Flashman, colonel in the British Army, and –"

"Spring told me that's what ye'd say, but you're a liar an' he ain't. Your name's Comber, an' in the States they've got warrants out for you for everythin' 'cept pissin' in the street – Spring told me that, too! So any hangin' there is, you'll do it."

"You're wrong, you fool! I'm telling the truth, you Yankee idiot – don't hit me –"

He stood over me, rubbing his knuckles. "Now, you listen, mister, 'cos I'm runnin' out o' patience. John C. Spring is my friend. *An'* when he pays an' trusts me for a job, I do it. *An'* you're goin' to Baltimore. *An'* we'll lay off Sparrow's Point a couple o' days while the letters he give me goes ashore, to let the traps know you're comin'. *An'* then *you* go. *An'* till then you'll work your passage, an' I don't give two cents' worth of a Port Mahon sea-horse's droppings if you're Comber or Lord Harry Flasher or President Buchanan! Savvy? Now you git up, and walk along easy to the focsle – it's that way – an' give your callin' card to Mr Fitzgibbon, who's the mate, an' he'll show you to your stateroom. Now – skat!"

Having felt his fist twice, I skatted, and so began several weeks of vile hard work and viler food, but if you've been a slave to the Malagassies, or lain in a bottle-dungeon in India, or been toasted on a gridiron, or fagged for Bully Dawson – well, you know things could be worse. I'd been a deckhand before, but I didn't let on, so I was never sent aloft; Fitzgibbon, and the skipper, whose name was Lynch, were first-rate seamen, so far as I'm a judge, and the last thing they wanted was some handless farmer hindering work, so I was tailing on and hauling and holystoning and greasing and painting and tarring and doing any of the countless unskilled menial tasks of shipboard – oh, I cleaned the heads, too – and because I knew better than to shirk, I rubbed along well enough, bar sea-sickness which wore off after a week, and inedible tack, and being played out with fatigue, and driven half-crazy by that hellish creaking and groaning din that never ceases on a sailing packet; you get used to that, too, though. The focsle gang were a hard-bitten crowd, Scowegians and Germans, mostly, but I was big and strong enough to be let alone, and I didn't encourage conversation.

You may think I make light of it – being kidnapped and pressed into sea-slavery, but if I've learned anything it's that when you have no choice, you must just buckle down to misfortune . . . and wait. It was all sufficiently beastly, to be sure, but d'ye know, I reckon Spring was cheated of that part of his vengeance; as I've said, I'd been through hell and back before in my chequered life, far worse than Spring had, and being a packet-rat was that much less of an ordeal to me than it must have been to him. He thought he was Godalmighty, you see, lording it over riff-raff by virtue of his "eminence" as he'd called it, by which I guess he meant his master's ticket and his M.A. and simply being the great John

66

Charity Spring, classical don and Fellow of Oriel, damn your eyes. Now, I *am* riff-raff, when I have to be, and so long as I can see a glimmer at the end of the passage, well, *dum spiro spero,** as we scholars say. Having his high-table arse kicked must have had Spring gnawing the rigging; I took care not to be kicked. His haughty spirit rebelled; I ain't got one.

Another thing that cheered me up was my belief that Spring, being mad as a weaver to start with, had let his harboured spite get the better of his few remaining wits; if he thought he was dooming me to death or the chain-gang by packing me off to the States, he was well out of reckoning. What he had said about my American embarrassments was true enough, but that had been a long time ago; it's a painful story, but in case you haven't read it in my earlier memoirs, I'll give you the heads of it here.

Ten years back, when Spring's slaver, the *Balliol College*, with Flashy aboard as reluctant supercargo, had been captured off Cuba by an American patrol, I'd deemed it prudent to assume the identity of Beauchamp Millward Comber (don't laugh, it was his name), our late third mate, who'd told me on his deathbed that he was an Admiralty agent who was only sailing with Spring to spy on his slaving activities. If you think I'm stretching, the U.S. Navy didn't; Comber's papers saw me through, but it was touch and go, so I'd slipped my cable and looked for a way home. I thought I'd found one when the Underground Railroad, a clandestine troupe of lunatics who ran escaped slaves to Canada, got their hands on me – they had ears everywhere, even in the U.S. Navy Department – and offered to help me North if I'd take an important runaway nigger with me to freedom.

That enterprise had ended with me going over one rail of a Mississippi steamboat while the darkie, with a slave-catcher's bullet in him, had gone over t'other. Subsequently I'd been overseer on a plantation, lost my situation for rogering the lady of the house, escaped North with a female octoroon slave who'd killed two men en route, been shot in

* While I breathe I hope.

67

the backside by pursuers while crossing the Ohio River, found refuge with Congressman Abraham Lincoln who'd dragooned me into testifying at the adjudication on Spring's slave-ship in New Orleans, been unwillingly reunited with my dear old commander who had then murdered one Omohundro in a pub, fled with him to seek shelter with a whore of my acquaintance who'd obligingly had old J.C. shanghaied . . . and had at last won back to England, home, and beauty via the Great Plains, an Apache village, and San Francisco, slightly out of breath. Honestly, I'd have been better going into the Church, or banking, or politics, even.

In any event, that's how the sparks flew upward on my first visit to America – and you can see Spring's point. In my brief sojourn I'd been an impostor and perjurer (as Comber), stolen slaves (under the names of Prescott, Arnold, and, I rather think, Fitzroy Howard or something like that), and was wanted for murders I hadn't committed in Mississippi, or it may have been Tennessee for all I know, as well as for aiding and abetting (which I hadn't done, either) Spring's stabbing of Omohundro. An impressive tally, I concede, and none the better for being all entirely against my will.

However, I doubted if the U.S. Navy was much concerned with the fugitive Comber at this late date, and I'd no intention of going near the Mississippi. I wasn't wanted in Maryland, where Baltimore is; let me present myself to a British consul there, or in Washington, which was only forty miles away, and I was on easy street. The great thing, you see, was that I *wasn't* Comber (or Prescott or those other chaps), but I *was* Sir Harry Flashman, not unknown by name and fame, and once I was under our embassy's[13] wing, warrants from far-flung states for the arrest of non-existent Combers, etc. would matter not at all. Not in Washington or the North, at least; if I were fool enough to venture South, where there might be witnesses to identify me, that would be a different and damned unpleasant kettle of fish; as Spring had pointed out, my rank and heroic stature at home wouldn't weigh much with a Louisiana jury.

So you can see why I wasn't over-troubled about what lay

ahead; indeed, my preoccupation was how to pay Spring out when I was safe home in England. The evil-eyed bastard had terrified, drugged, and kidnapped me, subjected me to the gruelling misery of packet-ratting, and done his damnedest to deliver me to an American gallows; well, he was going to rue the day. Straight prosecution was out of the question: it would take too long, likely uncover past history which I'd rather keep dark, and almost certainly fail in the end – the whole business was too wild, and the thought of returning to testify at the Cape, with Spring frothing at me across the court . . . no, I'd prefer not. Especially since the most artistic revenge had already occurred to me: a detailed account, to the address of J. C. Spring, M.A., of the contortions which his saintly Miranda and I had performed aboard dear Papa's yacht – that would bring a blush to his cheek. It would destroy him, wound him to the depths of his rotten soul, probably drive him crazy altogether. He might even murder her, and swing for it – well, the bitch deserved it. No . . . she'd swear blind that I was lying out of spite, and he'd believe her, or pretend to . . . but in his heart he'd always know it was the truth. Aye, that would teach him that Flashy's a critter best left alone because, as Thomas Hughes pointed out, he can find ways of striking home that you ain't even thought of.

Now I'll not weary you with any further relation of Life at Sea when Uncle Harry was a Lad, but hasten on to Chesapeake Bay, which I reckon we reached in about eight weeks, but it may have been more.[14] I made two further attempts to suborn Captain Lynch, promising him Golconda if he would put me down at New York or Boston, but I might as well have talked to the mast; I believe my speech and bearing, and my conduct aboard, had sown some doubt in his mind, for he didn't hit me on either occasion, but perhaps because he was a man of his word, as some of these half-wit shellbacks are, or more likely because Spring had a hold on him, he wasn't to be budged. "You're goin' to Baltimore even if the Chesapeake's afire, so ye can save your wind!" says he, and that was that.

We lay two days in the bay, and I didn't doubt that

Spring's letters had gone ashore with the pilot. Now that the grip had come, all my assurance had melted like snow off a dyke, and I was in a fine funk again, dreaming hideous nightmares in which I was swimming slowly towards a misty jetty on which stood Yankee peelers brandishing warrants made out for "the handsomest man in the Army" and jangling their handcuffs, and all my American ill-willers were there, singing jubilee – Omohundro, and the squirt Mandeville who'd caught me galloping his wife, and Buck the slave-catcher and his gang, and the poker-faced Navy man whose name I'd forgotten, and blasted George Randolph, the runaway nigger I'd abandoned, and vague figures I couldn't make out, but I knew they were the Cumanches of Bent's Fort and Iron Eyes who'd chased me clear across the Jornada, and then somehow I was in the adjudication court at Orleans, but instead of the wizened little adjudicator it was Spring on the bench, in gown and mortar board waving a birch and shouting: "Aye, there he is, the great toad who ravishes daughters and can't construe Horace to save his soul, *Flashmanum monstrum informe ingens et horrendum,** mark him well, ladies and harlots, for Juvenal never spoke a truer word, *omne in præcipiti vitium stetit,*† by thunder!" and when I looked at the jury, they were all the American women I'd betrayed or discarded – fat Susie weeping, Sonsee-Array sulking, the French nigger Cleonie whom I'd sold to the priest at Santa Fe, willowy Cassy looking down her fine nose, coal-black Aphrodite and the slave-women at Greystones, but their faces were all turned to the bench, and now it wasn't Spring who sat there, but Arnold in a pilot cap glowering at me, and then Miranda was tripping up beside him, swirling her hair about her like a cloak, giggling as she stooped to whisper in his ear, but it wasn't his ear, it was Congressman Lincoln's, and I saw his ugly face scowl as he listened, nodding, and heard his drawl as he said that reminded him of a story he'd heard once from an

---

* The monster Flashman, shapeless, huge and horrible (adapted from Virgil's description of Polyphemus).
† Every kind of vice has reached its summit.

English naval officer who didn't know what club-hauling meant . . .

*   *   *

I came back to waking very slowly, with sense stealing over me like a sunrise, almost imperceptibly, growing gradually conscious of a throbbing ache in my temples and a dryness in my mouth and throat that was truly painful. There was someone beside me, for I could feel the warmth of a body, and I thought "Elspeth" until I remembered that I was in a ship at sea, bound for Baltimore and that awful nightmare which thank God was only a dream after all, conjured up out of my fears. But there was no motion about the place on which I lay, no gentle rocking as there should have been as we lay at anchor in the Chesapeake; I opened eyelids that seemed to have been glued together, expecting to see the knot-hole in the floor of the bunk above me, as I'd seen it with every awakening for the past many weeks. It wasn't there, and no bunk either; instead there was a dingy white ceiling, and when I turned my head there was a bare wall with a grimy window.

I was ashore, then . . . but how, and for how long? I tried to conjure up my last memory of shipboard, but couldn't with the ache in my head, and to this day I don't know how I left the ship, drunk, drugged, or sandbagged. At the time, it didn't signify anyway, and even as I reached that conclusion a woman's voice said:

"Hollo, dearie! Awake, are ye? Say, didn't you have a skinful, though!"

An American cackle, piercing my ear, and I shuddered away by instinct, which was sound judgment, for if I felt dreadful, she looked worse, a raddled slattern grinning her stinking breath into my face, reaching out a fat hand across my chest. I almost catted on the spot, one thought uppermost.

"Did I . . . ? Have we . . . ?" It came out in a faint croak, and she leered and heaved herself half across me. The paint on her face looked about a week old, and her awful bulk was clothed only in a grubby shift.

71

"Ye mean . . . did you and me . . . ?" She loosed another braying laugh, displaying bad teeth. "No, dearie, we didn't . . . yet. You've bin snorin' your big head off all night. But you're awake now . . . so how 'bout my present . . . ?"

"Get away from me, you pox-ridden slut!" Another hoarse whisper, but I had strength enough to thrust her away, and tumbled over her to the floor. I scrambled up, dizzy, and almost fell again, staring about me at a big, unbelievably foul whitewashed room, in which there were about a dozen beds containing various beings, male and female, in squalid undress. The stench of stale tobacco and unwashed humanity took me by the throat, and I blundered for the door, falling over a frantically courting couple on the floor, and followed by shrill obscenities from my bedmate. I found myself on a bare landing, confronting a goggling darkie with a bucket in his hand.

"Where the hell am I?" I inquired, and had to repeat myself and take him by the collar before he stammered, rolling his eyes:

"Why, boss, you' in de Knittin' Swede's!"

Only later did I know what he'd said; at the time it sounded like gibberish.

"What town is this?"

"Why . . . why, dis Baltimo', boss! Yassuh, dis Baltimo', honnist!"

I let him go and stumbled down two flights of stairs, with no notion but to get out of this beastly place without delay. There were other doors, some of them open on to sties like the one I'd left, and various creatures on the landings, but I didn't pause until I bore up unsteadily by a big wooden counter on the ground floor, and I think there was a tap-room, too, but what mattered was that there was a street door ahead of me, and open air.

There were a number of seamen lounging at the counter, and behind it, sitting on a high stool, was a figure so unlikely that I thought, I'm still drunk or dreaming. He was big and ugly, with a nose that had been spread half across his face, probably by a club, there wasn't a hair on his phiz or gleaming skull, the huge arms protruding from his vest were

72

covered with tattoos, but what took the eye was that he was clicking away with knitting needles at a piece of woollen work – not a common sight in a waterfront dosshouse. He purled, or cast off, or whatever it is that knitters do when they want to take a breather, and nodded to a fellow in a striped shirt who was laying some coins on the counter. Then he looked at me, and I realised that the loungers were doing the same, in a most disconcerting way.

I had got some sense back now, and saw that this was plainly the receipt of custom, where guests settled their accounts and ordered up their carriages. Equally plainly, I'd spent the night on the premises, but when I put a hand to my pocket, the bald head shook emphatically.

"You paid for, Yonny," says the Knitting Swede. "You wan' some grub yust now?"

I declined, with thanks, and he nodded again. "You got a ship, maybe?"

I was about to say no, but one look at the loungers stopped me: too many ferret eyes and ugly mugs for my liking, and I'd no wish to be crimped a second time. I said I had a ship, and a greasy disease in a billycock hat and brass watch-chain asked:

"What ship would that be, sailor?"

"The *Sea Witch*, and I'm Bully Waterman,[15] so get the hell out of my way!" says I. Being over six feet and heavy set has its uses, and I was out in the street and round the corner before he'd had time to offer me a drink and a billy behind the ear. You didn't linger in establishments like the Knitting Swede's, not unless you fancied a free holiday in a whaler for the next couple of years. I walked on quickly, reflecting that it had been considerate of Lynch to pay my lodging; but then, it may have been a club rule that insensible members had to be settled for in advance.

I walked for two minutes, and felt so groggy that I had to sit down on a barrel at the mouth of an alley, where I took stock. I knew I was in sailortown, Baltimore, but that was all. The growth on my chin told me I hadn't been ashore above twenty-four hours. Whatever information Spring had sent to the authorities must have been in their hands for two

73

days by now, and no doubt it would contain an excellent description, even down to my clothes. These consisted of a shirt and trousers, boots, and a canvas jacket, the crease not improved by a night in that verminous hole I'd just escaped from. (I've since learned, by the way, that it was quite celebrated among the less discriminating seafarers; if you'd stopped at the Knitting Swede's you could dine out on it in every shebeen from Glasgow to Sydney.)[16]

Now, I doubted if the authorities would be scouring the streets for Beauchamp Millward Comber, but the sooner I was under the protection of my country's flag, the better. A port the size of Baltimore must surely have a British consul, or some kind of commercial representative at least, who shouldn't be too difficult to find; he might look askance at my appearance, but it would have to do, since Captain Lynch's generosity hadn't run the length of leaving a single damned penny, or anything else, in my pockets. It wouldn't make my bona fides any easier to establish, but I'd meet that trouble when I came to it.

Although I'd been in Baltimore before, with the U.S. Navy folk, I'd no notion of how the town lay, so I took a slant along the street, which was bustling with business round the chandlers' shops and warehouses, and approached a prosperous-looking old gent to inquire the way to the centre of town. I'd barely got a word out when he rounded on me.

"You goddam leeches, can't you work for a change!" cries he. "I declare you're stout enough!" He slapped ten cents into my hand and strode on, leaving me wondering if it would buy me a shave . . . and now that my head was clearing, I found I was almighty hungry . . .

D'you know, within an hour I was richer by four dollars, and a splendid new vocabulary – the first time I ever heard the word "bum" mean anything but backside was on that morning. The beauty of it was, I didn't have to beg, even: my dishevelled clothing, unshaven chin, and most charming smile, with a courteous finger raised to the brow, marked me as a mendicant, apparently, and for every nine who brushed past, a tenth would drop a few coppers in my palm. Damned interesting, I found it. Women were altogether

74

more generous than men, especially as I moved up-town; when I approached two fashionable young misses with "Pardon me, marm" and a bow, one of them exclaimed "Oh, my!" and gave me fifty cents and a fluttery look before they hurried away tittering. I left off, though, when I became aware that I was being watched by a belted constable with a damned disinheriting moustache, but I've calculated since that I could have cleared ten thousand dollars a year on the streets of Baltimore, easy, which is two thousand quid, sufficient to buy you a lieutenancy in the Guards in those days – and from the look of some of them, I'd not be surprised.

I was still no nearer finding the consul, and the constable had given me a scare, so after a shave and brush-up and a hearty steak and eggs at a chop-house, I looked for a fellow-countryman – and the sure way to do that in America in those days was to find a Catholic church. I spotted one, noted that the name of its priest displayed on the gilt board was Rafferty, made my way through the musty wax-and-image interior, and found the man himself delving like a navigator in the garden behind the church, whistling "The Young May Moon" in his shirt-sleeves. He greeted me with a cry of "Hollo, me son, and what can I be doin' for ye on this parky day?" a jaunty little leprechaun with a merry eye.

I asked my question and he pulled a face. "Faith, now, an' I don't know there's any such crater in Baltimore," says he. "Jist off the boat, are ye?" The shrewd blue eyes took me in. "Well, if 'tis diplomatic assistance ye're seekin', Washington'll be the place for you, where our minister is. He's new come, an' all, they tell me – Lyons, his name is, an English feller. He'll be your man, right enough. And what would ye say, yes or no, to a cup o' tea?"

Seeing him so affable, and with only two dollars in my pocket, it struck me that if I played smooth I might touch him for the fare to Washington, so I affected the faintest of brogues and introduced myself as Grattan Nugent-Hare (who was rotting safely in a cottonwood grove somewhere south of Socorro) of the Rathfarnham and Trinity College, lately arrived to join my brother Frank, who held a minor

75

position in a Washington bank. Unfortunately, I had been set upon soon after landing the previous night, and was without cash or effects. He opened eyes and mouth wide.

"D'ye tell me? Dear God, what's the world comin' to? An' you wi' your foot barely on the ground, and from Dublin, too! Have ye been to the police, man dear? Ye have – an' got little good o' them? Aye, well, they've a hard row to hoe, wi' some queer ones in this town, I'll tell ye! They wouldn't know of a British consul, neither . . . ? No, no . . . it's a wonder they didn't think to steer you to a feller-countryman, at least – there's enough of English and our-selves hereabouts, God knows. But they didn't; ah, well. But come away an' we'll have that dish o' tea while we think what's best to be done. An' how's the Liffey lookin', eh?"

I sat in his kitchen while he prattled Irishly and made tea. Since I'd never been in Dublin in my life, I found it safest to let him run on, with a cheery agreement from time to time, waiting an opportunity to state my needs, but he didn't give me one, being content to prose sentimentally about the "ould country", until:

"An' ye're in the banking line yourself, are ye?" says he at last. "Ah, well, ye're in the right furrow in Ameriky; fine grand opportunities for a gentleman like yourself, so there are; it's a commercial world, so it is, a commercial world, but none the worse for bein' that if the trade's honest an' the word's good! An' ye're a Trinity man, too!" He chuckled wistfully. "Ah, this is a country of grand prospects, but I wonder could a man do better than sit in the ould College court contemplatin' the trees on St Stephen's Green on a summer's evenin'? You'd be there about '45, am I right?"

I made a hasty calculation and said, rather earlier, '43.

"Then ye would know ould Professor Faylen!" cries he. "A fine man, that, an' a grand Hebrew scholar, so they said, not that I'm a judge. He would still be about in your day, was he not?"

I can smell a false lead as fast as anyone, but he was such a happy simpleton that I decided it was safe to say I hadn't studied under Faylen myself, but knew of him. He nodded amiably, and sighed.

"Ah, well, here am I blatherin' on, an' you itchin' to take your way to Washington. Aye, but with your pockets all to let. Well, man dear, I was after thinkin' yonder that I'd be makin' ye a small loan for your train ticket, but d'ye know, I'd be party to an awful sin if I did that, so I would. Ye see," says he, shaking his pawky old head, "the day ye find a priest sittin' in the court at Trinity is a day ye'll be able to skate over Dublin Bay from Bray to Balbriggan – an' as for seein' St Stephen's Green from the court, well, I doubt if even ould Faylen could see that far from heaven, where he's been this five-and-thirty years, God rest his soul. An' tellin' me ye were a banker," he added sorrowfully, "an' you wid spurs an' brass buttons stickin' out all over ye! Now, will ye take another drop o' tea . . . *soldier*, an' tell me all about it?"

"You wouldn't believe it if I did," says I, rising. "Thank'ee for the tea, padre, and I'll bid you a very good day."

"Stop, stop!" cries he. "Sit down, man dear, an' don't be takin' offence at an ould man jist because he knows Phoenix Park shoulders when he sees them! Come, now, be easy, an' drink your tea. Can ye not see I'm burstin' to know the truth of it?"

His smile was so eager and friendly that I found myself smiling in turn. "What makes you think I'll tell truth this time?"

"Why shouldn't ye? Ye'll come to no harm from me if ye do. An' if ye don't – well, am I to have no diversion at all? Now then – whut's this I wouldn't believe? Jist you try me!"

"Very well . . . I'm a British Army officer, I was on my way home from India, I was waylaid at Cape Town and crimped aboard a packet which arrived here yesterday, I'm destitute – but thanks to you I know where to find British authorities who'll help me back to England. And if you believe that –"

"And why would I not? It fits ye better than all that moon-shine about bankin' an' Trinity, I'll say that for it! What's your name, my son?"

There was no earthly reason why I shouldn't tell him – so I shook my head. Least said.

"An' why didn't ye ask direction from the first policeman ye saw?" I still said nothing, and he nodded, no longer smiling. I rose again to go, for the sooner I was out of this, the better, but he stayed me with a hand on my sleeve. "Ye'll tell me no more? Well, now, just bide a minute while I think about . . . no, don't go! Ye want the fare to Washington, don't ye?"

I waited, while he cogitated, chin in hand, eyes bright as a bird's.

"Tell ye whut I think. Ye're an officer, an' a bit of a gentleman – I know the look. An' ye're a runner – now, now, don't be addin' to your sins by denyin' it, for I had a parish in Leix in the Great Trouble, an' I know *that* look, too – aye, twice as long in the leg as ye would be if I put a fut-rule on ye! An', man dear, ye're a desperate liar . . . but who's not, will ye tell me? But ye're civil, at least – an' ye're Army, an' didn't me own father an' two uncles an' that other good Irishman Arthur Wellesley follow the flag across Spain togither – they did!" He paused, and sighed. "Now, ye're a Protestant, so I can't penance ye for tellin' lies. But since I'm dreadful afflicted wid the rheumatics, and can't abide diggin' at all, at all . . . well, if ye can sink your gentlemanly pride an' finish them two rows for me, why, t'will be for the good o' your soul an' my body. An' there'll be ten dollars to take ye to Washington – nine an' a half in loan, to be repaid at your convenience, an' fifty cents for your labour. Well . . . what say ye, my son?"

Well, I needed that ten dollars . . . but who'd have thought, when Campbell pinned my Cross on me, that seven months later I'd be digging a bog-trotter's garden in Maryland? Father Rafferty watched me as I turned the last sods, observing dryly that it was plain to see I was English from the way I handled a spade. Then he gave me a mug of beer, and counted ten dollars carefully into my palm.

"I'll walk ye to the station," says he. "No one'll look twice at ye when ye're keepin' step wid the Church. An' I can see ye don't get on the wrong train, or lose your money, or go astray anyways, ye know?"

He put me on the right train, sure enough, but the rest

of his statement proved as wrong as could be. Someone did look at us, but I didn't notice at the time, possibly because I was busy parrying Rafferty's artful questions about the Army and India – at least I could satisfy him I was telling the truth about those.

"Ask at the Washington station where the British minister's to be found," he advised me, "an' if they don't know, make your way to Willard's Hotel on Fourteenth Street, an' they'll set ye right. It's the great place, an' if they turn up their noses at your togs, jist give 'em your Hyde Park swagger, eh?

"But mind how ye go, now!" cries he, as I mounted the step to the coach. "T'will be dark by the time ye get in, an' 'tis a desperate place for garotters an' scallywags an' the like! We wouldn't want ye waylaid a second time, would we?"

Gratitude ain't my long suit, as you know, but he'd seen me right, and he was a cheery wee soul; looking down at the smiling pixie face under the round hat, I couldn't help liking the little murphy, and wondering why he'd been at such pains on my behalf. It's a priest's business, of course, to succour the distressed sinner, but I knew there was more in it than that. He was a lonely old man, far from home, and he was Irish, and had guessed I was on the run, and I was Army, like his father and uncles. And he had taken to me, as folk do, even when they know I'm not straight.

"I wish ye'd tell me your name, though!" says he, when I thanked him. I said I'd send him my card when I repaid the ten dollars.

"That ye will!" cries he heartily. "In the meantime, though – your Christian name, eh?"

"Harry."

"I believe ye – ye look like a Harry. God knows ye didn't look like – what was't? – Grattan? Grattan the banker from the Rathfarnham – the impidence of it!" He laughed, and looked wistful. "Aye, me – sometimes I could wish I'd been a rascal meself."

"It's never too late," says I, and he spluttered in delight.

"Git away wid ye, spalpeen!" cries he, and stood waving

79

as the train pulled out, a little black figure vanishing into the hissing steam.

I reckon Father Rafferty was one of those good fools who are put into the world to grease the axles for people like me. They charm so easy, if you play 'em right, and the bigger a scoundrel you are the more they'll put themselves out for you, no doubt in the hope that if you do reform, they'll get that much more treasure in heaven for it. You may be astonished to know that I did repay the loan, later on, but in no spirit of gratitude or obligation, or because I'd quite liked the little ass. No, I paid because I could easily afford it, and there's one rule, as a practising pagan, that I don't break if I can help it – never offend the local tribal gods; it ain't lucky.

It was dark when we pulled into Washington, and the conductor had never heard of the British ministry; oh, sure, he knew Willard's Hotel, but plainly wondered what business this rumpled traveller without a hat could have at such a select establishment. He was starting to give me reluctant directions when a chap who'd alighted from the train directly behind me said if it was Willard's I wanted, why, he was going that way himself. He was a sober-looking young fellow, neatly dressed, so I thanked him and we went out of the crowded station into a dark and dirty Washington evening.

"It's close enough to walk if you don't mind the rain," says my companion, and since it seemed only prudent to save my cash, I agreed, and we set off. It wasn't too damp, but Washington didn't seem to have improved much in ten years; they were still building the place, and making heavy weather of it, for the street we followed was ankle-deep in mud, and so poor was the lighting that you couldn't see where you were putting your feet. We jostled along the sidewalk, blundering into people, and presently my guide pulled up with a mild oath, glanced about him, and said we'd be quicker taking a side-street. It didn't look much better than an alley, but he led the way confidently, so I ploughed on behind, thinking no evil – and suddenly he lengthened his stride, wheeled round to face me, and whistled sharply.

80

I'm too old a hand to stand with my mouth open. I turned to flee for the main street, cursing myself for having been so easily duped, and after Rafferty's warning about footpads too – and stopped dead in my tracks. Two dark figures were blocking my way, and before I had time to turn again to rush on my single ambusher, the larger one stepped forward, but when he raised his hands it wasn't to strike; he held them palms towards me in a restraining gesture, and his voice when he spoke was quiet, even friendly.

"Good evening, Mr Comber. Welcome back, sir – why, you mayn't believe it, but this is just like old times!"

For a split second I was paralysed in mind and body, and then came the icy stab of terror as I thought: police! . . . Spring's letters, my description, the alarm going out for Comber – but then why had the young man not clapped his hand on my shoulder at the station . . . ?

"Guess you don't remember me," says the big shadow. "It's been a whiles – N'awlins, ten years ago, in back of Willinck's place. You thought I was Navy, then. I took you to Crixus, remember?"

It was so incredible that it took me a moment to recall who "Crixus" was – the Underground Railroad boss whose identity I never knew because he hid it under the name of some Roman slave who'd been a famous rebel. Crixus was the little steely-eyed bugger who'd dragooned me into running that uppity nigger Randolph up the river, and dam' near got me shot – but it wasn't possible that he could know of my presence now, within a day of my landing . . .

"He's waitin' to see you," says the big fellow, "an' the sooner we get you off the streets, the better. We've got a closed cab –"

"I don't understand! You're quite mistaken, sir – I know of nobody called . . . Cricket, did you say?" I was babbling with shock, and he absolutely laughed.

"Say, I wish I could think as quick as you do! Ten years ago, Billy," says he to his companion, "when we jumped this fellow, he started talkin' *Dutch*! Now, come along, Mr Comber –'cos I'd know you anywhere, an' we're wastin' time *and* safety." His voice hardened, and he took my arm. "We mean you no harm – like I once told you, you're the last man I'd want to hurt!"

82

Sometimes you feel you're living your life over again. It was so now, and for an uncanny moment I was back in the alley behind Susie's brothel, with the three figures materialising out of the darkness . . . "Hold it right there, mister! You're covered, front and rear!" I knew now it was no use bluffing or running; for good or ill, they had me.

"It wasn't Dutch, it was German," says I. "Very well, I'm the man you call Comber, and I'll be happy to take your cab – but not to Mr Crixus! Not until I've been to the British ministry!"

"No, sir!" snaps he. "We got our orders. An' believe me, you'll be a sight safer with us than in the British ministry, not if your whole Queen's Navy was guarding it! So come on, mister!"

God knew what that meant, but it settled it. Whatever Crixus wanted – and I still couldn't take in that he'd got word of me (dammit, he should have been in Orleans, anyway) or that these fellows were real – he'd been a friend, after his fashion, and was evidently still well disposed. And with the three pressing about me, and my arm in a strong hand, I had no choice.

"Very good," says I. "But you don't put a sack over my head this time!"

He laughed, and said I was a card, and then they were bustling me out of the alley and into a closed growler – mighty practised, with one in front, one gripping me, the third behind. The big man shouted to the driver, and we were lurching along, back towards the station, as near as I could judge, and then we swung right across a broad quagmire of a street, and through the left-hand window I caught a glimpse in the distance of what I recognised as the Capitol without its dome – they still hadn't got its bloody lid on, would you believe it, in 1859? – and knew we must be crossing the Avenue, going south. The big man saw me looking, and whipped down the blinds, and we bowled along in the stuffy darkness in silence, while I strove to calm my quivering nerves and think out what it all meant. How they'd found me, I couldn't fathom, and it mattered less than what lay ahead . . . what the devil could Crixus want with me? A

83

horrid thought – did he know I'd left Randolph to his fate on that steamboat? Well, I'd thought the bastard was dead, and he'd turned up later in Canada, anyway, so I'd heard, so it wasn't likely to be that. He couldn't want me to run niggers again, surely? No, it defied all explanation, so I sat fretting in the cab with the big man at my side and his two mates opposite, for what must have been a good half-hour, and then the cab stopped and we descended on what looked like a suburban street, with big detached houses in gloomy gardens either side, and underfoot nothing but Washington macadam: two feet of gumbo.

They led me through a gate and up a path to a great front door. The big fellow knocked a signal, and we were in a dim hall with a couple of hard-looking citizens, one of 'em a black with shoulders like a prize-fighter. "Here he is," says my big escort, and a moment later I was blinking in the brightness of a well-furnished drawing-room, only half-believing the sight of the bird-like figure crying welcome from a great chair by the fireplace. He was thinner than I remembered, and terribly frail, but there was no mistaking the bald dome of head and the glinting spectacles beneath brows like white hedgerows. He had a rug over his knees, and from his wasted look I guessed he was crippled now, but he was fairly whimpering in rapture, stretching out his arms towards me.

"It is he! My prayers are answered! God has sent you back to us! Oh, my boy, my brave boy, come to my arms – let me embrace you!" He was absolutely weeping for joy, which ain't usually how I'm greeted, but I deemed it best to submit; it was like being clutched by a weak skeleton smelling of camphor. "Oh, my boy!" sobs he. "*Ave, Spartacus!* Oh, stand there a moment that I may look on you! Oh, Moody, do you remember that night – that blessed night when we set George Randolph on the golden road to freedom? And here he is again, that Mr Standfast who led him through the Valley of the Shadow to the Enchanted Ground!"

With one or two stops at Vanity Fair, if he'd only known, but now he broke down altogether, blubbering, while my big guardian, Moody, sucked his teeth, and the black, who'd come into the room with him, glowered at me as though it were my fault that the old fool was having hysterics. He calmed down in a moment, mopping himself and repeating over and over that God had sent me, which I didn't like the sound of – I mean to say, what had he sent me *for*? It might be that Crixus, having heard of my arrival, God knew how, was merely intent on a glad reunion and prose over good old slave-stealing times, but I doubted it, knowing him. He might have one foot in the grave and t'other hopping on the brink, but the grey eyes behind his glasses were as fierce as ever, and if his frame was feeble, his spirit plainly wasn't.

"God has sent you!" cries he again. "In the very hour! For I see His hand in this!" He turned to Moody. "How did you find him?"

"Cormack telegraphed when he boarded the train at the Baltimore depot. Wilkerson and I were waiting when the train came in. He didn't give any trouble."

"Why should he?" cries Crixus, and beamed at me. "He knows he has no truer, more devoted friends on earth than we, who owe him so much! But sit down, sit down, Mr Comber – Joe, a glass of wine for our friend . . . no, stay, it was brandy, was it not? I remember, you see!" he chuckled. "Brandy for heroes, as the good doctor said! And for ourselves, Joe! Gentlemen, I give you a toast: 'George Randolph, on free soil! And his deliverer!'"

It was plain he didn't know the truth of how dear George and I had parted company, and I was not about to enlighten him. I looked manly as he and Moody and Black Joe raised their glasses, wondering what the deuce was coming next, and decided to get my oar in first. I didn't need to pitch him a tale, much less the truth; you see, to him, Comber was the British Admiralty's beau sabreur in the war against the slave trade; that was how he'd thought of me ten years ago, as a man of intrigue and mystery, and he'd not expect explanation from me now. So, once I'd responded with a toady toast of my own ("The Underground Railroad, and its illustrious station master!", which almost had him piping his modest eye again), I put it to him plain, with that earnest courtesy which I knew Comber himself would have used, if he hadn't been feeding the fish off Guinea since '48.

"My dear sir," says I, "I can find no words to express the joy it gives me to see you again – why, as Mr Moody said just now, it is like old times, though how you knew I was in Baltimore I cannot think –"

"Come, come, Mr Comber!" cries he. "Surely you haven't forgotten? 'An ear to every wall, and an eye at every window', you know. Not a word passes, not a line is written, from the Congress to the taproom, that the Railroad does not hear and see." He looked solemn. "It needs not me to tell you that you have enemies – but they may be closer than you think! Two days ago the police, here and in Baltimore, had word of your presence – aye, and of those brave deeds which our vicious and unjust laws call crimes!" His voice rose in shrill anger, while I thought, well, thank'ee Spring. "We have watched every road and depot since – and thank God, here you are!"

"And you're right, sir!" cries I heartily. "He has sent me to you indeed, for I need your help – I must reach the British ministry tonight at all costs –"

He jerked up a hand to check me, and even then I couldn't help noticing how thin and wasted it was; I'll swear I could see the lamplight through it.

"Not a word! Say no more, sir! Whatever message you wish to send shall reach your minister, never fear – but what it is, I have no wish to know, nor what brings you to our country again, for I know your lips must be sealed. I can be sure," says he, looking holy, "that you are engaged on that noble work dear to your heart and mine – the great crusade against slavery to which we have dedicated our lives! In this our countries are at one – for make no mistake, sir, we in America are purging the poison from our nation's veins at last, the battle is fully joined against those traitors within our gates, those traffickers in human flesh, those betrayers of our glorious Constitution, those *gentlemen* of Dixie –" he spat out the word as if it had been vinegar "– who build their blood-smeared fortunes with the shackle and the lash –"

86

At this point he ran short of air, and sank back in his chair, panting, while Moody helped him to brandy and Joe gave me another glower, as though *I'd* set the senile idiot off. He'd always been liable to cut loose like a Kilkenny electioneer whenever slavery was mentioned, and here he was, doddering towards the knackers' yard, still at it. I waited until he'd recovered, thanked him warmly, and said I'd be obliged if Moody could convoy me to the ministry without delay. At this Crixus blinked, looking uncertain.

"Must you go . . . in person? Can he not take a note . . . papers?" He gave a feeble little wave, forcing a smile. "Can you not stay . . . there is so much to say . . . so much that I would tell you –"

"And I long to hear it, sir!" cries I. "But I must see the minister tonight."

He didn't like it, and hesitated, glancing at Moody and Joe, and in that moment I felt the first cold touch of dread – the old bastard was up to something, but didn't know how to spring it; while all sense and logic told me that he could have no business with me, at such short notice, my coward's nose was scenting mischief breast-high – well, by God, he'd flung me into the soup once, and he wasn't doing it again. I rose, ready to go, and he gave a whimper.

"Mr Comber, sir, a moment! Half an hour will make no difference, surely? Spare me that time, sir – nay, I insist, you must! You shall not regret it, I assure you! Indeed, if I know you," and he gave me a smile whose radiance chilled my blood, "you will bless the chance that brought you here!"

I doubted that, but I couldn't well refuse. He had that implacable light in his eye, smile or no, and Moody and Joe seemed to be standing just an inch taller than a moment since. I gave in with good grace and sat down again, and Joe filled my glass.

Crixus studied a moment, as though unsure how to begin, and then said he supposed I knew how things stood in America at present. I said I didn't, since my work had taken me east, not west, and I'd lost sight of colonial affairs, so to speak. He frowned, as though I'd no business to be mess-ing with foreign parts, and I thought to impress him by adding that I'd been in Russia and India.

"Russia?" wonders he, as though it were the Isle of Wight. "Ah, to be sure, that unhappy country, which forges its own chains." I tried to look as though I'd been freeing serfs right and left. "But . . . India? There is no slavery question there, surely?"

I said, no, but there had been a recent disturbance of which he might have heard, and I must go where my chiefs sent me. He didn't seem to think much of India, or my irresponsible chiefs, and returned to matters of importance.

"Then you may not know that the storm is gathering over our beloved country, and soon must break. Yes, sir," cries he, getting into his stride, "the night is almost past, but the dawn will come in a tempest that will scour the land to its roots, cleansing it of the foulness that disfigures it, so that it may emerge into the golden sunlight of universal freedom! It will be a time of sore trial, of blood and lamentation, but when the crisis is past, Mr Comber, victory will be ours, for slavery will be dead!" Now he was at full gallop, eyes bright with zeal. "Yes, sir, the sands of pleading and persuasion are running out; the time has come to unsheath the sword! What has patience earned us? Our enemies harden their hearts and mock our entreaties; they stamp their foot with even grosser cruelty upon the helpless bodies of our black brethren!" I stole a look at our black brother Joe, to see how he was taking this; he was listening, rapt, and I'd not have stamped on him for a pension. "But the nation is waking at last – oh, its leaders shuffle and compromise and placate the butchers, but among the people, sir, the belief is growing that it is time to arm, that the cancer can be cut out only by the sword! America is a powder-keg, sir, and it needs but a spark to fire the train!"

He paused for breath, and since the real Comber would have raised a cheer, I resisted the temptation to cry "Hear! hear!" and ventured a fervent "Amen!" Crixus nodded, dabbing his lips with a handkerchief, and sat forward, laying his skinny hand on mine.

"Yet still the people hesitate, for it is a fearful prospect,

Mr Comber! Not for four score years have we faced such peril. 'It would destroy us!' cry the fainthearts. 'Let it be!' cry the thoughtless. Still they hope that conflict may be avoided – but given a lead, they will cast away their doubts! It needs a man to give that lead, sir – to fire that train!" He was staring at me, his talons tightening. "And God, in His infinite wisdom, has sent us such a man!"

For one horrible instant I thought he meant me. I've heard worse, you know, and I knew what this little fanatic was capable of when he had the bit between his teeth. I stared back, stricken, and he asked:

"What do you know of John Brown?"

That he's a hairy impertinent lout who can hold more hard liquor than a distillery, was my immediate thought, for the only John Brown I knew was a young ghillie who'd had to be carried home on a hurdle the day I'd gone on that ghastly deer-stalk with Prince Albert at Balmoral, when Ignatieff had come within an ace of filling me with buckshot. But Crixus could never have heard of *him*, for this, you see, was years before Balmoral Brown had become famous as our gracious Queen's attendant (and some said, more than that, but it's all rot, in my opinion, for little Vicky had excellent taste in men, bar Albert; she always fancied me).

I confessed I'd never heard of an American called John Brown, and Crixus said "Ah!" with the satisfied gleam of one who is bursting with great news to tell, which he did, and that was the first I ever heard of Old Ossawatomie, the Angel of the Lord – or the murderous rustler, whichever you like. To Crixus he was God's own prophet, a kind of Christ with six-guns, but if I give you *his* version, unvarnished, you'll start off with a lop-sided view, so I'll interpolate what I learned later, from Brown himself, and from friends and foes alike, all of it true, so far as I know – which ain't to say that Crixus wasn't truthful, too.

"Picture a Connecticut Yankee, a child of the Mayflower Pilgrims, as American as the soil from which he sprang!" says he. "Born of poor and humble folk, raised in honest poverty, with little schooling save from the Bible, accustomed as a lad to go barefoot alone a hundred miles driving

89

his father's herd. See him growing to vigorous manhood, strong, independent, and devout, imbued with the love of liberty, not only for himself, but for all men, hating slavery with a deep, burning detestation, yet in his nature kind, benevolent, and wise, though less shrewd in business, in which he had but indifferent success."

[Flashy: True, for his childhood, but omits that when he was four he stole some brass pins from a little girl, was whipped by his mother, lost a yellow marble given him by an Indian boy, had a pet squirrel, and a lamb which died. On his own admission, J.B. was a ready liar, rough but not quarrelsome, knew great swathes of the Scriptures, and grew up expecting life to be tough. As a man, his business career could indeed be called indifferent, since he made a hash of farming, tanning, sheep-herding, and surveying, accumulated little except a heap of debts, law-suits, and twenty children, and went bankrupt.]

"Then, sir, about twenty years ago, he conceived a plan – nay, a wondrous vision, whereby slavery in the United States might be destroyed at a stroke. It was revolutionary, it was inspired, but his genius told him it was premature, and wisely he kept it in his heart, shared only with a few whom he trusted. These comprehended his sons, on whom he laid, by sacred oaths, the duty to fight against slavery until it was slain utterly! That duty," says Crixus, "they began to fulfil when, grown to manhood, they sought their fortunes in Kansas, on whose blood-drenched soil was fought the first great battle between Abolitionist and Slaver, between Freedom and Tyranny, between Mansoul and Diabolus – and there, Mr Comber, in the scorching heat of that furnace of conflict, was tempered the soul and resolution of him whom we are proud to call Captain John Brown!"

[Flashy: We'll leave the "wondrous vision" for the moment, if you don't mind, and deal with "Bleeding Kansas", which like everything to do with American politics is difficult, dull, and damned dirty, but you need to know about it if you're to understand John Brown. The great question was: should Kansas be a free state or a slave one, and since it was up to the residents to decide, and America being devoted to democracy, both factions rushed in "voters" from the free North and the slave South (Missouri, mostly), elections were rigged, ballot-boxes were stuffed, and before you knew it fighting and raiding had broken out between the Free Staters and the "Border Ruffians" of the slavery party. Brown and his sons had joined in on the free side, and taken to strife like ducks to water. It was the first real armed clash between North and South, and you get the flavour of the thing from the Missouri orator who advised: "Be brave, be orderly, and if any man or woman stand in your way, blow 'em to hell with a chunk of cold lead!"][17]

"Nor was it long," says Crixus, "before Captain Brown's fame as a champion of freedom was heard throughout the land. Too late to prevent the wanton destruction of the town of Lawrence by Border Ruffians, he was moved to wrath by the news that the conflict had spread to the halls of Congress, where the brave Senator Sumner raised his voice against the despoilers of Lawrence, and was clubbed almost to death in his very seat by a coward from South Carolina! In the very Senate, Mr Comber! Conceive if you can, sir, the emotions stirred in the honest bosom of John Brown – and ask yourself, is it matter for wonder that when, a few hours later, he came on Southern bullies threatening violence to a Free State man, he should smite them with the sword? Yet there are those who would call this just chastisement murder, and clamour for the law to be invoked against him!"

[Flashy: Well, Crixus was only saying what he and most of the North believed, but the truth of the matter was that Brown and his boys had gone to the homes of five pro-slave men who weren't threatening anybody, ordered them outside, and sliced 'em up like so much beef with sabres; the men were unarmed, and it was done in cold blood. J.B. himself never denied the deed, though he claimed not to have killed anyone himself. That was the Pottawatomie Massacre, the first real reprisal by the Free Staters, and the most notorious act of J.B.'s life, bar Harper's Ferry three years later, and even his worshippers have never been able to explain it away; most of 'em just ignore it.]

"So now," says Crixus, "he was a hunted outlaw, he and

his brave band. They must live like beasts in the wild, while the full fury of the Border Ruffians was turned on the unhappy land. Men were slaughtered, homes and farms burned – two hundred men, Mr Comber, died in the fighting of that terrible summer of '56, property valued at thousands of dollars destroyed – but John Brown held the banner of freedom aloft, and his name was a terror to the tyrants. At last the Border Ruffians descended in overwhelming force on his home at Ossawatomie, put it to the torch, slew his son Frederick, and drove the heroic father from the territory – too late! John Brown's work in Kansas was done! It is free soil today, and shall so remain, but more, far more than this, he had lighted Liberty's beacon for all America to see, and shown that there can be but one end to this struggle – war to the bitter end against slavery!"

[Flashy: On the whole, I agree. J.B. hadn't ensured Kansas's freedom – the will of the majority, and the fact that its climate was no good for slave crops like cotton and sugar and baccy, saw to that. But Crixus was right: he had lit the beacon, for while he and his boys were only one of many gangs of marauders and killers who fought in "Bleeding Kansas", his was the name that was remembered; he was the symbol of the fight against slavery. The legend of the Avenging Angel grew out of the Pottawatomie Massacre and the battle at Black Jack, where he licked the militia and took them prisoner. To the abolitionists back east he was the embodiment of freedom, smiting the slavery men hip and thigh, and the tale lost nothing in the telling by the Yankee press. You may guess what the South thought of him: murderer, brigand, fiend in human shape, and arch-robber – and I'm bound to say, just from what he later told me himself, that he did his share of plundering, especially of horses, for which he had a good eye. But whatever else he did in Kansas, John Brown accomplished one thing: he turned the anti-slavery crusade into an armed struggle, and made North and South weigh each other as enemies. He put gunsmoke on the breeze, and the whole of America sniffed it in – and didn't find the odour displeasing.][18]

Crixus had paused for breath and another sip of brandy,

but now he leaned forward and gripped my hands in his excitement.

"Do you know what he said, Mr Comber, this good and great old man, as he gazed back at his burning home, his revolvers smoking in his hands, his eyes brimmed with tears for his murdered child? Can you guess, sir, what were those words that have rung like a trumpet blast in the ears of his countrymen?"

I said I couldn't imagine, and he gulped and raised his eyes to the ceiling. "He said: 'God sees it. I have only one death to die, and I will die fighting in this cause. There will be no peace in the land until slavery is done for. I will carry the war into Africa!'"

"I say! Why Africa? I mean, it's the dooce of a long way, and what about transport and –"

"No, no!" cries he impatiently. "By Africa he meant the South – the land of darkness and savage oppression. For now he knew that the time was come to realise his dream – that vision of which I spoke!" He was spraying slightly, and I could see that the great news was coming at last. "The invasion of Virginia – that, sir, was his plan, and the hour is nigh for its fulfilment, after years of maturing and preparation. He purposes an armed raid to seize a federal arsenal, and with the captured munitions and supplies, to equip the slaves who will cast off their bonds and rush to join his standard! They will withdraw into the mountain fastnesses, and there wage guerrilla war against their former masters – oh, he has studied the ancient wars, sir, and Lord Wellington's campaign in Spain! Formerly it was his design to found an independent black republic, but now his vision has soared beyond, for can it be doubted that once his army is in the hills, every slave in the South will rise up in arms? There will be such a rebellion as was never seen, and whatever its outcome, the greater battle will be joined! Free men everywhere will rally to the standard that John Brown has raised, and slavery will be whelmed forever in the irresistible tide of liberty!"

He was almost falling out of his chair with enthusiasm, and Moody had to settle him while Joe refilled his glass and helped him take a refreshing swig; neither of them said anything, but Crixus was staring at me with the eager expectancy of a drawing-room tenor who has just finished butchering "The Flowers on Mother's Grave", and awaits applause. Plainly this fellow Brown was a raving loose screw, and I knew Crixus was no better, but it behoved me to respond as Comber would have responded, and then take my leave for the British ministry. So . . .

"Hallelujah!" says I. "What a splendid stroke! Why, it will give these . . . these slavers the rightabout altogether! A capital notion, and will be well received . . . er, everywhere, I'll be bound! I suppose it's a well-kept secret at the moment, what? Just so, that's prudent – I'll not breathe a word, of course. Well, it's getting late, so –"

"It is no secret, Mr Comber," says he solemnly. "The where and when John Brown has yet to determine, but the intent is known, if not to the public at large, certainly to all who labour secretly for liberty – aye, even in Congress it is known, thanks to the treachery of Captain Brown's most trusted lieutenant. You stare, Mr Comber? Well you may, for the traitor was a countryman of your own, a rascal named Forbes, enlisted for his military experience, gained in Italy with Garibaldi. He it was who babbled the secret, abusing Brown's name because, he claimed, his pay was in arrears! Fortunately, those Senators in whom he confided were no friends to slavery, so no great harm was done, and Brown at least became aware what a viper he had nourished in his bosom.[19] Nor has he himself sought to conceal his design. Since leaving Kansas he has been about the North, preaching, exhorting, raising the funds necessary for his great enterprise, purchasing arms, rifles and revolvers and pikes –"

"Pikes, did you say?"

"Indeed, to arm the slaves when the hour strikes! Wherever he has gone, men have fallen under his spell, seeing in him another Cromwell, another Washington, destined to bring his country liberty! Everywhere he rallies support. Alas," he shook his head, glooming, "more have promised than performed; his treasury is low, his army stout of heart but few in number, and even those devoted leaders of opinion who wholeheartedly approve his end, shrink timidly at the mention of his means. Oh, blind! Do they think pious words can prevail against the shackle and the lash and the guns of the Border Ruffians? The dam' fools!" cries he, in unwonted passion. "Oh, they are sincere – Parker and Gerrit Smith, Sanborn and Higginson, members of the Secret Six who are heart and soul in the cause, yet fearful of the storm that John Brown's scheme would unloose! The North is with him in sympathy, Mr Comber, aye, many even in the halls of Congress, but when his hand goes to his pistol butt, they quake like women, dreading lest he destroys the Union – as if that mattered, so it is made whole again when slavery is dead –"

"But hold on – a moment, sir, if you please!" I tried to calm him before he did himself a mischief. "You say they know in Congress – in the government? And he goes about, er, preaching and so forth . . . well, how does he escape arrest, I mean to say?"

"Arrest John Brown?" He gave a bitter cackle. "Why, then, sir, we should have a storm indeed! The North would not abide it, Mr Comber! He is our hero! And he goes silently, without fanfare, appearing only in those public places where his enemies would not dare raise their voices, let alone their hands! Oh, Missouri has set a bounty of $3000 on his head, and that pusillanimous wretch who calls himself our President, and whose cowardice has rent the Democratic Party in twain, has sunk so low as to offer $250 – why not thirty, in silver, false Buchanan? – for his apprehension! But who in the North would try to claim such rewards?"

That's America for you: a maniac at large, threatening to stir up war and slave rebellion, and nothing done about it. Not that I gave a dam; what with brandy and sitting down I was feeling easier than I'd done all day, and was becoming most infernally bored with Captain Brown and his madcap plans for setting the darkies against their owners (with pikes, I ask you!), and anxious to be gone. So I shook my head in wonder, expressed admiration for Brown and his splendid activities, didn't doubt that he'd win a brilliant triumph, and hinted that I'd like to get to the British ministry this year, if possible. D'ye know, Crixus didn't seem even to hear me? He was sitting back in his chair, brooding on me with an intense stare which I found rather unnerving. Suddenly he asked me if I'd had food lately, and it came as a shock to realise that my last meal had been in Baltimore that morning . . . my God, it had been turmoil since then, with no time to think of eating. I was famished, but said I could wait until I reached the ministry; he wouldn't hear of it, reproaching himself for his thoughtlessness, bidding Joe rustle up sandwiches and drumsticks, waving me back to my chair, while Moody filled my glass and set a restraining hand on my shoulder, with a warning nod to me to humour the old buffoon.

So I sat, fretting, but wolfed the grub down when it came, while Crixus resumed his tale. It seemed that Brown, having squeezed as much cash as he could out of well-wishers, liberal philanthropists and rich free blacks, had lately returned to Kansas under the name of Shubel Morgan, and had set the border in uproar by raiding into Missouri, stealing eleven niggers, and bringing them to free soil, dodging posses all the way. (He also liberated several horses and a large amount of plunder, and left one unfortunate householder with his head blown off, but Crixus didn't see fit to mention that.)

"The gallantry, the audacity of the deed has won all Northern hearts, and spread terror through the South," says he. "From the very heart of the enemy camp he plucked them forth, shepherded them north through the bitter depths of winter, the pursuers baying at his heels, and brought them at last to safety. And only last month, Mr Comber, he saw them across the line to British soil – oh, my boy, does not your heart swell with patriotic pride at the thought that those poor fugitives, lately bound in the hell of slavery, dwell now in freedom beneath the benevolent folds of your country's flag?"

I assured him, between sandwiches, that I was gratified beyond all measure, and was mentally rehearsing a tactful farewell when he startled me by pushing aside his rug, rising unsteadily, and confronting me with a pointing finger and bristling brows. He spoke slow and solemn.

"But that raid, Mr Comber, was only grace before meat. For now, his little army tried and tested, he is ready for the great attempt. In his last letter to me – for we are in weekly correspondence – he tells me that the hour is nigh. Only one thing –" he flourished the finger "– is lacking, and in this one thing he seeks my help. The defection of the traitor Forbes has left him without a lieutenant, without a trusty deputy practised in arms to train and marshal his band of adventurers, for though their hearts are high they are not soldiers, sir – and soldiers they must be if they are to foray into Virginia, storm a federal arsenal, overwhelm its garrison troops, and form the Praetorian Guard of the greatest slave army since Spartacus challenged the power of Rome!"

He stooped towards me, bright-eyed and panting, and seized my wrist as I was in the act of raising a drumstick to my mouth. "A lieutenant he must have, a clear military mind – aye, or a naval one! – to plan and to order, to chart the course and lead the charge, a strong right arm on which to lean in time of trial. 'Find me a Joshua!' is his cry to me. It has rung in my ears these nights past, and until yesterday I knew not where to turn. Oh, I have prayed – and now my prayers have been answered beyond my dearest hope!" He was gazing at me like a dervish on hashish, clutching my wrist, his eyes burning with the flame of pure barminess, as I sat open-mouthed, the chicken leg poised at my ashen lips. "I say it yet again: God has sent you to us – a Joshua for John Brown!"

Looking back on life, I guess I can't complain on the whole, but if I have a grievance against Fate, it's that I seem to have encountered more than my fair share of madmen with a mission. Perhaps I've been unlucky, or possibly most of mankind is deranged; maybe it was my stalwart bearing, or my derring-do reputation, but whatever it was, they came at me like wasps to a saucer of jam. At this time in '59, I was already an experienced loony-fancier, having been exposed to the brainstorms of Bismarck, Georgie Broadfoot, the White Raja of Sarawak, Yakub Beg the Khirgiz, and sundry smaller fry, to say nothing of Crixus himself, ten years earlier, and I'd learned that when they unfold their idiocies to you, and flight is impossible, you must take time, decide what mask to assume, and rely on your native wit and acting ability to talk your way out.

Oddly enough, this wasn't a difficult one. For a split second his appalling proposal had frozen my blood, until I remembered who I was meant to be, and that I had a cast-iron excuse for refusal. Comber wouldn't have laughed in his face or told him what to do with his disgusting suggestion, or dived for the window; all I must do was play Comber to the hilt, and I was safe.

So I stared at him bewildered for a second, and then with great deliberation I set down my drumstick, wiped my lips, rose, and with a smile of infinite compassion gently pressed the old Bedlamite back into his chair. I adjusted his rug, knelt down, took one of his claws in both hands (an artistic touch, that) and gazed on him like a wistful sheep-dog.

"Oh, my dear old friend!" says I, fairly dripping emotion. "You do me honour far beyond my deserts. That you should

98

think me worthy to play a part in this . . . this great enterprise . . ." I bit my lip, trying like hell to start a tear. "I shall never forget it, never! But, alas, it cannot be. I have my own country's service, my own mission which I must fulfil, before all others." I sighed, shaking my head, while his wrinkled features sagged in dismay. "It grieves me to say you nay, but –"

"But you don't understand!" cries he. "Whatever your mission, it cannot compare to this! That it is worthy and honourable, I am sure, but don't you see – this is the crux, the vital moment! At one stroke, the whole rotten edifice of slavery will be cast down in ruin! America is its last vile stronghold! How can you hesitate? Oh, dear Mr Comber, all your work, all your valiant service in the cause, can be as nothing beside this crowning –"

"I'm sorry, sir! Believe me, it breaks my heart to deny you . . . but I'm bound by my duty, you see –"

"That's what you said last time!" cries he petulantly.

"I know that, sir, and it was true – but you prevailed on me then to turn from it for George Randolph's sake." Blackmailing old swine. "But this time I cannot in honour turn aside –"

"Why not?" he bleated. "What could be more honourable than John Brown's cause?" He twitched fretfully, like a baby denied its rattle, his dismay turning to anger. "You can't fail him! I . . . I shan't let you!" He tried another tack, stretching out a hand to me, whimpering. "Oh, my boy, I entreat you! Our need is desperate! Once before you served us, nobly and well – again, I implore you, for the sake of the great crusade which we both –"

"Ah, don't make it harder for me, sir!" groans I, in noble anguish. I stood up, and I'm not sure I didn't beat my fist against my brow. "I cannot do it. I must go to the British minister. If I could postpone or delay, I would, but I dare not. You won't stay me, I know."

You can't, was what I meant. Again, history was repeating itself, but with a difference this time. Ten years ago he'd threatened to throw me to the U.S. Navy traps, and I'd had no hole to hide in; now, I had the ministry, wherever the hell it was – and both Crixus and I were ten years older. I wasn't as easy to bully now, and his cold steel had lost its edge with age – he sat now plucking at his rug, fit to burst with vexation, looking in distress to Moody and Joe, both of whom were regarding me hard-eyed.

"No!" He struck his bony hand on the chair. "No! It can't be! I'll not have it! You have come to us by a miracle – I can't let you go, unpersuaded! I can't!" It sounded like a tantrum, and then he gave a sudden squeal; for a moment I thought he was having a seizure, but it was just inspiration from on high. "I have it!" He turned to me, bright with passion. "You must see John Brown himself! That's it – where I have failed, he shall prevail! Oh, my boy, once you have looked on his countenance, and heard him, and felt the power of his spirit – believe me, you will hesitate no longer. No one can resist him. Let me see – he's in upper New York at present, but I know he means to visit Sanborn at Boston – yes, in a few days, you could see him and –"

"I can't go to Boston, sir. I must report to my chief at once." I said it as firmly as I dared, and he shot me such a glare that I thought it best to have an inspiration of my own. "Of course," I added thoughtfully, "if the minister could be prevailed on to give me leave – to release me from duty . . . why, then . . ." I left it there, looking keen, thinking once let me inside that ministry and you won't get me out with a train of artillery, you selfish little bastard. For a moment his face lit up, and then his lip came out, and I knew he was calculating that there wasn't a hope in hell of the British minister giving me leave to join a foreign rebellion, and was wondering what card to play next.

"Yes," says he at last. "Yes, that would be best, I think. Yes . . . I could see Lord Lyons myself . . . yes, I shall! In the meantime, you should remain here." He gave a convulsive grimace that was meant to be a reassuring smile. "Yes, indeed, Mr Comber, you will be safer from prying eyes here – you may trust the Railroad, sir! And you lose nothing, you see, for I shall wait upon his lordship in the morning – first thing, sir, I assure you!" He forced a broader smile, half-pleading, half-cunning. "That's settled, then, eh? You'll stay, my boy, won't you?"

He was lying in his teeth, and I wondered why. Did he think that by detaining me he could somehow dragoon me into John Brown's hare-brained war? Possibly, for when you're as besotted a fanatic as Crixus you can believe anything, but more probably he was playing for time. One thing he was sure of: if he let me go, he'd have to find his hero another lieutenant, so he'd hold me, by force if necessary, and hope for the best.

For a moment I toyed with the idea of telling him who I truly was, and threatening diplomatic reprisals – but it wouldn't have served for a moment. Sir Harry Flashman would mean nothing to him, and God knew how he'd react when he learned that I wasn't Comber after all. And since I couldn't hope to tackle Joe and Moody together, I must pretend to submit, gracefully – and take the first opportunity to slide. If they thought they could hold Flashy for long, they were in for a surprise.

I sighed, spreading my hands, and gave him my rueful, affectionate smile. "Oh, Mr Crixus, you're too much for me! I believe you could wheedle a duck from a pond. Well, I guess the minister wouldn't thank me for waking him at this hour, anyway, and truth to tell, I'm too tired to think . . . But you'll see him yourself, sir, first thing?"

"Yes, yes!" cries the old liar eagerly, and after that it was good fellowship all round, and he must embrace me again with more of his babble about God having sent me, and from that he passed to praying, while we stood with bowed heads, and then Joe sang "Hark, the song of jubilee" in a rolling bass that billowed the curtains, after which Moody conducted me aloft to bed, not before time.

I kept my eyes open, noting that the stairs were uncarpeted, and the upper floors, so far as I could make out by candlelight, were bare as a crypt; evidently this was a station the Underground Railroad used only on occasion. My room, under the eaves, held only a bed, a chair, and a washing bowl and jug; there were bars on the window and the door bolted on both sides. At my request Moody brought me a clean shirt and shaving tackle, waiting while I scraped my chin and then carefully pocketing the razor. He hesitated before handing me the shirt, clearing his throat uneasily.

"This here shirt . . . you're a pretty big feller, an', well, the only one to fit you is this 'un . . . of Joe's. D'ye mind?"

I asked him what he meant, why should I mind, and he avoided my eye. "Well, Joe . . . I mean, he ain't white."

I'll be damned, thinks I, and on the Underground Railroad, too.

"He needn't worry," says I. "You can tell him I'm not lousy."

"What?" He stared bewildered. "No, no, you don't get it . . . Joe didn't say . . . what I mean," he stammered, "is him bein' . . . well, some folks wouldn't . . . I mean, I just thought I'd mention it . . . but if you don't mind . . ."

I gave him my most innocent smile, while he fumbled the shirt and then handed it to me, looking confused. He said if I needed anything I should stamp on the floor and holler, bade me a rather puzzled good-night, and left, shooting the outer bolt. I do love to twist tails, especially liberal ones; I wondered if his delicacy extended to black women.

I was so tuckered that I supposed I'd fall fast asleep as soon as I lay down, but my mind was in such a whirl that I lay waking, trying to make sense of it all. It seemed an age since I'd woken beside that awful whore in Baltimore, and so much had happened that it was difficult to order my thoughts. One thing, though, was paramount: thanks to Spring's informations, "Comber's" presence was known; it didn't surprise me, on reflection, that the Railroad had sniffed me out, for they were sharp men, but I wondered what other eyes might be on the look-out for me? I couldn't begin to imagine that, and once I'd escaped from my present hosts and reached the ministry, it wouldn't matter anyway.

From that my thoughts turned to what Crixus had told me, not only about the lunatic Brown, but about the state of play in the States generally, which had been absolute news to me. To hear him, the place seemed to be on the brink of civil war, and that was hard to take, I can tell you: such wars and revolutions were for foreigners – heaven knew,

102

we'd seen that in '48 – but not for us or our American cousins. I didn't understand, then, that America was two countries – but then, most Americans didn't, either.

As you know, it was slavery that drew the line and led to the war, but not quite in the way that you might think. It wasn't only a fine moral crusade, although fanatics like Crixus and John Brown viewed it as such and no more; the fact is that America rubbed along with slavery comfortably enough while the country was still young and growing (and getting over the shock of cutting loose from the mother country); it was only when the free North and the slave South discovered that they had quite different views about *what kind of country the U.S.A. ought to be* on that distant day when all the blank spaces on the map had been filled in, that the trouble started. Each saw the future in its own image; the North wanted a free society of farms and factories devoted to money and Yankee "know-how" and all the hot air in their ghastly Constitution, while the South dreamed, foolishly, of a massa paradise where they could make comfortable profits from inefficient cultivation, drinking juleps and lashing Sambo while the Yankees did what they dam' well pleased north of the 36' 30" line.

They couldn't *both* happen, not with Northern money and morality racing forward in tandem while the South stood still, sniffing the magnolias. Slavery was plainly going to go, sooner or later – unless the South cut adrift and set up shop on their own. There had been talk of this for years, and some Southerners had the amazing notion that left to themselves they could expand south and west (for cotton needs land, by the millions of acres), embracing Mexico and the Dago countries in a vast slave empire where the white boss would lord it forever. But their wiser heads saw no need for this so long as the South controlled the Congress (and the Army), which they did because their states were united, while the Northerners were forever bickering amongst themselves.

The situation was confused by a thousand and one political and social factors (but, believe me, you don't want to know about the Missouri Compromise or the "doughfaces" or the

103

Taney ruling or the Western railroad or the Democratic split or the Know-Nothings or the Kansas–Nebraska Bill or the emergence of the Republican Party or the Little Giant or gradual emancipation, you really don't). It's worth noting, though, that there were folk in the South who wanted an end to slavery, and many in the North who didn't mind its continuing so long as peace was kept and the Union preserved. Congressman Lincoln, for example, loathed slavery and believed it would wither away, but said that in the meantime, if the South wanted it, let 'em have it; if slavery was the price of American unity, he was ready to pay it. Being a politician, of course, he had a fine forked tongue; on the one hand he spouted a lot of fustian about all men being equal (which he didn't believe for a moment), while on t'other he was against blacks having the vote or holding office or marrying whites, and said that if the two were to live together, whites must have the upper hand.

But over all, the anti-slavery feeling grew ever stronger in the North, which naturally made the South dig its heels in harder than ever. The Fugitive Slave law for recovering runaways was passed in '50, to the rage of the abolitionists; *Uncle Tom's Cabin* added fuel to the fire; and Crixus wasn't far out when he said that it only needed a spark to the powder-train to set off the explosion. I didn't pay him too much heed, though; what I've just been telling you was unknown to me *then*, and I figured Crixus's talk of gathering storms and trials by combat was just the kind of stuff that he, being a crazed abolitionist, wanted to believe.

Well, he was right, and I, in my excusable ignorance, was wrong; the storm was gathering in '59 – but what astonishes me today is that all the wiseacres who discuss its origins and inevitability, never give a thought to where it really began, back in 1776, with their idiotic Declaration of Independence. If they'd had the wit to stay in the Empire then, instead of getting drunk on humbug about "freedom" and letting a pack of firebrands (who had a fine eye to their own advantage) drag 'em into pointless rebellion, there would never have been an American Civil War, and that's as sure as any "if" can be. How so? Well, Britain abolished the slave trade

104

in 1807, and slavery in 1833, and the South would have been bound to go along with that, grumbling, to be sure, but helpless against the will of Britain *and* her northern American colonies. It would all have happened quietly, no doubt with compensation, and there'd have been nothing for North and South to fight about. Q.E.D.

But try telling that to a smart New Yorker, or an Arkansas chawbacon, or a pot-bellied Virginia Senator; point out that Canada and Australia managed their way to peaceful independence without any tomfool Declarations or Bunker Hills or Shilohs or Gettysburgs, and are every bit as much "the land of the free" as Kentucky or Oregon, and all you'll get is a great harangue about "liberty and the pursuit of happiness", damn your Limey impudence, from the first; a derisive haw-haw and a stream of tobacco juice across your boots from the second; and a deal of pious fustian about a new nation forged in blood emerging into the sunlight under Freedom's flag, from the third. You might as well be listening to an intoxicated Frog.

It's understandable, to be sure: they have to live with their ancestors' folly and pretend that it was all for the best, and that the monstrous collection of platitudes which they call a Constitution, which is worse than useless because it can be twisted to mean anything you please by crooked lawyers and grafting politicos, is the ultimate human wisdom. Well, it ain't, and it wasn't worth one life, American or British, in the War of Independence, let alone the vile slaughter of the Anglo-Saxon-Norman-Celtic race in the Civil War. But perhaps you had to stand on Cemetery Ridge after Pickett's charge to understand that.

I put these thoughts to Lincoln, you know, after the war, and he sat back, cracking his knuckles and eyeing me slantendicular.

"Flashman the non-Founding Father is a wondrous thought," says he. "Come, now, do I detect a mite of imperial resentment? You know, paternal jealousy because the mutinous son didn't turn out prodigal after all?"

"You can't get much more prodigal than Gettysburg, Mr President," says I. "And I ain't jealous one little bit. I just wish our ancestors had been wiser. I'd be happy to see the Queen reigning in Washington, with yourself as Prime Minister of the British-American Empire." Toady, if you like, but true.

"Lord Lincoln . . . of Kaintuck'?" laughs he. "Doesn't sound half bad. D'you suppose they'd make me a Duke? No, better not – the boys would never let me in the store at New Salem again!"

He was the only American, by the way, who ever gave me a straight answer to a question I've asked occasionally, out of pure mischief: why was it right for the thirteen colonies to secede from the British Empire, but wrong for the Southern States to secede from the Union?

"Setting aside the Constitution, of which you think so poorly – and which I'd abandon gladly in order to preserve the Union, if you'll pardon the paradox – I'm astonished that a man of your worldly experience can even ask such a question," says he. "What has 'right' got to do with it? The Revolution of '76 succeeded, the recent rebellion did not, and there, as the darkie said when he'd et the melon, is an end of it."

And a few hours after that he was dead, the last but not the least casualty of that rotten war. It's fitting that my digression (which has some bearing on my present tale, though what it treats of was mostly hidden from me in '59) has brought me back to dear devious old Abraham, because he was in my thoughts as I lay waking in Crixus's attic; I was remembering how he'd got me out of another tight spot, when the slave-hunters came to Judge Payne's house, and if now my door had swung suddenly open to reveal his ugly, lanky figure, I'd not have minded a bit. He'd been a junior Congressman when I'd last seen him, but I'd heard nothing of him since . . .

The faint click of the bolt being slipped broke in on my thoughts, and as I sat up the door opened noiselessly, and someone slipped quickly in – it wasn't Congressman Lincoln, though, it was Joe the negro, the whites of his eyes glinting in the candleshine as he set his back to the door and raised a finger to his lips. To my astonishment he was in stockinged

106

feet; he listened for a moment and then sped silently to the window, raising it slowly to make no sound before beckoning me to join him. Wondering and suddenly alive with hope, I watched as he stooped to examine the bars; he gave a little chuckle, motioned me to stand clear, and bracing his sole against one bar he laid hold on its neighbour and pulled. He was a huge fellow, as tall as I and a foot broader, and I heard his muscles crack as he heaved to wake the dead, twice and then again, and the bar suddenly bent like a bow, snapping free with a sharp report at its lower end.

We waited, ears pricked, but there wasn't a sound, and Joe swiftly unwound a slender rope from his waist and passed one end to me.

"Ketch holt, an' I'll set tight while you slide down the roof," whispers he. "When you hit the gutter, it ain't but a little ten-fut drop to the groun'. Go out the side-gate, turn lef' up the alley, an' you's on the street. Turn lef' again, an' keep goin' till you meets a carriage comin' by – they's allus one aroun' this time o' night." His teeth glittered in a huge grin in the black face. "Then tell 'em where you wants to go. Git slidin', brother!"

You don't wait to ask questions. I shook his hand, whipped the cord round my wrist, and squeezed out on to the sill, scuffing his fine borrowed shirt in the process and tearing my jacket. The roof sloped sharply down for about fifteen feet from the window, but with Joe paying out the cord I slithered gently across the tiles and eased myself over the gutter. It was black as sin beneath, but I lowered my feet into the void, tugged on the gutter to test its weight, hung for an instant by both hands, and let go, landing on grass and measuring my length in what felt like a flowerbed. In a second I was afoot, listening, but there was no sound save that of the window being closed overhead. I waited until my eyes became accustomed to the gloom, saw the gate, and a moment later was striding up the alley and then left on the street to which the growler had brought me hours earlier.

What it meant I couldn't fathom at all. Why the devil should Joe turn me loose? Was it some wild ploy of Crixus's?

107

No, that made no sense – but then, nothing did any longer. What mattered was that I was free, and once I'd found a hack to convey me to the ministry, or Willard's Hotel, I was home and dry. I had no notion what time it was, somewhere in the small hours, probably, but I hadn't even had time to start doubting Joe's assurance that cabs were to be found in Washington suburbs at this o'clock when I heard the squeak of wheels ahead, and round the corner comes a one-horse buggy, its lamps shining dimly through the gloom.

I took a quick glance back at Crixus's house, no more than forty yards away, but it looked dead to the world, so I called softly and waved as I hurried towards the carriage. The driver reined in as I came up, and I was preparing to give him direction when I saw that he already had a fare, a vague figure barely visible in the faint glow of the side-lamps. I was about to wave him on when it struck me that the whole neighbourhood was about as lively as Herne Bay in November, with not a light in a house or a soul on the street, and no prospect of another conveyance; there was a warm drizzle improving the mud no end, so I approached the window in my best Hyde Park style.

"Your pardon, but I'm looking for a cab, and there seems to be none about – would it inconvenience you if I shared yours until we meet one?"

"Why, honey," says a soft feminine voice from the interior, " 'twill be mah pleasure to take yuh wheah-evah yuh wanna go," and a slender hand gloved in lace was extended through the window. "Why'nt yuh-all jump right in, now? It's real cosy in heah."

A cruiser, bigod, of all the luck! – though what custom she expected in this deserted backwater I couldn't imagine. I was inside in a bound, expressing my thanks to the neatest little cracker you ever saw, who rustled her skirts aside with a flurry of petticoats and slim fish-netted ankles to make room for me and made no effort to disengage her hand from mine. It was too dim to see much, but I could make out blonde curls and a small, rather childlike face behind the veil of her saucy bonnet; she was decidedly on the petite side, in a fashionably low-cut gown that felt like silk, and

108

her scent was subtle enough to be expensive – but then, she was one who could afford to ply her trade on wheels.

"An' what is yore destination, suh?" cries she pertly, showing neat little teeth and bright eyes behind the veil. "Or would yuh-all prefeh to leave that to me?" She transferred her hand to my thigh. "Ah know the most elegant li'l place."

I'd been about to say the British ministry, but paused – she'd probably never heard of it, anyway. Besides, I was in no mood to decline her invitation: I'd been two months at sea, remember, and celibacy's a double trial when your last rattle has been someone as delectable as Miranda. Her perfume was reviving all sorts of jolly memories, the touch of her fingers was distracting . . . and the ministry would be fast asleep. I hadn't a dollar to my name, but we'd fret about that later.

"I'm in your hands, my dear," says I. "Take me where you will."

"Ah won' jes' take yuh, honey," purrs she. "Ah'll transpo't yuh. Home, Andy!"

The cab lurched off, and I lurched on, so to speak, encircling her tiny waist with an arm and undoing her veil from the velvet neck-ribbon which secured it. It wouldn't come loose, and in my impatience I kissed her through it, which was a novel sensation, while she squeaked and giggled and said I was *so* vig'rous she feared I would do her an injury.

"Jes' you rest quiet a li'l bit," she protested, "an' quit chewin' up mah veil, you naughty boy! Theah – now it's out the way, yuh kin chew me instaid, yuh greedy ole thing! My, Ah nevah did know sech whiskers; you must be about the whiskeredest man in town, Ah reckon! Gently, now, honey, gently – Ah's fragile!"

I had lifted her bodily on to my knee, for she was the daintiest little bundle imaginable, and if the cab had been roomier I'd have done the deed then and there, for she kissed most artistically, and what with abstinence and encountering a little goer so unexpected, I was randier than the town bull. When I became more familiar, she wriggled and squealed, so I pinned her tiny wrists in one hand,

109

scooped out her boobies, and began nibbling, at which she became unmanageable, swearing that she'd *scream* an' *scream*, it was so *awful* ticklish, an' ifn I'd jes' *wait*, now, she'd show me the highest ole time when we got to her place.

We were on busier streets by now, with some traffic and passers-by, so I desisted, and she popped her bouncers away and patted my hand.

"Ah don' believe yore f'm Washin'ton at all," says she. "Yuh sure don' *taste* like Washin'ton, all of seegars, yuh know? An' Ah think Ah detect an English accent, ain't that so?"

Smart, too. I said I was Canadian, and she said, uh-huh, which is the most expressive word in the American language, surveying me through her veil as she adjusted it. She asked where I was staying, and I said Willard's, naming the only hotel I'd heard of. She said, "Well, lan's sakes!", and I guessed she was weighing my dishevelled appearance – creased pants, torn jacket, no hat or tie or choker even . . . and a finger of doubt began to stir in my mind. This was a twenty-dollar whore if ever there was one, yet she'd picked me up (most convenient, too) in my shabby condition, played up like a good 'un when I'd assailed her, and never a word about cash or her "present" to a client who looked as though he'd just crawled out of a hawsehole (which I had, more or less). Dooced rum . . . unless her maiden heart had been smitten by my manly address and Flashy charms . . . but even I ain't that vain. Something was amiss, and my coward's instinct was just considering whether to leap out and run for it, when the cab stopped, and she was smiling invitingly through the veil.

"Heah we are, honey! Home, sweet home!"

To my astonishment we had drawn up on a street broad enough to be the Avenue, outside a palatial building which was plainly a hotel – for a moment I wondered if it might be Willard's, and she expected to be entertained in my room. There was a fine marble frontage,[20] carriages were coming and going, with black porters holding doors, gas-flares sparkled on the jewellery and glossy evening tiles of the fashionably dressed folk crowding the steps, even at this ungodly hour; some grand function must be dispersing.

"Well, c'mon, honey, han' me down, why don't yuh!" cries my companion, so there was nothing for it but to jump out into the usual two feet of mud and the appalling stink of sewer gas. She hesitated on the step, drawing up her skirt with plaintive squeaks, so I swung her up in my arms and ploughed to the sidewalk, grateful to have my scarecrow duds shielded from the gaze of the throng.

"Don' set me down!" she whispered, and giggled. "Ah guess we cain't go in the front do' thisaway, kin we? Theah – down the alleyway, an' we'll go in the side-do'. Say, ain't this some fun, though?"

Some fun – what the deuce was I, Harry Flashman, V.C., and soon to be knighted by Her Majesty, en route from India to England, doing toting a tittering whore down a reeking lane in America's capital city? Well, the wind bloweth where it listeth, you see, and if it carries you up several flights of back stairs, along corridors where the air has been replaced by cigar smoke and the carpet fairly squelches with tobacco juice, and at last into a dimly lit salon whose ornate gilt-and-plush decor would do credit to a Damascus brothel, why, you must make the best of it and get her stripped and on to the bed before your luck changes. Which mine was about to do, with the most incredible coincidence that I can remember in a long career which has had more than its ration of freaks of chance. It had been staring me in the face, but lust is blind, alas, and I hadn't seen it.

I was undressing her with one practised hand and myself with the other even as I kicked the door to, and such is my skill in these matters that I had my pants round my ankles and her bare to her stockings by the time we reached the bed, where she tried to break free, breathless and giggling.

"Lemme take off mah hat, for mercy's sake!" cries she. "No, honey, jes' you hold on – Ah gotta see mah maid! Calm yo'self, do – Ah won' be but a second!" She slipped from my ardent grasp and scampered to an inner door, popping her head through and calling: "Ah'm back, Dora!", and then something in a lowered voice that I didn't catch – a maid, forsooth, and not just a bedroom but a suit of

111

apartments; my blonde charmer was evidently at the top of her tree. I could believe it, too, gloating at the white perfection of that little body as she closed the door, turning towards me and making a fine coquettish show of slipping off her garters and rolling down her stockings. She sauntered forward, stretching up to the chandelier chain to turn the gas up to its full brightness, and began to untie the bow securing her veil, all coy and playful.

"Well, now, big boy," drawls she, "let's have a real good look at yuh . . . my, Ah do declare Ah never . . ." And then she stopped, with something between a gasp and a cry, her knuckles flying to her veiled lips, starting back as I went for her with a lustful "Tally-ho!"

"No . . . no!" she faltered, and for an instant I checked in astonishment: the sight of Flashy stark and slavering might well strike maidenly terror in amateurs and virgins (my second bride, Duchess Irma, near had the conniptions on our wedding night) but this was a seasoned strumpet . . . and then I twigged, this must be her special ploy to rouse the roués, playing the helpless fawn shrinking before the roaring ravisher. Wasted on me, absolutely; cowering or brazen, it's all one to your correspondent; as she turned to flee, whimpering, I seized her amidships, tossed her into the air, planted her on hands and knees, and was installed before she could budge, roaring feigned endearments to soothe her pretended alarm and bulling away like fury. With two lost months to make up for, I'd no time to waste on further refinements, nor, I fear, did I treat her with that solicitude which a considerate rider should show to his mount, especially when she's barely five feet tall and half his weight. Having slaked what the lady novelists would call my base passion, I staggered up and collapsed on the bed, most capitally exhausted, leaving her prone and gasping on the carpet with her little bottom a-quiver, very fetching, and her hat and veil still in place.

What with weariness and contentment, I must have dozed off, for I didn't hear her leave the room. It may have been five minutes or twenty before I became drowsily aware of voices not far away; I stirred and sat up, but there was no sign of her. Gone to make do and mend, thinks I – and since I didn't have a red cent to requite her, it struck me as a capital time to resume my scattered togs and make tracks for the ministry. In a trice I had my shirt and pants on, and was slipping on a boot, well pleased at having had a most refreshing gallop for nothing, when a man's voice spoke loud and close at hand. Starting round, I saw that the door to the adjoining room was slightly ajar, and other voices were being raised in exclamation, the blonde whore's among them. For perhaps five seconds I sat stricken with wonder, and then the man's voice was raised again, sharp with impatience, and my blood turned to ice.

"What d'ye mean – he ain't Comber? O' course he's Comber – dammit, Joe heard that skunk Crixus call him so – didn't ye, Joe?"

My hair stood upright at the deep bass reply – for it was the voice of the nigger who'd broken me out of Crixus's house: "Sure he did, Massa Charles, over'n over! Ain't no doubt about it –"

"Don't dare tell me, you black fool!" That was the whore, shrill with fury – but where was the Dixie drawl? Gone, and in its place the voice of a Creole lady, sharp and imperious. "He's the wrong man, I say! I *know* him! His name's Tom Arnold! He ran off a slave wench from my husband's plantation ten years ago, and killed two men! He's wanted for murder and false bills and slave-stealing, I tell you! Damn you, colonel, do you think I don't know a man who's been my lover?"

I was over the bed like a startled hare, boots in hand, and was racing for the outer door when a huge black shape came storming in from the adjoining room, and Old Brooke would have picked him first of the Schoolhouse chargers, for he came at me in a flying lunge that would have had every cap in the air on Big Side. His shoulder took me flush on the thigh, and it was like being hit by the Penzance Express; I went headlong, smashing into the furniture and fetching up against the wall with a jar that shook every bone in my body. Joe was up like a cat, fists clenched as he stood over me, shouting:

113

"It's him, sho' 'nuff! You bet it's him – Comber! Ain't no doubt, Miz Annette!"

And there she stood in the connecting doorway, the tiny body wrapped in a silk robe, and as I saw her face in full light for the first time, I could only lie and stare in utter disbelief. The slim, childlike shape had filled out in ten years, she'd put on an inch or two in height, the sharp elfin features were fuller (and all the prettier for it, I may say), and her hair that had been fair was dyed bright gold, but there was no mistaking the icy little vixen with whom I'd rogered away the clammy afternoons at Greystones in her abominable husband's absence. Annette Mandeville, fragile blossom of the Old South, half-woman, half-alligator, who wore spurred riding boots to bed and whose diminutive charms I must have explored a dozen times – and now I'd just spent an hour in her company, conversing, kissing, caressing, carrying her bodily up five flights of stairs, rattling her six ways from Sunday – and never for a moment suspecting who she was!

Impossible, says you; even the coarsest voluptuary (guilty, m'lud) couldn't have failed to recognise her, surely? Well, consider this: in your lifetime you probably wear as many as three hundred pairs of boots and shoes, perhaps more; I ask you, if when you were forty your orderly laid out a pair of pumps which you'd worn for a week when you were thirty, would you remember 'em? No, you admit, likely not, unless there was something singular about them. You see my point: by '59 I'd known, in the scriptural sense, 480 women (I'd reckoned up 478 when I was confined in the Gwalior dungeon the previous year, and since then there'd been only the Calcutta bint and Miranda), so was it wonderful that I shouldn't recognise Annette Mandeville after ten years? I think not. Oh, you may point out that of all my prancing-partners she was by far the smallest, and that when I saw her in the buff, even with her face veiled, I should have recollected the tiny nymph of Mississippi. But against that I argue that the vulgar, cracker-voiced hoyden of Washington was as unlike the high-bred frigid midget of Greystones as could be. They were two different women (and I wasn't surprised to learn later that in the intervening years, after

114

the demise of the disgusting Mandeville, little Annette had earned a fine living on the boards, her doll-like stature being admirably suited to juvenile roles, including Little Eva, which she'd played with great success in Northern theatres). So I can't blame myself for being taken in.

It's not the only case of female double jeopardy that I've experienced, by the way. Elsewhere in my memoirs you'll find mention of a French-mulatto trollop with whom I dallied in my salad days, and who came to my carnal attention again twenty-seven years later, and I'm damned if I recognised *her*, either.

That's all by the way; what mattered, as I wallowed amidst the shattered furniture, was not that I'd failed to identify La Mandeville's dainty buttocks *in ecstatio*, but that she was here at all, and in company with yet another branch of the B. M. Comber Admiration Society, to judge by the snatch of talk I'd heard from the adjoining room a moment since. To add to my confusion, Black Joe, who'd been a friend an hour ago, had just tried to hurl me through the wall and was now standing over me sporting his fives in a threatening manner. I didn't know what to make of him, or her, or any damned thing – and now men were surging into the room, and Mandeville was pointing and shrilling:

"Comber or not, that man is Tom Arnold! He was our slave-driver. Let him deny it if he can!"

Black Joe took his eyes off me for an instant, possibly to contradict her, and I seized the opportunity to lash him across the knee with a broken chair-leg. He staggered, cursing, and I was up and past him, tripping in my blind flight but recovering and snatching for the handle of the outer door. I wrenched it open, and found myself face to face with a goggling darkie in a white jacket bearing a tray and beaming inquiry:

"Podden me, suh, but wuz you de gennelman whut sent for bourb'n an' seltzer?"

It checked me for a split second, which was long enough for Joe to seize my collar from behind, pluck me backwards, growl "Wrong room, boy!" and slam the door shut. I lost my balance and sprawled in the wreckage once more, and

115

before I could stir they were on me, two burly ruffians with bullet heads and no necks, one at either arm. I heaved one aside, and was wrestling with the other when I realised that three other men had emerged from the adjoining room and were advancing past Annette, and at the sight of them I 'vasted heaving and subsided, paralysed with horror.

To judge by their dress, they were thoroughly worthy citizens, bearing every mark of wealth and respectability: one wore U.S. Army uniform, with the epaulettes and double buttons of an infantry colonel; another might have been a prosperous professional man, with his immaculate broadcloth coat and heavy watch-chain across his bulky middle, and the third was an absolute Paris fashion plate in silk tailcoat, embroidered weskit, ruffles, and a gold-topped cane on which he limped slightly as he advanced – he'd have been the altogether dandy if he hadn't had the misfortune to be as fat as butter. They might have been three of Mandeville's richer clients, but for the mutual eccentricity in their appearance which froze me where I lay.

All three were wearing hoods over their heads, ghastly white conical things like gigantic candle-snuffers with eyeholes and blank gaping mouths.

Barring an illustrated edition of Bunyan's *Holy War*, with its fanged devils sporting their horns and tails in the infernal regions, the great terror of my infancy was a lurid coloured print entitled "All Hope Abandon", purporting to show what happened when the Spanish Inquisition got hold of you – which they undoubtedly would, my nurse assured me, if I didn't eat my crusts, or farted in church. It showed a dreadful gloomy vault in which a gibbering wretch, guarded by hairy Dagoes in morions, was cowering before three Inquisitors, one of whom was pointing to a fiery archway through which could be seen hideous shadows of stunted figures operating pulleys and wheels and brandishing whips; you couldn't really tell what they were doing, even if you squinted sidelong, but you could imagine it, you see, while your infant soul quaked at the visible terror of those three awful hooded Inquisitors, one of whom I was convinced was the Pope – nurses were sounder theologians then than they are now, I daresay. In any event, pointed cowls with empty eyes haunted my young nightmares, and the sight of them now, real and palpable, for the first time in my life, damned near carried me off. To make matters worse, I saw that the two thugs who had laid hold of me, and were now on their feet, had masks on their ugly phizzes, and Joe had a cocked revolver in his hand.

"Cover him, Joe!" barks the hooded soldier. "An' you, suh, lay right still theah! Ye heah?"

"An' speak up!" snaps the broadcloth figure, deep and harsh. "What's yo' name, suh? Out with it – Comber or Arnold?"

The broad Southern accents were the last thing you'd have

expected to hear out of those grotesque hoods, but my amazement redoubled when the fat dandy limped up and stooped his great bulk to inspect me through blank eyeholes.

"I'll lay seven to two he answers to both," drawls he – another Southerner, but where the others were broad Dixie, he was your refined magnolia, elaborately soft and courteous. "Good mornin', suh. Pray pardon this intrusion, an' our outlandish attire. No cause for alarm, I assure you."

It didn't assure me for a moment, with those three horrid masks looming over me, but the politely mocking voice stirred me to fury in spite of my terror. "Damn your impudence! Who . . . who are you, and what d'you mean by it – you and your infernal nigger, he's broke my bloody leg –"

"Hold yo' tongue!" snarled the colonel's hood, and he snatched Joe's pistol and levelled it. "Stir a finger an' Ah'll burn yo' brains –"

"Stow it, Clotho," says the fat hood quietly, and set the weapon aside with his cane. "Pistols, 'pon my soul – we're in a Washin'ton ho-tel, suh, not a Memphis boa'din' house. 'Sides, firearms ain't necessary . . ." He lowered his cane – and a glittering blade shot out from its ferrule, stopping an inch above my palpitating breast. ". . . are they? Have no fear, suh – just a precaution 'gainst any sudden outcry on your part, like hollerin' for help, or showin' fight." He gave a fleshy chuckle. "But you wouldn't be so foolish – would you now?"

Before that wicked point and soft-spoken menace I shrank back, gasping. "In God's name . . . what d'ye want with me? I'm a British officer, under the protection of my ministry, damn you –"

"Now, that you ain't," says he, gently chiding. "Oh, right dearly you'd *like* to be, but folks keep gettin' in the way, don't they? First the wo'thy Crixus, then ourselves." The blade clicked out of sight, and he leaned comfortably on his cane, all patient amiability – and I've never seen anything more sinister than that hollow-eyed white visor with the smooth voice issuing from its shapeless mouth. "Now, see heah . . . if you're reasonable no least harm will come to you, on my honour. All we seek is to talk with you, civil

118

an' quiet – but we have to know who we-all are talkin' to, you see? Joe heah, on good authority, says your name is Comber; Miz Mandeville, on t'other hand –"

"Why waste time?" Annette broke in, shrill and impatient. "If you want the truth from this snake, you'll have to twist it out of him!" She was at his elbow, eyeing me spitefully – coupling apart, we'd detested each other heartily in the old days, and my innards shrank as I remembered those spurred boots and the cruel pleasure she'd taken in the whipping of her plantation wenches.

"That's not what we want him for, Annette deah," sighs the fat horror. "You're lettin' outraged delicacy cloud your judgment." He chuckled again. "Cain't think why – I'll wager you relished eve'y lovin' moment of him jus' now; you always do." He shifted his game leg, wincing audibly, and tapped his cane sharply on my chest. "Now, suh, I'm gettin' right weary standin' heah when we could be settin' at our ease, so . . . are you Arnold, or Comber – or both?"

In my terror it didn't even cross my mind to tell him I was neither, but Flashy – when you're surrounded by Inquisition hoods with a swordstick at your throat, you tell 'em what they want to hear, believe me. And whoever this ghastly genteel apparition was, I know a killing gentleman when I meet one; everything about this oily fat flawn – his dandy clobber, his polite irony, the leer in his voice when he spoke to Annette – suggested a graduate of the Starnberg–Ignatieff school, and probably all the more vicious for being a flabby cripple.

"Both . . . blast you! Yes, I called myself Arnold on her husband's plantation – whatever the hell it is to you, whoever you are –"

"In Louisiana you called yo'self Prescott!" cries the hood with the colonel's uniform, and damned if he didn't sound indignant. "Fan me, ye winds, the feller's got mo' names'n Lucifer! Yore a damned rascal, suh! What else you bin callin' yo'self, hey?"

"It don't signify, Clotho," says the beau. He turned to the other hood. "He's our man, Lachesis."

119

"Then let's get to business," snaps the broadcloth one.

"You see any profit in it?" grumbles the colonel. "How we goin' to put trust in sech a scoundrel? Prescott, Arnold, Comber – lordy, whut next? An' Ah tell ye, Atropos, he don' look to me like the kind you kin bend to our pu'pose!"

"He'll bend, never fear," sneers Annette. "I know him. He would sell his own mother for railroad fare."

The dandy Atropos heaved a gusty sigh, and turned his hooded head to survey them. "I would remind you-all, Miz Mandeville an' gen'lemen, that we are lookin' to Mistuh Comber as an al-ly, not as an enemy. I trust that is cleah?" There was an edge to the silky voice, and they stood silent. He gestured to the two masked ruffians who had been hovering hopefully above my prostrate form.

"You two boys be off an' repo't to Hermes. Mistuh Comber will be discreet, I'm sure . . . won't you, suh? Joe, assist the gen'lemen to rise . . . theah, that's fine! My 'pologies for the rough handlin' . . . mere necessity, suh, an' much regretted." Bright eyes studied me through the holes of the hood. "Yeah . . . Now then, since we have established your . . . identities . . . and as we have a proposal to make to you, I think that as a token of confidence an' courtesy, I should remove my disguise. Then we can conve'se at greater ease."

He raised a hand to the white monstrosity on his head, and there were shocked exclamations from the two other hoods, which he silenced with a flutter of pudgy fingers. "Unlike you gen'lemen, I have no public po-sition to protect," says he. "I'm sure Mistuh Comber will have no objection to your remainin' covered."

He pulled off his hood – and I'm bound to say he'd looked better with it on, for his face was as gross as his body, and all the worse because under the jelly jowls, swollen cheeks, and bulbous nose were features that might once have been handsome. He was about forty, and his fine head of blond hair, which he'd taken care not to disturb in removing the hood, was artfully dressed in the style they used to call windswept; that, and the elegance of his duds, were in obscene contrast to the bloated face, but it was the eyes that

120

told me my first impression had been right in the bull: they were bold, blue, smiling, and amiable as fish-hooks.

"Your servant, Mistuh Comber," says he, and gave me his arm; his hand was soft and manicured, but when I perforce laid mine on his sleeve it was like touching a hawser in velvet; he didn't use scent or pomade, either. "Now, I b'lieve we'll be more comf'table in the drawin' room . . ."

I'll wake up presently, pray God, thinks I, for I'm certainly dreaming this, whatever it is. I was past wondering who or what they were, or what "proposal" they could have for me, or the meaning of those nightmare hoods and mythical names – one thing only I was sure of: they weren't lunatics or practical jokers, but damned serious gentry who knew what they were about, and wouldn't hesitate to silence me if I didn't behave. I'd developed a wholesome terror of the obese shark conducting me to the adjoining room, ushering me to an armchair, bidding Joe pour me a glass of the poison they mis-spell "whiskey", and begging me in that honeyed voice to be at my ease – with Joe looming behind me with his pistol in his waistband, if you please. I didn't undervalue the choleric Colonel Clotho or the grim-voiced Lachesis, either; there was authority and purpose in the way they sat themselves down at either end of a table, the hooded heads facing me; from what the fat monster had said, the hidden faces must be well-known, to Americans at least. Annette lounged on a chaise longue at one side, watching me sullenly, and the elegant tub of lard rested his ponderous rump on the table before me, his game leg thrust out stiffly, lighted a long French cigarette, and blew thoughtful smoke while I waited in scared bewilderment to learn what they wanted of me – or of Comber, rather.

"Now, then," says Beau Blubber, "you wonderin' who we are, an' what we want of you. Well, you jus' take breath while I tell you. But, first . . . does the word 'kuklos' have any meanin' for you?"

I racked my memory. "It's Greek . . . means 'circle', I think."

"You think right, suh, an' I daresay you are familiar with the classical names we three have adopted, bein' those of

121

the Parcae – Lachesis, Clotho, an' myself, Atropos – tho' I hope to convince you that those of the Eumenides would have been more fittin'.'' His liver lips parted in a hideous grin at his learned joke; he and Spring would have made a pair. "They are our secret names, as officers of the Kuklos, which is a clan-des-tine society of our southe'n United States,[21] de-voted to guardin' an' upholdin' those liberties an' institutions which our no'the'n fellow-countrymen are bent on destroyin'. I refer to slavery, Mistuh Comber, which they affect to abominate, but which we of the South hold to be a nat'ral condition which, for better or worse, is inevitable –''

A strangled oath came from within Clotho's hood. "Better or wuss, my ass! It's awdained by the will o' God, goddammit! Why, you sound like a dam' doughface, Atropos! Yo' pardon, Miz Mandeville, but Ah cain't abide that kind o' feeble talk!''

If I wasn't drunk or dreaming, I must be drugged again. I couldn't be sitting in an American hotel, listening to a well set up military man in an Inquisitor's hood, calling himself after one of the Fates, and apologising for coarse language to an aristocrat-turned-whore who used to be my mistress . . .

"I doubt if Mistuh Comber is im-pressed by the rhetoric of the camp-meetin', Clotho," says Atropos. "To resume, suh – the Kuklos is strong, widespread, an' capable. For eve'y friend the abolitionists, Underground Railroad, an' so-called freedom societies have in high places – we have two. They have many ad-herents 'mong the lowly, the nigras – so have we. Joe, theah, was born a slave on my family estate; he was my childish playfeller, then my body-se'vant – an' is my best friend in all the world. Is it so, Joe?''

"You bet, Mass' Charles!'' It sounded like a volcano rumbling.

"Atropos, Joe, Atropos, remember . . . ne'er mind. Well, suh, the Kuklos arranged for Joe to 'run' five yeahs ago. He became a 'passenger' on the Underground Railroad, an', in time, one of its most trusted 'conductors'. For two yeahs now he has been at Crixus's right hand, his loyal aide – who observes, listens, an' repo'ts to the Kuklos.'' He gave

122

a plump, satisfied simper. "Now you know, suh, how you come to be heah. We learned of your arrival at Baltimo' as soon as Crixus did – like him, we have agents within the po-lice an' gov'ment, who noted the anonymous info'mation which reached the autho'ities two days ago that one Beauchamp Comber, an officer of the British Admiralty, had reappeared in this country. It was a name already known to us," continues the fat smug, "from the access we enjoy to the reco'ds of Crixus *an'* the U.S. Navy, as that of the Englishman who, under the alias of James K. Prescott, ran the nigra George Randolph north in '48. It was, howevah, nooz to us that this same Prescott had been party to a murder in N'awlins in the followin' yeah – "

"That's a damned lie! I didn't kill Omohundro – "

He raised a plump hand. "Party, I said, Mistuh Comber. Howsomevah, the nooz of your arrival, an' of your activities as an an-tye-slavery agent yeahs ago, were of no more than passin' interest to us until we learned yeste'day – thanks to Joe theah – that Crixus was all on fire to secure your person an' enlist your services on behalf of John Brown of Ossawatomie. *Then*, Mistuh Comber," he pointed with his cane in emphasis, "*then*, suh, our interest in you became pro-found . . . an' urgent."

He paused, and I could hear my heart thumping. I'd listened in mingled confusion and alarm, understanding his words without finding the least explanation in them, but now I could sense hellish bad news coming. The blank eyes in the hoods of Clotho and Lachesis stared at me unnervingly, and I stole a glance at Annette Mandeville, coiled in the corner of her seat like a little white serpent, watching me through narrowed lids with that well-remembered sulky curl on her thin lips – at any other time I'd have guessed she was fancying me above half, but it seemed unlikely just now.

"So we made haste to secure you ou'selves," Atropos went on. "Joe released you, an' *chere* Annette met, beguiled, an' conveyed you – all mighty smooth, you'll allow. We three should ha' been heah when you arrived, but we were delayed, which I believe . . ." his great belly heaved with amusement, ". . . gave her the oppo'tunity to indulge her taste for mixin' business with pleasure – "

"Damn you, Charles!" She came upright, flushed with anger. "You bridle your filthy fat tongue – "

"But whatevah for, dahlin'? We-all know your lovin' weakness . . . an' Mistuh Comber was an old friend – which came as a right surprise to both of you, I collect." He took another cigarette, smirking. "Still, that acquaintance may prove useful to our pu'pose – eh, Annie deah?"

She answered nothing but a glare, and Lachesis drummed his fingers on the table. "Git to the pu'pose, then. Time presses."

Atropos struck a fuzee and applied it to his cigarette without haste, watching me carefully as he shook it out.

"Crixus told you that John Brown plans to invade V'ginia an' raise a rebellion of the nigras theah. An' he wants you, Mistuh Comber, to take the place of Colonel Hugh Forbes" – he pronounced it 'Fawbus' – "who was lately Brown's loo-tenant. Now, suh," he drew deeply on his cigarette, "we'd kindly like to heah what you-all think of that interestin' proposal."

At first the question made no more sense than all the bewildering drivel and wild events of the past twenty-four hours – was it only a day and a night since I'd come to in that stinking doss-house? And here I was, with a pistol at my back, in the grip of Dixie fanatics (and Annette Mandeville, of all people), and still no wiser. But at least I could answer – though what the deuce it could mean to this foppish monster was far beyond me.

"I'd not touch it with a ten-foot pole!" I told him, and Clotho gave a muffled grunt, while Atropos let smoke trickle slowly out of his nostrils, and nodded over my head to Joe.

"Good boy, Joe . . . you read him aright, even if Crixus didn't. So, Mistuh Comber . . . care to tell us why you wouldn't touch it?"

Being in a fair bottled-up taking, I exploded – and like an ass let my tongue run away with me.

"Great God, man, d'ye think I'm as crazy as Crixus? What the dooce have I to do with his hare-brained schemes? Look here, for heaven's sake – I don't know what you want with me, and let me tell you I don't care! I ain't American, I don't give a rap for your politics, or your slavery, or Crixus and his damned Railroad, or you and your infernal Kuklos, and I wouldn't go near this madman Brown for a bloody pension –"

Lachesis's hand slapped the table like a pistol shot, cutting me short. "What's that ye say? Heah's strange talk from a liberationist, on my word!" He was sitting forward, and I could see his eyes shining within the hood. "You don't care about slavery? Ah find that passin' strange from a man engaged by the Queen's Navy 'gainst the Afriky traders, who spied on them in the Middle Passage, an' worked for the Underground Railroad, runnin' Jawge Randolph to Canada –"

"An' dodged the patter-rollers to take a slave wench 'cross the Ohio!" Clotho was on his feet. "An' got shot doin' it! An' killed a couple men along the way, 'cording to what Miz Mandeville say!"

"You claim now yore *not* an abolitionist?" Lachesis rose in turn, accusing me like the lawyer he probably was. "That's not what the U.S. Navy reco'ds say – we've seen 'em, an' it's all theah, under the name Comber!"

I'd forgotten, in my fright and confusion, that I was meant to be Comber – bigod, was this the time to announce myself as Flashy? No, I daren't, for they'd never credit it – and if they *did*, God alone knew what they'd do. I'd been a political long enough to know that these secret bastards can't abide loose ends or innocent parties who stray into their beastly plots; it rattles 'em, and you're liable to find yourself head foremost in a storm drain with a knife in your ribs. Atropos wasn't the sort to think twice about slitting a throat, I was sure, the others were probably no better, and Mandeville was a callous little bitch – no, for my skin's sake I must cleave to what they believed to be true. I struggled for words – and noisy voices were passing the door, fading down the corridor . . . Jesus, four floors below careless diners would be wolfing steak and fried oysters in the breakfast-room – and those hideous white death's-heads were before me, Joe's

125

pistol was behind – and Atropos was restraining my questioners with a languid gesture of his cane.

"Easy, theah, gen'lemen; no call for heat." He sounded almost amused, and the gargoyle face was smiling inquiry at me. "Well, suh?"

I tried to brush it aside. "Why, that's all past and done with! I'm not with the Admiralty – haven't been for years . . . retired ages ago, on half-pay –"

Lachesis pounced. "That's not what ye told Crixus!"

"You said you wuz on a mission fo' the British!" cries Clotho.

"Ah wuz theah . . . 'member?" Joe's voice spoke behind me like the knell of doom, and I could only bluster.

"What I told Crixus is my business! Damnation, what's it to you? Who the hell d'you think you are to bullyrag me, rot you?"

I've no doubt they'd have told me, but Atropos intervened again, more firmly this time.

"Gen'lemen, you're wastin' breath. All this makes no nevah-minds. Whether Mistuh Comber is workin' for the British or not, don't signify a bit. You see, suh, we need you . . . an' we got you. All that matters is that Crixus wants you to go along with John Brown." He dropped ash from his cigarette, the ugly face regarding me blandly. "An' so do we."

God knows what I looked like as I digested those unbelievable words. For a second I didn't take them in, and when I did I was too dumfounded to speak, or laugh hysterically, or make a bolt for it. But I started to come to my feet, and Atropos raised his cane and gently pushed me back into my seat.

"If you had said 'aye' to Crixus, we could ha' left you with him to get on with it. But Joe figured you wanted no part of his plan – that you were tellin' him 'maybe' but thinkin' 'no' . . . so we had to lay hold on you. To persuade you."

I heard myself croak: "You must be as daft as Crixus! Why the hell should I do what you want?"

"Because," says he patiently, "it ain't far to Kentucky."

126

"What the devil d'ye mean?"

"There's a warrant – maybe a rope – waitin' there for Beauchamp Comber, on a charge of stealing a nigra wench con-trary to the Fugitive Slave Act. If that ain't enough, we could send you down the river to answer for the killin' in N'awlins that you didn't do." He glanced at Annette. "You say he killed two men in Ole Miss?"

"I remember their names: Hiscoe and Little. There was a reward poster billing Tom Arnold as the murderer." She was absolutely smiling, enjoying herself, the malicious slut. "Better still, there's a plantation in Alabama where he can be lost for the rest of his life –"

"I never murdered anyone, I swear! It was the wench, Cassy! I'd no part –"

"You nevah killed no one, did ye?" came the growl from Clotho's hood. "Haw! You sho' have the damnedest luck!"

Atropos gestured him to silence. "So you see, there appear to be com-pellin' reasons why you should do as we ask, Mistuh Comber. If you came to trial, I doubt if Lord Lyons would stir himself to save you; gov'ments don't relish that kind of emba'ssment. You're a long way from home, suh," says the flabby son-of-a-bitch with a mock-rueful grin on his repulsive face. "I reckon you got no choice."

He was dead right, and the tirade of protest and appeal and raving refusal died on my lips: I could submit, or be shipped south to the gallows – or worse still, the lonely Alabama plantation where Mandeville's swine of a husband had planned to have me worked to death in the cotton-fields. I didn't doubt their ability to do it – or to snuff me out here and now and save themselves the trouble. I could feel myself going crimson with terror – which I do, God knows why, and makes folk think I'm about to go berserk. Clotho saw it, for he called to Joe to look out, and the pistol was jammed into my back . . . and all the while I could hear the morning traffic rumbling in the street far below the curtained windows, and the distant knocks of porters rousing guests . . . and that merciless fleshy face and the vile white hoods were waiting. So I must pretend to agree, play for time, say any damned thing at all . . .

127

"But . . . you're *Southerners*, for heaven's sake – and you want me to help this half-wit Brown start a *slave rebellion*?"

It was the right note, for to them it suggested I was weakening. Clotho grunted, Joe took his piece from my back, and Atropos eased his bulk on the table edge and leaned forward.

"Theah's an 'lection next yeah," says he, "but since you don't value our politics it won't mean molasses to you if I tell you Seward an' his Republicans are like to win it –"

"Hey, whut 'bout Breckenridge?" protests Clotho.

"Breckenridge couldn't win with Jefferson on the ticket," retorts Atropos. "But it don't matter who's Pres'dent – Seward, Breckenridge, Douglas, or Jake the hired hand – after the 'lection, comes the crisis, Mistuh Comber." He nodded impressively. "This country will then *dis*-unite, into North an' South – with or without war. We of the South must break free, or see our way of life destroyed fo'evah. 'Twill be a mighty step, an' when we take it, we must be united as nevah before, or we perish. Well, nothin', suh, can do more to ensure Southe'n unity than an act of war committed by Northe'n abolitionists 'gainst a Southern State –"

"An act of brigandage!" mutters Clotho. "Dam' Yankee villains!"

Atropos ignored him. "If John Brown raids into Virginny, the South'll come togetheh as one man, 'cos they'll see it as sure proof that the Nawth'll stop at nothin' to crush us an' all we stand for – an' at the same time, such a raid'll split the Nawth wide open, with the doughfaces an' moderates an' save-the-Union-at-all-costs ninnies feelin' shocked an' shamed, an' the wild spirits hurrahin' 'Good ole John Brown!' an' quotin' Scripture." His affected calm had dropped from his fat carcase like a shed cloak, and his genteel accent was fraying at the edges: he was rasping "Nawth" like a cotton-broker, and dropping "r"'s right and left. "The Nawth'll be tore all ways, an' . . . well, who knows? Maybe we of the South will be able to cast off without a fight. An' that's why John Brown's raid *must* go ahead . . . you see, Mistuh Comber?"

I wasn't concerned about the sense of it then, though I can see it now; I had my skin to think of, and there were questions Comber was bound to ask.

"But if he raises a slave rebellion, and all the niggers go on the rampage – "

"He couldn't raise dust in a mill!" It came unexpected from Lachesis's hood. "He'll stick on the first step, which is the takin' of a federal arsenal, prob'ly Harper's Ferry, jus' over the Virginny line. He's been braggin' it for yeahs, tellin' that loudmouth Forbes, who tol' half Washin'ton! Why, ev'yone knows he's set on the Ferry – "

"So he kin arm the nigras!" Clotho's hood shook with his guffaw. "He 'spects they all come a-runnin' to fawm up in battalions behin' Napoleon Brown, an' go a-crusadin' through Dixie settin' all t'other nigras free! Well, suh, that they ain't! Virginny nigras too dam' well off, an' knows it – no Denmark Veseys or Nat Turners[22] in *that* section! Plen'y of Uncle Toms, though!" He ended on a snarl. "They oughta burned that bitch Stowe at the stake!"

I turned in disbelief to Atropos. "But if the government *know* where he's going to raid – dammit, they'll guard the place, won't they? And collar Brown before he can go near it!"

He shook his head. "Gov'ment don't take Brown that serious – not officially, anyways. An' they won't start a ruckus in the North by arrestin' him." That was what Crixus had said – and the lunatic thought crossed my mind: were there Southerners in the government who, like these Kuklos fanatics, would be happy to see Brown stirring up merry hell . . . ? Well, it mattered not one dam to me – and I realised that Atropos was watching me closely as he lighted another of his Regie gaspers.

"Theah you have it," says he. "Brown's raid'll fail – but not before it's served our turn: dividin' the North, unitin' the South."

"But . . . God help us, why should he need *me*?"

"Come, now, Crixus told you that. Brown needs a trained officer if he's to take that arsenal – why, the man's but a peasant, half-crazy, half-iggerant, leadin' a crew of

129

jayhawkers an' farmers, scrimmagin' in backyards an' rob-
bin' widder women. Forbes was his brain, to plan an' advise
an' whip Brown's gang into shape. But Forbes is gone, an'
Brown's at a loss for a captain – so he appeals to Crixus,
an' lo! – Crixus has the very man, a foreign free lance well
skilled in this kind o' work." The bloated features creased
in a triumphant smile. "An' I'm 'bliged to agree with him.
The man who ran George Randolph can surely run Old
Ossawatomie."

It's being six foot two and desperate-looking that does it,
you know; if I'd been short-arsed with no chin and knock-
knees, no one in search of a hero would have looked at me
twice. I cudgelled my wits for some other objection, and hit
on one that seemed unanswerable.

"But it won't do, don't you see? You've stolen me from
Crixus – so how the hell can he send me to Brown now?
Am I to roll up on his doorstep and say I'm ever so sorry
for escaping, but I've changed my mind, don't ye know, and
to hell with my duty and the British ministry . . . Ah, the
whole thing's folly! You're off the rails, all of you!"

Atropos shook his head, being patient. "The Kuklos don't
leap before it's looked real close, Mistuh Comber. See now,
heah's how it is: Crixus knew of your escape ten minutes after
you made it. Sure – Joe 'discovered' it, an' Crixus has a passel
o' men scourin' town for you right now . . . mos'ly aroun' the
British ministry." He gave another of his greasy chuckles.
"Joe hisself is one o' those searchers, an' presen'ly he'll sen'
word to Crixus that he's hot on your trail. An' then . . . Crixus
won't heah no more for a day or two . . . until he gets a telegraph from Joe *in Noo Yawk*, sayin' as he's run you down an'
reasoned you into enlistin' with John Brown –"

"Christ in the rear rank! You expect Crixus to swallow
that? See here, I know he's barmy, but –"

"He'll be-*lieve* it," says Atropos, "'cos he'll *want* to
believe it. It's what he's been strivin' after an' prayin' for
. . . God sent you, 'member? An' he trusts Joe like his own
son. When he gets that telegraph, he'll be too ove'joyed to
ask questions . . . an' he'll telegraph Joe to take you to
Brown without delay."

"That's why Noo Yawk is right convenient," puts in Lachesis. "Brown's up-state now, an' due in Boston soon, where you an' Joe kin join him –"

"And then," says Atropos, "you'll be on Brown's coattails all the way to Harper's Ferry."

I could say I'd never heard the like – but I had, all too often. When you've been pressed into service as "sergeant-general" of the Malagassy army, or forced to convoy a bog-trotting idiot figged up as Sinbad the Sailor through an enemy army, or dragooned into impersonating a poxed-up Danish prince – why, what's a slave rebellion more or less? You develop a tolerance, if that's the word, and learn that whatever folly is proposed – and this beat anything I'd struck – you must just seem to agree, and bend your mind to the only thing that matters: survival. So . . . they would send me North under guard, and I must submit to that – but if I couldn't slip my cable between Washington and New York (where I'd be well beyond the reach of Southern warrants, *bien entendu*) then my nimble foot had lost its cunning. Even if they kept a gun in my back (which ain't easy, even in American society) until I was under Brown's wing . . . well, he could try to hold on to me, and good luck to him.

Atropos's smooth voice broke in on my thoughts. "Now, it is surely occurrin' to you, suh, to *pre-tend* to give consent, an' make off when oppo'tunity serves. Dismiss that thought, Mistuh Comber. You will go north in company with Miz Mandeville an' Joe . . . an' other se'vants of the Kuklos whom you won't see, but who'll be theah, eve'y step o' the way. An' when you 'list with Brown . . . why, Joe'll be 'listed, too . . . an' again, he won't be the only one around. The Kuklos will be your guardian angel eve'y minute, an' if you was to . . . step aside or make any commotion, why," he gave me his fattest, smuggest smile, "you'd be dead . . . or boun' for Kentucky in a packin' case."

There's a moment, in any trial between two persons, whether it's a game or an argument or a battle of wits or a duel to the death, when Party A thinks he's got Party B cold. And *that*, believe it or not, is the moment when A is most vulnerable, if only B has the sense to see it. Atropos

131

thought he had me to rights. He was a damned shrewd secret political, and his task had been to coerce me (or Comber, if you like) into joining John Brown, for the reasons he'd given. No easy task, given the kind of fellow he knew (or thought he knew) Comber to be, but he'd set about it like a true professional, using approved methods – viz., scare, unsettle, and bewilder your man, impress him with the power and genius of your *bandobast*,* and convince him that he has no choice but to obey. Very well, he'd done that, handsomely – but it was all based on the assumption that Comber would have to be *forced* into compliance. It hadn't occurred to him that Comber might decide, on reflection, to be a *willing* party. Put that thought into Atropos's self-satisfied head, and he'd be took aback; he might even be so dam' subtle that he'd believe it. In any event, he'd be less cocksure than he was, and it never hurts to do *that* to an opponent. (I hadn't been a prisoner of the Russian secret service for nothing, I can tell you.)

So I said nothing for several minutes, but sat there, mum and blank, while they waited in silence. Then I raised my head and looked the fat brute straight in his ghastly face.

"It's a rum trick," says I, "but I don't doubt you're serious. Well, sir, I'm a serious man, too, you know. You've put your proposal, on what you account fair terms. Now you can hear mine." You could have heard a pin drop. "Ten thousand dollars. Or two thousand sterling. That's my price."

He didn't even blink. The others let out gasps and exclamations – Annette gave a shrill didn't-I-tell-you-so laugh – but Atropos just drew on his cigarette and asked:

"Why should we pay you when we can compel you?"

"Because a man well paid is a dam' sight more reliable."

"Don't trust him!" cries Annette. "He's a liar!"

"Ten thousan' dollahs! Ye Gods!" Clotho's hood was in danger of being blown off. "Of all the con-founded gall!" But Lachesis said not a word, only sat stock-still, sharp-eyed

* Organisation.

132

in his hood. Atropos considered me through his cigarette smoke.

I waited, then rose from my chair. "And I thought Americans were smart. Please yourselves – but remember you were the one who spoke of a free lance. That's what I am – and you may believe it, I'm a sight better than that ass Forbes, who sold out Garibaldi." I'd never heard of Forbes before that night, but I reckoned it was a neat touch. "And now . . . I've heard you out, I'm dog tired, and there's a bed next door. Servant, marm . . . gentlemen." I inclined my head and started for the bedroom, speaking over my shoulder. "Joe can guard my slumbers, if you're nervous . . . and you can decide among yourselves whether ten thousand dollars is too much to pay for uniting your precious Dixie."

"I'd not ha' given you one red cent!" says Annette Mandeville. "You'd be doing it for your miserable life, and been thankful for that!"

"Ah, but we know your generous nature, don't we? And suppose I'd refused?"

"You? Refuse? With your worthless skin at stake? You forget, I know the kind of cur you are – I heard you that day at Greystones, when my husband and his white trash caught you, and you whimpered and grovelled like a whipped nigra wench!"

"My, how you must miss the gracious life of the old plantation!"

"Whining for your life! And I'd thought you were a man!"

"Man enough for one eager little Creole lady, though, wasn't I? But then, I was probably a welcome change after your nigger fieldhands . . . gently, Annette dear, that fork is for dessert, not for stabbing . . . Anyway, we're not at Greystones now – and let me tell you, if your fat friend hadn't agreed to pay me, I'd be on my way to the British ministry this minute. Why, I'd not even have to go that far – there's a party of Englishmen at the corner table yonder, by the sound of them . . . who's to stop me joining 'em, eh? Or sending for a constable? Not your ridiculous Kuklos, I'll be bound! Or would they come rushing in, with their Guy Fawkes hoods –"

"You fool! Don't you know the kind of men you're dealing with – the danger you're in? If you were to move two steps from this table, they'd be the last you'd ever take –"

"Oh, fudge! What, in a hotel dining-room, crowded with

134

guests? Hardly the place for an assassination – what would the *maître* say?"

"Listen to me! There are two men in this room now, armed and watching you – try to escape or call for help and you'll be shot down without mercy. I mean it. This is not England – such things happen here. I've known the Kuklos kill a man on the steps of the Capitol, before scores of people, in broad day. If you don't believe me – run for the door! But if you value your life, you'll keep faith with them."

"My dear Annette! Can this be alarm on *my* behalf? Is that wifely concern I see in those bonny grey eyes?"

"I'm concerned that the Kuklos's work is done – and that I play my part in it, and you play yours –"

"Then you'd better stop whispering like some Dago conspirator and finish your pudding like a good little wife, Mrs Beauchamp Comber, and smile ever so sweetly at Mr Comber, and insist on cutting his cigar for him . . . why, thank'ee, my dear! Are we on honeymoon, by the way? If so, let's forego the savoury and coffee, and repair to our nuptial couch . . . no? Love's first bloom has faded, has it? Oh, well . . . coffee, waiter!"

I was testing the wicket, and finding it confoundedly sticky – as I'd known it would be the moment I'd awoken from my exhausted sleep and remembered where I was and what had happened. Any hopes that I'd dreamed the whole ghastly thing were dashed by the sight of Joe sitting by the bedroom door like a black nemesis, sporting his pistol. I was caught, for the moment, and could only hope that my little charade before retiring had taken some effect.

It was late afternoon when I came to, and someone had been busy while I slept, for beside the bed there was a new outfit of clothing – and damned if it didn't fit perfectly, even to the collar. But what sent a chill down my spine was the name on the tailor's tab: B. M. Comber; it was even stamped in the lining of the hat. I'd formed a respect for the Kuklos from the ease with which they'd spirited me away from Crixus, but these little touches told me they were formidable indeed.

135

While I dressed, Joe brewed me some coffee on a spirit stove, and directed me to the drawing-room. There was no sign of Lachesis and Clotho, but Atropos was writing at the table, and Annette was on hand, stony-eyed but mighty jimp in a gown that seemed to consist of flowers and gauze. He complimented himself on my appearance, and hoped I approved of the sober cravat he'd chosen for me. "Our colonial taste runs to more extrav'gant colours, but since your ac-cent marks you as English, why, you best look it," says he, chuckling fatly as though he'd never put a point to my throat in his life. "The suit's well enough, I guess, an' will serve for day an' evenin' – I fear we still lag behind London in our deplo'able failure to change after six o'clock. Now, suh, sit down, an' tend to what I say."

First of all, says he, five thousand dollars ("we felt your request for remuneration was reasonable, but stiff") would be placed to the credit of B. M. Comber in a bank of the New York Safety Fund, and might be drawn at either of two addresses in Washington and New York, "but only *after* the day on which the country is ringin' with the nooz that Old Ossawatomie has made an armed incursion into V'ginia." The gross cheeks creased in a sardonic grin. "Then all you have to do is present the draft which you'll find in the breast pocket o' that noo coat you're wearin' . . . Now I see it on you, I don't know as I can bring myself to like that collah . . ." He squinted critically while I examined the draft, on the Citizens' Bank of Louisiana, and my spirits soared. It was all window-dressing to be sure, and they'd never put a cent to Comber's account – but at least they were pretending to treat my offer of mercenary service seriously. Maybe they even believed it. Not that they'd trust me an inch . . . but they might be just a little less watchful. I pocketed the draft and told him the coat collar suited me to admiration.

"Well, if you're content . . . now, suh, you an' Miz Mandeville will travel to Noo Yawk by the Night Flyer, as Mistuh an' Miz Beauchamp Comber – you're bound to keep that name, 'cos it's the one John Brown will be expectin'. Joe will accompany you, as your slave, an' when he has telegraphed Crixus tomorrow that you've been 'found' in Noo Yawk, he will take you on to Boston or Conco'd, where you will meet Brown, prob'ly at the home of Franklin B. Sanbo'n, a prom'nent abolitionist. There you an' Joe will 'list in Brown's service. 'Tis all planned out, you see, neat as a Quaker's bonnet," says he with satisfaction. "By the by, 'til you leave Noo Yawk, you are in the care of Miz Mandeville – Miz Comber, I should say," he shot her a greasy smirk, "an' will obey any instructions she may give you. What these may be, I can only guess – "

"Keep to the business, you fat swine!" snaps she.

"Why, surely, dahlin' . . . an' see that you mind yours, an' the Kuklos's. Jus' remember you ain't takin' this trip for pleasure alone." There was an edge to the soft voice, and I thought, hollo, is someone's piggy carcase aglow with jealous passion for our tiny poppet? It conjured up a tableau too hideous to contemplate . . .

"So theah it is, Mistuh Comber. All you need do is go 'long quietly, do whatevah Brown requiahs of you, go with him right down the line to Harper's Ferry or wherevah it may be, put your trust in the Good Lawd . . . an' go home to England with five thousan' dollahs in your money-puss. An' again, an' for the last time," he gave me his blandest fat smile, "don't evah think you can jump off the wagon 'long the way. The Kuklos will be theah, always, an' if you play false by wo'd or deed . . . then suh, you are crow-pickin's."

He rose, smoothing his coat and shooting his cuffs, and stowed his writings in his pocket. "I b'lieve that is all, so I confide you to deah Annette – an' Joe, of course, an' your unseen guardians. Your se'vant, ma'am . . . honoured to have made your acquaintance, suh. I bid you adieu, an' good fortune . . . an' you take care, now, ye heah?"

D'ye know, when I look back on those bizarre few hours when the Kuklos took me by the neck and twisted me to their crazy ends, the rummest thing of all wasn't the amazing coincidence of Annette, or those grotesque hoods, or that obese monster so pathetically bang up to the nines, or even their incredible plot – but those last six words from Atropos:

137

after all the threats and blackmail, the gentle ritual of the Dixie farewell. God help me, I believe he meant it.

When he'd gone, it occurred to me to twit Annette that she had an admirer in our dandy hippo. I asked innocently if he was her lover, expecting a fine explosion, and was taken flat aback by her reply:

"He is my husband."

"Good God! He can't be – what, that great bag of jelly? What happened to Mandeville?"

"He died."

"And you married *that*? Well, I never . . . gad, what a wedding night that must have been . . ." I let out a yelp of horror. "But, my God . . . he *knew* . . . well, he suspected, I'm sure . . . what we'd been up to, I mean . . . before he arrived . . . you know, when we were . . ."

"He was already here, in this room. Watching us," says she, cool as be-damned before the mirror, tittivating her low-cut bodice. "You will see there is a spy-hole in the door to the bedroom."

"You don't mean it! But . . . but . . ." I had a terrifying memory of lying helpless beneath his swordstick – and he'd just watched me rattling his wife. "Godalmighty! But . . . you mean . . . he don't *mind*?"

"On the contrary." She patted her hair. "He insists."

"Well, strike me dead! I say . . . he must be a damned rum chap – phew! But . . . you, I mean – why the devil . . . ?"

"Do I do it, you would ask?" She took a last sneer at the mirror, and faced me. "He is the richest man in Louisiana. He is also the brain, though not the head, of the Kuklos. You've been singularly honoured by his personal attention, a measure of your importance." She gave me a withering look, up and down. "You probably think him mad. He is not. Whatever he plans, succeeds, and whatever he promises, he performs. Remember that, for your own sake. Now, it is past five o'clock, and I wish to dine before we leave." She drew herself up like a tiny Guardsman. "Give me your arm and take me down."

So I did, ruminating on the manners and morals of the Old South, and now that we'd broken the ice so splendidly we were soon chatting away in the dining-room like an old married couple, as I've described at the beginning of this chapter. I affected a carelessness I was far from feeling, because I wanted to test just how real were the threats that Atropos had made; her alarm told me all I wanted to know, and gave me some useful information: apart from Joe, who was lurking in the lobby while we ate, there were two Kuklos "shadows" watching me, and no doubt they or others would be on hand all the way to New York. I'd have to look damned slippy when the time came to run.

It was a mad pickle, you may think: held prisoner amidst all the bustle and confusion of civilised society – but if your captors know their business, and are ruthless enough, why, you might as well be chained in a dungeon. Rudi von Starnberg took me halfway across Germany against my will, simply by having a gun and a knife and being ready to use 'em if I so much as sneezed out of turn, and I'd no doubt the Kuklos would be equally unscrupulous. So I could only wait, and seem to play up – both of which I'm good at – and take comfort in the knowledge that they'd not harm me unless forced to, since I was no use to them dead or bound for Kentucky.

Being resigned, I felt easier, and even a touch light-headed, as we cowards will when we feel safe for the moment. The upshot was that, with bottle and belly-timber before him, Flashy became if not beastly, at least mischievously, drunk, enjoying himself in contemplating the charms of the choice little icicle across the table. I'd already noted that she'd put some elegant flesh on her elfin form over the years, and was altogether a juicier morsel than she'd been at Greystones; she might still wear the expression of an ill-tempered ferret, but that kind of viciousness on a handsome face has its own attraction, and I knew perfectly well that her artistic paintwork and stylishly coiled blonde hair had been designed for my benefit; she'd always loathed and lusted after me together, which only added spice to her allurement, and I looked forward as much as she did to the enjoyment of Mr Comber's marital rights.

On this happy thought I was content to idle my way

through the dinner, which like all American meals was gargantuan and over-rich; how the devil they can put away a
massive breakfast of steak, ham, eggs, terrapin, or giant
oysters, two dinners at noon and five, and still be fit to beat
their bellies at supper, is beyond me; even Annette, who
wasn't two pisspots and a handle high, worked her way
through five courses without breaking sweat on her pale
immaculate brow. Unlike most of her compatriots, she
didn't shout through her food, so I had leisure to listen to
the deafening chatter around us. From the trumpetings of
two portly curry-faced gentry at the next table[23] I gathered
that President Buchanan was a weak-kneed nincompoop for
not going ahead and "teachin' them dam' impident greasers
a lesson" by annexing half their country; war with Mexico
would, in the speaker's opinion, rally the public behind "Old
Buck", ensure a Democratic victory in next year's election,
and be "one in the eye for that slippery bastard Seward an'
his dam' Black Republicans."

"Ah heah Seward's goin' to England," says his companion.

"Bes' place fo' the nigra-lovin' sunnavabitch! Ah hope his
vessel sinks – Ah mean it, suh, Ah do! Kin you 'magine
President Seward? That's whut it'll come to yet, you mark
mah wo'ds!"

"Come now, suh, he may not git nom'nated, even!"

"You wanna wager, suh? Why, he's got Weed an' Greeley
in his pocket . . . whut's that ye say, 'Tilda? Give you ladies
the vote an' 'twill be President *Douglas*![24] Haw-haw! Why,
he ain't but a dam' dwarf! You'd like to cuddle him, ye
say? Ye heah that, Ambrose? 'Tilda thinks Douglas is right
cuddlesome! Waal, now, honey, Ah reckon his beauteous
Adele might have suthin' to say 'bout that; Ah jus' reckon
she might – an' so might yo's truly! You keep yo' cuddles
for papa, ye heah?" And the lecherous old goat laid a fond
paw on the arm of the languid 'Tilda, who might have been
his wife, but I think not, from the wanton freedom with
which she had been glancing in my direction.

"Ah declare 'Tilda would put Adele right in the shade!"
cries the other roué gallantly. "Nevah seen her in sech looks!

140

How you *do* that, 'Tilda? All the soirees an' parties, you oughta be clean wore out, but darn if you don't come up fresher'n dew on a lily! You got some magic potion, sweetheart?"

"Know whut she's got?" cries her escort. "She got this 'lectric rejuvenatin' contraption, an' a coloured wench to mechanic it – why, they all the crack wi' the smart gals, ain't they, 'Tilda? Puts the bloom right back in those damask cheeks in no time at all – an' all over, too! Haw-haw! Yessir, that's mah honey's secret!"

"Why, you make me soun' like some kinda monster works on 'lectric'ty!" drawls the fair 'Tilda, lowering her lashes at me and showing her profile. "But mah machine is right stimulatin'."

"Our train leaves in an hour," says Annette sharply. "You will wait in the lobby while Joe fetches a carriage – and keep your tongue and eyes to yourself, do you hear?" Her mouth was tight with anger, and there was a little flush on her cheek. "Do nothing to excite attention."

"Difficult, when we're such a handsome couple," says I, leering. "If we want to pass unnoticed, why the dooce are we parading before half Washington? Suppose one of Crixus's people is about?"

"We know them all by sight. And they will not be seeking you here, or at the station. Joe has seen to it. Stop guzzling that wine, you fool! Now . . . follow me out closely."

What with the booze, my natural taste for devilment, and confidence that I was perfectly safe as long as I didn't try to run for it, I felt a sudden urge to put turpentine on her dainty little tail and light it. So when I'd drawn back her chair, and she had made for the lobby without a glance at me, I navigated carefully in her wake, turned in the doorway, surveyed the glittering splendour of the dining-room and its chattering gluttons, drew a deep breath and let out a Lakota war-whoop at the top of my voice. A woman shrieked, men sprang to their feet, a passing waiter went up like a galvanised grouse and dropped his loaded tray with a tremendous smash – and then there was dead silence as a hundred mouths gaped and two hundred eyes goggled; every

141

head turned, in fact – save for a tall chap near the door who kept his eyes fixed on his plate, and another with his back turned who watched me like a hawk in a mirror on the far wall.

I strolled into the lobby, where Annette was standing rigid with fury; people were craning towards the dining-room to see what the row was. "Are you mad?" she hissed.

"You were right," says I, "the boys are in there. But the Kuklos ought to train 'em better, you know; 'tain't natural *not* to stare when a lunatic cuts loose in public. Now, then, where's that dilatory Joe with the carriage, eh?"

Her eyes were blazing, but she swept off without a word, leaving me to look about and wonder which of the throng in the lobby might be Kuklos "shadows" – for Joe had disappeared, and the two betrayed by my little ruse in the dining-room hadn't emerged, but I wasn't fool enough to imagine that I wasn't being watched. I gave up, though, for the patrons of Washington hotels in those days were such a mixed lot, my unseen watchers might have been anyone. There were the obvious politicos, standing about in knots puffing their cigars and disputing warmly, wealthy citizens with stout matrons dressed up like May Day cuddies, young blades in fancy weskits and amazing whiskers, with fashionable belles gushing and squealing on their arms, plantation aristocrats in their broad-brimmed straws with little nigger boys toting their bags, likely-looking fellows in city clothes but with the unmistakable silence of the frontier hanging round them like a shroud, barefoot slaves waiting patiently beyond the great doors leading to the marble porch, thin seedy fellows with ferret eyes questing for Senator This or Congressman That and muttering to each other before scurrying away like the political rodents they were, one or two top-drawer strumpets immediately recognisable by being the most tastefully dressed women in view, and everywhere the Great Curse of the New World, the American Child, in all its raucous, spoiled, undisciplined, selfish ghastliness, the female specimens keeping up an incessant high-pitched whine and the male infants racketing like cow-pokes on payday. There's nothing wrong with grown Americans, by and

142

large; you won't find heartier men or bonnier women anywhere, but the only remedy I can see for their children is to
run Herod for President.

Then Joe was at my elbow with a slouch hat and a long
coat, guiding me out of the throng and down a passage to
the same side door by which I'd entered the hotel, where a
growler was waiting with Annette inside, raging silently. She
said not a word as we bowled through the dusk to the station,
and when we drew up close by the train – they had platforms
in those days – she whisked out and into the carriage while
Joe signed to me to sit tight. He descended, spying both ways
before beckoning abruptly, and I strode quickly through the
wreathing steam with the bell clanging overhead, and
mounted into the sudden quiet of the train.

I wasn't well acquainted with American railroads at that
time, and was resigned to an uncomfortable long haul
through the night to New York, in one of those reeking long
coaches in which I'd travelled down from Baltimore, full of
noisy unwashed louts whose favourite occupation was spitting at the stove. But no such thing; here was a quiet corridor
with private compartments which they called "cabins", fitted
up in tip-top style. Annette was in Number 8, I remember;
I had a glimpse of an alcove bed with curtains drawn back,
a washstand and comfortable furniture, and then Joe was
hustling me into Number 7, which seemed smaller but had
a bed beneath the window. I asked him where he was going
to sleep, and he replied curtly that he wasn't. I made myself
comfortable while he slipped out, and presently I heard his
deep rumble in Annette's cabin, and the conductor saying
anything she wanted, ma'am, anything at all, she should just
send her boy, and it would be attended to right smartly.

Then Joe returned, sitting on the floor with his back
against the door, and a moment later the bell clanged and
the steam whistled and the conductor bawled that this was
the Night Flyer to Baltimo', Wilmin'ton, Philadelphia, Tren-
ton, an' Noo Yawk, and we jolted and clanked into motion
– and I reflected that my evasion would have to wait until
journey's end. I didn't fancy dropping from a moving train,
even if Joe hadn't been on hand; he was a big, ugly gyascuta,

143

that one, his sleeves tight on his enormous biceps as he sat with his arms folded on his barrel chest, the yellow-flecked eyes rolling at me whenever I stirred on the bed. I found myself studying him: he was your real jet-black Nubian, flat-nosed, thick-lipped, and could have walked into the K.A.R.* nowadays, no questions asked. Having nothing better to do for the moment, I indulged my idle curiosity.

"Joe," says I, "why are you with the Kuklos?"

He glowered suspiciously. "Whut you mean?"

"Well, you're Atropos's slave – yet you've been with Crixus on the Railroad, had the chance to escape to free soil. Why didn't you? You want to be free, surely?"

He studied me in turn, the black face expressionless. Then: "You got niggers in England . . . that so?"

"Yes, a few – and they're all free. So are the niggers in our Empire, in Africa and the West Indies. No one owns 'em, or can make 'em do what they don't like, or sell 'em down the river. Wouldn't you like that?"

He sat, apparently thinking, though you couldn't be sure with that face. At last he said: "Yo' English niggers . . . how many on 'em got a fine coat, like this heah?" He ran a finger the size of a truncheon down his lapel. "How many on 'em got a silver timepiece an' chain? How many got five dollahs in they pocket?"

"Why, Joe, you could have all those things, in Canada, say – and be free into the bargain! You could do whatever you liked, go wherever you liked, be your own master."

He digested this, staring at the floor, and shrugged his huge shoulders. "Ah guess so," says he slowly. "An' Ah cud be tret like black trash whenevah Ah liked, an' git out the way, nigger, whenevah Ah liked, an' go hungry whenevah Ah liked, an' beg mah bread'n go to jail whenevah Ah liked." He raised his bullet head and stared at me; it was like looking into the eyes of an ape in a cage. "Don' have none o' that wi' Mass' Charles. Ah his slave, but he treat me like a man – an' folks r'specks me, cuz Ah's his nigger. Don' git tret like no black trash, nossuh! Git good vittles,

* King's African Rifles.

144

git good clo'es like these heah . . ." He closed his eyes and gave a great growling sigh. "An' Ah gits to hump his li'l white lady whenevah Mass' Charles say so . . . oh, but she is prime white meat! None o' yo' free niggers gits that kin' o' pleasurin', Ah reckon."

I was shocked – not that I'm a prude, you understand, but because I knew the physical loathing that Annette had for black skin; why, at Greystones, any wench who'd had the misfortune to touch her by accident, hadn't been able to walk for a week. The thought of her with this human gorilla . . . well, my little French aristo was paying a price for being the richest woman in Louisiana, wasn't she just?

"You ask yo' Afriky niggers whether they'd ruther be free – or Joe," growls he, showing his gleaming teeth in a great wolfish grin. "See whut they tell yuh."

"Ah, but they don't know any better, Joe – you do. They're savages, but you're . . . well, civilised, I mean. I've seen how you carry yourself with Crixus – and with Atropos, too. You're not a common nigger . . . why, I'll bet you can read, can't you?"

He stuck out a sullen lip. "Some. Writin' an' figurin', though . . . they kinda tough."

It's not often you find yourself conversing with a caveman, and I was becoming interested. "But see here, if you can read a little, you can learn to write and . . . ah, figure, fast enough. Why, man, you could make something of yourself – and if you were free, you could buy all the white tarts you wanted. Mandeville's nothing special, I can tell you! You're a fool, Joe . . . but you needn't go on being one, you know. You can be something better than a slave –"

"Ah cain't be white!" growls he, shaking his head, and then he frowned, and a wicked glitter came into his eyes. "Say, Mistuh Comber . . . you tryin' talk yo'self out o' this? You tryin' to fool this po' coloured boy?"

"No such thing! Why, if I wanted to be 'out of this', as you call it, don't think that you could stop me. I'm here because I'm being paid – ah, there you have it! I'm free, you see, but you're not, because you're content to be bound

145

to that great fat slug, when you could be . . ." And then I caught the gleam in his eyes, and I stared for a moment, and then lay back on the bed, looking at the ceiling, anger giving way to amusement.

"Joe," says I at length, "you are a smart black son-of-a-bitch, aren't you, though?" I began to laugh, and so did he, the great black face split in a melon grin, his shoulders heaving. "Oh, you poor coloured boy! So writing and figuring are tough, are they?"

"Some," chuckles he. "Cain't hol' de pencil in mah big black fingers, nohow!"

"Oh, leave off! Begging your bread, forsooth, and mumbling like a fieldhand! What's the capital of Portugal?"

"Oh, lemme see . . . Ah gotta study dat! Tain't Madrid, nossuh, 'r Gay Paree . . . um, Lisbon, maybe? Say, though, which o' yo' li'l ole English kings got hisself mu'dered in de Tower o' Lunnon in fo'teen-eighty-three?"

"Don't be daft! Oh, very well – which one?"

"Edwa'd Fift'. He was jes' twelve yeahs old, an' his mammy wuz a lady called 'Liz'beth Woodville." He sat there chortling, the jolly darkie to the life, damn him.

"Yes . . . I should have remembered, shouldn't I, that anyone who can spy inside the Underground Railroad, and fool Crixus, knows more than picking cotton . . . Went to school along with Atropos – Master Charles – did you?"

"Niggers don' 'tend school. No, we had the same gov'ness, in the same nussery. Mass' Charles's papa was an . . . exper'mental gen'leman, so he raised us the same." He was smiling still, but the black eyes were expressionless. "Wanted to see how it came out, Ah guess."

"But see here . . . this is all the more reason why my question's good, Joe – why, being raised like that, and educated, and knowing what you do . . . why, in God's name, d'ye stay a slave? Don't you *want* to be free, for heaven's sake?"

Just for a second he avoided my eye, then his chin came up. "Ma answer's good, too, Comber." It came out in his harsh bass growl. "Ah don' *need* to be free. Ah serve Mass' Charles as a friend – his best friend, like he told you. He

146

trusts me, Ah trust him. The way he goes, Ah go. He wants me to work for the Kuklos, Ah work for the Kuklos. He wants me to keep a hold on B. M. Comber an' make sho' he earn that fi' thousan' dollahs . . ." The smile on the primitive face was a knowing glimmer now, and not pleasant. ". . . Ah keep a hold. Oh, maybe take a li'l rise out o' him, fo' fun, an' so we both know whut's whut, but that don' signify a bit. You stay held, Comber, all the way, make no mistake 'bout that!"

So there . . . Comber. Evidently my question anent slavery had annoyed him, and he was reminding me "whut" was "whut".

"Well, Joe, all I can say is that Master Charles is fortunate in the loyalty of his friend."

"That's right!"

"And tell me . . . when he says 'Hump my wife, for my entertainment', do you do it as a friend – or as an obedient slave?"

I'll swear his eyes glowed, and he wasn't a pretty sight. Then he smiled, and was even less pretty.

"It ain't no ha'dship – 'speshly 'cos she don't like it. She don' like it *at all*. She jus' cain't 'bide niggers, it seems."

"Ah, well, there's no pleasing some people, is there? Happy little menage you must all have together. Fortunately, however, she *can* abide white men . . . and I rather think she's expecting me." I swung my legs off the bed, and he seemed to flow upright like a genie towering out of a bottle. I feigned surprise. "Don't worry, Joe, I shan't run away."

He stood glaring down at me, undecided, and I wondered if he was going to assert his guardianship. But he had style, did Joe, in his own way, for after a long moment he stood aside, giving me his nastiest grin, and unlatched the door. "Sho' . . . you go right ahead, like an o-bedient free white man . . . yo' right welcome to the nigger's leavin's. An' Ah know you won't run, 'cos o' that fi' thousan' dollahs . . . an' this." He pulled back his coat to show the pistol butt. "You go along, now . . . an' enjoy yo'self, ye heah?"

"Why, Joe, Ah b'lieve Ah sho'ly will," says I. "Tell ye

147

sumpn else, Joe . . . so will she." I winked at him. "You think 'bout that."

And she did, so far as I could judge, which was never easy with La Mandeville, quite the most unsociable mistress I ever mounted. Most women I've known have exchanged seductive pleasantries beforehand, squealed and gasped during performance, and chatted comfortably afterwards (except my Elspeth, who gasses throughout, bless her). Not Annette; when I accosted her that night in her cabin, it was Greystones all over again – cold, clawing passion, and then sullen silence until she fell asleep. However, when the train bell woke her (at Philadelphia, if memory serves) she went to work like Poppaea on honeymoon, which I took as a compliment, before resuming her impersonation of a Trappist nun, if there is such a thing. It was at this stage that I succeeded in getting a snatch of conversation out of her, and most interesting it proved to be.

In the interval between rounds, so to speak, while she lay cold and quiet beside me in the cramped berth, I'd been reflecting on Joe's capricious behaviour. For a while there we'd got on rather well, he'd taken me in by playing the darkie simpleton, teased me cheerily – and then all unintended I'd touched him on the raw, probably by my impatient concern for his enslaved condition (Christ, you can't do right for doing wrong with these folk). So he'd turned ornery on me, been redoubled and set down, and from that moment we were sworn enemies. Well, the hell with him. At all events, in trying to coax some chat out of my tiny paramour after our final gallop, in which she'd drawn blood in two places, I mentioned Joe's name – partly out of curiosity, but mostly out of malice, I confess – and she started like a galvanised frog.

"What of him? What did he say?"

Aha, thinks I, guilty conscience; capital. "Oh, this and that . . . he's an odd chap. No fool, for all he looks like a backward baboon. Knows more English history than I do, anyway . . ."

"What? History, you say?" She was wide awake now. "What does that black beast know about it?"

148

"The name of Edward the Fifth's mother, for one thing. Quite extraordinary . . . aye, a most educated nigger, smart as paint. I'm surprised your husband trusts him."

She was silent a moment. "Why should he not?"

"Well, Joe's a slave, ain't he – and here he is, heading for the free states, so what's to hinder him lighting out for Canada? I would, if I were he – but when I put it to him, he said your husband was his best friend, and he'd not dream of running from him . . . you know, loyalty, that sort o' thing . . ."

"Loyalty! What do animals know of loyalty?"

"Oh, I dunno . . . dogs are loyal, they say, 'tho I never found 'em so. My Aunt Paget had one of those damned poodles, when I was a kid – stank, but she swore it was faithful. Took a great lump out of my arse when I tried to sick it on to some hens –"

"What else did the brute tell you?"

"Oh, nothing." I yawned, and when she had turned away and settled down, I gave a drowsy chuckle. "Nothing much, leastways . . . oh, yes, I gather Joe likes white women . . . unwilling ones, for choice."

She lay dead still – so still, I could sense the sudden tension of her muscles. Good luck to you, Joe, thinks I, if ever Atropos kicks the bucket unexpected and you become the widow's property. I waited for her fury to vent itself in shrieks of rage or fine French oaths, but nothing came for at least a minute, and then the most astonishing thing happened. She turned slowly towards me in the berth, and her hand stole across, searching for mine, and to my amazement she nuzzled her head on to my shoulder. Her tiny body was trembling, and damned if I didn't feel wetness trickling on my skin – she was absolutely weeping, with a soft murmuring wail that I could hardly hear until it turned into a faint broken whisper: "Oh-h-h . . . hold . . . me . . ."

I couldn't credit it – Annette Mandeville, the spurred succubus, hard as a diamond and vicious with it, whimpering like a lost child. I slipped an arm about her, marvelling, and she clung closer still, pushing her blubbering face under my chin. "Oh-h-h, hold me . . . close . . . close . . . oh, please . . ." Well, naked tits never appeal to me in vain, so I drew her over me with her small rump in my one hand, for she was the veriest fly-weight. She lay there, keening away, bedewing my manly bosom with her tears. Baffling, I found it, but rather jolly; I disengaged the clasp of her fingers so that I could work at her poonts with one hand and her stern with t'other.

"No . . . no . . . not that," sobs she. "Only . . . comfort me . . . oh, please . . . hold me close!" She was crying hard now, with a great yearning misery. "Please . . . comfort me!"

So I did, stroking her hair and petting her in a bewildered fashion, asking myself if I'd ever understand women. She clung like a clam, and after a while her weeping subsided into little sniffs and sighs, and I guessed she was dropping off to sleep. So then I cheered her up properly.

Some cynic once observed that it was impossible to see the sights of New York City because there were no cabs to take you about, but it didn't matter because there were no sights to see anyway.[25] I can't agree; whether there were cabs or not in '59 I didn't have time to find out, but for sights, well, there may have been no St Paul's or Rialto or Arc de Triomphe, or mouldering piles of stone or dreary galleries stuffed with the rubbish of centuries, but there was something far more moving, inspiring, and aesthetically pleasing to the eye than any of these, and you didn't need a cab to see 'em either, as they sashayed along Broadway past the old Astor House by the Park, resplendent in their silks and satins and furs, with those ridiculous fetching hats and parasols above and the extravagantly high heels below. I refer to the women of New York, who for beauty of face and form, elegance of dress, and general style and deportment, are quite the finest I've struck – until they open their mouths, that is, which they do most of the time, but even that incessant nasal braying can't rob them of their exquisite charm. I don't mean only the trollops, either, of whom there were said to be two thousand in a population of three-quarters of a million in '59 (and who counted 'em I can't imagine, some clergyman, no doubt) but the respectable women of every class. I was enchanted at first sight, and if I were condemned to spend my dotage sitting in Stewart's store or the Metropolitan lobby, contemplating the passing peaches, I wouldn't mind a bit, provided I was furnished with earplugs against the cackling laughter and cries of "You bet!" "Be blowed!" and "Okay, bo!" But they

151

probably have different cries nowadays, and no powdered hands or Grecian bends, alas.

They absolutely ruled the place then; New York was a woman's town, and let no one tell you different. They were the queens of the world, and didn't they know it, not that they were pushing, you understand; they were just freer and bolder and more forward and independent than any women I'd seen elsewhere, taking it for granted that men existed to serve and minister to them, and not t'other way about. For example, you could be on an omnibus, going through the inconvenience of paying the driver through his little window, and three or four dolly-mops would come on chattering and laughing behind you, drop their money in your hand, and expect you to pay it over and bring 'em their change – perfect strangers, too. Mind you, the reward of a free and easy smile and "Thanks, chief!" from a pert New Yorker is a delight; given time, I'd have been haunting that omnibus yet.

Everything was for their convenience, too: hotels had their ladies' entrances and dining-rooms, so that the dears wouldn't be offended by the reek of cigars and the conversation of horrid men; every other shop seemed to be dedicated to cosmetics, female finery, and jewellery, from quality establishments like Ball and Blacks to the seedier stores on Water and Mercer Streets; they had their own cake-and-coffee houses where no male dare enter, and there were even gambling hells for ladies only (and I mean society women, not cigar-store tarts from below Fourteenth Street) where they "bucked the tiger"* and blued their menfolks' dividends at faro and billiards. And their husbands, sweethearts, and paramours seemed to be all for it, and treated 'em with a regard and deference you'd never find in Europe.

Why this should be, I don't know; New York men are certainly no more chivalrous than any other. It may be that women were scarce in colonial times, and so grew to be particularly treasured, but my own theory is that, the U.S.A.

* Play for high stakes (prob. from the tiger sign used to denote a gambling-house).

being all for progress and liberty, and New York in the vanguard of everything, its women have become emancipated sooner than their sisters elsewhere. They've usurped not a few masculine habits, too: anywhere in the world you'll see roués with fast young women in tow, but only in New York was it common to see fashionable ladies of mature years settling restaurant bills and buying gifts for handsome young clerks; they picked 'em up over department-store counters, I was told. And the New York female grows up at a startling rate: my first day there I was astonished to see a party of society schoolgirls, the kind whose parents live on Fifth Avenue and have the brats educated at Murray Hill, driving along in a basket wagon with a "tiger" on the step – none of 'em was above twelve years old, and all were got up like women of twenty, even to the languid airs and gestures.

So that was my first impression of New York, gained in a few brief hours: splendid women on the go, but nothing else out of the ordinary, for the town itself was a sort of larger Glasgow – there were no sky-scrapers then – and chiefly remarkable for being paved apparently with peanut shells, which were sold by swarms of urchins and crackled underfoot wherever you turned, even in the lobby of the Astor House, to which we drove from the station. It was *the* place in New York just then, and large even by American standards, a great barracks looking east across Broadway to the Park, with a shaving mug and brush in each room; talk about luxury, if you like.

If my impressions are sketchy,[26] I can only plead preoccupation. New York was where I was going to have to cut stick, not only eluding the Kuklos but hiding out from them, preferably with a British consul who'd see to my passage home once he found out who I was. It was maddening (and frightening) to drive through crowded, bustling streets, to look about the busy lobby of a great hotel, to sit in the suit of rooms which had been reserved for us – and to know that I daren't stir a foot for fear of the unseen eyes that were following me everywhere. Soon after we arrived, when Joe had gone below stairs to chivvy the porters about our bags, and Annette and I were alone, I excused myself to visit the privy along the way. She didn't even turn her head as I slipped out into the passage, which seemed empty except for a couple of darkies clinging somnolently to their brooms – and then at one end there was a nondescript white man who turned his back just a shade too hurriedly at the sight of me. I strode smartly the other way – and became aware of a chap lounging in an alcove ahead, with a round hat tilted over his eyes. Of course, he may have been an innocent citizen – but I didn't know that. I stepped into the thunder-house, palpitating; it was empty so far as I could see, but it was six floors above ground, and by this time I was convinced that there was probably an armed dwarf crouching in the bloody cistern.

Right, thinks I, we'll have to wait until dark; if I'm not a better night-stalker than anything the Kuklos can show, it's a poor look-out. Meanwhile, we'll be a docile little prisoner, and keep our eyes peeled. I headed back for our rooms, and bore up sharp at the door, which was ajar, for voices were being raised within, Annette's and Joe's.

Following her astonishing behaviour the previous night, when she'd crept into my arms blubbing like a baby, I'd looked to see a softening of her manner in the morning, but no such thing. The Annette who woke as we pulled into New York was her old shrewish self; when I referred to our tender interlude, she simply turned her back and ordered me out in her iciest tone so that she could get dressed. It was the same on the drive to the hotel, with Joe on the box, and at breakfast in the coffee-room; she either ignored my remarks or replied in cold monosyllables, staring past me. And now, as I eavesdropped, she was in fine withering form with Joe, who was fighting a dogged rearguard action, by the sound of it.

"I gotta wait fo' a reply at th'Eastern 'lectric," he was protesting. "Crixus cain't git ma message till aft'noon, an' cud be evenin' 'fore he telegraphs back. Might have to wait till mawnin', even –"

"What of it? D'you think I intend to sit here waiting for you?"

154

"Might be best, ma'am. Cain't leave Comber heah on his lone – one of us oughta be with him –"

"Don't be a fool! Of course I shan't leave him here! He'll come with me. Hermes's men will have him in view every moment – there are two of them, are there not?"

"Even so, ma'am, he'll be safest right heah! He's a right slippy mean feller, an' dang'rous! Ah know it –"

"You know it! Who are you to know anything, you black dolt! You'll remember your place, which is to do my bidding! D'you hear? Now, get to the telegraph office – and don't return until you have Crixus's order to take him to Boston! I don't care if you have to wait until tomorrow, or the day after!"

He muttered something which I didn't hear, and she fairly hissed in fury. "Don't dare question me – don't dare! Comber is my concern – not yours, you insolent offal! Do you hear? Answer me, when I address you! Do you hear?"

"Yes, ma'am." His deep voice was shaking. "'Sposin' Ah git word f'm Crixus this aft'noon – where Ah find yuh?"

"You don't! Wait till I return. Now, get out!"

I met him in the doorway, murmured, "Ah, Joe – how many free niggers get *that* kind of pleasuring, eh?", and received a murderous glare before he strode off. Annette was putting on her bonnet before the mirror, but when I inquired where she was going I was told curtly to hold my tongue and wait, which I did obediently, while she fussed with her appearance, referring every few minutes to the little gold watch which she kept in her reticule. She was paler than usual, and twitchy as a nervous sepoy, drawing her gloves off and on and fiddling with her toilette – something's up, thinks I, but after a while she seemed to settle, and it was a good half-hour before she looked at her watch for the last time, stood up, and informed me that we were going out.

"I have business in town. You will come with me, and don't move a yard from me at any time, do you understand? Whatever I do, wherever I go, don't leave my side for a moment, and do not contradict anything you may hear me say. No, do not ask questions!" She rapped it all out like a

155

tiny drill sergeant, steady enough, but I guessed that she was up to high doh within, and striving to hide it. "You are being watched, remember! Do not look around for . . . for anyone – they are there. Do nothing out of the usual, you hear? Your life depends upon it!"

It was nothing she hadn't said in Washington, but the manner was new: she was scared, and I couldn't believe it was only on my account. I started to ask her what was amiss, but she bit my head off.

"Be quiet! Do as I say – no more! We are man and wife out in New York, so try to behave in a natural manner!" That was rich, coming from her. She took a breath, and handed me some change. "That is our streetcar fare, three cents apiece. Pay the conductor. Now, give me your arm."

It was like walking with a badly wound up clockwork doll as we descended to the street, but once we were out in the sunshine and the chattering Broadway crowds she became easier, possibly because I showed no tendency to cut and run or bawl for a copper. There's a great air of up and doing about New York; everyone seems to be in a cheerful hurry, and even my apprehensions about the Kuklos bravos who, I was sure, were dogging our steps, receded in that jolly bustle. We mounted one of the long cars which ran on rails on the broad thoroughfare; it was crowded to the doors, but half a dozen gallants begged Annette with much tipping of tiles and "Do me the honour, ma'am!" to take their seats, and I'm bound to say she played up like the actress she was, smiling prettily as she accepted and even referring demurely to "her husband" to discourage one young blade who was being over-attentive. He gave me an apologetic grin and offered me a chew from his tobacco case, which I declined; fortunately the press was too thick for him to start the relentless inquiry to which Yankees are wont to subject perfect strangers as to their origin, business, habits, and destination, and after a couple of stages Annette informed me that "this is our stop, Beauchamp", and we transferred to one of the omnibuses which ran on the cross-streets.

Here I had my encounter with the dolly-mops who used me as a conductor; one of them exclaimed flirtatiously that

156

I'd given her too much change, so I said gravely that in the presence of so much beauty I invariably became confused, and she should return any over-payment to my wife, who handled all my financial affairs. That sent them into blushing whispers and giggles, with sidelong glances at Annette, who gave me a sharp look as I took my seat beside her, but said nothing. The girls lost interest in me after that, and fell to discussing a party which one of them had attended, "on Park Avenoo, you never seen such style, it was a *yellow* en'ertainment – sure, everythin' yellow, linen, glass, plates, an' all, I swear even the lampshades were yellow, but then Mrs van Vogel, she's Harold's boss's wife, y'know, why, she's just drownin' in money – Harold reckons that party cost her fifteen thousan' dollars!"

Cries of "You don't say!" "Well, I swan!" and "Gosh a mercy!"

"Harold *hated* it, tho', 'cos he couldn't smoke or chew, he was fit to be tied –"

"Say, Harriet, did you have to wear yellow, too?"

"Why, sure, you think I'd go in green or blue to a *yellow* party? An' we danced, an' there was a magician, an' an English breakfast, an' I never saw more policemen outside a house in my life, to keep the crowds back from the carriages. 'Course, Harold and I, we walked . . ."

Annette gripped my wrist. "Come!" snaps she, and made for the door. We were at a stop, some passengers had just descended, and the driver was about to strap up the door again; he raised a great bellow of complaint at our tardiness, but Annette squeezed out with me on her heels. I looked back at the cursing driver in time to see him close the door on another latecomer, a cove in a brown suit and bowler who was demanding that he open it again, but jarvey wasn't having any, and the bus rolled off with the fellow staring after us through the glass.

"This way – do not hurry, and do not look round!" Annette's fingers were tight on my arm as she guided me along the crowded sidewalk, her heels clicking smartly. We were on one of the Avenues, lined with fashionable shops, and before you could say Jack Robinson she had whisked into

157

one of them, a splendid emporium with two large glass doors, one bearing the word "Madam" and t'other "Celeste" and with fat gilt Cupids capering on the lintel above. One moment we were in the crowded bustle of the street, the next in the hush of an opulent interior, the street noise cut off as the doors closed behind us.

For a moment I thought it must be an exclusive brothel, for we were in a great salon all plush and gilt and mirrors, with thick carpet and velvet divans and curtains looped back by silver cords, and Junoesque females of perfect complexion drifting about. The air was heavy with perfume – and then I realised that I was the only man in the place, and that the Junoes were shop attendants waiting on society women of all ages. My astonished gaze fell on a polished counter displaying alabaster pots of "Mammarial Balm", travelled to a glass cabinet containing – did my eyes deceive me? – corsets enhanced by globular objects labelled "Madam Celeste's Patent Bosom Balloons, with Special Respirator", dwelt in disbelief on a plaster cast of the Venus de Milo attired in "Eternal Youth Pumped Cups", and came to rest on a double doorway consisting of an enormous oil painting of splendidly endowed females in gauzy costumes teasing the god Pan who was bound to a tree and not thinking much of it; above the doorway was a gilt sign: ENAMELLING STUDIO.

I'm too young for this establishment, thinks I, but before I could speak we were accosted by a dark soulful beauty who'd have been the picture of elegance if she hadn't been chewing like a longshoreman – not baccy, but a curious grey pellet like candle-wax which she removed daintily as she approached and secreted in a lace handkerchief before inquiring languidly if she could render assistance to "maydam".

"I am Mrs Comber," says Annette. "I have an enamelling appointment with Madam Celeste."

"Sure," drawls the beauty. "Would maydam be requirin' facial treatment only, or face'n shoulders, or face'n shoulders'n buzzum?"

"What do you mean?"

"Face," repeated the young lady patiently, "or face'n

158

shoulders, or . . . ," she fluttered graceful fingers at Annette's upper works ". . . the whole shebang?"

"I shall discuss that with Madam Celeste!" snaps Annette. "Kindly send for her at once."

"O-kay," sighs the beauty, and spoke as one in a trance. "If-maydam-will-please-to-be-seated-an'-study-our-tariff-she - will - see - we - offer - the - $25 - weekly - application -the- $75-monthly-application-an'-our-special-$500-application-guaranteed-for-one-full-year-'tis-a-capital-economy-much-favoured-by-our-reg'lar-clienteel –"

"I said I shall discuss it with Madam Celeste!" Annette kept her voice down, but it was quivering with impatience. "She is expecting me – Mrs Comber! I must speak with her privately, do you hear?"

"Privately, huh?" The beauty raised a knowing brow, gave a sly glance at me, and leaned forward confidentially. "Is . . . ah . . . messoor to be present durin' th'application?"

"What? Yes, yes – now will you fetch Madam Celeste?"

"Well, sure! Right away. Perhaps maydam an' messoor would care to study our choice of shades while you wait." She presented us each with cards bearing coloured illustrations of scantily clad females with varying complexions. "Indian Ivory is 'specially becomin' for facial application," she murmured. "On t'other hand, Rose Blush for the buzzum is a prime fav'rite with gennelmen, we find . . ." She tapped my card delicately. "Perhaps messoor has a pref'rence?"

"Eh?" says I, startled. "Oh, I don't know . . . what flavours have you got?"

"Bring Madam Celeste this instant!" snarls Annette, and the beauty gave me a wondering look and swayed off, smirking, while my companion made seething noises and glanced quickly over her shoulder towards the door; her knuckles were white on the handle of her parasol.

"If you're looking for the cove in the brown suit, he's still on the bus," whispers I, and she started, eyes wide with alarm. "He was Kuklos, was he? Look here – what the devil's up, and what are we doing in this place? Are you *trying* to give 'em the slip?"

159

She stared at me wildly, lips trembling, but before she could speak, a tall beak-nosed female, with the beauty in tow, was bearing down on us, crying apologies for the delay, and would Mrs Comber kindly step this way? She bustled Annette off through the enamelling studio doors,[27] and as I followed the beauty stood aside to let me by; she was retrieving her chew from her handkerchief, popping it between rosebud lips, and I must have looked mystified for she smiled brightly and said: "Spruce gum. 'Tis real succulent – you wanna chew?"

There was a sudden commotion at the street door. A tall burly man, with another behind him, was pushing in, looking around the salon, thrusting past a girl attendant who tried to bar his way. I heard Annette give a little scream; she was staring back white-faced from the enamelling studio doors, and at that moment the burly cove spotted us and started forward at a run, barging a customer aside and overturning a table laden with pots – Mammarial Balm, probably, but I didn't wait to see; I was through the studio doors like a whippet, and Annette was crying: "Quickly, for your life! This way!" as she and Madam Celeste disappeared round a corner ahead of me.

I followed, full tilt, and found myself facing a short flight of stairs leading upwards, but no sign of fleeing females. There was a door ajar at the stair foot, though; I dodged into it, and now it was my turn to scream as I found myself confronting four women, naked to the waist and painted entirely white, seated in barber's chairs with girls in overalls lathering them in some kind of plaster from buckets; for an instant we stared in mutual amaze, and then someone shrieked "Peeping Tom!", they rose as one enamelled female and scurried for cover, and Flashy tactfully withdrew and legged it upstairs four at a time. I heard the studio doors crash open behind me, booted feet pounding, oaths and screams as my pursuers encountered the Plastered Poonts Society, a roar of "This way, Jem!", and panic lent me wings as I shot up another two flights – and here was Madam Celeste on a landing, grim as a Gorgon, but pointing towards an open doorway.

160

"Through there!" cries she. "They're waiting in the far attic! Run! I'll bar the door!"

Some chaps might have paused to offer gallant assistance, or inquire who "they" might be, but if you're me, and have no notion what the hell is happening, but only that you're a short stairway ahead of murderous pursuit, you do as you're bid and let chivalry take care of itself. I bounded through, heard the door slam and the lock grate behind me, and found myself in an immensely long studio gallery with a glass roof, full of lumber under dust-sheets. Annette was ten paces ahead of me, pausing in her flight to wave me on; I was beside her in a second, bellowing for enlightenment as she fumbled in her reticule and stamped her tiny foot in dismay.

"Where are they?" cries she. "McWatters! *A moi!*"

There was a distant shout from the far end, and then a splintering crash as the door was burst in behind us. I had a glimpse of Madam Celeste being hurled aside by the burly villain, and then he and his mate were hallooing at the sight of us, the leader drawing a revolver – and Annette had a Derringer in her fist and was letting fly, once, twice, the sharp reports no louder than exploding caps, and God knows where the shots went, for he stood unharmed, covering us and roaring:

"Give up, Comber! Hold there, or you're dead, by thunder!"

His muzzle swung to me as I heard Annette's hammer click on an empty chamber – and there was only one thing for it. Quick as light I gripped her by the waist and swung her bodily before me as a shield, his gun boomed like a cannon in the confined space, I felt the wind of the slug past my cheek, and as I flung myself back, clasping her to my bosom, an absolute salvo of revolver fire sounded from behind us, the burly man threw up his hands and pitched headlong, his mate fell back, clutching his arm, and now the gallery seemed full of men running past us, six-shooters at the ready, bawling to our stricken pursuers to surrender. One of the newcomers, a white-whiskered file in steel spectacles, dropped to his knee beside us and seized Annette by the arm.

161

"Are ye hit, wumman?" cries he, in a broad Scotch accent, and she plainly wasn't, for she struggled from my nerveless grasp, demanding furiously why he hadn't been on hand when needed, and then she became aware of the smoking Derringer in her fist – and went into a dead swoon. The Scotchman swore and demanded if I was wounded; I reassured him, and he promptly abandoned me and hurried off to supervise the apprehension and manacling of our two assailants, who were bleeding all over the shop and being deuced noisy about it – and so far as I could think at all, I was reflecting, well, if this is New York, they may keep it for me. Sixty seconds earlier I'd been quietly weighing the relative merits of Indian Ivory and Rose Blush as knocker cosmetics, and here I was lying winded in an attic reeking with gunsmoke, sober men in large boots were pocketing revolvers and shouting at each other, one was hauling me to my feet and enjoining me to take it easy, and Annette was lying comatose while Madam Celeste waved a bottle of salts under her nose.

One thing only penetrated my dazed mind: she'd led my Kuklos shadows into a carefully laid trap in this unlikely tit-painting emporium – but why? And who were these hard-faced gentry who had emerged to smite the Amalekites in the nick of time? There wasn't a uniform among 'em, but they were far too official to be anything but police or govern-ment; one, a brisk, bearded chap in a hard hat who seemed to be the leader, was barking orders – and, bigod, he was another haggis-fancier; no getting away from the brutes, wherever you go.

"Right, McWatters, awa' wi' them tae the Tombs," he was telling the white-whiskered cove. "Pickering'll have the third yin by now – they're tae be kept apart and solitary, mind that! Now, the black fellow, Simmons, will still be at the telegraph office, and Casey's seein' tae it that no message from Washington will reach him till tonight – your men are to observe him in the meantime, but let him alone, ye fol-low?" He gestured at Annette, who was stirring feebly, eye-lids fluttering, and snapped his fingers at the man beside me. "Johnson – carry her down. I'll attend tae Mr Comber mysel'

162

– ye're no hurt?" he added to me. "Capital, I'll be wi' ye
directly!" He clapped McWatters on the shoulder. "Away
ye go, then, Geordie! A smart morn's work, my boy, and
so I'll tell the commissioner!"

So they *were* police – and suddenly I was so weak with
relief that my legs buckled, and I sat down heavily on a pile
of lumber. I was safe at last, and could sit there panting
gratefully while the man Johnson swung Annette gently up
in his arms and bore her out to the stairs, with Madam
Celeste in attendance, my two would-be murderers were
carried out, dripping gore, McWatters ordered his men away
– and then the bearded man and I were alone in the silent
gallery, with the powder smoke still wraithing in the sun-
beams from the glass roof, and the blood wet on the planks.
He pulled a flask from his pocket and handed it to me.

"Tak' your time," says he, "and we'll have a wee crack,
you and I." He was a nondescript fellow, in his shabby suit,
but with an eye bright and unwinking as a bird's questing
over me and missing nothing, and while he wasn't above
middle height I guessed that anyone who ran into him would
come away bruised.

"You're police?" says I, when I'd swallowed and gasped.

"Officer McWatters and his men are from the New York
force," says he, with a sour glance at his flask. "For mysel'
. . . let us say that I serve the United States."

"Thank God for that!"

"Ye can thank Mistress Mandeville, too, while ye're about
it. She's in the same employ . . . that startles ye? Aye, weel,
tak' anither pull at the Glenlivet, if ye like. She never said
cheep to ye, did she? And right she was; the less ye knew,
the better."

"She's an American . . . agent? I'll be damned . . . but,
lord, she's married to that fat scoundrel –"

"Count Charles La Force, who calls himsel' Atropos.
Aye, she is that. It's a great convenience. I'll have the flask
back now," he added dryly. "Good malt's scarce on this side
o' the water."

I handed it back, marvelling. Annette Mandeville spying
for the government on her own husband's conspiracy? Just

163

as Black Joe, in Crixus's confidence, was a spy for the Kuklos
. . . dear God, was no one in this bloody country what they
seemed to be? My bewilderment must have been a sight to
see, for my companion was looking sardonic and benign
together, rot him.

"A tangled skein, eh?" says he. "But not tae my agency
– ye see, Mr Comber, we've been following your progress
ever since Moody picked ye up in that Washington alley,
and every word ye've spoken and heard since then has been
reported tae me. We know all about your conference wi'
Crixus, and how Atropos had ye lifted, and how they both
schemed tae send ye to John Brown (who is a friend o' mine,
I'm proud tae say), and about Harper's Ferry, the whole
clanjamfry." He had that complacent know-all air which is
so objectionable in Scotchmen, especially when it's justified.
"Oh, aye, the Kuklos and Underground Railroad pride
themsel's on their secret intelligence . . . weel, sir, they're
no' the only ones."

He paused, to see how I was taking it, but I was mum,
so he went on:

"Needless tae say, once we knew of your presence, we
referred to our official records, and identified ye as the
British Admiralty agent who was active – aye, uncommonly
active! – in this country ten years ago." He gave a knowing
smile. "Never fear, Mr Comber. We have no interest in that,
ye'll be glad to hear; our concern wi' you is here and now."
He regarded me with eyes like amiable gimlets. "So . . .
why are ye in the United States?"

Not a question, you'll allow, to which I could give a short
answer – but I didn't need to. Since they weren't concerned
with my murky American past, my course was clear.

"There's no secret about it. You're welcome to the whole
story – but not until I'm under the protection of the British
minister, either here or in Washington." I gave him my
Flashiest smile. "Very good?"

It wasn't, of course. "I'd remind ye, Mr Comber," growls
he, "that ye're in no position to make conditions – having
entered this country secretly, and associated wi' two clandestine and illegal bodies –"

164

"Associated my eye! They kidnapped me – as your eavesdroppers have certainly told you! And I'm not an Admiralty agent, and never was, and my name ain't Comber –"

"I dare say! Prescott, is it? Or Arnold, or Howard? Or have ye another one?"

"You're damned right I have! It's Flashman – and I'm a colonel in the British Army! And believe it or not as you choose, I was on my way home from India to report to Lord Palmerston when I was . . . why, what's the matter?"

For he had recoiled a step, staring down at me in the oddest way – not as though he didn't believe me, but as though he *did*, and couldn't credit his senses.

"Flashman, did ye say? Flashman – the Afghan soldier?"

Well, this was gratifying – I'd not supposed my fame had carried so far. But of course he was British-born, by his voice, and must have heard of me years ago.

"The very same!" cries I, laughing. "I know it must sound damned unlikely – and I've no papers, or anything of the sort, and I don't know a soul here to vouch for me, but a telegraph to our minister in Washington – Lord Lyons, I believe –"

"Stop you!" He leaned forward abruptly. "We may not have tae seek so far. Tell me – sharp, now! – what was your wife's maiden name?"

"What? My wife's . . . what d'ye mean –?"

"Answer!" snaps he. "Her maiden name!"

"Why . . . Morrison! But –"

"An only child, was she?" He rapped it out, face close to mine, and I found myself answering:

"Why . . . no – she had three sisters –"

"Their names?"

"What the devil! Now, see here –"

"Answer! Ye say ye're Flashman! Prove it! Her sister's names!"

"Why . . . Mary . . . and Agnes . . . yes, and Grizel –"

"Where were ye married?"

This was staggering. "In Paisley Abbey – but how in God's

165

name do you know?" I was on my feet now. "Who the devil are you? D'ye mean to say ye know me?"

"I do that," says he, and the sudden bark and blazing stare that had jolted the answers out of me were gone, and he was regarding me with grim astonishment. "I could wish I didn't. But we'll mak' siccar – what took ye to Paisley in the first place?"

"Why, I was training militia –"

"That ye were! What for?"

"To . . . to help to put down the Chartists – there was rioting among the mill people –"

"When they read the Riot Act at Morrison's mill – what like horse were ye ridin', and what colour were your breeks?"

"Eh? How the . . . hold on, it was a white mare, I think . . . and my pants would be cherry-pink . . . My God, you were there?" In my mind's eye were the dirty yelling faces, the shaken fists, the hail of clods and brickbats that had knocked the Provost's hat off, the Peninsular veteran sergeant bawling to the wavering militia to hold their line, the snarling obscenities as the mob gave back sullenly before the bayonets, your correspondent near to soiling his fine Cherrypicker "breeks" with fear . . . and this glowering inquisitor with his rasping voice and peeler's eyes remembered it, too. And here we were, twenty years after, facing each other in a New York attic . . . where his timely intervention had probably saved my life.

"Aye, I was there," says he. "Was I no'? Man, I was the ring-leader! No, ye won't mind me – it's my trade, no' bein' noticed. And there were no warrants out for Allan Pinkerton in those days, tae drive him from his native land!" His eyes glinted angrily, and then he shrugged. "At least ye didnae fire on us, like those fools at Monmouth Castle!"

His name meant nothing to me; he wasn't the most famous detective in the world, then.[28] But the great thing was that he knew and could vouch for me, and speed me to the British ministry; in my delight I gripped his hand and pumped it, congratulating him on his splendid memory; he said curtly

166

that it was easy enough to remember going hungry on a cooper's wages, and when I cried jovially that I meant his remembering my wife, and her family, he replied unsmiling that no one in Paisley was ever likely to forget Morrison and his brood. He wasn't sharing my high spirits, I could see; in fact he was looking damned sour, frowning and tugging his beard like a man who doesn't know what to do next.

"It's no' that simple!" snaps he, when I spoke of telegraphing Lyons. "Oh, aye, I ken fine who ye are, and a' about the Crimea and the Light Brigade – I still see the old country papers! Didn't I read lately about your great deeds in India and the Victoria Cross!" He ground his teeth. "And ye spoke of Palmerston – I suppose ye're far ben wi' the Queen, too!"

Being married to Elspeth, I understand Glaswegian, so I could agree that I had the honour of Her Majesty's close acquaintance – but why should that upset him?

"Because 'Comber' was a poor crater of no account – but Flashman, V.C., is anither kettle o' fish a'thegither!" cries he, becoming Scotcher by the minute. "And my orders are tae hold 'Comber' for my chiefs, and no' let him near the British ministry!"

"Well, I ain't Comber, so your orders don't count –"

"Do they no'? That's where you're wrong!" He rounded on me. "Comber or Flashman, the United States want ye, and that's the end o' it!" He added quietly: "So ye'll please to consider yoursel' in my custody."

"What? You told me a moment since they don't give a dam about ten years ago, and by God, I've done nothing since . . ." My astonishment gave way to fury at the insolence of it. "Custody be damned! Who the dooce d'ye think you are? Since I was railroaded into this bloody country I've been assaulted, kidnapped, threatened, blackmailed, and dam' near killed – and you've known all about it, damn your eyes, and never lifted a finger until now! Well, Mr Allan Pinkerton, I've had enough of it, and you'll take me to the British minister or consul or whoever-the-hell it is here and now, or I'll –"

"Or ye'll what?" says he, and as I gargled to a stop before

167

that ruthless stare, he pushed me unresisting back to my seat – I'm as persuadable as the next man, you know.

"There's no help for it," says he. "My chiefs may take a different view when they learn who ye are – but I doubt it. There's too much at stake, and it all turns on what has happened tae ye in these few days past." He regarded me sombrely. "The fact is, we need ye."

"Well, you damned well can't have me, d'ye hear? I never heard such moonshine – what the blazes can you need me for?"

"Perhaps tae preserve the union of these United States," says he steadily. "But that far ahead I cannae see. Now, I'll take ye to my chiefs – who are among the highest in the land, I may tell ye – and they'll inform ye further." He chewed his lip, considering. "This much I'll tell you now, since the scheme is mine: for reasons quite different from those of Crixus and Atropos, whose infernal plans must be frustrated at all costs . . . my superiors would have ye enlist with John Brown."

They say that Yankees are the smartest salesmen in the world, and I'll not deny it. I'd not have believed, when Pinkerton spoke those appalling words, that any advocate on God's earth could have talked me into joining Brown of my own free will – Crixus had tried by moral 'suasion (which he'd certainly have augmented with blackmail, if necessary), the bloated fiend Atropos by naked threats, and now this steely-eyed bastard was announcing it as the policy of the U.S. authorities – he didn't say why, and I didn't ask, because the whole thing was outrageous. I mean to say, while Crixus probably, and Atropos certainly, had the means to compel me into the service of a mad farmer bent on starting a war, the United States hadn't – *they* couldn't hold an eminent British soldier against his will, deny him the protection of his embassy, and force him into criminal activity, could they? And yet . . . I finished up at Harper's Ferry. Why? Because a certain shrewd New Yorker understood the true art of persuasion, which lies in convincing the gull, against all reason, that he can't afford *not* to buy – salesmanship, that's the ticket.

I'll come to that presently; my immediate response, when Pinkerton sprang his mine, was to question his sanity and decline at the top of my voice, pointing out that if he didn't drum up Lyons instanter, Palmerston would have a fit, the Queen would be *most displeased*, we might well burn Washington again, and he, Pinkerton, would find himself selling matches on the street corner. To which he replied bleakly that I'd better come along quietly.

I said I'd swim in blood first, so two minutes later I was being escorted down the backstairs by two of his stalwarts, standing on my dignity and doing what I was bid, in the sure knowledge that I was on a sound wicket, and the longer they held and hindered me, the more crow they'd have to eat in the long run. They put me in a Black Maria in the alley behind Madam Celeste's bouncer repair shop (which I guessed was what the secret service call a "cave", and Madam herself in government pay) and so to a brown building overlooking the river, nothing like a police station or jail, but staffed by sober, silent civilians who conducted me to a comfortable enough chamber which was something between a parlour and a cell (carpet on the floor, bars on the window), gave me a disgusting luncheon consisting of a cake of fried chopped beef smothered in onions and train oil, and left me to my own devices for a couple of hours.[29]

Believe it or not, by this time I was quite enjoying myself. I was *safe*, you see, gloriously safe, after all my trials nobly borne, and certain of eventual deliverance. Poor old Charity Spring's scheme for my undoing had gone agley altogether, now that it was known who I really was (thank God for Pinkerton and his memory!). There could be no question now of my answering old charges in the distant South (the diplomatic stink would have been tremendous), the Kuklos couldn't come near me, and poor old Crixus simply didn't count. By now, I reflected happily, Pinkerton would be dismaying his chiefs with the news that the lowly Comber, whom they'd hoped to bend to their nefarious will (though why they should want him to join Brown's ragged regiment was still beyond imagination) was none other than the admired Flashy, darling of the British Empire, and quite beyond their touch; I even had a jolly daydream in which I was summoned to the White House to receive President Buchanan's apology for the lunch.

Pinkerton's reappearance brought me back to earth. He had a couple of civilians in tow, and as soon as I clapped eyes on them I smelt "government". One was a swell ministry ruffian, a genteel lantern-jaw with a flowered weskit and brass knuckles in his fob, no doubt; the other was your complete politico, with the pudding face of a bad-tempered baby and no nonsense. Pinkerton called him "Senator", and

170

he plumped down in a chair with his fists on his knees, scowled, cut my protest off short, and pitched right in.

"Pinkerton tells us you claim to be an English army colonel named Flashman." He had the harsh, nasal rasp of New England. "Says he recognises you, from twenty years back. It won't do, sir! Not good enough. He may be mistaken. He also says you refuse to give any account of yourself until you've seen your minister. Well, sir," he stuck out his fat chin, "that won't do, either! *After* you've explained yourself, and your connection with the Englishman who masqueraded in this country ten years ago under various names – and satisfied me that you are who you claim to be . . . *then* we'll see about the minister." He sat back, folding his hands over his guts. "Now, sir . . . you have the floor."

I'd been all set to sail into him with demands that I be released forthwith, but the steady look of the shrewd eyes in that stubborn, podgy face, and the flat assurance of the man, told me it wouldn't answer: they'd keep me here until hell froze or I talked – as I was certainly going to have to, sooner or later, to Lord Lyons, who'd be bound to pass it on to them, so why not save him the trouble? And I love telling a tale about myself, and startling the whiffers . . . so I decided to shelve my protests, asked for something to wet my whistle, warned them it would be a long story, and fired away.

Well, you know it by now, from my being pressed aboard Spring's vessel, my masquerade as Comber, adventures on the Mississippi, slave-running, slave-stealing, Underground Railroad, Lincoln, and so on, to the point where I'd fled westward after Spring killed Omohundro. My peregrinations beyond the wide Missouri I dealt with only briefly, dismissed the Crimea and Mutiny in a modest sentence or two, and so came at last to my present misfortunes, all the way from the Cape to Madam Celeste's, omitting only the tender passages . . . and I'm bound to admit, it is one hell of a tale, which I'd not believe myself if I hadn't been there, every ghastly foot of the way.

They heard me out in silence, and I was croaking hoarse

171

when I finished. The Senator had barely moved, but his petulant glower had grown deeper as I talked; Pinkerton had listened intently, nodding and sniffing now and then and occasionally prowling about to view me from different vantages. The lantern-jawed sportsman had been out of my line of sight, but when I'd done he was the first to break the silence.

"It fits," was all he said, and the Senator grimaced and eased himself in his chair, shaking his jowls in perplexity.

"You may say so!" growls he. "By Gadfrey, it's the wildest thing I ever heard, I'll say that!"

"Too wild to make up."

"Oh, well, now! You mean you believe it?"

"I guess I know the papers on Comber by heart," says lantern-jaw, "and he hasn't contradicted 'em. Not once. What he's added to what we knew already . . . well, sir, as I said – it fits. Every time."

The Senator scowled harder than ever. "Where's Lincoln just now?"

"Not in New York. But, you know, he couldn't speak to this . . . this gentleman's being Colonel Flashman."

"No, dammit!" The Senator swung round in his chair. "See here, Pinkerton – are you sure of him?"

"Beyond any doubt whatever, sir. This is Colonel Flashman."

"You'd take an oath on that?"

"It's no' a matter of oath!" Pinkerton was impatient. "I *know*!"

The Senator drummed his fingers, brooding, and then threw up his hands. "What the Hades, whichever he is, he's all we have, in any event!" He rose and faced me. "Very well . . . Colonel Flashman! I make no apology for doubting you, sir, for if ever a man brought suspicion on himself . . ." He paused, breathing hard, and suddenly burst out: "Confound it, sir – do they know of this in England? About Comber, and impersonation, and slave-running, and . . . and heaven knows what?"

"No, sir," says I. "I was on leave, you see."

"My God!" He stared helplessly at the others, and then,

squaring his shoulders, he sat down before me again, full of stern resolve.

"I'll not waste words. We've had a deal too many already – but we had to be sure who you were. Now that we know," says he, without much confidence, I thought, "I am still bound to ask the question I'd have put to you if you were Comber." He took a deep breath. "Are you prepared to place yourself at the disposal of the United States for an extraordinary service?"

"You mean to help this mad bugger Brown to start a war?" I had my answer ready, you may be sure. "No! Dammit, if I told Pinkerton once, I –"

"No, sir!" cries he. "Quite the contrary! To make sure that Brown does not start any such thing!"

I could only gape – by God, he was serious. "What on earth d'you mean? Make sure he *doesn't* . . . how could I do that? In heaven's name, if you want him stopped – why, arrest him, or shoot him, or banish him to Timbuktu –"

"That can't be!" It was the lantern-jaw. "Crixus and Atropos both told you. For political reasons, we daren't touch him."

"But we can restrain him, given the means tae hand," says Pinkerton. "Yoursel', colonel."

"Me? Restrain him? Why, my good ass, I don't even know him . . . thank God!" Something Pinkerton himself had said flashed into my mind. "You said Brown was your friend! Well, *you* restrain him, then! I can't, even if I wanted to, which I dam' well don't –"

"Hear me, sir!" cries the Senator, raising a statesmanlike hand. "You misunderstand entirely. No one can reason with John Brown. He is a man possessed, sir, not to be moved by persuasion. But he could be prevented –" he leaned forward dramatically "– *by a lieutenant in whom he reposed absolute trust!* A deputy, a counsellor on whom he relied completely for the military skill and knowledge which he himself lacks, could so hinder and delay his terrible design that it would die stillborn. He is a simple man, when all is said. And the events of this past week have conspired to make *you* –" he stabbed a finger at me "– and only you, that lieutenant,

173

that deputy, who can frustrate him. Why, already Brown is looking to you, the man chosen for him by his trusted friend Crixus. And Crixus and the Kuklos, from far different motives, have set you on the path to the same dreadful end that they both seek. We are asking you to follow that path, so that their infernal machinations may be confounded!" So help me, it's what he said; Senatorial oratory, you see. He took his finger out of my weskit and flourished it aloft. "There must be no abolitionist raid on Southern soil! The consequences would be too hideous to envision – war, sir, civil war, might well follow! That is what hangs in the balance, do not you see? But it can be prevented, sir, without loss of life, without so much as a tremor to disturb the tranquillity of –"

"Not by me! Man alive, d'ye know what you're saying? I'm a British officer, sworn to my country's service – or have you forgotten that? I can't meddle in –"

"You have not heard me out – but you must!" He stood firm, jowls and all. "The peace of a nation is at stake! Very well, you may say that you are not an American, that this is no concern of yours or England's – but you would be wrong as can be! As a man of honour –"

"Honour? Honour, d'ye say?" A splendid horizon of humbug suddenly unfolded before me, and I sprang to my feet, John Bull incarnate. "What's honourable about bamboozling this barmy peasant, I'd like to know? Hoodwinking, by George, playing Judas! Of all the caddish tricks – pshaw! And you talk about honour – dammit, you Yankees can't even *spell* it!" I'm not sure I didn't stamp my foot. "Oh, the blazes with this! I've heard enough! I demand to see the British minister – and that's my last word to you!"

He was swelling for another burst of eloquence, and Pinkerton was flushed with anger, but the lantern-jaw motioned them aside, and they conferred in urgent whispers while I stared nobly out of the window – mind you, I kept an ear cocked, and caught a few murmurs: ". . . no, no, 'twould be fatal – Lyons would be bound to refuse . . .", ". . . must prevail on him somehow – why, he's heaven-sent! . . .", ". . . oh, he'll see him, right enough –

174

he's set on the thing, heart and soul . . .", ". . . aboard the ship, then, out of sight, couldn't be better . . .", which was all very mysterious. Not that I cared, now; for once, I was savouring the novelty of being able to face a group of selfish zealots who were intent on flinging me into the soup, and present a dead bat to all their urgings. I was quite cock-a-hoop, I can tell you. As they emerged from their confabulation I turned to look them blandly in the eye, and the Senator addressed me, magisterial but sour.

"Very well, sir . . . since you are not to be moved, we have no choice but to place you in the charge of your consular officials, who will doubtless arrange for you to see Lord Lyons in Washington." I could have cheered, but confined myself to a grave inclination. "In the meantime, there is an eminent personage in this city who desires to speak with you. I shall take the liberty of presenting you to him forthwith."

It gave me pause for a second; after all, my true identity had been known only for a few hours, and to a limited circle, I'd have thought; what "eminent personage" had got wind of me? Still, I've never minded being lion-hunted, so I waved a courteous assent, asking only who it might be.

"Notwithstanding your deep interest in American affairs," says the Senator with a sarcastic sniff, "I doubt if his name is known to you. Let us simply call him the next President of the United States."

* * *

For a moment I wondered if he meant Lincoln (and that was a prophetic flash, if you like) since he was the only American of any note I'd ever met, bar Kit Carson, and it wasn't likely to be *him*. Then I remembered they'd already said Lincoln wasn't on hand; besides, the Abraham of my acquaintance, while a handy man to have at your side when you've a bullet in the buttock and the slave-catchers are closing in, hadn't struck me as a likely candidate for high office; too good-natured a rascal altogether, and dressed like a scarecrow.

It didn't signify, anyway, whoever it was; in a few hours I'd be among my own folk, preparing to shake the dust of

America from my feet forever, and glad of it. So now it was back to the Black Maria again, with a sullen Pinkerton for company, and the other two in a carriage behind; we were borne swiftly along the waterfront to a quiet quay where a trim little sailing-cutter was waiting, manned by Navy tarpaulins, Pinkerton ushered us aboard, and in no time we were scudding out on to the crowded river, with my curiosity rising by the minute.

There was any amount of water-traffic about Manhattan Island in those days – steam-launches, sailing craft, paddle-steamers, three-deckers even, and rowing boats, and what with the salt air and sunshine and cheery bustle, it was quite capital; I sat on a thwart drinking it all in, not minding the spray or the heaving, content to admire the view and wonder which river we were on, for I didn't know East from Hudson and still don't. We seemed to be making for the far shore, cutting through the water at a great rate, with the steamboats shrilling their hooters and passengers crowding the rail to look down on us; as we neared the shore-line of wharves ahead, there seemed to be some jamboree in progress, and the sound of brass bands was mingling with the steam whistles and the cry of the sea-birds. A little flotilla, gay with bunting, was making for a big sea-going paddleboat, there were banners flying, and people waving and hurrahing, and a tug was squirting its hoses high into the air, making watery rainbows in the sunlight, very pretty to see.

Some great swell taking his leave, thinks I, for the folk on the smaller boats were singing "Auld Lang Syne" and giving three cheers, again and again, and as we stood off I could see a knot of people on the big paddle-boat, waving their hats. We seemed to be waiting, and then there was a great volley of orders, and our sail cracked like a gunshot, and we went swooping in under the paddle-boat's stern, and round to her lee, where we hooked on.

"Put this on," says Pinkerton, handing me a big wide-awake hat. "And turn up your collar. Right, come on!"

He led the way up the side-ladder, with two of his fellows fore and aft of me, and others ahead shouting to the people to stand clear; we bustled through them, and I was shown into a small cabin, and bidden to wait.

Which I did, for a good half-hour, wondering but not alarmed, until Pinkerton reappeared and conducted me without a word to a door where the Senator was waiting; he rapped on the panels, a voice cried to come in, and we were in a large stateroom in the presence of a wiry little gentleman in his shirt-sleeves, smoking a cigar as big as himself, and sighing with relief as he eased off his boots with his feet, and kicked them aside.

"Ah, Henry!" cries he. "So this is the gentleman! Colonel Flashman, I am happy to make your acquaintance; my name is William Seward.[30] Sit down, sir, sit down." He exchanged a nod with the Senator, who went, and Seward grinned apologetically. "Forgive the informality of my feet, won't you? They protest at this time of day."

I felt quite let down; hang it, I'd been expecting someone ten feet tall, and here this "eminent personage" was a slight, dapper bantam in his stocking-soles; brisk enough, with a head of greying reddish hair, bright blue eyes under bushy brows, and a curiously husky voice, but his only striking feature was a nose like a battleship – he looked not unlike a clever parrot, or an amiable Duke of Wellington, if you can imagine any such thing. Next President of the United States, though? I couldn't see that – and, as we know, he never was, and who's heard of him these days? Still, I can say I've been bullied by Bismarck, diddled by D'Israeli, cajoled by Lincoln, charmed (believe it or not) by Palmerston, and bored to submission by Gladstone – and not one of 'em was harder to resist than William Henry Seward. He was civil, pleasant, easy – and the most vicious arm-twister I ever struck – he didn't even hint, let alone threaten, just showed you the inevitable, ever so amiable. Which, of course, was why he'd asked to see poor unsuspecting Flashy, when all other persuaders had failed.

He soon had me settled with whisky and cigar, crying how pleased he was to meet such a distinguished soldier of whom he'd heard so much – that disarmed me to start with, I admit. Then he was full of India, of which he knew a surprising

177

deal, questioning me about the Mutiny, wondering how the natives would take to Crown rule instead of John Company's, asking how Christianity was doing in the country – not my style at all: if he'd asked how the Bombay *bints* compared to the Punjabi *bibis*, I could have set him right. Had I visited the Holy Land, as he hoped to do when he got to Europe? Waterloo, too, he must see Waterloo, and Stirling Castle, and look up his relatives in Wales – oh, he'd visited England before, as a lad, and sneaked in to have a look at old King William at Windsor, ha-ha!

All this as he pottered about, setting his books in order, placing the flower-vase just so, tapping the glass, smoking like a chimney, and at last settling himself in an armchair, remarking how grand it would be to see "the homeland" once more.

"For that's what it is, you know, to an American – why, I feel as excited as a child again, going on a visit to granpapa's house." Puff-puff on his cigar. "Or ought I to say grand-*mama's* house? No, 'twould be ungallant to your gracious queen to saddle her with that venerable title yet awhile." He chuckled, and grew thoughtful. "Ah, yes . . . old England. . . new America. Has it ever occurred to you, colonel, that our two nations are the only ones on earth who have a *natural* claim to each other's sympathy and affection? The truth is, you see, we're not two different *nations* at all, but merely two separate *states* . . . the European and American branches of the British race." Puff-puff. "I say that with all respect to the Dutch, German, and French citizens of this country, of course. We Americans are still part of the British family – as you are." He smiled at me through the smoke. "Don't you agree?"

I made some idle remark about the War of Independence, and he burst out laughing. "My dear sir, my grandmother's family fought for the *King* on that occasion! Grandpapa Seward chose the right side, though; yes, sir, he was a colonel in Washington's army, a true-blue American patriot . . . and a Welshman to the end of his days, I'm told." Puff-puff. "No, colonel, political differences don't run in the veins."

He lit himself a new cigar, and waved it philosophical-like. "What does polity matter, after all? Republic . . . monarchy . . . England was a republic once, long before there were United States." Puff-puff. "As for those differences of which so much is made – accent, social custom, and the like – why, they are no greater, surely, between Devon and Delaware than, shall we say, between Cornwall and Caithness." He regarded me with smiling blue eyes. "Now, you have travelled widely in this country, and while I dare say it has not felt *quite* like home . . . still, I would venture to wager that you have felt more *at home* here, than in France or Italy or Spain. Isn't that so?" It was the first sidelong mention of my American activities that he'd made, and I wondered what was coming next, but he went cheerfully on: "Why, I dare say if you were to stop a man on Fifth Avenue – or better still, on the Oregon Trail! – ten to one his name would prove to be Smith or Jones, if it were not Mac-Pherson or Clancy . . . ah, you smile – you've found it so?" In fact I'd been thinking of my Far Western acquaintances, and he was right: Wooton, Carson, Maxwell, Bridger, Goodwin . . .

"Or take your own profession," he went on. "If someone were to exchange your British Army List for our own, who could tell which was which, eh?" Puff-puff. "No, colonel, we may have our rivalries and jealousies, all those tiresome jests and jibes about the top-lofty Briton and the brash Yankee, but let me tell you, sir, the smart travellers who publish their 'impressions' and disparage the 'differences' between us, see only the surface of our countries. Beneath, we are one people still. One language, one law, one *thing*, as our Norse ancestors would say." He gave a little grunting laugh. "As a politician and statesman, I confess I have frequently opposed British policy, even sought to frustrate British interest, but do you know . . ." he was leaning back, that beak of a nose pointing at the ceiling ". . . if ever the day came – which God forbid! – when the being – aye, the very existence! – of that dear old land were in danger, then I, as an American, would give my life to keep it whole." He paused. "Nor do I doubt that an Englishman would do

179

as much for my country . . . ah, your pardon, colonel, I see your glass is almost out."

If you have illusions, Seward, prepare to shed them now, thinks I, as he plied me with more liquor. For it was plain as a pikestaff whither he was bound, and if he thought he could come round me with his blood-brotherhood fustian, he was well out of court. I thought of keeping mum, to see how he would come to cases at last, but my natural mischief decided me to play him up, so I observed innocently that the occasion wasn't likely to arise, surely?

"In the United States?" He pushed out a lip as he set down the decanter. "A young country, at the crossroads, facing the awful question whether it shall be a free nation or a slave nation . . . whether slavery shall wither gradually, peacefully, and with compromise, or be slain suddenly in the terrible arbitrament of war . . . that is a country in grave peril, colonel. Oh, it may be that given time and moderation, the withering process will take place . . . unless some evil chance, some terrible folly, should bring the irrepressible conflict suddenly to a head."

Like some loony invading Virginia, for example – why the devil couldn't he say it, instead of tiptoeing coyly about? We both knew what he wanted, that this was the last vain attempt to coax me into joining Brown – was he too scared to come straight out with it, or did he suppose that if he gassed long enough, about it and about, I'd be mesmerised into changing my mind? It was quite amusing, really, and I was content to smoke his excellent cigars and sip his indifferent liquor while he skirted delicately around the point. Hollo, was he getting there?

". . . if such a catastrophe should threaten," he was saying, pacing slowly to and fro and contemplating his cigar ash, "and it lay with an Englishman to avert it – if he alone had been given, by chance, the power to avert it, at no peril to himself . . . would he feel himself bound, I wonder, to answer the call of blood, to put aside the petty, man-made trammels of mere citizenship, and do the little service that would mean so much . . . to his kinsfolk?" He'd be quoting Magna Carta in a minute. "What would you think, colonel?"

I'll tickle you, you insinuating little bastard, thinks I. "He'd not hesitate a moment," I said. "In like a shot – I mean to say, he couldn't refuse, could he? Unless, that is, he was prevented by his duty – if he was a soldier, say. That would rule him out altogether."

He didn't blink, or start, or do anything but nod solemnly. "True . . . it depends, though, does it not, on one's interpretation of that elusive word, 'duty'?" He cocked his head. "To his Queen . . . his country? To his . . . race? To humanity, even?"

"Nothing about humanity in Queen's Regulations, I'm afraid." I gave him my regretful grin, and he sighed and shook his head.

"I've no doubt you're right. And yet . . ." he resumed his seat and went into another of his philosophic trances at the ceiling ". . . I wonder how the Queen – whose Regulations they are, after all – would view the question? What advice, do you suppose, would she give to one of her officers if he had the opportunity to render such a signal service to the young cousin-country for which she and her people feel such a warm affinity?" Puff-puff. "If he could save it from the horror of civil strife . . . perhaps even from destruction? Where would she – and Prince Albert – conceive that his duty lay? I wonder . . ."

He heaved another reflective sigh and sat up, stubbing out his cigar. "Well, we can't say, can we? You know her, of course, which I do not . . . but I look forward with the keenest anticipation to the honour of being presented to her, at Court, in a few weeks' time." The blue eyes regarding me steadily were as innocent as a babe's; he even smiled. "Oh, even a staunch republican feels his pulses quicken at the prospect of . . . conversing . . . with your gracious Queen, and her Consort. I shall also be meeting your Prime Minister, Lord Duhrby – oh, I must remember, Lord Darby, I should say! And Lord Palmerston, who takes a close interest in American affairs . . . you know him, I believe? I must tell him that you and I have spoken . . ."

I've received quite a few vicious thrusts in the low lines in life's fencing-match, but this was the real navel-slasher.

It was beautiful, effortless, and deadly – not once had he said directly what he was after, or even mentioned John Brown, or *me*, for that matter, but the moment he'd spoken of being presented and "conversing", the murderous black-mail was out, and a frightful scene was before me: the Queen, all goggle-eyed dismay, bloody Albert stuffed and shocked, Pam's false teeth fairly popping out in agitation while the Next President of the United States sighed and shook his head: ". . . no, ma'am, we couldn't move him . . . country on the brink . . . peril of civil war . . . our fate in his hands . . . said it was no business of his, deaf to all entreaties . . . God knows what'll happen now . . . his name, Your Majesty? Flashman . . . how's that, Prince? . . . oh, F-l-a-s-h-m-a-n . . ."

I'd be ruined. My promised knighthood would be dead as a tent-peg, and my career with it. I'd be shunned by St James's, cut in Society, discarded at Horse Guards – for it wouldn't be a damned bit of use pleading that America's troubles weren't my *indaba*,* or that as a serving officer I was positively forbidden to meddle in 'em. No, I'd be the villain who had spurned the appeal of our colonial cousins in their hour of dire need, cold-shouldering their President-elect, standing wilfully by the letter of the law when honour demanded that I should be guided by its spirit, and (horror of horrors!) *embarrassing Victoria and dear Albert*, and in front of the Yankees, too! I could see Elspeth's lovely fea-tures dissolving in anguish as she learned that she'd never be bidden to tea at Balmoral again . . .

"It's not public knowledge yet, I believe, but the Prince of Wales is to visit Washington next year." Seward was beaming at me like a happy ferret. "The first British royalty ever to stand on American soil – another precious link in the chain that is being forged anew . . ."

And a fat chance there would be of *that* once Flashy's churlish refusal had fouled the transatlantic cable . . . no, it was unthinkable. This smooth-spoken blackmailing little swine had got me by the essentials – and John Brown was

* Affair, concern (Swahili, council).

182

going to get his lieutenant. That was that, and no help for it . . . and my nature being what it is, I did a lightning reckoning of the possible advantages that might follow. If I did what they wanted, and could keep this idiot Brown from flying off the handle (and heaven knew I had enough experience of disaster to be able to scupper the half-baked military ambitions of a pack of backwoods yokels, surely?), if, in a word, I rendered this "signal service" to the Great Republic . . . by gum, but Mr President-in-waiting Seward would have a different tale to tell to little Vicky and her awful husband, wouldn't he just?

". . . volunteered like a shot, ma'am . . . knew it was irregular, but felt sure Your Majesty would wish it . . . sacred task . . . blood thicker than water . . . who would true valour see . . ." "We are *most gratified*, Mr Stew-hard . . . so *obliging* of the dear colonel, was it not, Albert? . . ." "Hoch-hoch, yess! Colonel Flash-mann to Rugby School wass going, ja!"

Gad, I might get a title out of it . . . but no, it would all have to be kept mighty quiet and unofficial . . . still, there would be whispers, and knowing royal smiles when I got home . . . and no doubt a confidence from Her Majesty to Elspeth over the tea-cups . . . and stern questions, followed by a rebuke for form's sake and a wink and clap on the shoulder, from old Pam.

It ran through my mind in seconds, while Seward busied himself clipping another cigar, and when I stood up those bright eyes searched my face for several seconds before he glanced at the clock and said, why, how time had run past, and he expected they would be casting off soon.

"I thank you for coming to see me," says he. "We have had a most valuable talk, I'm sure." He paused. "I expect to be in England for two months at least; perhaps I may have the pleasure of your company again – or have you decided to prolong your stay in America?"

Well, two could play at that game. "By George, Mr Seward, I'd been intending to take the first ship, but you've roused my curiosity, don't ye know? I rather think I'll stay on a while – see something of the country, what?" And just

183

for devilment I added: "Any special sights of interest you think I ought to see? Some people have urged me to visit Virginia, but I've a notion it might be rather warm at this time of year, eh?"

It took him aback, but only for a second. "That is my understanding, too," says he. "Good-bye, colonel, and God speed."

They tell me he was a man quite devoid of principles, whatever they are, but I'd put it another way and say he was a consummate politician. Clever, no question; he knew exactly how to turn me round in short order, which argues some kind of capacity, I suppose, and there's no denying he saved the United States a few years later when he wriggled out of the Trent Affair. He was no friend of ours, by the way, for all the humbug he'd given me, and I can think of only one good reason for wishing he'd become President: Lincoln wouldn't have got shot.[31]

The fellow with the lantern-jaw was called Messervy, and as soon as I stepped out of Seward's state-room and announced my change of heart, he took charge, cutting off the Senator's cries of satisfaction and reminding Pinkerton, who surprised me by clasping my hand, that there was a day's work to do in two hours, so good-bye, Senator, and let's go. Then it was ashore in haste to the Black Maria, which was beginning to feel like home, with Pinkerton firing instructions at me as we rattled along, while Messervy sat aloof, stroking his moustache.

"Mandeville an' yoursel' will return to the Astor House tonight as though nothin' had happened, and wait for Black Joe Simmons. He sent a telegraph tae Crixus this mornin', sayin' ye'd been found and were willin' tae enlist wi' Brown; Crixus's reply has been at the New York telegraph office this three hours past, but Joe hasnae seen it yet – and won't, until you're safe back at the hotel. We've seen it, though – sure enough, Crixus is over the moon, haverin' on about the returned prodigal, an' biddin' Joe take ye tae Concord wi'out delay, where ye'll be presented tae Brown at the house of Frank Sanborn. So ye'll be off tomorrow, likely – an' neither Crixus nor Atropos will have an inkling o' what's happened today." He permitted himself a sour grin. "The three Kuklos men who followed you this mornin' are safe under lock an' key, and will not see the light o' day until this whole Brown business is by and done wi' – "

"And when'll that be?" In the rush of events I'd given no thought to it. Messervy spoke without looking round.

"Weeks. All summer, maybe."

"What? But, my God – "

185

"Wheesht, and listen!" snaps Pinkerton. "Once you an' Joe have left for Concord, Mandeville will return tae Washington tae inform Atropos that all's well. It'll be days afore he begins to wonder what has happened tae his three bravos – an' we'll have one or two ploys tae keep him guessin', never fear. The main thing is, he'll be satisfied that you're safe wi' Brown, workin' your mischief – he thinks. Crixus will be under the same misconception." He glanced at Messervy. "That's my part done, I think."

Messervy nodded, and we sat in silence until our paddy-wagon drew up behind the big brown building. It was growing dusk, and as we alighted Pinkerton turned to me:

"I'll bid ye good-bye, colonel – but I'll be keepin' an eye on ye until ye leave for Concord." He hesitated, and held out his hand. "Glad ye're wi' us. Take what care ye can of auld John Brown. He's worth it." He wrung my hand hard. "An' my respects tae your good lady when ye see her. She'll no' mind me, but I carried her portmantle once, tae the Glasgow coach."

Then he was gone, and Messervy swung his cane idly as he looked after him. "There goes a worshipper of John Brown . . . h'm. Follow me, colonel."

In my time I've been sent into the deep field by some sharp politicals – Broadfoot, Parkes, Burnes, and Gordon, to say nothing of old Pam himself – but Messervy, the long-chinned Yankee Corinthian with his laconic style, was as keen as any and straight to the point, coaching me briskly even before we'd sat down, turning up his desk-lamps as he spoke in that lordly half-English accent that they learn in the best Eastern colleges.

"Whatever you've heard, Brown's not mad. He's a simple man with a burning purpose. His admirers like to think of him as a latter-day Oliver Cromwell. He is no such thing. He's not a fool, but he lacks all capacity to organise and direct. His strength –" here he sat down, shooting his cuffs as he clasped his fingers before him on the desk "– which you would do well to remember, is a remarkable gift of inspiring absolute devotion, even in men far above him in education and ability – Pinkerton, for example, and the

186

Eastern liberals who furnish him with money and arms. But it is among his personal followers – his gang – that this loyalty is most marked."

He drew a sheet from a stack of papers at his elbow, and pushed it across.

"Those are their names – you can study them later. They are almost all young men, staunch abolitionists for the most part, and dangerous beyond their years. They include several of Brown's sons; the others are adventurers, jacks-of-all-trades, a crank or two, some free blacks and escaped slaves; a number of them have been soldiers, one was a militia colonel, and most of 'em have fought in the Kansas troubles. Only one or two are what you would call educated." He considered. "They're tough, eager, and love nothing better than shooting up slave-owners, as they did a couple of months ago when they rescued a few niggers from Missouri and chased the militia. But for the most part they camp in the woods, do a little drill or target practice, a few gymnastics, and sweetheart the local girls. Brown will be looking to you to lick 'em into shape and plan his great stroke in Virginia."

"How," says I, "d'you suggest I stop him?"

He indicated the paper in my hand. "There aren't above a dozen names on that paper – that's his weakness, lack of numbers. Many have come and gone; those names you may regard as permanent. He's never been good at recruiting – when he was camped out in Iowa, rallying support, he managed to muster the grand total of nine. It may well be that his want of men, his inability to plan anything sensible, and his habitual indecision, will be his ruin – with a little judicious hindrance from you, skilfully contrived. One thing you must *not* do, and that is try to undermine his men's loyalty: it would be fatal. They love him; no other word for it."

"What weapons has he got?"

"That we know of, two hundred revolvers and two wagon-loads of Sharps rifles. And you heard about the thousand pikes."

"Yes, to arm the niggers when he invades Virginia. It all

187

sounds damned unlikely," says I, "but you take him seriously."

"Like nothing since the Revolution," says he quietly. "He's a man on fire, you see. And if the fit suddenly takes him, he may go storming into Virginia at half-cock, with his handful of gunfighters . . . and it just might start a war."

"And you say he isn't mad! Has he got any money?"

"He's spent much of the past two years, when he hasn't been raiding or writing half-baked constitutions, trying to drum up funds here in the East. Said he needed $30,000, and may have got close to a third of it, but in arms and equipment rather than hard cash." He shrugged. "In other ways, though, I suspect he's found it rewarding work. Unless I'm in error, his vaunted simplicity masks a substantial vanity: he seems to like nothing better than being received in abolitionist Society, playing the Old Testament prophet, preaching the wrath of God – he's a poor speaker, by the way – being adored by maiden ladies from Boston who know *Uncle Tom* by heart, and admired by social superiors who treat him as another Moses. That's one of them . . ."

He took a card from his stack of papers and pushed it across to me: a daguerre print of an earnest weed with flowing locks and a wispy goatee, like a poetic usher.

". . . Frank Sanborn, one of the so-called 'Secret Six', the committee of influential abolitionists who are Brown's leading supporters.[32] You may meet some of 'em when you're presented to him at Sanborn's place in Concord. They hang on Brown's lips, applaud his speeches, pass the hat, shudder deliciously when they think of him sabring Border Ruffians, go into prayerful ecstasies whenever he runs a nigger across the British border – and are in mortal terror that he'll do something truly desperate." He stroked his silky moustache. "Like attacking Harper's Ferry."

"They know he means to?"

"He told 'em so, a year ago – and they almost had apoplexy. You see, they thought the cash and arms they'd been giving him were to be used in the Free Soil campaign in Kansas; when he sprang it on 'em that he was planning to

188

invade Virginia, arm the blacks, set up a free state in the hills, hold slave-owners hostage, and dare the U.S. Government to come on . . . you may guess what effect *that* had on our pious idealists. They besought him to give up the idea, he thundered Scripture and told them slavery is *war* and must be fought, they pleaded, he stood fast . . . and they gave in, like the old women they are. However, he decided to postpone his invasion when your compatriot, Hugh Forbes, his right-hand man, fell out with him over money, and betrayed the whole plot to various Republican senators . . . among them Mr Seward, whose eloquence so charmed you, I'm sure, this afternoon." He raised an eyebrow at me, studied his nails in the lamplight, and went on:

"Seward's a true-blue abolitionist, but he's not a fool or a firebrand – and he has Presidential ambitions. He warned the 'Six' they were playing with fire, and must leave off. That set them shivering . . . but instead of cutting off Brown without a penny, they renewed their tearful pleas to him not to do anything rash, but if he did, please they'd rather not hear about it beforehand."

Messervy sat back in his chair, and arched his fingers together. "And there, colonel, you have the liberal abolitionists of the North, in a nutshell: half hoping Brown will go wild, while they pull the blankets over their heads. Seward has more sense. He wants Brown stopped, which is why he spoke to you today, once we'd convinced him that you were the likeliest means of doing it. At the same time," he added drily, "Senator Seward finds this a convenient moment to make the Grand Tour of Europe, which is a capital place for the Republicans' favoured candidate to be while Brown is rampaging around breathing fire."

"Hold on," says I. "You say 'we' convinced Seward – by which you mean the secret service, and don't tell me different! Aren't you meant to be working for President Buchanan, who I believe is a *Democrat*? Not that I understand American politics –"

"I work for the United States," says he coolly, "whose next President will *not* be a Democrat. My task is the peace and security of this country, by any means, despite the efforts of its politicians."

"Spoken like a man!" I was beginning to take to this chap. "But if it's peace and security you're after, and you can't stop Brown by arresting him, or openly interfering with him, for political reasons . . . tell me, as one government ruffian to another, why don't you just shoot him quietly in the back of the head some dark night?"

"And have all hell break loose – North accusing South, the government itself (which is headed by a 'doughface',* remember) suspected of political assassination, people like Pinkerton outraged and demanding inquiry, the wild men calling for bloody retribution? God knows where it would end." He gave a faint smile. "In any event, I don't work for Lord Palmerston – my political masters didn't learn their ethics at Eton College."

"Oh, you're out there! I've a notion Pam was at Harrow . . . what are you grinning at?"

"A kindred spirit, I suspect." He rose, shed his coat, and loosed his cravat. "Please, be comfortable. Will you join me?" He produced a bottle – Tokay no less, and poured. "Now we can get down to cases," says he, settling himself. "By the by, how much of the yarn you spun us this afternoon was true – and how much did you leave out?"

"Every word of it – and about half as much again."

He nodded. "I guess that qualifies you. Well, here's confusion to John Brown . . . one way or another." He sipped, and sighed, a frown on the long clever face. "Now then – I've told you about him, and his gang, and his supporters; at least you know what to expect. If you can keep him quiet, by fouling his traces for him and helping him *not* to make up his mind – which, with your experience, you very well may – then that's fine. But . . ." he set down his glass and gave his moustache another thoughtful tease, ". . . just suppose you fail . . . and Brown does cut loose and raises cain in Virginia for a day or two – for he'll last no longer than that, you may be certain –"

* A Northerner sympathetic to the South.

190

"You're sure of that? Even if he were to take Harper's Ferry? Damn it all," I demanded, "why don't you put troops into the place?"

He made a disdainful noise. "The *official* answer to that is that we can't be sure he's still set on the Ferry – Forbes's blowing the gaff may have scared him off it, he may be thinking of some other target altogether, and we can't guard the whole Mason-Dixon line. Myself, I'd say a squad of Marines at the Ferry wouldn't hurt – but try telling that to Washington mandarins who are too lazy or too dense or too smug to take Brown seriously." He shrugged. "But ne'er mind that. Consider, I repeat, what happens if Brown *does* invade Virginia, tries to stir up the niggers, and shoots a few Southern citizens? What then?" Without waiting for a reply, he went on, tapping off the points on his slim fingers.

"I'll tell you. The South will explode with fury and accuse the Republicans of being behind it. The Republicans, including the two Senatorial gentlemen you met today, will deny it. The North will bust with ill-concealed delight because Simon Legree has been kicked in the balls. The Southern States will raise the cry of 'Disunion or death!' . . . and then?"

"Then the bloody war will break out, according to you and that fat Senator!" says I, impatiently, and he nodded slowly and sipped the last inch from his glass.

"Yes, it very well may. I'd lay odds on it. But then again . . . there's a chance – oh, a very slim one – that wiser counsels might prevail, provided . . ." he raised a finger at me ". . . provided Brown had been killed or lynched along the way. You see, if his raid had been a fiasco, and he had met his just deserts – well, it might take a little heat out of the South's temper. And Northern rejoicing might be a little muted – oh, they'd go into mourning for their hero, and Mr Emerson and Mr Longfellow would write odes to the saint departed, and the Secret Six (having disclaimed Brown faster than you can blow smoke) would beat their breasts in public and give thanks in private that dead men can tell no tales . . . but many sober Yankees would be appalled and angry at the raid, and condemn Brown even while they

191

mourned him. Many would say he'd been proved wrong, and that violence is not the way." He shrugged again. "Who knows, in that mood, common sense might assert itself. The country might shrink back from war . . . provided John Brown were dead."

"I don't see that," says I. "What odds would it make whether he was dead or alive?"

"Considerable, I think. Here, let's finish the bottle." He tipped the remains into my glass. "You see, if Brown survived the raid, and was taken, he'd stand trial – probably for treason. I'm no lawyer, but when a man writes constitutions for black rebel states, and fires on the American flag, I guess I could make it stick. But whatever the charge, one thing is sure: they'll hang him."

"Well, good luck to 'em!"

He shook his head. "No, sir. Bad luck – the worst. Right now, I doubt if one American in five has even heard of John Brown – but let him make his crazy raid, and swing for it, and the whole world will hear of him." He smiled with no mirth at all. "And what will the world say? That America, the land of liberty, has hanged an honest, upright, God-fearing Christian whose only crime was that he wanted to make men free. A man who could stand for the archetype that made this country – why, he could pose for Uncle Sam this minute. And we'll have put him to death – the damnedest martyr since Joan of Arc! And there will be such an outcry, colonel, such a blaze of hatred throughout the North, such a fury against slavery and its practitioners . . . and there is your *certain* war ready-made, awaiting the first shot."

He hadn't raised his voice, but just for a moment the cool *nil admirari* air had slipped a trifle. He smiled almost in apology.

"There are many 'ifs' along the way, to be sure. I'm envisaging the worst. Brown may not ride into Virginia this summer; his own incompetence and indecision, encouraged by you, may delay him long enough – if he doesn't move before fall, I doubt if he ever will. He can't hold his followers together forever, living on hope deferred, and fretting to get home for the harvest."

192

He rose from his chair and went to a cupboard by the wall; his voice came to me out of the shadow beyond the pool of light cast by the desk-lamps.

"If you can keep him bamboozled for a couple of months, why, all's well. But if you can't, and if he does light out for Dixie with his guns on, and comes to grief . . . then for the sake of this country, and for tens of thousands of American lives, he must not survive for trial and martyrdom at the hands of the U.S. Government. No . . . John Brown must die somewhere along the road . . . oh, bully for us! – I knew there was another bottle!"

*   *   *

You will wonder, no doubt, why I'd remained cool and complacent during the conversation I've just described. I'll tell you. Seward, in making it plain that if I didn't toe the line he'd blacken my fair name to our sovereign lady and her ministers, had used a phrase which had quite altered my view of things. "At no peril to himself", meaning me. You see, what had been proposed by Crixus and Atropos was that I should be one of a whooping gang of cutthroats invading the South to storm arsenals and stir up bloody insurrection – the sort of thing I bar altogether, as you know. The proposal made by the Senator and Pinkerton, hinted at by Seward, and illuminated by Messervy, was quite the opposite: I was to restrain, hinder, and prevent anything of the kind, and while the prospect of passing several weeks in the company of a pack of hayseeds, showing 'em how to shoulder arms and dress by the right, and discussing strategy with their loose screw of a commander, was not a specially attractive one – well, I'd known a lot worse. It would be hard lying and rotten grub, no doubt, but I'd be earning the gratitude of the next President, for what that was worth, and adding to my credit at home when the story reached the right ears – as I'd make dam' sure it did. Above all, it would be safe – "at no peril to himself". Not that I'd trust a politician's word for the weather, you understand, but Messervy's information had borne him out . . . until he'd made it plain that if the worst befell, I'd be expected to put Mr John Brown quietly to rest.

Fat chance. A scoundrel I may be, but I ain't an assassin, and you will comb my memoirs in vain for mention of Flashy as First Murderer. Oh, I've put away more than I can count, in the line of duty, from stark necessity, and once or twice for spite – de Gautet springs to mind, and the pandy I shot at Meerut – but they deserved it. Anyway, I don't kill chaps I don't know.

But it wouldn't have been tactful – indeed, it would have been downright dangerous – to say this to Messervy, so I received his disgusting proposal with the stern, shrewd look of a Palmerston roughneck who took back-shooting in his stride. I may even have growled softly. (And, d'ye know, I accepted it all the more calmly because I didn't believe for a moment that there was any chance of the matter arising: Messervy and Seward and the others might regard Brown as a dangerous bogyman, but from all I'd heard he was a mere bushwhacker whose talk of invasion and rebellion was so much wind. Oh, I'd do my best to humbug him, but my guess was he'd stay quiet enough without my help. As for starting a war, it was too far-fetched altogether. Well, I was wrong, but I can't reproach myself, even now; it *was* damned far-fetched.)

Anyway, I nodded grimly as he brought his bottle to the desk.

"You take the point?" says he, looking keen.

"Quite so," says I. "Which reminds me, the sooner I have a gun in my pocket the better. Oh, and a decent knife – and a map of Harper's Ferry, wherever it is."

"Colonel," says he, "it's a pleasure doing business with you. Excuse me." He went out humming and I punished the Hungarian until he returned with a neat little Tranter six-shooter, a stiletto in a metal sheath, and a map which he insisted I study on the spot and leave behind.

"There's the Ferry – just inside Virginia, and only fifty miles from Washington." He came to my elbow. "The odds are you'll never see the place, but if Brown does go for it, and you have to do . . . what needs to be done, then your best course afterwards will be to make tracks for Washington and your ministry. The militia will round up the rest of

194

Brown's gang, and that'll be that. You'll have no difficulty with Lord Lyons, by the way; he'll be given notice of your coming, with an assurance from a high quarter that you have rendered a signal service to the United States in a domestic matter, and we are most grateful. We shan't tell him, officially, what the service was, and I'm sure he won't ask, officially. But I'm sure he'll speed your journey home."

He folded the map. "If, as is most likely, John Brown spends a quiet summer, and nothing untoward takes place . . . well, when he starts to disband his followers, you can desert him at your leisure. Again, Lord Lyons will be advised to expect you, with our expressions of gratitude, et cetera. Very good?"

"I don't know Lyons," says I, "but I'll bet he's nobody's fool."

"He isn't," says Messervy. "Which is why, whatever course you have to take, all will be well." He took another turn at his moustache. "It's in a dam' good cause, colonel. You know it, we know it, and Lord Lyons will know it."

I thought it wouldn't hurt to play my part a little. "You Yankees have a blasted cheek, you know. Ah, well . . . I say, though, when I'm out in the bush, with Brown, how do I –"

"Send messages to me? You don't – too dangerous. Brown and his people might get wise to you; so might the Kuklos. Just because we've got three of their men in the Tombs doesn't mean there won't be others watching you – they'll certainly have people keeping track of Brown himself. If either side suspected you were secret service . . ." He gave me a knowing look. "Quite so. Anyway, the fewer of our people who know we've got an agent with Brown – and a Briton, at that – the better. We'll be keeping an eye on things, though, and if need arises, I'll get word to you."

He took a small purse from a drawer and tossed it over. "That's $50 to keep in your money belt . . . if Joe should wonder how you came by it, Mrs Mandeville gave it you." He frowned. "That's another thing. Brown will welcome you with open arms –"

"Just suppose he doesn't – what then?"

"He will, no question; you're a gift from God. The point is, he'll also welcome Joe; he's all for black recruits. Well, I don't have to remind you that Joe is a Kuklos man, and a good one."

"He's a damned rum bird," says I. "Oh, I know he and Atropos have been chums in the nursery and all that tommyrot – but hang it, he ought to be all *for* Brown and black freedom, surely? I don't fathom him at all."

"Some of these darkies who belong to the old Southern families are mighty loyal. They think of themselves as kin to their owners – and many of 'em are, though I doubt if Joe is. But all we know of him confirms that he's staunch to Atropos." He shrugged. "Maybe he reckons he's better off slave than free, living high in the tents of wickedness rather than being a doorkeeper in the house of a God who'd expect him to earn his own living." And having a free run at massa's white lady from time to time, thinks I. "Anyway, beware of him," says Messervy. "He'll be watching you like a hungry lynx." He glanced at his timepiece. "It's half after eight, and Mrs Comber will be waiting. She hasn't been told your real name, by the way. No need for her to know that."

The building seemed to be deserted, and we went down the echoing stone stairs to a room on the ground floor where Annette was waiting, with a nondescript civilian who faded from view at a nod from Messervy. She seemed none the worse for her swooning fit of the morning, and didn't give me a glance, let alone a word, as Messervy conducted us to a closed carriage in the back court, where he handed her in, bowed gallantly over her hand, and gave me his imperturbable nod. "Joe won't be given Crixus's message for another hour. By that time you'll be having a quiet supper after a day's sauntering and shopping on Broadway." He indicated a couple of band-boxes on the floor of the cab. "Your purchases, Mrs Comber. One of our lady operators chose them, with regard to your taste, I hope." The Yankee secret service evidently left nothing to chance. "Good luck, Comber . . . and," he added quietly, "if need be, good hunting." Cool as a trout, rot him, doffing his tile and knuckling his lipwhisker as we drove away.

Annette sat like a frozen doll for several minutes, and then to my astonishment broke out in a low hard voice: "You saved my life this morning. When that creature fired on us. My . . . my courage failed me. But for you, I would have been killed. I . . . thank you."

I didn't twig for a second, and then it dawned that she must have quite misunderstood why I'd seized hold of her when the lead started flying. Oh, well, all to the good. I waved an airy hand.

"My dear, 'twas nothing! I wasn't going to be a widower so soon, was I?" I slipped an arm about her and kissed her soundly. "Why, it's I should thank you, for steering me clear of those Kuklos villains. But, I say, you took me in altogether, you clever little puss – never a word that you were working for Brother Jonathan* all the time! And you a Southern Creole lady, too! How's that come about, eh?"

"If you knew what it was to be married to that devil, you would not need to ask!" But she said it automatically, her mind still fixed on that fateful moment at Madam Celeste's, sitting stiff as a board while I munched at her cheek. "I never shot at anyone before! I . . . I was in terror, not think-ing what I was about or –"

"Nonsense, girl!" says I, squeezing her udders. "Why, you blazed away like a drunk dragoon – winged him, I shouldn't wonder! Gave him a nasty start, leastways. But here we are, safe and sound, so . . . take that, you little peach!"

But it was like kissing a dead flounder. "I might have killed him!" she whispered, staring ahead. "It would have been murder – mortal sin! Thou shalt not kill! Oh, let me be, damn you!" She beat at my hands, trying to struggle free. "Have you no feeling? Can you think of nothing but . . . but your filthy lust – oh, when I might have had *that* upon my soul?"

I was so shocked I absolutely let them go. "Upon your *what*? Heavens, woman, what the dooce are you talking about?"

* Synonymous with "Uncle Sam".

197

"I tried to kill him!" She turned on me, eyes blazing. "I had murder in my heart, can't you understand?"

"And he didn't, I suppose? My stars, he might have done for both of us! What the devil's the matter?" I stared at the pale little face, so tight and drawn. "Ain't you well? It's all past and done with, we never took a scratch! Ah, but you're still shaken – it's the shock, to be sure! Come here, you goose, and I'll put it right!"

"I might have killed him! I wanted to kill him!" She closed her eyes, and her voice was almost too faint to hear: "I would have been damned!"

Now, I've seen folk take all kinds of fits after a shooting scrape, or a battle, or a near shave, and the shock can be hours in coming on, but this was a new one altogether. Her eyes when she opened them were full of frightened tears, staring as though she were in a trance. "Damned," she whispered. "Damned eternally!"

They don't usually say that sort of thing until they're at death's door, and she was as fit as a flea. I wondered how to bring her out of it – she was too frail to slap, petting her hadn't answered, and I couldn't very well ravish her in a carriage on Broadway. So I tried common sense.

"Well, you didn't kill him, and you ain't going to be damned, so there's no harm done, d'ye see? I know – we'll try putting your head between your knees –"

"In my heart I murdered him!" cries she.

"Well, it didn't do him a penn'orth of harm! Heaven's alive, you never came near hitting the fellow –"

"The will was the deed! I would have killed him – I, who never thought to take life!"

This was too much, so I took a stern line. "Oh, gammon and greens! What about those black wenches of mine at Greystones? You had them *half*-killed – 'twasn't your fault they didn't kick the bucket, and you never thought twice about damnation! Anyway, who says there's a Hell? Twaddle, if you ask me!"

It seemed to reach her, and she stared at me as though I were mad. "This was a *human being*!" cries she. "If I had killed him . . ." She closed her eyes again, and began to

198

tremble, turning away from me. I waited for the waterworks, but they didn't come, and I saw there was nothing for it but the religious tack.

"Now, see here, Annette, you didn't kill him, and if it's the *wish* to kill that's troubling you, well, you're a Papist, ain't you? So if you tool along to the nearest priest, he'll set your conscience right in no time." I thought of my little leprechaun in Baltimore, and dear drunken old Fennessy of the Eighth Hussars. "If he's got half as much sense as the padres I know, he'll tell you that self-defence ain't murder in the first place. And if you want to thank me," I added, "you'll do it best by recollecting that in a little while we'll be seeing Black Joe, and we can't have him wondering why you're looking like Marley's ghost!" I patted her hand. "So draw breath, there's a girl, and forget about damnation until you see old Father McGoogle in the morning and get your extreme unction or whatever it is. The worst is past, and if you play up now – well, you'll be doing your fat swine of a husband a dam' bad turn, what?"

Possibly because of my healing discourse, possibly because we'd pulled up at the Astor House, she suddenly snapped her head erect, white as a sheet but *compos mentis*, and began to behave normally, but mute. As I followed her up to our suite, and presently down again to the dining-room, I found myself wondering if she was quite sane – and to this day I ain't sure. I'd known her, by turns, a vicious tyrant, a voracious bedmate, a superb actress, a forlorn child, a gun-toting secret agent, and now, of all things, a penitent in terror of hell-fire because she might have shot a chap but hadn't. Well, as they say in the North Country, there's nowt so funny as folk – but I'd never have credited Annette Mandeville with a conscience. Nursery education, no doubt; God, these governesses have a lot to answer for.

She said not a word at supper – which she attacked with a fine appetite, I may say – but when we returned to our room and found Joe waiting, she was quite her old imperious self, and talked according. He was in a fine excitement, thrusting Crixus's telegraph message into her hand; it was in code, and at length, but its purport was precisely what everyone, from Atropos to Pinkerton, had predicted: Joe was commended for his zeal in running me down, and helping me to see the light – not that Crixus had ever doubted I would come round in the end, even after I'd lit out, for he knew my devotion to the cause, and that reflection would guide me to a just and righteous conclusion, God bless me a thousand times. (I'd been doubtful, as you know, whether Crixus would swallow the tale that I'd been persuaded to change my mind, but Atropos had been proved right: he believed it because he *wanted* to, and it fulfilled his fondest hopes.) Finally, Joe was to lose no time in conducting me to Concord and our Good and Trusty Champion, that the Lord's Will might be accomplished and His Banners go forward in Freedom's Cause. Amen.

"We got no time to lose," says Joe, all eagerness. "They's a train leavin' fo' Boston fust thing, an' –"

"You'll take a later train, and reach Boston after dark," snaps Annette. "You'll stay the night there, and keep under cover, going on to Concord next day – and again, you'll arrive after dark." Joe would have protested, but she shut him up. "Do you think Sanborn wants you to be seen entering his house in broad daylight? Don't you know he's watched by government operators, you black dolt?"

"They don' know us –"

"They'll know you even less if they never see you! Oh, why did they entrust this business to a clod like you! Get out, and fetch me a train schedule – not now, in the morning!"

He could gladly have broken her in two, but all he did was mutter that he hadn't seen Hermes's men about the hotel, and did she know where they were? She told him curtly to mind his own business and let them mind theirs, and he left with a venomous glare – but no suspicion, I'll swear, that there was anything amiss; her tongue-lashing performance had been altogether in her best style.

So then it was bedtime, and since I didn't expect much carnal amusement chez Brown, I was determined to make the most of it. After Annette's earlier vapourings, I half expected reluctance, but she was all for it, and if her conscience was still troubling her, she kept it on a tight rein, addressing heaven only in secular terms when amorous frenzy got the better of her. That interested me, for her usual form was to gallop in grim silence; more astonishing still, she was ready to talk afterwards, briefly enough at first, but little by little at greater length, until we were conversing almost civilly. Whether it was gratitude for having her life saved (as she thought, heaven help her), or I was in prime fettle, or she'd made her peace with God, or was just getting used to me, I can't tell, but out came Annette Mandeville, Her Life and Times, and diverting stuff it was.

I'd known already that she came of impoverished bayou aristocracy who had literally sold her, aged fifteen, to the disgusting redneck Mandeville, with whom she'd been living at Greystones when I hove in sight in '48. After my departure, Mandeville had drunk himself to death, leaving a heap of debt and Greystones mortgaged black and blue. As a personable enough young widow, she'd had offers a-plenty, but Mandeville had sickened her of marriage, if not of men, and after a succession of lovers she had decided that a career as a mistress was no great shakes, and had determined to try her luck on the stage – she'd been born with a talent for mimicry, and being vicious, immoral, and vain, she had taken to the theatre like a pirate to plunder. And it had taken to her; in a few years she was playing the principal houses in the States and Canada, making and spending money, mostly on men.

Then, during an engagement in Chicago, her company had been the victims of a daring robbery, and who should be called in when the police had failed but Allan Pinkerton, then making his mark as a private detective. He had been impressed by the help she'd given in pointing the way to the thieves, and identifying them, and had remarked that if ever she tired of acting, she might do worse than police work; it had been lightly said, and she'd forgotten it the more readily because a new and brilliant prospect had opened before her soon afterwards.

It was in a comedy at Orleans that she had caught the lustful gooseberry eye of Charles La Force, and while the very sight of him had set her shuddering, the size of his fortune, and the ruthless determination with which he'd pursued her, had made her think twice about repulsing him: he'd plied her with priceless gifts, haunted the theatre, and finally killed her beau of the moment in one of those ghastly knife-and-pistol duels which the Louisiana gentry favoured in those days, stalking each other through the bayous by night. After which his offer of marriage, with a royal cash settlement, had finally conquered her far-from-maiden heart, and she had trotted up the aisle with him, to her abiding regret.

For she had soon discovered that beneath his revolting exterior there lurked a monster whose depraved tastes would have had Caligula throwing up the window and hollering for the peelers; enforced bouts with Joe and other menials, while the husband of her bosom cheered them on, had been the least of it, and to make matters worse she had been drawn into the dark affairs of the Kuklos. But where any other wife would have lit out with whatever she could carry, Annette's one thought had been to vent her hatred on him, and she had been hesitating between poison and a knife in bed when Pinkerton had again emerged, discreetly, upon the scene. By now he was undertaking occasional work for Washington, and had a finger on every pulse in America; he had kept her in mind, and when she had married Atropos he had seen her as an invaluable agent within the Kuklos, if she could be persuaded. She had leapt at the chance, and had been betraying Atropos happily ever since, until the present emergency had caused Pinkerton to employ her in more active work. And so, here we were.

It was plain from her account that loathing of Atropos was the ruling passion of her life, and knowing her cold and selfish nature, I found that odd. Granted she was compounded of equal parts of malice and cruelty, I'd still have thought she'd have preferred to decamp with his money and pursue her theatrical and amorous careers in France or England, rather than devote her existence to doing him despite. It didn't seem to weigh with her, either, that in betraying him she was probably helping to destroy the way of life in which she'd been raised – the South, slavery, plantation

202

society, and all that gracious magnolia stuff; no, she was wreaking vengeance on Atropos, and that was enough for her. Well, I'm a ready hater myself, God knows, and take the keenest pleasure in doing the dirty on deserving cases, but I'd never make grudgery my life's work; I reckon you have to like, or love, something worth while, even if it's just trollops and beer, or, if you're lucky, cash and credit and fame . . . and Elspeth. It occurred to me, as I put Mandeville through her final mounting drill, that she wasn't fit to fill my dear one's corset, and I felt a great longing for those blue eyes and corn-gold hair and silky white skin and so forth, and for that brilliant simpleton smile of welcome and the witless prattle which would follow. At least I had that to look forward to; Annette Mandeville had nothing but her revenge. Oh, aye, and her eccentric conscience.

She was in a vile mood in the morning, snapping at me and roasting Joe, and for the last hour before he and I left to catch the train north, she sat in stony silence, staring out of the window. At the last, when Joe was putting our valises out in the passage, she closed the door quickly on him, and turned her pale elfin face to me; she was biting her lip, and then the tears came, and suddenly she was clinging round my neck, the tiny body shivering against me.

"Have a care!" she sobbed. "Oh, have a care!" Then she kissed me fiercely and ran into the bedroom, slamming the door behind her.

I have only three memories of the trip from New York to Concord: Joe's ugly face, under his plug hat, glowering at me from the opposite seat of a railroad car; the creaking bed-springs of the cheap rooming-house in which we stayed in Boston; and an advertisement poster of a young lady crying: "Oh, Ma, I gave my back the awfullest strain, dancing with Billy!" and fond mater replying: "Mustang Liniment, judiciously applied, will ensure certain relief, my dear!" The rest is blank, from the closing of Annette's door to the opening of Sanborn's, presumably because I was too used up to notice anything. They hadn't been idle days, exactly, and Crixus, Atropos, and Mandeville had seen to it that my nights weren't tranquil either, so it was small wonder I was tuckered out – I had sense enough, though, before we reached Boston, to tie the Tranter to my knee beneath the trouser, in case the watchful Joe decided to search me as I slept. A wise move, as it turned out, for when I woke in the rooming-house my stiletto had disappeared, but the Tranter was still in place.

It was Joe's hammering at Sanborn's knocker that brought me back to life, I think, reminding me that it was a case of on stage again, with a part to play, and no room for missed cues or bungled lines, with that black nemesis at my elbow. I remember thinking he must have telegraphed ahead, for it was Sanborn himself who opened the door and greeted us by name on the spot.

"Mr Comber, sir, welcome – welcome to Concord!" cries he, and I saw that the daguerreotype had not lied, for he was as intense and poetic as could be, with his fluffy whiskers and anxious eyes. "And this is Simmons, to be sure!"

Abolitionist he might be, he still knew a mister from the riff-raff. He ushered us into a hall stuffed with furniture and smelling of birdseed, and sped ahead to close the door of a room from which came the rumbling conversation of worthies with beards and gold watch-chains across their weskits – you can always tell the quality of unseen company by the noise they make, and I was willing to bet that at least half of the "Secret Six" were on hand.

Sanborn led us into another room across the hall, moving with quick, agitated steps. "Captain Brown is with us!" says he, in a confidential whisper. "Do you know, we are celebrating his birthday today? Yes, indeed, he is now in his sixtieth year, but gentlemen, his frame and spirit are those of a vigorous youth! Yes, indeed, although," he frowned, "he has lately been somewhat indisposed, a result, no doubt, of the privations endured on his recent glorious raid of liberation 'into Africa', as he calls it. Yes, indeed," he rubbed his hands, a nervous habit which I realised was always accompanied by his favourite phrase. "Yes, indeed, he is only now recovering from a malarial ague. But he is in good heart, I assure you! Yes, indeed!"

I asked if they'd tried quinine powder, and he beamed. "There spoke the man of action – the practical man! Oh, Mr Comber, you cannot know how it rejoices me to see you!" And he absolutely wrung my hand again. "We have heard so much from our good friend in Washington – you know who I mean, I'm sure! And of the worthy Simmons . . . er, Joe, isn't it? Yes, indeed! Yes, Joe!" He was one of your tiptoe babblers, I could see, smiling, fidgeting, and suddenly remembering to offer us refreshment, with more prattle about the fatigue of travelling, and the crowded condition of railroad cars. If this is a sample of our abolitionist conspirators, I can see American slavery flourishing for a century or two yet, thinks I; Joe, I noticed, was regarding him like a cannibal inspecting an under-nourished missionary. He gave us a toddy apiece, promised there would be supper anon, muttered about seeing if Captain Brown was still occupied, and was away like a shot, leaving the door ajar. We sipped our toddies in silence, inspecting the

antimacassars and potted plants, and presently I was aware
of a child's voice in the hall asking:

"Please, sir, may I have your signature?"

I glanced out, and there was a lad of about eight holding
up a paper and pencil to a man who had just come out of the
other room, with Sanborn at his shoulder; I had a glimpse of
a fine shock of hair and a full beard, both grizzled, and then
he was speaking to the lad.

"What's this, my boy?" says he. "Not an order to pay the
bearer, I hope?"

"Oh, no, sir," squeaks the kid. "I want to pay *you*, if
you'll take my pocket money as a trade for your name. It's
but six bits," he added, digging out his coin, "an' it's all I
have, but Pa says every cent is blessed that goes to the good
cause."

A practised toad, this one, with a soapy smile and his hair
slicked down.

"The widow's mite," says the bearded man to Sanborn,
and laid his hand on the infant's head. "Bless you, my boy."
He pocketed the six bits and scribbled his name.

"Young Stearns has started quite a fashion!"[33] cries Sanborn. "Yes, indeed! There, now," says he, as the child took
the paper, fawning, "you have a name that will live down
the ages, and for only six bits, too!"

I'd already guessed who the owner of the beard was, and
as he stepped into the room I was sure of it. From all I'd
heard in the past three days, I'd formed a picture of John
Brown as a towering figure with flowing white locks, glaring
like a fakir and brandishing an Excelsior banner in one fist
and a smoking Colt in t'other; what I saw was an elderly
man, spare and bony in an old black suit, like a rather seedy
farmer come to town for market. He had a long aquiline
nose, large ears, and deep-set eyes under heavy brows. An
imposing enough old file, you'd have said, but nothing out
of the ordinary – until you met the gaze of those eyes, clear
bright grey and steady as a rock. Gunfighter's eyes, was my
first thought, but they weren't cold; you knew they could
blaze or twinkle (and I was to see 'em do both), but what I
remember most was their level certainty. No one was ever

206

going to make this man drop his gaze, or talk him out of anything.[34]

He came forward with a measured step, holding himself erect, and took my hand in both of his; his grip was rough and strong, and he spoke slowly, in a deep, rather harsh voice.

"Mr Beauchamp Comber," says he – pronounced it Bo-champ. He gave Joe the same hand-clasp. "Mr Joseph Simmons. Welcome, gentlemen." I realised that he wasn't as tall as he looked, a little over middle height. "My good friend Crixus tells me that you are an Englishman, Mr Comber, and that by joining us you risk being in disfavour with your own government. Have no fear of that, sir. I pledge my word not to reveal your presence among us, by speech or writing, and my friends –" he glanced at Sanborn "– pledge themselves also. That goes for you, too, Mr Simmons." He nodded at Joe. "Indeed, the names of Comber and Simmons are forgotten from this moment.[35] Crixus refers to you, sir, as Joshua; that's good enough for me. Joshua . . . and Joe, it shall be henceforth." He seemed pleased with that, and it must have been his patriarchal manner that called to my mind the verse about God seeing every thing that He had made, and behold, it was very good. "Joshua and Joe," he repeated solemnly, and took hold of our hands again, one in each of his, and looked from one to the other of us, nodding like an approving bishop – and I knew upon instinct that here was one who, in his own modest way, was as big a humbug as I am myself. Only on later acquaintance did I come to realise that – again like me – he *knew* it.

Don't mistake me: I'm not saying he was a hypocrite, or a sham, because he wasn't. God help him, he was a sincere, worthy, autocratic, good-natured, terrible, dangerous old zealot, hard as nails, iron-willed, brave beyond belief, and possessed of all the muscular Christian virtues which I can't stand. He was a humbug only in the public performance he put on for his supporters back East, playing the part of John Brown, the worthy simple son of the soil with greatness in him, the homespun hero whose serenity was all the more

207

impressive because it was so at odds with the berserk savagery of his reputation on the wild frontier. It was a performance which he thoroughly enjoyed (for he was quite as vain as Messervy suspected) and for which he was naturally equipped, with his deliberate manner, calm searching eyes, strong handshake, and quiet tolerant humour – oh, it was worth paying money to see him lay it on (and they paid, too). That I found wholly admirable, for I couldn't have done it better myself, and I'm an expert at being lion-hunted. In his own backwoods way, he had great style, and, odd though it may seem in one whose historical image is that of the Ironside fanatic, he also had considerable charm. Anyway, for all his virtues, he was a bloody hard man to dislike.

I didn't sum all this up in a minute, of course, but I got the first whiff of it, and having both style and charm myself, and being a born crawler to boot, I responded to his welcome as befitted a bluff, honest, British crusader.

"Thank'ee, Captain Brown," says I, guessing that my use of the title would flatter him sick. "Proud to be with you at last, and honoured to be accepted. They tell me, sir, that it's your birthday. Warmest congratulations, and many of 'em. Now, I hope you won't take it amiss," I continued heartily, "if I offer a small gift to mark the occasion. I'd not dream of doing it if I didn't know that you won't keep it for yourself, but will apply it to the great cause we're all privileged to serve." I hauled out Messervy's fifty dollars and handed them over. "It's all I have on me, I'm afraid, but . . . well, I can't do less than that manly little chap I saw out in the hall just now, can I, what? So . . . many happy returns, skipper!"

Shocking bad form, you'll agree, but this was America, and I'd weighed my man: he snapped it up like a trout taking a fly, looking moved and furrowed, and told me with another hand-clasp that I had bought shares in freedom, and he'd not forget it. I didn't grudge the fifty bucks; that was my sturdy, open-handed character established, and I'd be living at his charges for several weeks, anyway.

Then, in case anyone thought he was neglecting the nigger, he turned to Joe, and told him that his presence there, as a coloured man eager to fight for the liberty of his oppressed brethren, was a birthday present in itself, and one whose value couldn't be reckoned in money. He asked Joe where he came from, and when Joe said he was an escaped slave who had worked for Crixus on the Railroad, and that his family were still on a Southern plantation, Brown gripped him again, and put a hand on his shoulder, swearing that he wouldn't rest until that unhappy family had been plucked from the teeth of the wicked, whose jaws would be broken. He got quite warm about it, and for the first time I saw that gleam beneath his brows, and heard the rasp in his voice, which somebody described as being like a volcano disguised by an ordinary chimney flue.

Joe didn't know what to make of it, but looked confused, and when Brown let go his hand I saw him wince as he worked his fingers. Sanborn, who had been listening in rapture, took Joe out, and Brown settled his coat and begged me to be seated, so that we might talk. He pulled up a chair close in front of me, put his big gnarled hands on his knees, looked me over carefully, and then said: "Well, now, friend Joshua, tell me who you are, and what you know, and what you have done."

For one horrid instant I thought he'd found out about me – that I was Flashy, and the Yankee secret service, and all the rest – and then I saw it was just his manner of speech, with that grave look that stern pedagogues give to naughty children to convince 'em that lying's useless. What he was after was "Comber's" story, and to inspect me.

So I described my "life" in the Royal Navy, and how I'd spied on the slavers, and run into Crixus, and brought George Randolph north – he lit up at that, calling it the "bravest stroke" he'd ever heard of, so I embellished Comber's record with my own service with that maniac Brooke against the Borneo pirates. He asked if they held slaves in Borneo, and I said, droves of them, and that was why I'd been there in the first place, to turn the poor buggers loose and proclaim liberty throughout the land, or words to that effect.

He drank it in with stern approval, saying I surely had

209

fine experience of irregular warfare; he mentioned Toussaint and Spartacus, and asked if I'd studied Wellington's campaign in the Peninsula, and the ways of the Spanish guerrillas "who were much in my mind when I surveyed the field of Waterloo, pondering how the great captain would have gone about the task of liberating our black brethren held in cruel bondage by evil laws." Knowing the late Duke Nosey, I could have said that he'd certainly not have put pikes in their fists and told 'em to take to the hills, but thought it better to express toady interest in his visit to Waterloo.

He said it had been during a tour he'd made to study European fortifications, so that he could acquire the knowledge necessary if he was to build strongholds in the Alleghenies for revolting darkies; I nodded solemn agreement, reflecting that Messervy had been quite wrong – this fellow wasn't only mad, he was raving, in a quiet sort of way. Alas, he hadn't been able to pursue his military studies at any length, since his time had been taken up with selling wool in London, where he'd won a bronze medal for his wares – and here he pulled it from his pocket, chuckling that it had been *some* set-down for the smart Londoners, a poor rustic Yankee winning their prize. He became quite jolly in his recollection, and went into a long story of how some English wool-merchants had tried to take a rise out of him by asking him to feel a sample and give an opinion.

"Say, though, they were out to hoax me – why, it wasn't wool at all! No, sir, it was *hair from a poodle-hound*, with which they hoped to take me in! So I teased it, and pulled it, mighty solemn, and told them if they had machinery for working up *dog-hair*, it might do very well! *That* took 'em aback, I can tell you! Yes, sir, they had to admit they couldn't *pull the wool* over my eyes! They were cheery men, though, and meant it all in fun, so we had no hard feelings. *Poodle* hair, can you imagine that?"[36]

It's how I see him still, laughing deep in his throat, slapping his thigh, the great beard shaking and his eyes dancing with merriment – old Ossawatomie, who sabred five unarmed men to death in cold blood, and blew hell out of Harper's Ferry.

210

He got back to business after that, saying soberly that I mustn't think he would harbour any feeling against me, as an Englishman, because of the shabby way he'd been served by my fellow-countryman, Forbes. "I blame myself for trusting him," says he, "rather than him for his betrayal. His heart was not in the work, as yours is, and he was distracted by the plight of his wife and little ones in France, wanting bread and a place to lay their heads. If he betrayed me . . . well, we must not judge him too hardly."

Dreadnought Comber wasn't having that. I cried out in disgust that I couldn't credit chaps like Forbes; it was too bad and didn't bear thinking about, the bounder was a disgrace to the Queen's coat and ought to be drummed out. Brown leaned forward and laid a forbearing hand on my sleeve.

"You're timber from a different tree, Joshua. You are what Crixus said you would be, and your story – aye, and what I see before me – speak for you." Believe that, old lad, and we'll get on famously. "But now, tell me . . ." He tightened his grip on my arm. "Crixus has told you what I purpose, and the disappointments and delays I have suffered, and my resolve that this time there shall be no turning back from the gates of Gaza." The grim bearded face was so close now that I could see my reflection in his eyes, which is a sight nearer to John Brown than you'd want to get. "Can you show me how best this great thing can be done?"

It was more than I'd expected, and my heart jumped. "You mean, how to take Harper's Ferry?"

His lids came down like hoods. "That's a name best left unspoken just now." Tell that to the rest of North America, thinks I. "In this house, at least. But . . . yes, that is the goal."

"When?"

"July the Fourth. What better day to found the new United States?"

"Oh, absolutely!" Less than two months away. "I'll have to study it. I must know what force, what arms you have, what you mean to do afterwards. You see, captain," says I

211

soberly, "given preparation, any fool can take a place –
holding it's another story. And using it."

"That is all determined!" cries he, glowing.

"Then I've a question."

"Ask away, my boy!"

"Very good," says I, all business. "Am I to carry out your
orders without question? Or will you look to me for advice?"

He threw his head back, frowning, and I knew I must
follow up at once. "I'm a man of war, Captain Brown. It's
my trade – but I practise it against only one enemy – slavery.
Did you know," says I, "that William Wilberforce was my
uncle? Oh, it don't matter; I only tell you so that you may
understand the . . . the force within me." I was the one
leaning forward now, going red in the face with holy zeal,
and just a touch of the fanatical stare. "I am with you
because you are Liberty's champion in America. It all rests
on you whether the oppressed black people of this land are
brought forth into the light, or languish in bondage. You
must not fail!" I gave him my grim, do-or-die smile. "I'll
not have you fail! When we strike, it must be a sure, shattering blow – not a pin-prick, not a hasty foray which miscar-
ries for want of planning, but the breach in the dyke through
which the flood of freedom will surge to sweep away the
foul growth of slavery forever!"

It's listening to folk like Crixus that does it, you know;
they supply the words, and I'm the boy who can carry the
tune. I was out to convince Brown that I was as crazy as he
was, and that if I found fault with his plans, it wouldn't be
from half-heartedness or lack of abolitionist frenzy. I was
the seasoned professional, you understand, but with the fire
in my belly. Having let him feel the heat, I collected myself
again, with an apologetic shrug.

"I beg your pardon, sir. I'm presumptuous – and to you,
of all people! But, you see . . . I must be *sure* of victory –
oh, not for myself, but for those thousands of poor black
souls crying out for deliverance!"

Ringing stuff, and he took it like a man, mangling my
fingers again. "We shall win that victory!" cries he. "And
we'll win it with your good counsel, be sure of that! Why,

212

Moses hearkened to *his* Joshua, didn't he?" He chuckled and clapped me on the shoulder, saying I'd turned his hope to certainty. And now it was time for me to meet "our friends – good men one and all, bound to the cause . . . but not men of action," says he with a sigh. "Still, we depend upon them, and it will put heart into them to see you take the oath."

This, it turned out, was a rigmarole which Joe and I had to repeat before the company in the other room, a motley bourgeois crew of about a dozen, male and female. Among them were three of the "Secret Six" – Sanborn; a truly enormous beard which went by the name of Stearns; and Dr Howe, a keen-looking citizen who had in tow the only passable female present, a spanking little red-head with a sharp eye.[37] They were affability itself, but I guessed they were wary of me and Joe, possibly because we looked fit for spoils and stratagems; they beamed approval when Brown bade us raise our hands and swear to fight slavery with all our might, and keep secret all our transactions, but while the women clapped and murmured "Amen!", I wondered if one or two of the men were altogether easy about witnessing the men of blood getting their baptism, so to speak.

I played strong and silent, and Joe, of course, didn't say a word, but it didn't matter, for the purpose of the gathering was to pledge money, which apparently they'd already done, and thereafter to admire Brown, to the accompaniment of coffee and sandwiches. Sanborn took the lead by reading a press report by one Artemus Ward of a meeting which Brown had addressed in Cleveland some weeks earlier, after his triumphant return from the Missouri raid in which he'd snatched eleven niggers and various horses.

"Listen to this, will you?" cries Sanborn, adjusting his glasses. "'A man of pluck is Brown. You may bet on that. (Cries of "Hear, hear!" and "I should say so!") He must be rising sixty, and yet we believe he could lick a yard full of wild cats without taking off his coat. (Laughter) Turn him into a ring with nine Border Ruffians, four bears, six Injuns and a brace of bull pups, and we opine that the eagles of victory would perch on his banner!'"

213

Loud laughter and applause, and Sanborn cries: "He writes further that Captain Brown is 'refreshingly cool', and could make his jolly fortune by letting himself out as an ice-cream freezer!" Delighted cries from the ladies, while Brown stood gravely regarding the carpet. "What d'you say to that, captain?"

"He has one thing right," says Brown drily. "I'm rising sixty."

At this they all cried, no, no, Ward had hit it dead on, and clustered round him, filling his cup and offering sugar cookies. He took it all pretty cool, with that stern modesty that's worth any amount of brag. One shrill old sow in a lace cap said she had been told that at that same meeting Captain Brown had said that the only way to treat Border Ruffians was as though they were fence-stakes, and whatever had he meant by that? Brown looked down at her, stroking his beard, and asked, what did she suppose people did to fence-stakes?

"Why, they strike them, I suppose!" says the beldam.

"Just so, ma'am," says Brown. "You drive 'em into the ground, so that they become permanent settlers."

She cried "Oh, my!" and fanned herself, while the other women tittered, Sanborn said "Yes, indeed!", and the men chortled that it was the only way. One said he had much admired Captain Brown's reply to a heckler who had accused him of stealing horses and looting the property of pro-slavery people; Brown had answered that since the pro-slavers had started the war in Kansas, it was only right that they should defray its expenses.

"But even better," cries a small snirp with a cow-lick and glasses, "was your hit at the expense of the wiseacre who questioned your right to sell horses taken from Missouri!" He beamed at Brown. "Do tell the company, captain, what you retorted!" He nudged his female companion. "Listen, Sally, 'twas the neatest thing!"

"Why," says J.B., very serious, "I believe I told him they were not Missouri horses, but abolitionist horses, since I had converted them!"

This had them in fits, while I watched with approval, for

214

I knew this game of old, having played it myself a hundred times in the days when I was being hero-worshipped. It's almost a ritual: they flatter you by praising your words or actions, and you play it easy and modest, but just giving a hint every now and then, in a humorous way, what a desperate fellow you are, because that's what they love above all. We had a prime example of it that night when a young fellow came in with the news that one Governor Stewart was expected in Boston soon, at which there was a sensation, for this Stewart was the man who'd put a price of $3000 on Brown's head in Missouri. The women squealed, and the men looked anxious; Brown, standing by the fireplace, asked the young chap, whose name was Anderson, if it was Stewart's intention to set the U.S. marshal after him, and were the reward posters up in Boston?

"You bet, cap'n," says Anderson, who was a jaunty bantam. "But I reckon you may stand under 'em, and the marshal won't trouble you."

"Indeed, he'd better not!" cries Howe. "Massachusetts won't stand for any Missouri warrants being served here!"

"I think Massachusetts need feel no alarm," says Brown. "There were posters in Cleveland, and I stood under *those*, and made myself conspicuous outside the marshal's office down the street. But he chose to ignore my presence, I can't think why." He was resting an arm on the mantelpiece, and now he turned so that his coat fell open, to reveal an enormous Colt strapped to his hip. "I guess it was just civility on his part, in case I'd feel embarrassed."

There was a great whoop of laughter, and arch glances at the pistol, while they nudged each other and agreed that it would have been *real* embarrassing – for the marshal, ha-ha! The old biddy in the lace cap said it was monstrous that *Southern* reward posters should be permitted in a Northern city, and what would happen if the marshal and his "government hounds" should try to arrest Captain Brown – "why, they might have the gall to try it in one of our very own houses!"

"If they do, ma'am," says Brown, "we shall bar the door against them. I should hate to spoil your carpet."[38]

That seemed to set them in the mood for a few blood-thirsty hymns, with Sanborn thrashing the harmonium; one was about a small, weak band going forth to conquer, strong in their captain's strength,[39] which was sung with approving smiles in our direction, and a scrawny female had the impudence to press my hand in encouragement; if she'd been worth it I'd have arranged a prayer meeting with her later, for there's nothing like religious fervour to put 'em in trim, you know. I gave her my brave, wistful smile instead, and devoted my energies to "Who Would True Valour See?", which concluded the soiree, with Brown in great voice, eyes shining and beard at the charge, as he roared defiance at the hobgoblins and foul fiends.

When the guests had gone, Sanborn gave us a slap-up supper in his kitchen, during which Brown made a point of engaging Joe in talk, plainly to make him feel at home, and an equal member of the band – which was ironic, in its way, since Joe was a sight better educated than Brown or, as it turned out, any of his other followers. He took care not to show it, though, which wasn't difficult, since Brown prosed on at length, telling him that when they'd been in Chicago, and a hotel had refused to take the coloured people who were along with him, Brown and his gang had trooped out en masse, and hadn't rested until they'd found a place where there was no colour bar. It amused me to see Joe trying to look impressed by this earnest recital, but I didn't overhear much more, for young Anderson, who was seated next to me, had that curious American compulsion to tell you his life-story, as well as his views on everything under the sun.

He was an engaging lad, fresh-faced and full of beans, with a Colt in his armpit and that restless eye that you develop from years of learning not to sit down with your back to the door. He called me "Josh" right away, told me he was "Jerry", that he'd fought on the Kansas frontier as lieutenant of an irregular troop of Free Soilers, skirmished with the U.S. Cavalry, been jailed by pro-slavers, ridden on the recent Missouri raid, and thought Brown was the next best thing to God. He was one of your true-blue hell-fire abolitionists, and itching to prove it.

216

"It's this way, Josh," confides he solemnly, "I reckon this fight is more mine than most folks' – 'cos my family held slaves once, till my daddy came up North, so I figure I have to wipe the slate clean, don't you see? Maybe you can't understand that, bein' Canadian – oh, sure," grins he, winking, "I guessed that straight off, from your ac-cent – but *I* feel it in my *heart*, don't ye know? I just wish I could make everyone feel that way. Why, those poor black folk are cryin' out for help down yonder – but does anybody listen? Oh, I know there's lots o' good people, like we seen tonight, who'd wish slavery away tomorrow, an' they talk, an' 'tend meetin's, an' take up collections – but they don't *do* anythin'!" He had dropped his voice, so that Sanborn didn't hear; now he gritted his teeth. "Well, there's a few of us ready to *do*, an' *dare* – people like you an' me – an' we'll be enough, you'll see! Yes, sir, when Cap'n Brown gives the word, we'll shake this land of liberty and equality clear to its centre!"[40]

I hope the rest of the gang are your sort, my son, thinks I – young and full of ideals and without a brain among you when it comes to sober planning; the last thing I wanted was older and wiser heads competing with me for Brown's ear. Fortunately, the old man seemed to have taken to me; he wrung my hand fiercely at parting – he and Jerry were staying at a hotel in Concord, but Joe and I were to bed down in Sanborn's attic – and assured me that as soon as he'd finished his work in Boston, the two of us would start to plan "the campaign", as he called it. Joe pricked up his ears at that, and as soon as he and I were alone under the eaves, where mattresses had been provided, he rounded on me.

"What did Brown say to you befo' – when you was alone?"

"Well, Joe, I don't know that that's any of your concern," says I, just to provoke him, but before he could do more than glare, I went on: "If you must know, he wants to be in Harper's Ferry by the Fourth of July. There, now. Does that satisfy you?"

He came swiftly, stooping under the beams, and squatted down by me, whispering.

"Fourth July! You reckon the others know – them as was heah tonight?"

217

"I doubt it. I don't think they want to."

He nodded; he was quite smart enough to guess that Sanborn and his friends were scared of the whole business.

"He say how many men he's got? How he's gonna do it?"

"No. He's waiting for me to show him. That's bound to take time – and I don't know how long it'll take to assemble his men, or how many he can count on, or what arms he's got, or what money. I don't know if he can be ready, in just two months –"

"Listen!" His ugly black face was thrust into mine, whispering furiously. "You better see he's ready, you heah me? An' you –"

"Now *you* listen!" I hissed, as loud as I dared, giving him back glare for glare. "The sooner we have this straight, the better! I'm being paid five thousand dollars to see that this damned farmer takes Harper's Ferry – and no blundering black fool is going to queer my pitch! I know how to do it – you don't! If it takes me all summer to make it sure, that's my affair! I'm his lieutenant, not you – and the farther you stay clear of me, the safer we'll both be. D'ye think you can prowl at my elbow, looking like my bloody keeper? D'ye want to make 'em suspicious of us?" I sat back, sneering. "How long d'ye think we'd last if they guessed you were a Kuklos spy? Why, we –"

Before I knew it I was staring into the muzzle of a cocked revolver, his eyes rolling with rage behind it.

"The day they guess *that*, *Mistuh* Comber," hisses he, "yo' *gone*! An' case you think you kin get up to any shines with me . . . jes' remembah . . . I ain't the only one watchin' you! So now!"

I forced myself to look unmoved down his barrel, with my bowels doing the polka – by God, he was a quick hand with a barker – and then to fetch an elaborate sigh as I stretched out on my mattress.

"You're a fool, Joe. You don't understand me at all, do you? Why, if I'd wanted to split on you, I could have done it when I was alone with Brown, couldn't I? But I didn't, because I've got five thousand good reasons, and when I make a deal, I keep to it. Now go to sleep – and in the morning, do try to remember that you're not my watchdog but a grateful darkie abolitionist who's fairly sweating to set his brethren free. Give 'em a chorus of doo-dah-day, why don't you?"

He stood looming over me for a long moment, then stirred his hand, and the pistol had vanished. He turned on his heel, and went without a word to his mattress – but not to sleep with a tranquil mind, as I became aware in the small hours, when I woke, discovered that there wasn't a piss-pot to be had, descended the attic ladder to a window where I relieved myself into the night . . . and turned to find him within a yard of me, pistol in hand and glowering as though he'd just escaped from Sinbad's bottle. It gave me a horrid scare, but I got my own back by offering to hold the pistol and keep a look-out while he took his turn at blighting Sanborn's geraniums. He wouldn't, though, and when I dropped off to sleep again I guessed he was still brooding watchfully, wondering what to make of me, no doubt.

In fact, I didn't sleep that long; there was too much to think about, and this was the first real leisure I'd had to do it. Brown was an odd case; I'd expected a brimstone-breathing fanatic, and instead I'd met a steady, pretty decent, but plainly determined old man with an admirable gift for modest showing off. There was no doubt that he was fixed in his resolve; he'd invade Virginia if it was the last thing he did – which it probably would be, if he ever got round to it. But that was out of the question, for the simplest of reasons: he didn't have the brains for it. He was a slow thinker, if ever I saw one, and a dreamer; Messervy was right – I doubted if he could have directed a nursery tea. Rampaging into Missouri and grabbing the first niggers and horses he saw was his mark, but planning a military raid . . . no, I couldn't credit it. That aside – where were his men? Scattered, visiting supporters, raising funds, working at odd jobs, or just loafing, from what Anderson had told me. And I'd *heard* about money and weapons . . . well, I'd believe them when I saw them.

As I lay there, staring up at Sanborn's skylight, my thoughts kept jumping between hope and dread. One

219

moment I felt my confidence growing that I could keep Brown busy, planning and dreaming and getting nowhere, for as long as need be . . . and then doubts would creep in, and I'd have to tell myself fiercely that I was in the business now and no turning back; I'd been a helpless cork, borne on the tide, until my meeting with Seward – then, I'd had a plain choice, and made it, and while it had landed me in this ridiculous galley, it had been the right one . . . and it was too late to run now, anyway, with this black gunslick watching my every move . . .

I was too hot and clammy to go back to sleep now – it's wonderful how fears can sprout in the dark, when you're as naturally windy as I am. As I writhed fretfully on the lumpy mattress, it struck me as damned sinister that Messervy hadn't arranged some means whereby I could get a message to him – why, I could have let him know that Harper's Ferry was the *certain* target, and he could have had the Marines deployed around the place, and word of that would surely have reached Brown, and caused him to give up the business altogether . . . my God, was it possible that Messervy and his "superiors", whoever they were, absolutely *wanted* Brown to raid the Ferry, for some ghastly political reason which I didn't understand? Never – in that case, why the hell were they employing me to stop him? Well, Flashy, you fool, to kill him, for taking six bits off that infant . . . for it was plain as print that Lincoln and Palmerston were in the thing, too, and it was all a devilish plot to make the Queen withhold my knighthood, as she certainly would do once Seward had told Prince Albert that I'd pissed in Charity Spring's flowerbed . . .

At which point I awoke with a wordless cry, lathered in cold sweat, to discover that it was growing light, and that I was in bursting need of another visit to the window below, so I rolled out, cursing, and clambered miserably down the ladder again – and blow me if Simmons didn't follow me every step of the way.

There's a photograph which may still be kicking about somewhere, showing John Brown enthroned in an armchair, with Joe seated scowling alongside him, while Jerry Anderson and your correspondent stand behind wearing expressions of ruptured nobility, each of us resting a comradely hand on Joe's shoulders – although, as Jerry observed, from the look on Joe's face you would think we were trying to hold him down. The reason for the picture was that Brown wanted a new hat, and in those days daguerreotypers used to dispense free headgear to their sitters, with a miniature copy of the plate attached to the inside lining. The hat was rubbish, but Brown reckoned it was a saving; he had no more money sense than my beloved Elspeth, and was always short, and it's my belief that we only had our "likenesses took" so that he could sit there looking like Elijah, with his faithful followers about him, the darkie being given the other chair to show that all men are equal in the sight of God and daguerreotypers.

It was posed in New York in that strange month of May, 1859, which I still look back on with wonder. I'd been harried halfway round the world, through the strangest series of chances, and now, after one of the most topsy-turvy weeks of my life, I found myself loafing about in the wake of an eccentric revolutionary, with nothing to do but wait to see what might happen next. Most odd, and my recollection of it is fairly incoherent, with one or two episodes standing out in relief.

This time, you see, was the last tranquil twilight in the remarkable career of John Brown of Ossawatomie, when he was saying his farewells to his Eastern friends, scrounging his final subscriptions, and preparing for the great day which probably he alone believed was coming at last. It was a sort of royal progress in which he addressed meetings, shook hands with legions of admirers, and stoked up the support which he hoped would burst into a great Northern crusade once he'd lit the fire in Dixie; it took us from Boston to New York and various places around, and since I'd decided that my own eventual profit and present safety would be best served by going along quietly, I used the time to study the man and take the measure of his prospects.

An encouraging sign was that his health was none too good; he complained of what he called ague, and I had hopes that he'd be in no shape to start a war that summer. But he was a tough old bird, and wouldn't pamper himself; he was a great one for Spartan living, and at one place we stayed the maid of the house found him at daybreak fast asleep on the front steps; she made the mistake of shaking him, and found a Colt presented at her head. Even up here, surrounded by a friendly population, he never went unarmed, usually with Jerry as bodyguard, an office which gradually passed to me, for Jerry dressed like an out-of-work scarecrow, and didn't fit too well in the Boston hotels or the halls where J.B. harangued the faithful.

Messervy was proved right: he wasn't a good speaker, but he had a presence, and the mere sight of that Covenanter figurehead, with its flashing eyes and rasping voice, was enough to set them stamping and rummaging in their purses. His message was plain: talk was futile, it was time for action – and sure enough, some oratorical gesture would give them a glimpse of the gun-butt under his coat. Once or twice he waxed philosophical, and came adrift: I remember him pouring scorn on those who felt that their strength lay in the greatness of their wrongs, and so neglected action; his point was that the negro had the greatest wrongs of all, and a fat lot of strength that gave him – you could see the folk wondering what he was talking about, and fidgeting, but when he came out thundering that whoever took up arms to defend slavery had "a perfect right to be shot", they raised the roof. Ringing phrases about striking off the shackles, and troubling Israel, and Hell being stirred from beneath, were received with wild applause, but what moved them to wrath and tears (aye, and excitement) were his accounts of blood and battle in Kansas, and his promise of more to come. It was after one of these addresses, when they were crowding round to bless him and shake his hand, that I heard someone say that his speech had been "like that of Cromwell compared to an ordinary king."[41] That delighted him; Cromwell was one of his heroes, and people were forever likening him to the old warthog.

When he wasn't speechifying or paying calls, he was writing letters to all and sundry. One I remember him composing at the U.S. Hotel in Boston, reading it aloud with particular care, because it was to his five-year-old daughter; I looked it up in his biography the other day, hoping to edify my own grandlings, who need all the morality they can get. It will give you some notion of his style:

> My Dear Daughter Ellen,
> I will send you a short letter. I want very much to have you grow good every day. To have you learn to mind your mother very quick; & sit very still at the table; & to mind what all older persons say to you that is right. I hope to see you soon again; and if I should bring some little thing that will please you; it would not be very strange. I want you to be uncommon good-natured. God bless you my child.
> Your Affectionate Father,
> John Brown

Couldn't punctuate worth a dam, you see, and used to say he "knew no more of grammar than the farmer's calves", but there ain't a man of letters in my time who could have put it better. My grandbrats received it in polite silence, and then John said "We-l-l . . . what was she to do when an older person said something *wrong*?", Jemima asked if Ellen was pretty, Alice wanted to know what the promised "little thing" was, and Augustus belched. God help Miss Prentice, I say.

The rest of his time he spent in talk, and since I was a

223

new listener I had to endure a good deal of his prosing in those first weeks. Silly cracker-barrel stuff, mostly, although he had a curious store of half-learned knowledge; Bunyan was a favourite, and he was well up on Napoleon and Caesar and assorted military history. He was thirsty for anything that might be of use in fighting slavery, but had no time for soldiers or soldiering, and had gone to all lengths to avoid service in his youth, the notion of drilling and training to kill being anathema – until the abolitionist bug had bitten, and he'd found an enemy to hate. And when he got onto the subject of his first encounters with slavery – look out. A change would come over him, and from talking in his usual opinionated style he would go into a sort of brooding study, staring ahead and growling as though a steam-kettle was coming to the boil inside him. It was an unnerving sight, I can tell you, and I shan't forget the first time I saw it, one evening when we were seated alone on some front porch or other.

"I was twelve years old," says he, gritting his teeth, "and had druv some cattle a long way to the house of a gentleman with whom I had to stay for a spell. He was a good man, kindly and feared God, and made a great pet of me, and showed me off to his folks, saying what a smart brave little chap I was, to come a hundred miles alone. Well, that was fine. But you know, he had a young black slave boy, just my age, and bright as a brass button – and I tell you, the way he tret that child would ha' broke your heart! Oh, it was the best vittles for *me*, and a seat at table nearest the fire, but for that little coloured lad – why, he barely fed him but scraps, and beat him like a dog, with a stick, or a shovel, or any old thing at hand! He didn't have pity on him at all!"

He choked on that, and sat with his great hands working on his knees; when he turned on me, there were tears in the blazing eyes, and his voice was hoarse as though he were on the brink of a seizure. That was the moment when I first understood how the man who wrote that letter to his daughter could also be the man who'd massacred the pro-slavers at Pottawatomie; he was a man possessed, no other word for it.

224

"I didn't see how God could let such things be!" cries he. "Or could put such fell cruelty into the heart of that good, kindly man – why, he was a U.S. marshal – yes, he was! He heard my prayers at night, and gave me a spinning top, the first I ever had! I asked him, if God was *my* Father, wasn't he Father to the little black boy, too, and he told me not to trouble my head about such things! Not to trouble!"

It wasn't canny, those eyes, and the huge hawk nose and heaving beard, all directed at me as though *I* was the bloody U.S. marshal; he seemed to be inviting comment, but all I could think to say was that it was pretty rotten, and had the fellow been tight, perhaps?

He didn't seem to hear me, luckily, so I let it be, and after a while he sighed and launched into a tale about a runaway nigger whom he'd hidden from the slave-catchers a few years later. The darkie had crawled into a wood, and when the alarm was over, he'd gone to look for him.

"Can you guess how I found him?" says he, and the fit seemed to have passed, for while he gripped my arm in his talons, he spoke quite calmly. "He was lying deep in the bushes, in terror of his life . . . and I located him by the sound of his heart *beating*! Yes, and it's a sound that has stayed in my ears these many years, that awful drumming of a human heart, in agony and fear!"[42]

Well, I didn't believe it for a minute; if a beating heart could give you away when you're cowering in cover, I'd have been dead meat before I was twenty. But I said that was an astonishing thing, the poor chap must have been in a dreadful funk, but he'd got over it, had he?

"I vowed in that moment that I would never rest until the last slave had been set free," says he solemnly. I said hear, hear, and he asked me what had been *my* moment of revelation. Since I hadn't had one, I had to choose at random, and said it had been when I'd first watched blacks being packed aboard on the Dahomey coast, bucks to starboard, wenches to port – with the shapeliest females nearest the hatches, for convenience, but I didn't mention that.

He shook his head and murmured something about the waters of Babylon, but a moment later he was telling me

225

about a dinner to which he'd been bidden the next night, and would I care to accompany him, and when he bade me good-night he was absolutely cheerful again. It left me quite shaken, though; for a moment he'd looked as though he was ready to foam at the mouth, and I concluded that if he wasn't barmy, as Messervy claimed, there was still a screw loose somewhere.

Mostly, though, he was as calm and measured as you could wish, going about his business of paying calls and spouting claptrap, writing letters, gassing to Joe and Jerry and me – but never a word of substance about the great stroke we were meant to be preparing; no talk of planning or gathering men and arms, or any of the work that should have been going ahead. Of one thing I became surer by the day: if he *was* bent on taking Harper's Ferry, it wouldn't be by the Fourth of July. Reflecting on that, it seemed a pity that I'd no way of conveying the glad news to Messervy – and then by a sheer fluke I was presented with the perfect opportunity.

I mentioned a moment ago a dinner to which J.B. had invited me; it was at one of the big Boston hotels, full of quality and local bigwigs, and the two of us were guests of Dr Howe. We'd barely stepped into the lobby when he cried to J.B. that here was someone he must meet – and who should it be but the podgy Senator who'd tried to dragoon me into this business in the first place, and whom I'd last seen outside Seward's cabin.

We bore up short at the sight of each other, but he kept his countenance, paying me no heed beyond the usual courtesies of presentation, and fixing on J.B., who seemed to know who he was but took no joy of the knowledge, for he drew himself up tall, looked down his nose, and says, pretty cool:

"I have heard, Senator, that you don't approve of my course of action."

I could have told him that our fat friend wasn't the sort to take any damn-you-me-lad airs. He stuck out his jowls and came straight back.

"If you refer to your recent rash foray into Missouri – no, sir, I do not!"

J.B.'s beard went up a couple of notches. "Indeed, sir. My friends tell me also that you have spoken in condemnation of it."

"That I have!" snaps the Senator. "I regard every illegal act as doing very great injury to the anti-slavery cause."

"Freeing slaves injures the cause – is that so?" growls J.B., and the Senator started to swell and go crimson.

"Let me tell you, sir," says he, "it was an imprudence that might have cost countless lives! There was a time, sir, not long ago, when such a thing might have led to the invasion of Kansas by . . . by a great number of excited people, sir!"

J.B. made a rumbling noise, his hand twitched at his coat, and for an awful second I thought he was going for his gun, but he just hooked his thumbs into his weskit.

"Well, I think differently, sir!" says he. "I acted right, and it will have a good influence, you'll see. Good-night to you, Senator!"

"Good-night to you, Mr John Brown!" cries the Senator, and they bowed and stalked off opposite ways, leaving me wondering how I might seize this unexpected chance. I daren't go after the Senator, but within ten seconds I was in the deserted lavatory, scribbling frantically: "Tell Messervy – Harper's Ferry *for certain*. July 4". I daren't go out for a waiter, not knowing who might be spying on me, so I sent the black attendant to fetch one. He brought another darkie, in a liveried coat, on whom I pressed the note, telling him to deliver it to the fat, ugly Senator with the yellow flower in his buttonhole, and he cried: "Sho' nuff, suh!" and bowled off, chortling. But whether the note ever reached the Senator, I never found out; if it did, he must have ignored it, or else Messervy did – and you may make of that what you will. Anyway, I'd done my best.[43]

*   *   *

It was in early June that I started to earn my corn as a military adviser, when J.B. took me into Connecticut to see the pikes which he'd commissioned two years earlier; he

227

was full of misunderstood nonsense about Swiss infantry and Greek phalanxes and Scottish schiltrouns, and plainly had visions of niggers forming squares to repulse cavalry charges. I couldn't believe my eyes when the blacksmith hauled out half a dozen which he'd got up as samples, amazing instruments six feet long with bowie blades clamped to their ends, but asked my opinion, I said they were capital weapons – the more money J.B. spent on trash, the less he'd have for serious equipment. He ordered a thousand on the spot, and the smith said admiringly that he hadn't realised that Richard the Lionheart was operating in Kansas, but a thousand would cost $450, and he couldn't deliver until August. Farewell July 4th, thinks I, this is splendid. J.B. was well pleased, though; you could see he was itching to fight Bannockburn o'er again in the Blue Ridge Mountains.

A few days after this we said adieu to New England, J.B. going north to visit his family, while Jerry, Joe and I were packed off to Ohio to join two of his sons who were supposed to be recruiting in that state. They were the first of his celebrated brood that I'd met, and I found them vastly reassuring: Owen Brown, J.B.'s right-hand man, was big, tough, genial, and fat-headed, and John junior, the oldest son, was a poor critter in low spirits, plainly bound for Bedlam. Like all the Brown boys they were strapping, fine-looking fellows, but you'd not have trusted either of them to light the fire. Owen would have made a fairish corporal, given no work more taxing than lifting heavy weights and advancing into the cannon's mouth, but Junior had always been slightly wanting, Jerry told me, and the Kansas fighting had sent him off the rails altogether. He'd never got over his father's butchery at Pottawatomie, and soon after had fallen into the hands of Border Ruffians who had chained him and flogged him sixty miles over hard going, which had reduced him to raving idiocy. He was better now, Jerry opined, but J.B. would never have him in the field again, so he'd been made quartermaster and chief of recruiting, at which he was making no headway at all.

If these two are a fair sample, thinks I, we'll have a quiet summer of it – but there was a third man in Ohio, whom I didn't meet until J.B. returned from up north, and as soon as I shook his hand and met his eye I scented two qualities we could have done without: brains and bravery.

He was a Switzer, though American-born, named Kagi, and he was to prove to be the only man in Brown's conspiracy who knew what he was about. He was in his middle twenties, dapper, sharp, well-read, and keen, and if there had been half a dozen like him . . . well, American history books might have a chapter today about the great Virginia slave uprising. He'd been a teacher and had fought in Kansas, where he'd distinguished himself by shooting a judge – who in turn had put three slugs into Kagi, which gives you some notion of what life at the American bar was like in those days.

"My Gideon," says J.B. in high good humour, putting one hand on Kagi's shoulder and the other on mine, "and my Joshua, who together shall be a scourge of Midian, yea, and of Canaan," and from Kagi's quick, cool smile I knew that this smart, clean-shaven youngster (who was styled "Secretary for War", by the way) was itching to steer his chief into action. He lost no time in drawing me aside and showing me a map of Harper's Ferry (hand-drawn, but far better than Messervy's) and asking if I had formed any plan for taking it, and for the campaign that must follow. I said J.B. hadn't asked for one yet, but as I understood it, taking the place was the least of it.

"You're right," says he briskly, and tapped the map. "See here: armoury, rifle works, arsenal, all within a half-mile. No troops on guard, only watchmen. I know the place well, 'twill be easy as pie –"

"Given the men, the arms, and secrecy," says I, and decided to impress him. "Then, strip the arsenal and armoury; have wagons and mules to carry the stuff to a prearranged rendezvous in the hills; food, bedding, clothes and boots for the slaves when they come in; despatch scouts to watch for the nearest militia companies and bring word of their movements; cut the wires; blow the railroads . . ." I paused for breath. "But that, of course, is just for a beginning."

229

I'd expected his face to fall, but he was beaming. "Thank God!" cries he. "A man who knows his business!"

"If I didn't, I wouldn't be here," says I, the grim professional. Then I grinned, to show him I was human. "See here, though . . . John Henry, isn't it? Aye, well, answer me this, John: these slaves J.B. is counting on to run away and join us. How many? How soon? How does he intend to bring 'em in to us? We're going to need 'em quick – but they mustn't know too soon that we're coming, or the whole South will know it, too. Then they'll have to be fed, clothed, armed, and trained. I can plan for all of that – given the assurance of men and equipment. But getting 'em moving in the first place – that's the key to this whole affair, my boy. That's where we stand or fall!"

D'ye know, it was only while I was talking that the sheer lunatic impossibility of the whole ridiculous business rose up and hit me a facer for the first time. You see, until now, I hadn't thought beyond J.B.'s intended capture of Harper's Ferry – why should I, when I didn't believe it would ever happen? But now, in showing off for this bright spark, I found myself considering the sequel – a slave uprising, followed by a guerrilla campaign – and when I did, I wanted to burst out laughing. To put it plainly, J.B. was hoping that thousands of slaves would rise up spontaneously, which seemed unlikely – and suppose they did, how in God's name did he hope to feed, clothe, equip, house, doctor, and train the poor buggers – probably the worst raw material on earth – to fight the American Army?

J.B., of course, had the answer: the Lord would provide. Kagi, being blessed with common sense, could see that the Lord would need considerable help, but being an optimistic disciple of J.B., *and no soldier*, he probably hoped that all would come right on the night – after all, this brilliant fellow Comber was taking the thing seriously, so it must be feasible. I knew it wasn't, not for the Duke himself, let alone these rustic dung-slingers.

But it wasn't for me to say so – my task must be to let the impossibles appear, slowly but surely, until Kagi saw the thing was hopeless. It would take time, and delicate

230

handling, but from the respect that J.B. showed him, I realised that he was the one to convince; if Kagi cried quits, that would be the end of it. I found myself revising my view of him: far from being a dangerous nuisance, he should be a godsend who unwittingly would help me to kill J.B.'s plan stone dead. I didn't know, then, how reckless a canny Swiss can be when he hears the bugles.

To my question about stirring up the slaves, he frowned, and said we had a man in Harper's Ferry already who was looking into it. I asked him about arms, and he showed me the cases of carbines which the Brown brothers had hidden in a warehouse, under a pile of coffins. They were good weapons, but I doubted whether there would ever be men to use them; Junior was in despair because the fellows who'd been ready to march the year before weren't turning up as expected. Left to him, the whole scheme would have been abandoned, but he daren't say so for fear of the old man, and when Kagi reminded him that there were hosts of free niggers up in Canada just waiting to answer the call, he pretended to perk up, saying he'd see to them when he'd collected all the weapons and shipped them down closer to the border.

It was the unlikeliest beginning to a desperate venture that I can remember in a lifetime of lost causes – I think of doddering old Elphy Bey before the Kabul retreat, changing his mind by the minute; Custer twitching and unshaven in his tent on the Rosebud, determined to have his way; Raglan imperturbable in his refusal to admit that he didn't know what the devil he was doing; Wheeler grey with fatigue and old age, tying his britches up with string as he prepared to surrender at Cawnpore. Each going to hell in his own way, torn between hope and despair, but at least they understood warfare and had good advisers about them. J.B. didn't have the understanding or the men; and for all his iron purpose he was no James Brooke or Fred Ward or Charlie Gordon.

I have a memory of a room somewhere, in Akron or Youngstown perhaps, with J.B. haranguing us about how well things were going, what with arms to hand, money in the bank, everyone back East cheering us on, and God letting the light of his countenance shine on our enterprise –

and Owen Brown, bearded and massive, hanging on Pa's every word; Junior looking glum and running his hand through his hair; young Oliver Brown, who had joined us, staring before him in his dreamy, soulful way; Kagi twitching with impatience; Jerry Anderson yawning and picking threads from his ragged sleeve; Black Joe watching J.B. with an intent, puzzled scowl that I couldn't read . . . all told, it was a damned uninspiring sight, and I found myself wondering what Guy Fawkes and the boys must have looked like on November the Fourth.

When J.B. wasn't lecturing us about troubling Israel and letting the foxes loose in the Philistine corn, he was on the go in the towns around the Ohio–Pennsylvania line, which was strong abolitionist country, assuring the people that the dawn was nigh, and he was girding his loins to invade Virginia – he made no secret of that, although I don't recall that he mentioned the Ferry by name, and he certainly glossed over the fact that his great slave insurrection would be in effect a rebellion against the U.S.A. and its Constitution. If the good folk who cheered, and pressed round to shake his hand, and sent Jenny scurrying home to fetch the ten dollars in the cookie jar for the good cause, had realised that he was ready to shoot the Stars and Stripes to ribbons, I reckon they'd have thought twice.

All this aimless jaunting about the country was fine by me. It wasn't the Grand Tour, what with passable food, middling accommodation, and no hope of vicious amusement, but I tolerated it in the knowledge that I'd be homeward bound presently having earned the gratitude of next-President Seward and the approval of Her Majesty. In the meantime I conferred endlessly with J.B. and Kagi, listening straight-faced to the old idiot's fierce enthusiasms, conscious that Kagi was watching to see how I took them, and I had to be on my guard not to approve anything too half-witted. For example, J.B. had a great bee in his bonnet about building forts in the hills from which his vast army of liberated darkies would sally forth like Boer commandos; I didn't remark that such forts would have taken a battalion of sappers weeks to build (give me the men and I'll do it, was

232

my line), but when he said the forts must have underground tunnels of communication between them, I had to point out that liberated slaves might not take too kindly to hacking their way through several hundred feet of granite, and anyway there wouldn't be time to spare from their military training (God forgive me). J.B. glowered like a spoilt child, for Kagi backed me up, and our discussion was pretty strained until he got his way on another ridiculous point – the establishment of a school in the hills for piccaninnies. Then he was happy again.

We had four or five of these staff meetings as we travelled about, and while I took care to hide my disgust, I could see Kagi's frown deepening by the day. J.B. talked interminably and vaguely, as though he didn't know what to do next, there was no sign of more recruits, and I'd made it plain that our operations must depend on numbers, black or white; I acted as though I expected them to roll up in troops at any time, but meanwhile, I said privately to Kagi, I could only plan in theory, and wait for J.B. to give his orders.

It was after the last of these talks, at a place called Chambersburg, that Kagi asked me to come for a walk. It was a lovely summer afternoon, and we strolled along the dusty road out of town – with Joe, I noticed to my amusement, dogging us at a distance. Kagi sat down under a finger-post and asked me straight out:

"Joshua – can we do this thing?"

Time to start sowing the good seed, so I answered right back.

"Take the Ferry? Given the men, certainly. Fight a campaign in the hills? If the blacks rise in sufficient numbers . . ." I shrugged.

"Sure . . . *if* they rise," says he, and started pulling petals off a flower. "Oh! . . . truth to tell, there ain't all that many blacks around the Ferry – and they ain't like the plantation nigras down south. They're farmhands, mostly, and house slaves – not much cotton thereaway, you see – and pretty much part of their masters' families. I don't know whether they'll *want* to rise!" He pitched the flower away irritably.

233

"Maybe after the harvest . . . that's when they're at their orneriest, and the suicides happen – "

"Suicides, for heaven's sake?"

"Yes, sir – see, when the harvest's in, that's when they're liable to be sold. South, maybe, with cotton-picking time coming on. So families are parted, and they get depressed and mean. But that's not till fall." He kicked absently at the dust. "I wish J.B. would make up his mind."

"Hasn't he?"

"Oh, sure, I guess so. I *ought* to know him by now, I s'pose . . . how he talks, and moons around, and then – bang! he's raiding Missouri! It'll be the same this time – when the Canadian blacks come in, and the other fellows who've promised." He turned his clever, troubled face to me, hoping to be reassured. "I just hate waiting . . . and I wondered what *you* thought, d'you see?"

It was no time to cheer him up, so I brooded a bit and said the five most depressing words in the language: "We are in God's hands." But so he'd never be able to say I'd discouraged him, I added sternly, with a hand on his arm:

"Never forget, John, that 'tis not the beginning, but the continuing until it be thoroughly finished, that yieldeth the true glory." And six feet of cemetery, as often as not. Arnold had made me write it out a thousand times for loafing in a pot-house when I should have been chasing 'cross country at Hare and Hounds.[44] Kagi said it was a fine sentiment, and he'd remember it.

As we rose to walk back, I chanced to look up at the signpost, and he followed my glance and said it was a pretty place, but quite a piece down the road, and much too far to walk. The name stayed in my mind, for no reason, as such things sometimes do. Gettysburg.

I should have jumped the train the moment the conductor took Joe's ticket, glowered suspiciously, and asked him to account for himself. Better still, I should never have boarded the train at all – and might not have done, if I hadn't mislaid my map. I'd bought it in Boston, to keep track of our random jauntings back and forth, and had traced our progress from New England to Ohio most satisfactorily, but after I lost it (in Pittsburgh, I think), why, like a careless ass I was content to roll along in happy ignorance of where we were. At Chambersburg, I knew we were in Pennsylvania, which was fine, and when J.B. said we were going to Hagerstown, I never thought twice; I'd never heard of the place, and had no notion where it lay.

There were six of us on the train: J.B., his sons Owen and Oliver, Jerry Anderson, myself, and Joe; Kagi had gone off north somewhere, and John junior had been left brooding in Ohio. It was a baking hot journey, with the sun turning the car into an oven, and even playing cards was too much of a fag. J.B. prowled up and down, accosting strangers to hector them, Owen was snoring like the great ox he was, Jerry was trying to get off with a girl across the aisle, and Oliver was boring me to blazes. He was the baby of the Brown family, a stalwart young Adonis of twenty, shy and given to books, but a chance remark had brought him out of his shell to tell me about his wife, Martha, who was up north, and by his account was a cross between Portia and Helen of Troy. I was dozing off when the conductor's harsh question roused me: "Whut's yore name, boy?", and I saw he was regarding Joe with a mistrustful eye. Joe told him.

"Joe Simmons, eh? An' just where are you from, Joe?"

235

J.B. was on the scene at once, beard bristling. "Some trouble, mister conductor?"

"You know this nigger?" says the conductor.

"I know this free coloured man," says J.B. sternly. "He is in my employ."

In his travelling duds, with their frayed sleeves and air of having been slept in, he didn't look like an employer, and the conductor sniffed.

"He is, is he? An' who might you be, mister?"

"My name is Isaac Smith," says J.B. "This is my servant, and these –" he indicated the rest of us "– are my sons, Owen, Oliver, Joshua, and Jeremiah." Well, if he chose to adopt me, I didn't mind. "Mrs Smith is not travelling with us," he added, with fine ponderous sarcasm, "or I'd be kindly proud to present her to you, too."

The conductor blinked uncertainly; J.B. tended to have that effect on folk, and the four of us were sufficiently large and ugly to daunt the stoutest ticket-walloper. "No offence, Mr Smith," says he hastily. "On'y there's been a couple o' runaways from Frederick lately, an' me seein yore boy here . . . well, I thought maybe . . ."

"That he might be one of them . . . taking the train *south*?" says J.B., mighty droll. The conductor scratched his head, and laughed apologetically, and said come to think of it, that wasn't likely, was it, ha-ha? J.B. said, no, it wasn't, and if the conductor was now satisfied that we weren't slave-stealers going in the wrong direction, perhaps he'd care to go about his business. The fellow cried, sure, certainly, no offence, mister, and went off like a scared rabbit, with J.B. glaring after him. I asked Oliver what the row was about, and he looked grim and said that was Dixie for you, all over.

"Dixie?"

"Sure – we crossed the line into Maryland a while back, didn't you know? If they're looking for runaway slaves, why, they think they can stop and question any black man they like!"

That gave me a start. I'd assumed, you see, that my charade with J.B. would be played out in the nice, safe, abolitionist North – and here we were, in the slave South, and

236

I'd never known it. Not that there had ever been warrants out for me in Maryland, and we were still a long way from the scene of my exploits of ten years ago, but it was enough to start me sweating, and I took the first chance that came to ask J.B., casual-like, what there was to interest us in Hagerstown. His reply, in a confidential undertone, but with an alarming glint in his eye, didn't quiet my fears a bit.

"You smell the battle afar off, Joshua?" He glanced round to make sure he wasn't overheard. "Have patience, my boy. The time is drawing nigh when we'll be done with talk and waiting at the doors of timid men! Yes, sir, we're approaching the scene of the great war from which there'll be no discharge. We're going to spy out the land," says he, with a grin that froze my marrow. "What did Moses say to *his* Joshua, eh? 'Get you up this way *southward*, and get you up into the mountain, and see the land what it is, and the people that dwelleth therein, whether they be strong or weak, few or many.' And Joshua and his eleven spies did just that, remember?"

I didn't, in fact; the only thing I recollected about Joshua and spying was two chaps being sent to a harlot's house . . . but this was appalling news I was hearing. I asked him what he meant.

"Why, we'll lie up a day or two at Hagerstown," says he, "and then it's just a few miles down the river to where we want to be at."

"Where's that?" says I, trying not to croak.

"Why, Harper's Ferry, to be sure! We'll take a good look at the country along the way, and – what's that? Restrain your language, sir! And keep your voice down!" He was glaring disapproval, and darting nervous glances at the nearest passengers. "There's no call for excitement," he whispered angrily, "or that kind of foul Navy talk! I won't have it!" Then he patted my knee, like a forgiving uncle. "I know you're eager – I've watched you chafing these past weeks, and I promise you won't have to wait much longer. Once we've seen how the land lies, we're going to find ourselves a nice out of the way place between Hagerstown and the Ferry, and there we'll make our final plans. And when the men have come in, and the arms . . ." He sat back, nodding his great bearded head, eyes gleaming, while I fought manfully to retain my breakfast. To find myself in Maryland had been bad enough, but the news that we weren't a kick in the arse from Harper's Ferry was shocking. Oh, I'd seen it on the map, often, but it had always seemed a safe distance away – America's such a big place, you get into the habit of thinking you're miles from anywhere – and I hadn't realised, in Chambersburg, how close we were getting. Now, without warning, we were almost there.

When my guts had stopped fluttering, I reflected that it might have been worse. For a horrid moment, when he'd mentioned the name, I'd thought he was contemplating a sudden wild onslaught, but plainly it was just to be a scout, before we retired to some hole in the ground for another jolly discussion about Greek phalanxes or forts with connecting tunnels. I could tolerate that – not that I had any choice, with Joe at my elbow.

For now that we were south of the line he took to sticking close again, possibly because he believed the great day was approaching. I continued to doubt it, for when we reached Hagerstown J.B. was back in his indecisive mood; he took us trekking about the country for a couple of days, inquiring for properties to buy or rent, and then it was all aboard the train again, and on a bright July day we rolled across the bridge into Harper's Ferry, and I had my first sight of that strange little town where a parcel of ragamuffins were to change the course of American history.

It's an odd place, lying on flat land at the tip of a peninsula where the Shenandoah and Potomac rivers meet, with heights of some grandeur on either side, so that the town seems to be at the bottom of a gorge. Behind, the peninsula runs up to a third set of heights, the rearmost houses climbing the slope, with steps cut into the hillside. In those days there was a covered road and rail bridge over the Potomac from Maryland to the town, which lay in Virginia,* and a smaller bridge over the Shenandoah.

* Now West Virginia (see town map on p. 269).

238

It's changed a good deal, having been battered and burned in the war, but in my time, as you came in over the Maryland bridge, there was a great stretch of armoury buildings running for near half a mile along the Potomac bank, quite unexpected in that kind of farming country. I'd imagined a sleepy hamlet, with a store and ferry-boat, and a few barefoot loafers snoozing and spitting in the sunshine, but here was a bustling little industrial community of three thousand souls, with neat houses and workshops, and my first thought was that you'd need a regiment to take this place – and a brigade to hold it, for a less defensible position I never did see. Those commanding heights would be a besieged garrison's nightmare, and when the bridges went, why, you'd be like a mouse in a bottle.

But it was the sight of J.B. and his boys, wandering about like a party of tramps looking for a place to doss down, that moved me to silent mirth. They gaped at the great spread of armoury workshops and the arsenal building, gazed up the Shenandoah shore to the rifle works half a mile off, considered the number of workmen moving briskly about the sheds, and the activity about Wager's station hotel by the railroad tracks – and you could see in their eyes the question to J.B.: how the devil do we take this place? True, there wasn't a soldier to be seen, but there were several score of likely labourers, and any number of townsfolk. I could just picture J.B. hammering at the arsenal door and getting a bucket of water over him for his pains, before the lads of the village swarmed out to chase us back over the bridge, probably in tar and feathers. As for the notion of carrying off arms and ammunition to the hills while the populace stayed obligingly in bed . . . well, I'd always thought the projected raid was daft, but only now did I realise it was ridiculous.

My spirits were further raised by our conference in Galt's saloon, where we met Johnny Cook, who was J.B.'s man on the spot. He'd been at the Ferry for a year, teaching school among other things, and God help the children's education: a pleasant fellow enough, but garrulous as a Welsh parson, and I'd sooner have trusted a secret to Elspeth. Like

239

Kagi, he was fretting about whether the slaves would rise, and wanted to take soundings among 'em. The thought of this babbling ass tooling about asking niggers if they felt like mutiny had J.B. almost biting his tea-cup (yes, tea, in a saloon; he and Oliver were strict temperance). He told Cook, with some vigour, on no account to meddle with the slaves. Cook was crestfallen.

"But how they goin' to know, an' be ready, without we tell 'em? Can't have a nigra uprisin' if the nigras don't *know*, can we? How we goin' to get them in?" He raised a foolish laugh, and J.B. ground his teeth.

"When we strike, they will know it, and they will come in to us, I tell you, and they shall be legion!" He was wearing his mad Isaiah look, as he always did when contradicted. "The Lord will guide them to us, and they will be like the standing corn for number – so don't you fool with 'em, John Cook, you hear me?"

And that, you should know, was the last that was ever heard about stirring up the slaves – a task which could never have been done in secret anyway; George Broadfoot would have turned his face to the wall at the mere thought.

The next thing was to find a lonely spot on the Maryland side where we could set up shop, pretending to be farmers while we girded our loins, planned, trained, drilled, accumulated arms and recruits, and generally played out J.B.'s dreams. After putting it about that we were settlers who hoped to bring in cattle from the North, he found the ideal place about four miles from the Ferry, a ramshackle three-storey farmhouse which he rented from someone named Kennedy; it had pasture and outbuildings and lay away from the road, shielded by shrubbery, in pleasant wooded country at the foot of the hills. Just the spot for a few eccentrics to waste time fooling themselves that they were on the brink of great things.

And there we stayed, God help me, for three solid months – and if you ask me what happened in that interminable time, I can only say that dusty summer drifted endlessly into golden autumn, our clothes got seedier, and our leader talked and talked and brooded and wrote letters North for money, and accomplished . . . absolutely nothing. While in the world outside (which I began to doubt still existed), Pam became Prime Minister again, Blondin walked across Niagara on a tightrope, someone invented the steam road-roller, people read *A Tale of Two Cities* (I know these things 'cos I looked them up in an encyclopedia the other day), and my loving Elspeth, I have reason to suspect, misbehaved in a potting-shed at Windsor Castle with that randy little pig the Prince of Wales, who at that time was just beginning to notice that girls were different from fellows, somehow.

And not far away from the Kennedy Farm a chap called Emmett was composing a catchy little ditty, which was rather ironic, when you consider that we were preparing to set the South ablaze: it was called "Dixie".

* * *

You may ask, how did I stand it, and why? Easy: I'd no choice. So far as I knew, the Kuklos were still keeping a leery eye on me, and Joe certainly was. Still, I might have tried to slide out, but for one thing – I never believed it could last. Only when you *know* you're in for a long haul do you grow desperate; I didn't, because each day I could tell myself that tomorrow, or next week, *must* see the end, surely; J.B. would realise his folly, and give up, or go loco entirely, or the plot would leak out altogether . . . or something would bring the whole farce to a quiet conclusion. One thing I grew increasingly positive about: there would be no raid and no uprising.

I became convinced of this in the first two weeks at the farm, which I spent, at J.B.'s request, in writing plans for the great invasion. I did it in best staff-college style, covering reams of paper with instructions for the initial taking of the vital points in the town (a simple task in itself), and the development of the rebellion – a glorious exercise in impossibility, since it took for granted a force of at least a hundred well-trained men, properly equipped and led (a total which I took care not to state in bald terms), and assumed that hordes of ferocious fugitive niggers would flock to join us; it might encourage them, I suggested, if we sent riders round

241

the country with fiery crosses – and if you think that was stretching credulity, you don't know J.B.

He was delighted. This was what he'd needed all along, he said, a clear laying-out by an expert; there had been nothing like me since Hannibal. He read it over and over, sighing with satisfaction as he turned the pages by the light of the oil-lamps, his great lion head tilted back to scan them through his reading-glass. The fiery crosses brought an explosion of admiration, and a fist thumped on the table, and I reflected that feeding dreams is like flattery: you can't lay it on too thick. If I'd had a spark of decency I'd have felt sorry for the credulous old clown, humbugging him so, but I didn't – hang it all, it's my livelihood.

Such a masterpiece had to be discussed, of course, ad infinitum, in every minute, futile detail. A copy must be sent to Kagi, who was now at Chambersburg awaiting the shipment of arms from John junior in Ohio, and Cook had to be summoned from the Ferry so that he, too, could be dumfounded by my genius. It was all there, he agreed, plain as print; he'd have to take a look up in the hills to select likely spots for the forts, but he could get tar and turpentine right away for the fiery crosses, you bet. One omission in my plan disappointed him, though: no mention of hostages. What hostages, I asked.

"Did I not tell you, Joshua?" says J.B. "When we have taken the Ferry we must lay hold on the principal slave-owners, as security for any of our people who may fall into the hands of the enemy." By "enemy" he meant the U.S.A., if he'd only thought about it.

"I know a prime case," says Cook. "Old Colonel Washington – he's George Washington's great-grandsomethin'-or-other. Has a fine place close to town – an' hasn't he got slaves, though!"

"We must take him without fail," says J.B. "It will mean much to have that great name, the name of our country's founder, as a hostage."

"He's a real fine gentleman, a proper arist-o-crat!" says Cook, pleased to be approved for once. "Say, you should see his house, though – that's the bang-uppest place! The things he has there – why, there's a pistol that Lafayette gave to George Washington, an' Frederick the Great's sword!"

"Are you sure – you've seen them?" J.B. fairly glowed. "Oh, to have those when we raise the flag of freedom over Harper's Ferry! Precious symbols in our country's history – Lafayette's pistol in my belt . . . great Frederick's sword in my hand . . ."

It kept him happy for a couple of days; if only Harper's Ferry had also contained Franklin's lightning-rod and Jefferson's commode, he'd have been in wonderland for a week.

*   *   *

We were just a party of six when we moved into the farm, but soon we were joined by Oliver's wife, Martha, and J.B.'s daughter, Annie, who were to keep house for us and the recruits who arrived at intervals thereafter. The two girls were bright, cheery lasses in their late 'teens, and I should put your minds at rest at once by stating that I never had carnal designs on either; they weren't my style or passable above half – and you don't fool with the womenfolk of John Brown of Ossawatomie, believe me. Martha was a capital cook, and little Annie a sharp sentry; it was J.B.'s great dread that we'd arouse suspicion among the local people – for Americans are the nosiest folk on earth, prying into every newcomer's business, trying to get sight of his furnishings and guess how much money he's got (being neighbourly, they call it), and the arrival of six mysterious stalwarts was enough to set the countryside agog.

Later, when more recruits came in, little Annie had to be on the look-out constantly, crying warning and rebuffing visitors, for it would have been fatal if the gossips had learned there were a score of men in the house. I've seen a dozen of us at dinner having to lift the cloth at a moment's notice and carry it off, dishes, scoff, and all, from the big common-room off the kitchen, up into the sleeping loft. And all because Mrs Huffmaster, a barefoot slattern with half a dozen snottering brats at her heels, "came a-callin'", peeping round Annie on the porch to get a look inside, and remarking slyly "what a smart lot o' shirts your men-folk

243

has", when we'd carelessly put all our washing out at once, and there were clothes for fifteen or twenty fluttering on the green.

These recruits came by twos and threes at intervals during the summer, but I'll list 'em all together for convenience. At first I worried in case J.B. might assemble a formidable force, but twenty proved to be the full count, far too few for the business he had in mind, and only one or two first-class experienced men. Mostly they were Jerry Anderson over again: young, eager, sworn abolitionists full of tripe about liberty and black equality, and all under the spell of J.B., for most of them had been with him in Kansas or up north, and had dispersed after last year's postponement.

The one formidable customer was Aaron Stevens, a big black-avised rascal who at thirty was the oldest; he'd served in Mexico, been sentenced to death for mutiny, broken out of Leavenworth, and fought the slavers in Kansas, where he'd been colonel of a militia troop. He and a fellow called Taylor, a Canadian, stuck together, for they were both spiritualists, and would prose away for hours about the beyond; Stevens was sane enough, but Taylor was next-door to a padded cell – he believed his dreams and would tell you cheerfully that he'd be dead by Christmas. He was, too.

Watson Brown was another of J.B.'s boys, tall and good-looking, with a dandy beard and a gentle manner; he'd left a wife and baby up north and was yearning to get back to them. Al Hazlett and Bill Leeman were wild young blades, forever sneaking out when J.B.'s back was turned to spark the local girls or get up to larks even down in Harper's Ferry, but Leeman was a favourite because he'd shot it out beside the old man when the Ruffians drove them from Ossawatomie. And Charlie Tidd was an ugly young brute with a temper to match.

There were two sets of brothers, the Thompsons and the Coppocs, just raw youngsters, but all I remember of them is that Dauphin Thompson was a fair-haired cherub who blushed like a girl, Bill Thompson was a jolly soul with a great fund of stories, and Ed Coppoc was a sober youth with nursery manners who called me "sir". And aside from Joe

244

there were three or four blacks, but they joined late in the day, and the only ones of whom I have any image were Emperor Green, an eye-rolling yes-massa critter, and a middle-aged Scotch-mulatto with the astonishing name of Dangerous Newby.[45]

Those, then, were John Brown's "pet lambs", as I remember them – lively youths without much schooling, but fanatics to a man, and as I note them down, pictures of memory rise before me: Leeman, slim of face and figure, lolling with his feet on the table, cigar at a jaunty angle, talking big; Hazlett haw-hawing at Bill Thompson's jokes; the three Brown brothers playing nap, Oliver's fine profile and curly hair in the lamplight, Watson intent on his cards, Owen like a benign bullock; Jerry Anderson snapping checkers across the board, telling young Ed Coppoc he knew nothing about the game; the blacks muttering quietly in a corner, except for Joe, who often as not would be in the kitchen, listening to J.B. prosing away in his chair by the stove – the old man was always there of an evening because, he said, he didn't like to damp the spirits of the young men by his presence in the common-room; Martha peeling potatoes for next day's dinner, pushing the hair out of her eyes with a damp hand; Stevens and Taylor on the porch, discussing the hereafter; little Annie perched on her stool, keeping an eye on the distant road fading into the dusk.

All gone now, every one, and I wonder if the Kennedy farm is still there in peaceful Maryland, or if it has crumbled into a ruin of planks and shingles, overgrown in that lonely field, or perhaps there's a new farm altogether, whose tenants wonder what those strange conspirators were like, so long ago.

I have another strong memory of J.B. conducting communal prayers night and morning, the great bearded head with its fine mane of greying hair thrown back, eyes closed while he exhorted God fit to shake the roof; or reading aloud some blood-and-thunder passage from the Old Testament. Often he would give us a brief sermon, usually on a text describing the destruction of the Amalekites or another of those unfortunate tribes who were forever being smitten hip and thigh.

If you'd seen him then, in full cry, you'd have believed all the stories about his fanaticism, yet at other times he could be as jolly as Punch. We occasionally played games on the meadow before the house (with Annie keeping watch), baseball or Tom Tiddler, and I taught them football as played at Rugby in my time, with a bladder for a ball; they took to it like sailors to rum, charging and hacking in fine style, and J.B. roared and hurrah'd and laughed so much he had to sit down. He would sometimes wrestle with his sons, and beat Watson and Owen easily, but Oliver nothing could shift. I wrestled with J.B. once myself, at his invitation, thinking I'd best go easy on the old fellow, but it was like being wrapped in wire hawsers with a scrubbing brush buried in your neck, and he grassed me before I knew it.

Sometimes he cooked breakfast, to give Martha a rest, skilleting out the eggs and ham in his shirt-sleeves – that was the time I noticed his toes sticking out of his old boots, and on that same occasion he lost his temper: he'd brewed tea for all of us, Watson wanted coffee, words were exchanged, Watson sassed him, and J.B. suddenly blazed up and let drive a fist. Watson skipped away, they glared at each other, and then J.B. fairly bawled him to bits about duty and respect for elders and ungrateful children. Watson was on the verge of tears, but still came back at him, shouting: "The trouble is you want your sons to be brave as tigers, but still afraid of you!" J.B. glowered at him a full minute, and then took Watson's head in the crook of his arm and held it against his breast, ruffling his hair and smiling, and damned if Watson didn't start blubbing in earnest.

I reckon he'd summed the old man up pretty well. J.B. was a natural tyrant, and his sons treated him as the Children of Israel served God, with terrified affection. Watson told me an astonishing story of how he'd punished them in childhood: he'd announce a number of strokes of his belt, say twelve, but he'd give them only *six*, and then *they* had to give *him* the other six. "'Twas the most awful punishment anyone could give a child," says Watson. "Imagine, havin' to lick your own *father*! I tell you, Josh, it near broke my heart. Say, didn't it keep us good, though!"

It wouldn't have kept *this* infant good; I'd have laced the old bugger till his arse fell off. But then, I never had any proper filial regard, and if you'd ever met my guv'nor you'd understand why.

While I remember, J.B. had a great way with animals; he knew horses and they knew him, and he could quiet a barking hound just by glancing at it. But the strangest thing was when a brace of wrens flew into the common-room where he was writing, fluttering about his head. When he went upstairs, they flew away, but later, when he was writing again, back they came to pester him. At last he went outside, and they flew ahead, twittering, to their nest in the brush – and there was the ugliest copperhead you ever saw, hissing and buzzing its tail. J.B. blew its head off with one shot – and when next he sat down to write, damned if the wrens didn't bowl in, perching on his table, even hopping on to his sleeve, doing everything but shake his hand. "They know a friend when they see one," says he, and for weeks afterwards, when he was writing, the wrens would look in to pass the time with him.

Another critter whose regard for J.B. piqued my interest as the weeks went by was . . . Joe. In all our time at the farm I doubt if he ever strayed ten yards from me, but he played it well, and no one ever suspected he was my watchdog, ready to bite. He was at pains to conceal his intelligence and schooling, too, taking the silent dignified line, but always showing willing – he was the keenest hand in our football games, scrimmaging with the best of them – and was pretty well liked, especially by J.B. What intrigued me was that Joe seemed equally taken with the old man; I've told you how he'd listen to J.B.'s gassing in the kitchen of an evening, and in the talks where we all sat round debating half-baked philosophy and how society ought to be put right, or religion and military tactics, and J.B. started laying down the law, I'd catch Joe watching him with a strange, intense look in those awful bloodshot eyes. And when J.B. got on his slavery hobby-horse, as he always did, Joe would sit back with his lids half-closed, and I would wonder what was going on in that shrewd black mind.

247

The arms arrived in August, fifteen cases of Sharps rifles and the revolvers. Owen Brown had been our teamster in the early weeks, driving the wagon up to Chambersburg to take letters to Kagi, and to pick up supplies discreetly in villages along the route; now Joe and I went with him to collect the arms, and while Joe and Owen stowed them in the wagon, Kagi drew me aside, looking grave.

"This plan of yours," says he. "I'll allow it's sound – but you're counting on a hundred men! Joshua, I don't see us raising half that number!"

I asked, what about the free blacks in Canada, who were supposed to be in a great sweat to join us, and he grunted.

"Junior's up there now – you may guess how many he'll raise! Oh, I should have gone myself, instead of wasting my time here, being a postmaster! And no sign of funds coming in, either; you'll be out of food shortly, and the boys daren't look for work down yonder." He shrugged angrily, then brightened again. "Still there's hope yet, for money *and* men – you know J.B. is coming up here to meet Frederick Douglass next week?"

Even I had heard of Douglass, the greatest black man in America, an escaped slave who moved in the highest circles, published his own newspaper, lectured all over, even in Europe, and was the nearest thing to a black messiah since Toussaint l'Ouverture.

"J.B. hopes to persuade him to join the raid," says Kagi. "Oh, if he but could – why, it would change our fortunes at a stroke! Every black in America and Canada would flock to him . . . well, enough, anyway! The trouble is, he's always

248

declared against violence, blast it! We must just see what J.B. can do with him."

This was the worst news I'd heard in months. Suppose this infernal nigger *did* throw in with Brown, and brought even fifty with him? The old buzzard would be into Harper's Ferry like a shot – and where would poor Flashy be then? Skipping for the timber, that was where . . . with the likes of Joe Simmons looking to put a bullet in my back. But, steady on – Douglass most likely wouldn't come to scratch, and all would be well. One thing was sure: when J.B. met him at Chambersburg, I was going to be on hand.

Luckily, J.B. was all for it, saying it was right and useful that Douglass should meet "our strategian", as he called me, and when Joe, inevitably, asked to come along, he agreed right off; it would be good for Douglass to see such a fine upstanding man of colour in the forefront of the cause, he said.

The meeting took place in great secrecy, because J.B.'s fears of betrayal were mounting by the day, what with neighbours prying and our young men behaving carelessly, showing themselves about the farm and writing indiscreet letters to wives and sweethearts, making no secret of what was afoot. I remember Leeman reading aloud an effusion to his mother, about "our secret association of as gallant fellows as ever pulled trigger", and how we were soon going to "exterminate slavery", and J.B. overhead him and pitched right in.

"It isn't enough that folk come spying about us, stopping us on the road, demanding to know our business – you have to write this kind of foolishness, too! Think of the burden of secrecy you put on your mother! And the rest of you, writing to girls, and special friends, telling of our location and all our matters! We might as well get it published in the *New York Herald* and be done with it! Now, drop it, d'you hear?" He scorched them with a look, and stumped off, and Leeman rolled his eyes and told Dauphin Thompson that he'd better mind what he wrote to those saucy little snappers of his; the infant blushed like a beetroot.

So we stole into Chambersburg by night, J.B. and Joe in the wagon, myself on the mule, and lay up in a deserted quarry. The old man was more nervous than I'd ever seen him, probably because he was in such a sweat to enlist Douglass – and I nearly caught a bullet as a result. It was around dawn that Joe and I heard someone coming, and when Joe shook J.B. awake, damned if he didn't come to with his Colt in his fist, loosing off a shot that blew splinters from the rock beside my head. It shook the old fool as much as it did me, and he was fairly twitching by the time Kagi hove in view, with Douglass and a young nigger in tow.

Douglass was one of those mulattos who are more white than black; but for the wiry hair he might have been Spanish or Italian, and I found myself reflecting yet again on the oddity that the smallest visible touch of the tar-brush in a white man makes him "black", but a trace of European in a negro don't make him "white". Douglass was altogether white in speech and style, but I doubt if he knew it or cared; he had a fine sense of his own dignity, which would have irked me whatever colour he was, but while he talked down his fine straight nose at least he had none of the resentful spite or childish airs that had made George Randolph such a confounded bore.[46]

It soon became plain that he was far too level-headed to be swayed by J.B.'s nonsense, or to beat about the bush. He listened soberly while the old man told him that the die was cast, it was Virginia or bust, and what did Douglass think of that? Douglass told him, straight, that it was not only wrong, and crazy, but downright wicked: it was an attack on the U.S.A., it would rouse the country against the abolitionists, do untold harm to their cause, and be fatal not only to Brown and his gang but to every slave who was fool enough to run off and join the rebellion. I wanted to cry hear, hear, and wondered why none of Brown's supporters had had the spirit to say it to him long ago.

J.B. said he didn't care two cents if the country was roused; it needed rousing. And Douglass couldn't conceive what the taking of Harper's Ferry would mean – why, it would be a sign to the slaves that deliverance was at hand, they would burst their chains and rally to his banner in thousands, not only in Virginia but throughout all Israel, amen! He was in his best raving style, pacing about the quarry, arms flailing and eyes flashing, while Douglass waited stern-faced for him to run out of wind. When he did, Douglass asked me to describe the men and means at our disposal.

It was my chance, and I took it, telling the simple truth without opinion, while J.B. stood nodding triumphantly as though to say: "There – you see!" Douglass sat back against the rock and looked up at him.

"I can't debate the cause with you, John; I'm no match for you in such matters. But from what your comrade tells me of the place, and all you've said, I'm convinced you are going into a perfect steel trap. You'll never get out alive, you'll be surrounded with no hope of escape –"

"If we're surrounded we'll find means to cut our way out!" cries J.B. "But it won't come to that – we'll have the leading men of the district prisoners from the start! With such hostages we can dictate our terms, don't you see?"

Douglass stared in disbelief. "You can't think it! Why, man, Virginia will blow you and your hostages sky-high rather than let you hold Harper's Ferry an hour!" He turned to me. "Is that not so, Mr Comber? You are a soldier, I believe –"

"He's a sailor!" roars J.B. "Oh, can you not see, Douglass, that even if we were destroyed altogether, we should have won the victory? The fire would have been kindled, the flag unfurled, the nation shaken from its slumber . . ."

And so on, ranting and pleading by turns, while Douglass exclaimed in anger or shook his head in despair. They argued back and forth for hours, J.B. insisting on a sudden war-like stroke, Douglass trying to persuade him that if he must go south he should do it gradually, helping slaves to escape to havens in the hills and so building a resistance that couldn't be ignored. They left off only at dusk, agreeing to meet again next day, and when we parted Douglass stepped aside to shake my hand.

"You are English, are you not? Well, sir, I must tell you that your country is dear to me beyond all others, for it gave me sanctuary from my enemies here. Indeed," says he, looking stuffed, "I owe my name to Scotland, and my liberty to England. 'Douglass' I borrowed from 'The Lady of the Lake', and English friends purchased my freedom." He

251

sighed, with a wry smile. "Ironic, is it not? America cast off a royal tyranny to found a free republic, yet it was the land of royal tyranny that bought my liberty from the free republic which had stolen it."

"Ah, well," says I, "always happy to oblige, don't ye know." It sounded a bit lame, so I added: "Cost a bit o' brass, did it?"

He blinked. "Seven hundred and ten dollars," says he, rather stiff. "And ninety-six cents."

"Bless my soul!" says I. "Well, there it is. Easy come, easy go, what?"

He gave me an odd look, and a brief good-night, and steered clear of me when the meeting resumed next day. He and J.B. were still altogether at odds, and when the old man begged him to join the raid, Douglass refused point-blank; much as he loved and respected J.B., his conscience wouldn't let him. Aye, thinks I, we've heard that tale before. Still J.B. wouldn't let up, putting his arm round his shoulders and breathing zeal.

"Come with me, Douglass!" cries he. "I will defend you with my life! I need you, my friend, for when I strike, the bees will start to swarm, and I shall want you to help hive them! Oh, think what it will mean to them if you, of all black men, aye, with the stripes of the lash upon you, are there to greet them sword in hand amidst the smoke of battle!"

That's the way to drum up recruits, thinks I. Douglass, sensible chap, wouldn't have it, but he told the young darkie he might go along if he liked, and to our surprise the fellow, Emperor Green, snuffled and muttered: "Ah guess Ah'll go wid de ole man." He looked as though he'd sooner have gone to China, but I suspect that word of J.B.'s plan had spread among the wealthier free blacks, and they were eager to have as many coloureds in the business as possible, so poor old Emperor may just have been doing what he was told.

It was a fine cheery trip back to the farm, I don't think, with J.B. deep in the dumps; he'd been so sure he could persuade Douglass, and all he'd got was a complete damper and one run-down nigger. To make matters worse (or rather better), we soon had word from Kagi that John junior had made nothing of the Canadian blacks, and that various white men on whom J.B. had been relying weren't coming – some wanted a definite date, others wanted to get the harvest in, or didn't fancy Virginia, and one had decided to study law instead. But the worst blow of all to J.B. was when two of his sons, Salmon and Jason, who were up north, wrote that they weren't joining. Salmon was quite brutal about it, saying that he knew the old man, and he would just dally until he was trapped.

So there it was, as autumn advanced: no more men, no more money, J.B. in the sullen frets and growling about betrayal, our situation at the farm growing more precarious by the day, and the young men restless and writing ever longer letters home – I couldn't have wished for a better state of affairs, and looked forward to the enterprise being abandoned any day.

It was interesting to watch the nerves starting to fray with the uncertainty. It's always the way: men facing a definite task, however desperate, are manageable, but give 'em a leader who can't make up his mind and they go all to bits. Quarrels became more frequent, Bill Thompson ran out of jokes, Leeman and Hazlett no longer got up to larks, and for the first time I heard murmurs that the raid should be given up, that it was madness with no more men coming in, and Harper's Ferry would prove a death-trap. The youngsters, who'd been so full of ginger a month before, were looking uneasy, Watson Brown confided to me that he wanted nothing but to be home with his wife and baby, and even Oliver, the coolest of hands, wore a tired frown on his handsome face – I'd seen dried tears on Martha's cheeks, and knew she'd been trying to talk him out of it.

To add to the gloom, she and Annie went back north in September, but one who wasn't missed was J.B. himself on the occasions when he went up to Chambersburg to confer with Kagi. He was at his wit's end for funds, and bit the heads off Leeman and Tidd just for lighting cigars, crying that if he had half the money that was wasted on smoking, he could have outfitted an army. Leeman threw down his weed in a temper, and Tidd flung out of the house, saying he'd had enough. He came back, though, after three days spent croaking to Cook down at the Ferry. Meanwhile J.B. was off to Chambersburg again, and the general feeling was that he could stay there, and the rest of us could go home.

No such luck. He drove up next day, bringing the famous thousand pikes with him, and tried to make it an occasion for rejoicing, saying here was proof that our friends had not forgotten us, but the mere sight of that great heap of lumber and metal lying in the yard sent everyone's spirits into their boots. He drove us to work fitting the pike heads and stowing them in the loft, and then had Stevens call a drill parade; we'd been getting slack in his absence, he said, and must brisk up directly, for the time was coming when we must prove ourselves in earnest.

"Sure, next summer, maybe," mutters Jerry Anderson, and Bill Thompson cried no, no, we mustn't be in such a rush, 1869 would be soon enough, if we weren't all dead of boredom by then. The niggers haw-hawed at this, but Joe rounded on them, telling them to mind what they were about, and fall in like the captain said. Stevens marched 'em up and down for an hour, while I watched from the veranda (chiefs of staff don't drill, you see), and a more ill-natured parade I never saw. Now's your time, Flash, says I to myself, and when they'd fallen out and eaten supper in sullen silence, I joined Stevens, who was having a brood to himself in the yard.

"Aaron," says I, mighty earnest, "I'd value your opinion. This plan of mine . . . I've done it as best I known how, J.B. is all for it, and so, I believe, is Kagi – but you're the only real soldier in this outfit." I looked him in the eye. "Straight, now – what d'ye think of it?"

"Well, it's a real fine plan, I guess," says he, in his slow way. "For a full company of soldiers. For our poor few . . ." He shrugged his big shoulders. "I reckon Harper's Ferry could be a right pretty place to die."

I nodded solemnly. "So think I. Well, my life don't matter." God, the things I've said. "And I know you don't count yours – like me, you feel it's a small price to pay for the cause. But . . ." I paused, a noble soul troubled ". . . what of the younger men – and the blacks? Is it right that they should be sacrificed? You see my plight, old fellow – it's my

254

plan that is dooming them . . . their deaths will lie to my account . . . ah, that's what burdens my spirit!"

This kind of soul-lashing was small talk at Kennedy Farm that summer, and meat and drink to mystic idiots like him. I knew I'd hit pay-dirt when I saw his jaw tighten; he shook his head sternly.

"Everyone counted the cost before he came," says he. "They'll give their lives gladly – after all, there is a better life beyond, and the door is always open. To pass through is but a small step," continues the great loony, "and if in passing it falls to us to do a noble thing, then who shall mind a moment's affliction, knowing that in death lies victory, not only for us but for the thousands enslaved and oppressed?"

"God bless you, old fellow!" cries I, and wrung his hand. "Gad, but you put it well! You've lifted a weight from my mind, I can tell you!" I hesitated. "See here, Aaron, will you do something for me?"

"What's that, Joshua?"

"Talk to the others . . . the younger men . . . as you've talked to me – you know, about passing through, and victory, and . . . and so on. They'll heed you, because . . . well, you have such faith, you see, and a gift of words! I mean, if I were to say to 'em: 'We're all dead men, but it's worth it' . . . well, there you are, you see! I don't put it too well, do I? But you can, old boy! Oh, 'twill raise their hearts – why it may make all the difference, and ensure that dear old J.B.'s dream comes true!"

You see my game: being a respected senior, and a spiritualist, he was just the man to put the wind right up our younger enthusiasts with his reassuring chat about the life to come; with luck he'd reduce the low spirits of Kennedy Farm to absolute zero. Well, he did more than that; God knows what he said to them, *privatim et seriatim*, over the next two days, but it dam' near caused a mutiny. Suddenly, Harper's Ferry was finding no takers at all on 'Change. Owen got wind of the disaffection, and reported to J.B., reminding him glumly of what happened to Napoleon when he marched on Moscow against the popular will, and the old boy took his head in his hands and groaned. Then he

255

called us all into the common-room, and brooded at us like a vulture on a tombstone.

"I hear," growls he, "that with the exception of Kagi, who I know is staunch, you are all opposed to striking the blow at the Ferry. I feel so depressed that I am almost willing to abandon the undertaking for the time being." He threw back his head, waiting, but only Owen contradicted him, saying we had come too far, and must go ahead.

"Must we?" grunts J.B., and glanced at me. "Joshua?"

I drew myself up, all Horse Guards, and spoke with deep feeling. "You know my sentiments, captain. But since the plan is mine, I don't feel entitled to a voice. I must beg to be allowed to abstain."

Rather neat, I thought, but one who obviously didn't think so was Joe. He was glaring at me fit to kill – my abstention looked to him like a rank betrayal of my engagement to the Kuklos. He burst out: "Well, Ah ain't abstainin'! Ah say we go, like cap'n says!"

J.B. stared, frowning in astonishment – it came as a shock to him, I think, to be reminded that Joe knew all about the plan – the other blacks didn't, you see, being mere cannon-fodder who hadn't been admitted to our councils. No one else spoke; even Stevens stood mum, and I could only conclude that in talking to the young men he had realised their deep reluctance, and lost heart himself. Personally, I was offering up a silent thanksgiving, for I was sure that in the presence of those sullen, uneasy faces, J.B. was going to have to call it a day at long last. He gave Joe a weary, wintry smile.

"I thank you for your trust and loyalty, Joe," says he, "but I fear that you and I and Owen and Kagi – and Joshua, too, I believe – can hardly do the thing alone. For myself, I have only one life to live, and to lose, but I am not so strenuous for my plans as to carry them through against the company's wishes." He paused, sighing, and rubbed his forehead. All over, thinks I – and then the cunning old bastard faced his hole card. "Very well . . . I resign. We will choose another leader, and I will faithfully obey him, reserving only the right to advise when I see fit."

256

There was a gasp of dismay. J.B. bowed his head and walked from the room without another word . . . and would you credit it, within five minutes that pack of brainless sheep had re-elected him! Unanimously, too – for when I saw where they were going, two of the youngest shedding tears of remorse, the others shamed into a renewal of holy zeal, you may be sure I cast my lot with the majority. I could have throttled the old swine; the whole crazy scheme had been within a shaving of collapse, and he'd swung them round simply by passing the decision to them. I still say he wasn't a good leader, but he was one hell of a farmyard politician.

You'd have thought, with that moral victory under his belt, that he'd have gone for the Ferry then and there, while the boys were still excited in their reaction, and indeed for a couple of days I was in a mortal funk that he would do just that. Kagi, who must have got wind of our little mutiny, was writing urgently from Chambersburg, insisting it was now or never: the harvest had been good, so we'd have ample forage in Virginia, the moon was right, and the slaves were restive because the suicides had started.[47] Further, Kagi pointed out, we didn't have five dollars left even to buy food – we daren't delay any longer.

Neither, I decided, dare I. All of a sudden, thanks to the mutiny producing the opposite effect to what I'd expected, the raid seemed to be on the cards for the first time, and my thoughts turned to the horse stabled beneath the house, and the road to Washington. The fly in the ointment was Joe, whose suspicions of me had become thoroughly roused; his baleful eye was on me every minute, and he had taken to sleeping across the doorway in the loft. I evolved and rejected half a dozen schemes for evading him – and still J.B. gave no sign of making up his mind. If anything, he was more sunk in despond than ever, fearful that at any moment we might be discovered, and on the other hand fretting that we daren't move without what he called "a treasury to sustain our campaign".

"There's a bank in Harper's Ferry, ain't there?" cries Jerry Anderson, and J.B. exploded.

"We are not thieves!" cries he. "Oh, for a few hundred

dollars! I shall write to Kagi again – he must find us something!"

And Kagi, damn him, did.

*   *   *

It was a dirty October night when the blow fell. J.B. was in the kitchen, writing, and the rest of us were yawning and snarling after a day which had seen us mooning indoors, confined by the driving rain, with nothing to do but clean weapons and make do and mend and croak at each other. Supper had been a meagre affair, and I was noting with satisfaction that the feverish burst of enthusiasm which had followed J.B.'s re-election had dwindled altogether after days of inaction. What had damped everyone's spirits most of all had been an announcement from the old man that he was contemplating "a decisive act in two or three weeks" – we'd heard *that* before, and as Leeman pointed out, in less than a week, never mind two or three, we'd be forced to disperse, if only to find some grub . . . and then there was a clatter of boots on the veranda, every hand was suddenly reaching for a rifle or revolver, the lamp was doused, and Stevens was challenging: "Who goes there?"

"It's Santa Claus – old Kriss Kringle, and see how you like it!" laughs an exultant voice, and in an instant the bar had been slipped and the lamp rekindled, and Kagi was standing grinning all over his face in the doorway, with the rain pouring off his shawl. There was a tall fellow with him, and as Kagi ushered him into the light I saw that he limped heavily and had one eye missing in his pale, sickly face.

"This is Frank Meriam!" cries Kagi. "Where's the captain?"

J.B. emerged from the kitchen. "Captain Kagi! What does this mean? Why are you not at Chambersburg?"

"Chambersburg, nothing, I've just come from the Ferry!" Kagi was afire with excitement. "Frank just came in by train today – oh, go ahead, Frank, show 'em!"

The tall fellow pulled out a satchel from beneath his coat, undid the strap, and opened it over the table – and out poured a cascade of dollars, glittering and jingling. There

258

were cries of amazement as Kagi stirred them on the table, laughing, and J.B. plumped down in a chair, staring in disbelief, while Kagi explained that Meriam was a friend from the North who had heard of J.B.'s dire need of funds, and here he was, at the eleventh hour, with his personal contribution to the cause. J.B. rose with tears in his eyes and seized Meriam's hand.[48]

"God has sent you!" cries he. "He has seen His children's need and filled their measure, yea, to overflowing! How much is there?"

"Six hundred bucks!" cries Kagi, and J.B. laid his hands on the gelt and raised his shaggy head in prayer, praising the Lord that He had furnished means to take His servants over Jordan and loose the whirlwind in Israel . . . and it seemed to me to be just the right time, as they all stood with bowed heads, muttering their amens, to slip quietly out of the still-open door, button my coat, vault over the veranda rail, and make a bee-line for the stable door at the end of the lower storey.

For I'd known, when the first coin clattered on the table, that all my hopes of many months had been dashed at the last minute: he would go to Harper's Ferry, and I'd never get a better chance to light out for Washington and safety; I'd done my best, I had my boots on, my Tranter in my belt, and a clear road to Frederick (or any station bar Harper's Ferry) where I could board a train south. As I fumbled for a match, lighting the stable lamp, I was telling myself that once I'd ridden a hundred yards I'd be free, for there wasn't but the one horse, a sorry screw, but he'd do. I saddled him in feverish haste, soothing him as I slipped the bridle over his head . . . ten seconds and I'd be out and away, and I was leading him to the door, gulping with excitement, when I bore up with a whinny of terror and stood rooted. Black Joe was standing in the doorway, hands loose at his sides, looking like the Wild Man of Borneo.

"You stinkin' snake!" says he. "I always knew you'd run at the last! Git yo' hand away f'm yo' belt!"

There was no point in pretending I was taking the beast out for exercise. I lifted my hands.

259

"Don't be a fool, Joe!" I croaked. "You don't need me
– he's going to the Ferry, dammit! That's all Atropos wanted
– it don't matter whether I'm there or not! Look, if you let
me go, I'll –"

"I ought to burn yo' brains!" snarls he, taking a pace
forward. "An' git away f'm that hoss! Now, *Mistuh* Comber,
you come ahead good an' slow – an' git yo' dirty ass back
inside that house!"

"What for? For Christ's sake, man, see sense! He can run
his bloody raid without me – or you! Look, we can both
slide out –"

"You made a deal, you dam' traitor! Fi' thousan' dollahs,
'member? An' yo' goin' through with it, the whole way!" I
must have moved a hand, for suddenly there was a pistol in
his fist, the hammer back. "An' you know *why* you's goin'
through with it, *Mistuh* Comber? 'Cos that good ole man up
theah, he's a-countin' on you! *He* needs you, 'cos they ain't
another man in his jackass outfit can plan or plot wo'th a
dam, 'cept you!" The hideous black face split in an awful
grin. "So yo' goin' to be at his side . . . *Joshua*, to keep him
right in his raid, *an'* when he takes to the hills with the
coloured folks, *an'* when he rides south to set the people
free! All the way, *Joshua*, you heah me?"

I was so flabbergasted I could hardly find words to protest.
"You're crazy! He'll never raise a rebellion! He'll come
adrift before he's clear of the Ferry, you fool! His raid'll be
a farce – but it don't matter! The raid *itself* is all that Atropos
wants –"

"– Atropos!" cries he. "– him an' every other lousy
slaver! You think Ah'm doin' his dirty work?" He lunged
towards me, waving the pistol in my face. "You think Ah'm
jes' 'nother yes-massa nigger, don't yuh? You think Ah'm
a chattel of that fat bastuhd M'sieu Atropos Goddam La
Force, 'cos he petted me an' let me screw his woman, an'
done me all kinda benefits? Well, mebbe Ah was once, but
not no mo'!" His breath hit my face like a furnace blast,
and the dreadful yellow-streaked black eyes rolled in frenzy.
"You know why? 'Cos Ah foun' me a *man* – a real man, a
simple, no-'count ole farmer that tret me like a man, an'

260

talked with me like a man! Not like Ah wuz dirt, or a pet dog like when Ah was in the schoolroom with that – Atropos La Force that allus got fu'st pick o' the sugar cookies an' to ride the rockin'-hoss while Ah wuz the goddam *groom!*" He stepped back, shaking, and lowered the pistol from beneath my petrified nose. "An' he's gonna set ma people free! John Brown's gonna do that! An' yo' gonna see he does, too, oh, right sure you are, *Mistuh* Joshua Comber! An' Ah'm gonna be right theah to see you do it!"

His hand flickered, and the pistol was gone. Another flicker, and it was in his hand again. He grinned at me, nodding. "See?"

Another bloody madman – my God, was anyone in America sane? In a flash I understood the way he'd watched Brown, and hung on his words, and sat in the kitchen listening to his babblings – why, the old bugger had converted him! I couldn't credit it – not Black Joe, the shrewdest, wickedest, best-read nigger in Dixie, whose slavery had been a rosebed compared to anything he could hope for as a free man? But it had happened, plainly; one look at those blood-injected eyes told me that, and God knows I'd seen enough of human lunacy not to waste speculation on the why's and wherefore's. And I was to be driven to sure destruction, just because this demented darkie had seen the light! I hadn't a hope of running now, with this fearsome black gunslick dogging my every move. But I could still try to reason with him.

"Joe, in God's name, listen! You're wrong! He doesn't have a hope, I tell you! He's going to his death – so are all the rest of 'em! Nothing I can do will save him! Damnation, man, you've heard the talk – the slaves won't rise, and he'll be –"

"Shut yo' lyin' mouth!"

"It's the truth, man! Dammit, you say yourself I'm the only one who can make a plan and reckon the odds – d'ye think I don't know, you bloody fool?"

He hit me a back-hander that sent me sprawling on the straw, then leaned down to drag me to my feet. "We goin' to the Ferry, you an' me, 'long o' the ole man – an' then to

261

the hills!" says he, his face close to mine. "You play false
– you even *look* false, an' Ah kill you dead!"

A voice shouted, outside and overhead; it was Stevens.
"Joshua, you down there? Josh?"

Joe let go and stepped to the door. "Jes' seein' to the
wagon, Mass' Aaron! We be theah d'reckly!" He beckoned
to me, stepping aside to let me pass out into the rain. "Dead
. . . 'member?"

*   *   *

Some wiseacre once said that the prospect of death concentrates the mind wonderfully, but I'm here to tell you that
the chance to work for a reprieve concentrates it a whole
heap more. I was in the true-blue horrors when I came up
from that stable, with Joe looming at my heels, and was no
way cheered by the celebration taking place in the common-
room. That pile of cash seemed to have acted like a tonic,
heaven knows why, and all around were smiling faces and
bustling activity, Kagi was pumping my hand and crying, at
last, at last!, and J.B. was like a man transformed, eyes
shining fiercely and beard bristling as he stood by the table,
fingering the dollars while he dictated to Jerry Anderson,
whose pencil was fairly flying across the paper. Tidd, I
remember, was singing "The Girl I Left Behind Me" in his
fine tenor, and the younger men were joining in and larking
about – and all because it was now certain that in a few
hours they'd likely be getting shot to pieces and dying along
the Potomac or Shenandoah. I'd seen it before, the hectic
gaiety that can take hold of young fools at the imminent
(but not too imminent) prospect of action after they've
waited long; I've never been prone to it, myself. I had my
work cut out keeping the upper lip in good order, while
asking myself fearfully how the devil I was going to keep a
whole skin this time.

There was only one way that I could see, and I bent my
mind to it with everything I knew. If Harper's Ferry could
be taken with no heads broken – and I knew it could be,
just, provided my plan was followed to the letter, and nothing went amiss – then there must arise a moment, surely,

262

when I could give Joe the slip. A few seconds was all I'd need (it's all I've ever needed), and I'd be into the undergrowth and going like hell's delight, on foot if need be. He couldn't watch me every second, not with the confusion that must occur in taking the armoury gates, the arsenal, and the rifle works. So that same evening, when J.B. was poring over my plans and consulting with Kagi and Stevens, and next day when (after a damned sleepless night, I can tell you, with Joe on a hair-trigger at my side) the final preparations were made, I worked on every last detail of the scheme as though my life depended on it – which it did . . .

Kagi and Stevens to silence the watchman on the Potomac bridge as we approached – they were the best men, for the most vital task. The surly Tidd, next best, to cut the telegraph wires, with the garrulous Cook, who knew the Ferry well, to show him the way. Oliver, the best of the Browns, to take and guard the Shenandoah bridge; his brother Watson to guard the Potomac bridge. (The third brother, Owen, I insisted must stay at the farm, to hold our base – the truth was that I wanted him as far from J.B. as could be, because he was the kind of ass who'd argue with the old man and set him dithering with indecision.) With the bridges in our hands, I'd see to the armoury gates myself, with J.B. and Stevens . . . then to the arsenal across the street, leave Hazlett on guard, with anyone but Leeman (they were too harum-scarum to trust together) . . . the rifle works were nearly half a mile off – aye, Kagi could see to them . . . and that would be Harper's Ferry receipted and filed . . . for a few hours at least. Provided the bridge and armoury watchmen could be dealt with quietly, there was no reason why we shouldn't remain undetected until daybreak . . . and long before then I'd have slipped Joe, if I had to kill him to do it, and be on my merry way.

I didn't consult or argue about these dispositions, but rapped them out in my sharpest style, with J.B. nodding alongside, and the fellows accepted them without a murmur. They spent that last day cleaning weapons and assembling gear, and Stevens and I inspected 'em to the last button, while J.B. did the really useful work – writing out our com-

263

missions, if you please! Half the men were "captains" in his army, and the others "lieutenants", except for Taylor, the Canadian, who was too cracked for anything, and of course the niggers, who were all privates. I was a "major", you'll be charmed to know . . . and I have the faded paper beside me as I write, with "John Brown, Commander-in-Chief" in his spidery hand at the foot. I keep it in my desk, alongside my appointment as "Sergeant-General" in the Malagassy army, my Union and Confederate commissions, the illuminated scroll designating me a Knight of the San Serafino Order of Purity and Truth (Third Class), the Order of the Elephant which I picked up in Strackenz, and all the other foreign stuff. Gad, I've been about, though.

Anyway, I left nothing to chance, talking to each man in turn to be sure he knew his duties, and J.B. doled out the "commissions" and read his Constitution, and administered his oath of allegiance to the late-comer Meriam and a couple of the blacks, who hadn't taken them before. Only once was there a cross word, when J.B. tried to interfere with my arrangements for the town; he said our first task must be to detach a party to take hostages, but I put my foot down hard, insisting that it must wait until we had both bridges and the three vital targets – armoury, arsenal, and rifle works – all secure.

He thrust his beard at me, glittering. "My will must prevail in this, Joshua!"

"No, Captain Brown, it must not!" says I. "The hostages can wait a few minutes, until our dispositions are complete. I'll not answer for our safety, or our success, unless the plan is followed to the letter."

It took him aback, but Stevens backed me up, and said he'd 'tend to the hostages himself when the time came. J.B. gave in, sulkily, and then in a moment he was off on another tack, telling Stevens that when he took Colonel Washington hostage, he must on no account forget to bring away Lafayette's pistol and Frederick the Great's sword, and see to it that Washington *in person* handed the sword to one of our blacks. "If he doesn't care for that, no matter. It is symbolic, and right and fitting that the sword of liberty should be placed in a coloured hand." That was J.B. all over.

And then, before I knew it, dusk was falling, and we were sitting down to our last supper in the Kennedy Farm. It was blowing up a wild night outside, and the rain was leaking in – almost as fast as my courage was leaking out, for I was scared as I've seldom been in my misspent life. The last desperate venture of this kind that I'd sweated over had been when the Hyderabadi Cavalry had charged the breach at Jhansi so that I could be deposited, disguised and petrified with funk, inside the fortress wall, there to worm my way into the presence of the delectable Lakshmibai . . . my God, that had been only last year, on the other side of the world! And here I was again, on the lion's lip, forcing my dinner down with Joe's noisy chewing sounding like a deathknell at my ear.

Then supper was over, and we sat about in silence, waiting. There were no jokes now, and the only smiles were nervous grimaces on the fresh young faces round the table. It struck me harder then than it had ever done before, what babes they were, half of 'em with barely a growth of beard on their cheeks, torn between fear and the crazy belief that they were doing the Lord's work, and I felt a sudden anger at bloody John Brown who was leading them to it – and what was a sight worse, leading me. I can see the faces still – Watson Brown poring over a letter from his wife, Oliver's fine features pale in the lamplight, Leeman drumming his fingers and chewing an unlit cheroot, Hazlett sitting back, brushing the fair hair out of his eyes, Tidd scowling as he traced a finger in a puddle of spilt coffee on the board, Aaron Stevens with his hands clasped behind his head, staring up at the ceiling, Kagi pacing about, tight as a coiled spring, old black Dangerous Newby whittling at a stick, the youngest men stifling those yawns that are born not of weariness but of fear, Charlie Cook cursing the rain, Bill Thompson whistling softly through his teeth . . . and Joe seated against the wall, never taking those baleful eyes off me.

J.B. came out of the kitchen, putting on his coat and hat.

"Get on your arms, men," says he. "We will proceed to the Ferry."

There were twenty of us, two by two, and J.B. driving the wagon, which held the pikes and tools for forcing the armoury gates. Every man-jack of us, fifteen white men and six blacks, carried a Sharps rifle and forty rounds, and two revolvers; against the blinding rain we had our hats and loose shawls, and before we were out of the lane and on to the road, we were sodden through. I cast a glance back as we reached the road: Owen and Meriam and one of the youngsters were still on the veranda, outlined against the light from the open door, Owen with his hand raised, although he couldn't have seen us in the dark, and I remembered something he'd said as he shook hands with Watson and Oliver in the moment of parting: "If you succeed, Old Glory'll fly over this farm some day; if you don't, they'll call it a den of thieves and pirates," and Oliver replying with a laugh: "Why, Owen, you can start shaping up a flagstaff right now!"

Neither of 'em believed it. Only two men in that company truly wanted to go to the Ferry – J.B. and Kagi, and of those two only one expected to come out alive, because he was sure God must see him through. One other was *determined* to come out alive, and you may guess who he was, striding resolutely through the wet night with his guts dissolving, conscious of the looming black genie at his shoulder.

Six of us marched before the wagon, Cook and Tidd out in front, then Kagi and Stevens, and last Joe and I, and as we sloshed on through the dark, barely able to see the muddy road before us, I found myself harking back to other desperate night forays – with Rudi Starnberg in the silent, snow-clad woods of Tarlenheim, on our way to carry out

Bismarck's mad design to put me on a European throne; stealing through the pandy lines at Lucknow with Kavanagh, and him figged out as Sinbad the Sailor with his cloak covered in blacking; riding with Mangas Colorado's band of Mimbreno Apaches to descend on a sleeping hamlet of the Rio Grande; hand in hand with Elspeth through that dark garden at Antan' where we'd lain doggo in the bushes and a Hova guardsman had trod on her finger and broken it and the little heroine had never so much as squeaked . . . and at the thought of her golden beauty and warm soft body entwined with mine on the green moss of the Madagascar forest, and now so far away and lost to me, perhaps, forever, I could have raved aloud at the sheer blind cruelty of chance that had landed me in this beastly business – while she was snug and safe in dear old London, aye, and like as not rogering her brainless head off with some fortunate swine, the little trot. I thrust the unworthy thought aside, as I'd done a hundred times in the past, for I've never been sure, you see . . . but whether or no, it didn't matter, I could still see that splendid milk-white shape reclining on the bed at Balmoral, the blonde glory of her hair spilling on the pillows, bright blue eyes wide and teasing, red lips kissing at me over the fan of crimson feathers that was the only thing between me and heart's desire . . .

No, by heaven, I refused to say farewell to all that magnificent meat; I'd win back to her somehow, though hell should bar the way, and give her loving what-for until the springs broke, in spite of J.B. and Joe Simmons and J. C. Spring and every other son-of-a-bitch who was trying to do me down – why, hadn't I taken on a black rascal every bit as big and ugly as Joe that night in Antan', and won through, just as I'd won through all those other terrifying scrapes with Rudi and Kavanagh and the rest? A great rage surged up in me as I blundered along, compounded of lust for Elspeth and hatred against the gods; I was damned if after all I'd suffered it was going to end in a two-bit pest-hole like Harper's Ferry . . .

A low whistle from the dark ahead banished my fond visions: there, a scant mile away through the murk, lights

267

were twinkling dimly – the lights of the little township, and below them, the faint glow of the few lamps that marked the armoury buildings along the Potomac shore, and cast a barely-seen glimmer on the river surface. Left of the armoury, and closer to our line of approach, I could just make out the loom of the covered bridge over the Potomac, with a lamp at either end – that was our first target. The whistle had been the signal that Tidd and Cook were breaking off to cut the first telegraph lines, and now we were hastening down the slope, the wagon jolting behind us, to the near end of the Potomac bridge. The timbers boomed beneath our feet in the wooden tunnel through which ran the Baltimore and Ohio railroad tracks as well as the road; we were running now, and a babble of voices was coming from the far end, where Kagi and Stevens were dealing with the watchman, who seemed to think it was all a joke – "Say, what are you fellers about – t'ain't Hallowe'en for a couple o' weeks yet . . . Goddlemighty, man, take care with that piece!"

I had a glimpse of his scared white face beneath the lamp, and Kagi holding a rifle to his breast, as I ran past, Joe at my elbow, and turned to face the covered bridge entrance. The wagon came rumbling out, with the boys running in file either side of it, and as I called my orders they wheeled away like good 'uns, each to his station. "Watson and Taylor – take the watchman, keep him quiet! Kagi and Stevens, close on the wagon! Halt her there, captain! Oliver – Shenandoah bridge, smart as you can, and quiet!" Oliver ran past me, with Dangerous Newby and Bill Thompson at his heels, and vanished under the trees at my back; J.B. reined in, and Kagi and the others closed round him. Taylor was covering the terrified watchman at the Potomac bridge mouth, and Watson waved his rifle to me in acknowledgment.

Now before I go any further, you should look at my map, which is done as best I can remember, for many of the old landmarks are gone now, so I can't be dead sure where everything was.[49] I've told you how the town lay, and you can see for yourselves, but I must impress on you just how

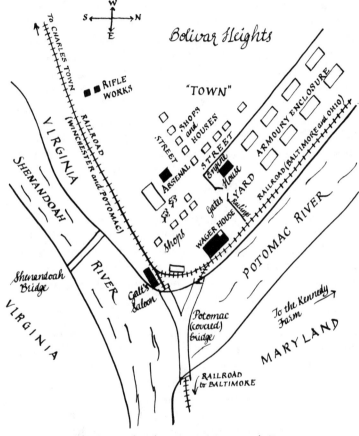

Flashman's sketch-map of Harper's Ferry,
Virginia, scene of John Brown's raid,
October 16-18, 1859

small was the space in which our little drama was to be played out. Coming out of the right fork of the Potomac bridge, you were looking at the Wager House hotel, a large gabled building with two storeys and a basement; it was part of the station and hard by the railroad where it branched right from the covered bridge. To your left, beyond the other railroad track and part-screened by trees, were the Shenandoah bridge and Galt's saloon. Directly ahead of you was the arsenal building, and to the right the gates and railings of the armoury enclosure. Beyond the arsenal and armoury were houses and shops and the town proper. All these places lay within an area not much bigger than a football field, perhaps eighty yards by a hundred, and from the upper floor of the Wager House you could see pretty well all of it, unless there happened to be a tree or a freight car in the way. The space between the hotel and the armoury gates was fairly open, as I remember, and I think part of it was cobbled; there were trees here and there, and I dare say some buildings I've forgotten, but nothing to signify.

"Joe, get the crowbar from the wagon! Aaron, take the sledge! Follow me!" I was legging it for the armoury gates, and J.B. jumped down from the wagon and kept pace with me, the others following. The rain was lighter now, but it was still pretty dark, save where a pool of light was cast by the lamps on the armoury gate-posts. A figure emerged from the shadows, staring towards us, and J.B. lengthened his stride, whipping out his pistol, calling to him to stand. There was a confused babble of who the hell are you, and give me the key this instant, and I'll be damned if I do, and then we were at the big double gates of iron railing, and Joe was snapping the retaining chain with one mighty heave on the crowbar, the gates were thrust back, and Stevens led the rush of half a dozen of our fellows into the yard. There were shouts ahead as two watchmen came running from the nearest buildings, but they stopped short at the sight of the weapons and were surrounded neat as a wink.

I whistled up the wagon, now driven by one of the blacks, and ordered it into the yard. I looked round for J.B., expecting to see him making for the arsenal across the street, but he had his piece to the breast of the first watchman, and was haranguing him in fine style.

"I am Isaac Smith," he was proclaiming himself, "and you are my prisoner! Submit peaceably and no harm will come to you, but if you resist your blood will be on your own head!"

"Ye're drunk, ye old fool! And on a Sunday, too!" cries the other, pushing the gun aside, but Jerry Anderson ran up and clapped a pistol to his head, and he just sank down in the mud, squawking. A voice called out of the misty darkness, from the direction of the town, asking what all the row was about, and I wheeled on Kagi.

"Take three men, round up anyone on the street over there, and bring 'em here, quick and quiet! Leeman, run to the Shenandoah bridge, see if all's well with Oliver! Bring the watchman back here! Dauphin Thompson, fetch the watchman from the Potomac bridge. And both of you – keep 'em quiet, d'ye hear?" Jerry was hustling his stricken watchman to the armoury yard, and J.B. was stalking after them, muttering; I called to him, but he didn't seem to hear – well, someone was going to have to secure the arsenal, and quickly.

"Hazlett, and you, youngster, follow me! Bring the crowbar!" I ran across to the arsenal building; behind me there was a babble of voices at the armoury gate, J.B.'s among them, and Stevens was snapping: "Silence, all of you! Another sound and we'll put you in eternity!" Hazlett came running with the crowbar, and I snatched the lantern from above the door to give him light; he shoved the bar into the jamb, and with a splintering of timber the lock was burst in. It was pitch dark within, but with the lantern I had a glimpse of rifles racked and ammunition boxes piled high; I shoved the lantern into Hazlett's hand.

"Stay here – and keep that glim outside or you'll blow the town sky-high!"

I ran back to the armoury gates just as Kagi arrived, herding three or four complaining citizens with their hands in the air; they seemed to think it was some kind of practical joke until they saw the captured watchmen in the yard, surrounded by levelled rifles, and J.B., beard bristling and eyes glittering, laying down the law in his best pulpit voice.

"Be silent, all of you! I come from Kansas to this State of slavery! I mean to free every negro slave, and to that end I have taken your armoury! If the citizens interfere with me I must only burn the town and have blood! Now, sit down upon the ground, and be quiet all."

They sat, too, scared and staring, all except one old codger who faced up to J.B.

"You're crazy, mister! What d'ye mean, scarin' folks half to death? Now, you put down that gun – why, you're as old as I am, and ought to know better!"

"Hold your tongue, friend, and do as you are bid!" growls J.B., but I heard no more, for at that moment came whooping and laughter behind me, and it was those noisy idiots, Cook and Tidd, to tell me proudly that the wires were cut, both sides. I shut them up fast enough, and then Dauphin was back with the guard from the Potomac bridge, pushing him into the yard. A moment later Leeman came striding across from the trees, flourishing his pistol at a terrified watchman and two fellows whom Oliver had picked up on the Shenandoah bridge.

"All's well!" cries Leeman. "Say, this is a lark, ain't it –"

"Shut up and put those men in the yard! And send Kagi to me – jump to it, man!" There was still the rifle works to attend to, six hundred yards up the Shenandoah shore – a matter which J.B. seemed to have forgotten; he was still hectoring the captives, now about a dozen strong, who were watching him like so many rabbits before a snake. Kagi came running, and I told him to take two blacks to the rifle works, send one of 'em back with the watchman, and sit tight until he heard from me.

He jerked a thumb in J.B.'s direction. "What about the captain? I've been telling him that our first task must be to clear the arsenal, and find wagons to carry off the arms, but all he talks about is his damned hostages! You must tell him, Josh – we ought to be loading up right soon, 'fore we have the town about our ears!"

272

"I'll talk to him when he's got his bearings. Stevens can collect his precious hostages and wagons together, and I'll get J.B. to go through the arsenal in the meantime."

"All right," says he, worried. "But, Josh – don't let him delay, will you? You know what he's like! We must be out of here by daybreak!"

"We will be, never fear!" I knew one who was going to be. "Off with you, John! Good luck!"

He went, with another doubtful look towards J.B., and I strode across to the arsenal, where Hazlett was standing in the doorway, rifle in hand, and took a quick survey around – I could just see Watson Brown under the Potomac bridge lantern; all was quiet towards Galt's saloon, its lights blinking through the trees, and there wasn't a sound from Oliver's station on the Shenandoah bridge; the curtained windows of the Wager House glowed crimson in the dark, and I could hear faint voices and laughter; J.B. and Stevens were in conference under the armoury gate lantern, and beyond them the captives were squatting silent, guarded by Leeman and the others. I looked towards the town: nothing stirred, a few lights shone in the houses only fifty yards away, but there wasn't a soul to be seen; no one was calling out, or coming to see what was amiss, or doing anything at all, apparently, except prepare for bed on a Sabbath night. It had stopped raining. We had taken Harper's Ferry.

I'm quite proud of that, still. Very well, it wasn't Sebastopol – but my plan had gone like clockwork, those gormless boys had played up like old soldiers, and we'd sealed the bridges, cut the wires, taken our three objectives, the town unsuspecting, and all within the hour. God knows I hadn't been a willing performer, and would have been over the hill but for Joe's presence – but, dammit, when you've no choice but to go ahead, your pulses start racing whether you like it or not, and excitement grips you, even though you're scared sick, because you want like hell to accomplish the thing you've set your hand to, however reluctantly. As I stood in the chilly dark, my heart hammering, I felt a great unreasoning exultation, just for an instant before sanity returned, and Joe must have felt it, too, for he grunted "You

273

done that pretty good, Comber", which, considering our relations, was not a bad compliment.

By this time Stevens, Cook, Tidd and a couple of blacks were hurrying off to kidnap the owner of the Washington Farm which lay a few miles up the Potomac shore, with J.B.'s insistence that they bring back Frederick's sword ringing in their ears. He was in an odd state: outwardly very calm, but strangely detached, as though his thoughts were far away; when I reported all well, he just nodded offhand, and when I asked if we should clear the arsenal, he said he would see to it presently, when the hostages had come in. I hinted, delicately, that haste might be advisable, since at any moment some stray citizen might happen by and raise the alarm, but at this he just frowned, stroking his beard, and muttered that we had time enough . . . and gradually it began to dawn on me that *he simply didn't know what to do next*, about finding wagons, or collecting arms, or rousing the slaves, or taking to the hills while our luck held. Now, of all times, he was stricken again with indecision, and retreating into his dreams by the look of him.

Well, it was nothing to me. I'd done my part perforce, and all that mattered now was throwing off the grim black shadow at my side and hitting the high road. I must just wait my chance, so I leaned against one of the gate-posts, smoking a weed and wondering, in an academic sort of way, when J.B. was going to take advantage of the capital start I'd given him.

Time's an odd thing. We hit the town about ten-thirty and secured the strongpoints, and then followed that eerie, tranquil interval of J.B.'s irresolution which no one has ever been able to explain, and which seemed to last forever – in fact it was a bare thirty minutes, until midnight. That was when things began to come adrift, and we had several hours of bloody and farcical confusion until daybreak – yet to me they seemed to pass in a few moments, one crazy incident on top of another in no time at all.

Picture the scene, gentle reader, as midnight approaches. Harper's Ferry drowses placidly 'neath the pall of night, the last gleams of light in its windows blink out one by one as citizens seek their repose, the town drunk nestles contentedly in his gutter, the liberators of Virginia stand around in picturesque uncertainty while their venerable leader contemplates the stars like a fart in a trance, the prisoners mutter sullenly in one of the armoury sheds, and not one solitary soul (least of all J.B. himself) seems to be aware that the revolution has begun. Flashy smokes and sweats, and wishes to heaven that Joe would turn his back just for half a minute – and hark! a shot rings out . . . and believe it or not, no one pays the slightest bloody attention.

It came from the Potomac bridge where, unseen by us, that Canadian halfwit, Taylor, was putting a bullet through the top hair of an inopportune railway guard who had happened along, been challenged, shown fight, and got his skull creased for his pains. We heard *him*, soon enough, bolting out of the covered bridge, roaring and bleeding, and taking refuge in the Wager House – and, so help me, no one emerged to protest or even inquire, the town slept on undisturbed, J.B. left off contemplating to stare towards the hotel, but did nothing, our fellows confined themselves to intelligent questions like "Who the hell was that?" and "Say, did you hear shooting?" . . . and nothing further took place until there came a distant whistle from far down the Baltimore and Ohio track, and presently in steams the east-bound night train for Baltimore, clanking past the armoury and coming to a slow halt near the Wager House only fifty yards from where I stood, at which point the wounded railwayman erupted from the hotel, clutching his bleeding scalp and bawling that there were road agents on the loose, the train engineer, silly ass, got down to investigate, Watson Brown and his idiots opened fire for no apparent reason, an unfortunate nigger (not one of ours) came striding down the track, was challenged by Watson, turned to run and was shot in the back, the engineer leapt back into his cab and reversed twenty yards with great blasts of steam, some stout parties in the coaches began blazing away at Watson's party, passengers were screaming and tumbling from the train, Harper's Ferry began to wake up at last, J.B. strode to the train bellowing for everyone to hold his fire and be calm, and your correspondent began to wonder if this mightn't be a

275

good time to retire – and would have done if Joe hadn't been holding a pistol in each hand and demanding to know what the hell was happening.

Either because of J.B.'s thundering, or more probably because neither side could see properly what they were shooting at, the firing died away after a few moments, and there followed a remarkable conversation between our leader and the engineer. It began, predictably, with J.B. announcing that he had come "to free the slaves at all hazards and in the name of universal liberty, God helping", and the engineer calling him a liar, a lunatic, and a damned jayhawking rascal who'd swing for this, and by the eternal the engineer would be there to see him do it, too. J.B. rebuked him for blasphemy, assured him that no harm was intended to the train or its passengers, and that he would let them proceed so that the railroad authorities should understand that the town was closed to traffic henceforth. The engineer damned his eyes and said he'd swim through seas of blood rather than budge before dawn, when he would inspect the bridge "to see what mischief you infernal scoundrels have done to it". J.B. agreed, and promised to walk over the bridge before the train (which he did, by the way) to show that it was safe.

This discussion took some time, with frequent interruptions, for you must imagine it taking place in darkness illuminated only by the train's headlight and the feeble lamps of the nearest buildings, against a background of babbling passengers being helped into the Wager House, men shouting, females screaming, the shot darkie being carried away, a church bell belatedly sounding the alarm, bewildered citizens seeking enlightenment at the tops of their voices, and some of the bolder spirits who emerged from the shadows for a closer look being seized by our fellows at the armoury gates and sent to join the prisoners in the shed.

But no one from the town showed fight, for several good reasons – it was too dark to tell properly what was taking place, a rumour had spread through the town that we were over a hundred strong, and while the arsenal was bursting with weapons, there was hardly a gun in the town except

276

for a few fowling pieces and the like. So while we held our positions (and J.B. continued to do nothing), the people kept their distance – except for one cool hand, a doctor, who approached the arsenal, was given the rightabout by Hazlett, and then crossed the street bold as brass to demand of J.B. what he thought he was about, and, on being told, denounced him for a murderer.

"The only black you've liberated so far is one who was free already – the poor fellow you shot down on the tracks!" He was a peppery medico this, with a jaw like a pike, and the darkie's gore all over his hands. "Look at that! He's dying this minute, with your bullet in his lung, you old blackguard!"

J.B. said he was sorry for it, but the man had run when called on to halt, and the doctor must consider himself a prisoner.

"Just try it, mister!" cries the sawbones. "Or shoot *me* in the back, why don't you!" And he stamped off to the Wager House, stopping on the way to survey us, and Hazlett at the arsenal, and if ever a man was taking stock, he was – sure enough, two hours later he was riding hell-for-leather for the nearest town to turn out the militia . . . and meanwhile J.B. was waiting and doing nothing, hardly answering when spoken to, and our fellows were fidgeting and muttering, and Joe was growling at me, why wasn't the cap'n takin' a-holt o' things, and why didn't I *tell* him? I said I'd told him, hadn't I . . . and every moment my gorge was rising higher with panic as I wondered if I dared make a run for it . . .

There was a clatter of wheels from the dark, and here came a fine four-horse vehicle wheeling in to the armoury gates, with three white men and about a dozen darkies aboard, and Stevens jumping down, rifle in hand. He helped down one of the whites, a bluff old cove in a grey coat who I guessed was Washington, and I heard him sing out: "This is Ossawatomie Brown of Kansas!" as J.B. strode forward to meet them. One of our darkies jumped down after them, brandishing a sheathed sabre, and calling out: "Here 'tis, cap'n – here de ole sword, sho' 'nuff!" and J.B. seized on it and stood with it in his hand as he told Washington that

277

he had been taken for the moral effect it would give to our cause, but he would be shown every attention, "and if we get the worst of it, your life will be worth as much as mine", whatever that meant. Washington took it mighty cool, saying nothing, and presently he and the two other whites, a man and a youth, were put in the yard, and J.B. supervised the distribution of pikes to the slaves in the captured carriage, telling them they were free men now, and must defend their liberties, and the poor black buggers stood in terrified bewilderment, looking at the pikes as though they were rattlesnakes. A fine rebellion we're going to have, thinks I; ah, well, they'll shape better, no doubt, when they've built their forts in the hills and dug communicating tunnels.

I kept clear of all this, but so did Joe, damn him, and my gorge rose another couple of notches, for the dark was beginning to lift slowly, and I could see clear to the nearest houses of the town, where people were peeping out, and some even gathering on the corners, staring across at us. There were faces at the windows of the Wager House, and hard by it, where the train stood, passengers were climbing aboard, with scared glances in our direction. In the armoury yard all was confusion, for the prisoners had been let out of their shed and were mingling with the newcomers in a great babble of voices, the niggers with the pikes looked ready to weep, and our men were watching anxiously as Stevens and Tidd clamoured around J.B., who now had the sword girt round his middle, and was exulting over a brace of barkers, presumably the property of the late Marquis de Lafayette.

"Why, we got more prisoners here than there is of us!" Tidd was exclaiming, and Stevens was arguing with J.B. about loading up from the arsenal, and getting nowhere; J.B.'s notion was to send Washington's carriage, which was larger than our wagon, over into Maryland, to collect the Kennedy Farm weapons, which Owen would have shifted by now to a school-house closer to the Potomac, and bring them back to supplement the arms in the arsenal. Stevens frowned in dismay.

"But, cap'n, 'twill be full light in an hour! See here, why don't we load up the carriage *an'* the wagon from the arsenal

278

now, with everythin' we need, call in Kagi an' Oliver, an' all of us hightail it out o' here – we can pick up Owen an' the arms from the school-house, an' be in the hills 'fore noon!" He gestured towards the houses, where more people were assembling, watching us. "Look at them folks yonder – how long they goin' to let us alone, you reckon?"

J.B. gave him a stern look. "You forget, Captain Stevens, that it is here, at the Ferry, that the slaves will rally to us. Why, if we were to leave now, we should be abandoning them! No more of that, sir!"

"Well, I don't know that the slaves are coming!" says Stevens. "We saw no sign of 'em when we came in just now, I can tell you!"

"An' it'll take three hours, easy, to get to the school-house an' load up an' come back here again!" cries Tidd. "Then we got to clear out the arsenal – cap'n, it'll be noon 'fore we can get out o' town! Why, the militia'll be here by then!"

"An' come dawn, these folks are goin' to see how few we are!" I could see Stevens was keeping his temper with difficulty. "They ain't goin' to stand by!"

J.B. stilled them with a raised hand, like a patient parent. "The hostages are our assurance of safety. The people will dare nothing against us for fear of harming them. And I will not desert the negroes!" He became peremptory. "Captain Tidd, you and Captains Leeman and Cook will take the carriage away, and receive our pikes and rifles from Owen –"

"But they're three of our best men, sir!" Stevens was near despair. "I beg you, send but one, and some of the slaves!"

But J.B. was deaf to all common sense, and presently the carriage rolled off over the Potomac bridge with Cook at the reins and Tidd and Leeman marching alongside, with a gaggle of the freed darkies in the back. Stevens pleaded with J.B. at least to start clearing the arsenal.

"First I must keep my promise to the engineer," says J.B., and off he went to the train, his rifle cradled in his arm and his sword trailing in the mud, holloing to the engineer that he might get up steam. The townsfolk across the way set up a murmur at the sight of his commanding figure striding

279

towards the tracks, but he paid them no mind at all, and presently the train was chugging slowly on to the covered bridge, with the old man striding ahead of it, and the crowd before the Wager House fallen silent.

"By gad, he's cool!" says Stevens to me. "Too dam' cool! I tell you, Josh, we ain't got but a couple of hours 'fore we'll have to shoot our way out! What ails him? He acts like we was in a town meetin'!"

It was true, and everyone who was through Harper's Ferry will tell you the same – the chancier things got, the calmer grew J.B., as though he were in the grip of some soothing drug. Stevens swore through his teeth. "We've got to get John Kagi down here – he'll take heed of Kagi!" And pat on his words there was a commotion at the Wager House, and one of our niggers came running from under the trees, brandishing his Sharps. The folk scattered to let him through, and he came panting up to tell us he was from the rifle works, and Kagi wanted to know when J.B. planned to retire from the town, because he'd seen a rider galloping along the Charles Town road.

"Damnation, what'd I say?" cries Stevens. "It's but eight miles off! Two, three hours, we'll have the militia on us –"

The crack of a shot interrupted him, sending us scurrying behind the armoury railings, and then came two more, from somewhere in the town. There was a shrilling of women as the people gave back to the houses, except for one fool who made a dart across the street towards the arsenal. One of our men – the younger Thompson, I think – loosed a shot at him, and he threw up his hands and flopped down in the mud, to a chorus of screams and oaths from the Wager House. A couple of men ran out, crouching, and hauled him away, Stevens bawled: "Stand to, men!", and every rifle was trained on the town, but now J.B. was striding towards us from the Potomac bridge, coat flapping, calling to hold our fire.

A man came hurrying from the Wager House, waving his hands as though appealing for calm, and J.B. stopped to talk to him, and presently nodded and came on to us, while the other scampered back to safety. No further shots came, but our fellows stayed at the armoury railings, and behind them the prisoners cowered down, all save old Washington, who stood his ground, arms akimbo.

"Those were only squirrel rifles," says J.B., unconcerned. "There will be no more of that, but be at the ready, men, and keep up a bold front."

"Cap'n," says Stevens, "this won't do. We're in no case to fight, just a handful here an' the rest spread all over –"

"There will be no call to fight," says J.B. "The prisoners are our security."

"If you count on that, sir, you are in error!" It was Washington, loud and steady, not stirring a foot. "Captain Brown, you must give over this madness! Either lay down your arms or avoid the town!" Odd word to use, I remember thinking. "Look yonder, sir! You have put the people in fear, you have shot a man down, you hold us captive here – all to no purpose! Give it up, sir, before worse befalls!"

He was full of spunk and sense, the old soldier,[50] both of which were wasted on our ragged Napoleon. He lifted a commanding hand to Washington.

"Be silent, sir! I have my purpose, as you shall learn – you and all others who live by human bondage! Not another word, sir!"

He stood a long moment, glaring like the wrath of God, and then looked about him, taking a slow survey of the scene, turning on his heel, his rifle at the port. It was full light now, and all plain to see – our men kneeling or standing behind the railings, pieces presented; behind them, Washington four-square among the prisoners; across the street to our right, the houses with people peering out of the alleys in nervous silence; the arsenal, with Hazlett and his chum in the door-way, rifles ready; the Wager House, with faces at every window and at least a score of folk on the porch, and others under the trees beyond, where Galt's saloon could be seen with a couple of fellows sitting on the roof; a few more by the railroad tracks. Hidden from our view by the Wager House, Watson and Taylor were on guard at the Potomac bridge.

And not a sound, except for the distant wail of the train whistle far away on the Maryland shore. A light rain was falling again, pattering in the muddy puddles. Everyone just

281

stood, waiting on that gnarled, bearded old scarecrow in his soiled coat and ragged hat, his ridiculous sabre trailing at his side. He finished his survey and fixed Washington with a grim burning stare.

"If any are in fear it is a judgment on the sins of their guilty land! If any die resisting a just cause, then they have brought it upon themselves! As to the purpose of your own captivity, I have told you it was a moral one, and also because, as aide to the Governor of Virginia, you would have endeavoured to perform your duty, and perhaps you would have been a troublesome customer to me!" He thrust a finger like a handspike towards Washington. "I shall do my duty also, and to a higher power than a slave State! I shall be very particular to pay attention to you, sir, on my word!"

He paused, growling deep in his chest, and turned to Bill Thompson at the railing. "Captain Thompson, how many hostages are under guard? Thirty, you say – so many! Why, that is twice our own number. Well, now, we must take account of that!"

He leaned his rifle against the gate, and stood glowering at the prisoners with his hands resting on his pistol-butts, his lips moving as though in calculation, and I felt the hairs rise on my neck.

"Sweet Jesus, what's he about?" gasps Stevens. "Is he crazy?"

A rhetorical question if ever I heard one, with the old death's-head glaring like Dragfoot the Hangman, and then he swung towards our group, hitching his sword-hilt out of the way and fumbling in his pants pocket. He lugged out a handful of the eagles Meriam had given him, glancing across at the Wager House as he sorted the coins on his palm.

"Joe Simmons," says he, "here is fifteen dollars. I want you to go to the hotel yonder, and tell them we require hot breakfasts for forty-five persons, to be served to us here. Oatmeal and milk, and some of their Southern fry of eggs and ham, whatever they have, you understand . . . oh, and Joe! They'll send coffee, no doubt, but tell them I desire a pot of tea also."

282

I suppose Cardigan's "Walk—march – trot!" at Balaclava is the most memorable battlefield command I've ever heard, but J.B.'s order for breakfast at Harper's Ferry runs it close. For a moment I didn't believe it, and neither did Joe, for he stood gaping at the coins in J.B.'s hand – and then his glance flickered in my direction, and I knew at once what he was thinking, that if he went off to the Wager House, who was going to keep an eye on slippery B. M. Comber? For a second he hesitated, and then the clever beggar saw his way out.

"Why, cap'n, Ah cain't do that!" says he. "They won't pay no heed to a coloured man, no suh. They'll mind what Mass' Josh says, though – an' Ah kin go 'long an' help carry, mebbe!"

And some fools say they're not fit to vote. The hope that had leapt in my breast died in a smouldering inward rage as J.B. nodded and handed me the money . . . only to revive again at the thought that the crowded confusion of the Wager House might give me the opportunity I'd been praying for. All I'd need was a split second to get out of reach (and range) of Joe . . . and then either try to flee the town or declare myself to some responsible citizen as a government agent . . . bigod, that would be risky, they'd never believe me . . . J.B. broke in on my thoughts.

"Leave your rifles and revolvers. They will offer you no violence, knowing that we hold their friends hostage."

I didn't hesitate, but drew the two Colts from my hip-holsters and passed them to Stevens, along with my Sharps. Joe's eyes rolled, and his ugly mouth tightened, but then he too passed over his pistols, J.B. said "Remember the tea,

283

Joshua", and we set off side by side across the open ground towards the Wager House, one of us casting wary sidelong glances, the other with the reassuring pressure of the Tranter tucked into the back of his waistband under his coat.

It was an interesting walk, in its way, under the astonished eyes of the citizens wondering what the deuce it meant, two of the desperadoes who were holding their town to ransom suddenly strolling over to their hotel. For a moment the crowd on the porch stood goggling, and then there was a flurry of skirts and squealing as the women shrank away, and some of the men drew back, although most stood pat, hostile but scared. I played up, tipping my hat and calling a cheery good-morning as we mounted the steps, and one of the men even thrust the door open for us to pass through, crying "John! Someone get John Foulkes, quick! They're a-comin' in!"

For a moment it was like upsetting a bee's nest as we strode in, for the lobby was full of anxious citizens, as was the dining area off to one side, and the advent of a stalwart ruffian with whiskers and a massive black of forbidding mien had them almost clambering over each other. I calmed them with an upraised hand and my best speech-day style, assuring them they had no cause for alarm, that Captain Brown presented his compliments and would be withdrawing from their delightful township presently, and that in the meantime they should remain at ease while I spoke to a waiter. There was a moment's stunned silence, and then cries of "He's a foreigner!" and the like, and a red-faced worthy in a tile hat shouted: "What d'you mean by it? What d'ye want of us – and who are you?" and a woman fainted, and another woman screamed, and all was confusion until I raised my voice again, and presently a small bald trembler in a white apron and an extremity of terror emerged, and I gave him my order for forty-five breakfasts. Strangely enough, it seemed to have a calming effect on the assembly, if not on the hash-slinger: his teeth chattered and he closed his eyes, babbling that he didn't know if Cookie could handle that many, at such short notice, and he'd have to see, and oh my God, he'd do his best, and finally (this is unvarnished

284

truth), in a shrill whinny: "Say, m-m-mister, how d'ye want the eggs?"

"At your discretion, my boy," says I, and he stared witless before scurrying away muttering "Discretion?" (and for all I know they're serving *oeufs à la discretion* in Harper's Ferry to this day), while I took a quick slant about me – fifty folk if there was one, pale faces and round eyes, women shrinking, men resolute but doubtful, every head in the dining section turned to stare, whispers and scared murmurs . . . no other door off the lobby, but one beyond the dining tables, obviously to the kitchen . . . straight ahead of me a big bar counter, with gilt mirrors behind, a staircase leading to a balcony above the lobby, a young negress looking down over the rail – and here I paused in astonishment at the bizarre contrast of bottle-bright red hair tumbling about shining ebony cheeks, a plump black hand clutching a silk peignoir round a form which would have done credit to a Turkish wrestler, and bold protruding eyes regarding me with (unless I was mistaken, which I seldom am) awakening interest. I stared, and received an unexpected dazzling beam of white teeth in return . . .

"How many more of us ye aimin' to kill, ye damned brigand?" It was my red-faced worthy again, waving a fist in my face. "There's a corpse a-layin' in back yonder, an' a nigger like to die –"

"An' that's Brown th'abolitionist out yonder!" cries another. "Him an' his gang o' Kansas murderers – an' you, ye skunk, an' this black villain got the gall to bust in here, askin' to be fed –"

"Shame, shame on you!" squawks a female, and then they were surging about us, spitting and cursing, a fist swung at my head, I ducked and my assailant blundered into Joe, tumbling him over, my hand was on the Tranter – and Joe, sprawling, was conjuring a Colt from his armpit! A fellow dived on him, grabbing his wrist, the squawking woman was belabouring me with her gamp, Joe was hurling his attacker aside . . . but by that time I was going through the dining section like Springheeled Jack, sending a table flying as I plunged through the kitchen door. One backward glimpse I

285

had of Joe, rearing gigantic and bellowing as the mob fell back before his pistol, and then I was face to face with a wizened black granny flourishing a skillet, a kitchen in uproar, and my little waiter on his knees crying: "'Twon't be but a moment, mister, honest!" There was a door ajar to my right: I leaped through, slamming it behind me and found myself in a passage with a door to the open air and a flight of stairs running up, and I was just about to choose the former when there was a tremendous crash and screaming from the kitchen, with Joe bawling: "Where'd he go? You see a white man, woman?"

He wasn't five seconds behind me: if I broke into the open he'd nail me for certain. I bounded up the stairs, through a door at the top, and crouched, wheezing with terror, in a deserted passage, while the sound of a raging blackamoor bursting from the hotel in vain pursuit sounded below. Then I tiptoed forward past closed doors on either side, wondering where the hell I could hide, came to the end of my passage – and dropped prone as I realised it opened slap on to the balcony above the lobby! There was uproar down yonder, and someone was clattering up the main staircase towards me . . . I had no time to retreat, there was a closed door to my right, I grabbed in panic at the knob, rolled hastily within, thrust it shut, and came to my feet, Tranter in hand and an ear to the panels, my heart pounding as I heard the steps go past . . .

Someone gasped in the room behind me, and I whipped round with a yelp of fear to find myself confronting my dusky amazon of the balcony, hennaed hair a-tumble, hands raised in amazement. I gave a frantic croak of "No – don't call out!", and she blinked, eyes popping at the Tranter, but she didn't faint or have hysterics, and when I shoved it back beneath my coat she rolled her eyes and let out an elaborate sigh of relief, followed by a shrill giggle.

"Well, heah's a go! My, cain't you move aroun', though!" She raised a whimsical eyebrow. "You jes' passin' through, or you kin'ly plannin' to stay . . . Ah hope?"

I'd no time to marvel at the presence of a gaudy and eccentric negress *en déshabillé* in a Southern hotel, or the nonchalance with which she greeted an armed intruder. "Madam!" cries I. "Don't be alarmed, I beg! I mean no harm, I swear, but . . . I'm in a slight pickle, you see – hold on, do!" I sped to the front window and peeped through the curtains – there, not fifty yards off, were the armoury gates, with J.B. and Stevens in plain view and the fellows at the railings. To the left was the arsenal with the town houses beyond; there were a few citizens by the houses, and one bold spirit was shouting and shaking his fist in J.B.'s direction.

"Whut in creation's happenin' out theah?" demands the Queen of Sheba. "An election? Sounds like Sacramento on Fourth July! Who you runnin' from, handsome – the Vigilantes?"

I hopped to the room's other window, which overlooked the railroad tracks and the Potomac (it was a corner room, as you'll see from my map), and started back as Joe suddenly appeared beneath, by the side of the hotel, Colt in hand, staring about him. There was a knot of people by the tracks, scattering away from him as he turned and shouted, and I realised he must be addressing Watson at the bridge entrance, behind the hotel. Then he set off for the armoury gates, waving and shouting to J.B., no doubt asking him how he'd like his eggs. I crouched, watching, until a husky voice spoke reproachfully behind me.

"Well, you sho' know how to flatter a fine coloured lady! Or is the view out theah mo' pleasin' than the one in heah?"

I turned, still breathless, to find her regarding me with a quizzy amusement that took me even more aback than her extravagant appearance. This was the South, mind, where darkies knew their place, but here was one, young, sassy, and black as your boot, who carried herself like a Dahomey duchess and looked the white boss in the eye with cheerful insolence. She must have read my thought, for she tossed that astonishing fiery head.

"Ah's *free*, case you wonderin'!" says she tartly. "An' Ah'm waitin'."

When in doubt, grovel. "I beg your pardon . . . ma'am.

287

Believe me, I can explain. Those men yonder are abolitionist raiders – "

"So Ah been told," says she coolly. "You likewise?"

"No, no, not at all! I'm . . . oh, lor' . . . the fact is, I'm a government man. I was with them to . . . well, to observe them, you see – find out what they were up to – "

"You don' say! Well, think o' that!" Her eyes widened in mock wonder. "Gov'ment man, huh? Like a po-lice detective?"

"It's true, I swear! I had to get away from them – but the people downstairs, they don't know what I am, you see . . . and they might not believe me . . . if they found me, I mean . . ."

"Uh-huh . . . So, you got to lie low for a spell . . . right heah? Is that it?" Her smile broadened, and I could have cried out in relief.

"Yes, yes, exactly!" I gave her my most appealing leer. "If I might stay for just a little while, I'd be most grateful, I assure you, ma'am . . ."

"Call me Hannah . . ." chuckles she, ". . . an' jes' try to leave!" She swayed majestically forward to lean on the four-poster in what I can only call a worldly attitude, teasing an amber tress between her fingers and pushing out her lower lip, and as I recovered my wind and appraised her at close quarters, inhaling a gust of sweet heavy scent and noting the ravenous glint in her eye . . . why, d'you know, all of a sudden it was like coming back to life again after months in another drab and dismal world, and my immediate terrors, and those of the past few hours, were dwindling away . . . By heaven, though, she was overwhelming, sixteen magnificent stone if she was an ounce, but light on her feet as a dancer, pug-faced pretty in an overblown way, and with a jolly sensuality in the thick purple lips and flaring nostrils spread across the fat shiny cheeks. Not my vision of Venus, exactly . . . but it seemed as though centuries had passed since Mandeville, my randy imaginings of Elspeth were still fresh in mind, and as I contemplated those enormous endowments fore and aft, and the massive shapely thigh thrust out of her peignoir,

288

I came all over a-tremble, pointing like a gundog. Her languid smile became a hungry complacent smirk.

"Say, that's bettuh!" purrs she. "Ah wuz beginnin' to think you wuz anothuh Popplewell."

"Another what?"

"Popplewell – ma lawful wedded, two days back, in Pittsbu'gh. Fu'st time fo' him, third for me . . . but ma fu'st white husband, you unnerstan'," she added proudly, drooping a plump hand to display a stone the size of a fives pill on her ring finger. "Rich li'l runt, too – how else you think he cud bring his *nigguh wife* to a V'ginia ho-tel? S'posed to be takin' me honeymoonin' in Washin'ton – oh, don' fret, honey, he's long gone . . . vamoosed on that train aftuh the shootin', pale's a ghost, the dirty dawg! Lef' me flat – an' this was goin' to be ma weddin' night, too!" She glanced regretfully at the bed, and heaved a sigh which shivered her top-gallants, causing me to grunt sharply in sympathy. "An' me tricked up in ma prettiest things, an' all," she continued plaintively. "You'd ha' thought he'd ha' stayed, wouldn't you?"

And before my enraptured eyes she shrugged off the peignoir, put her hands on her hips, and stood there bursting out of a flimsy corset which would have been tight on Mandeville. She leaned forward, bulging magnificently, and pouted at me with lips like cushions.

"Well?" says she, soulful-like. "Wouldn't you?"

*   *   *

No doubt about it, I've been lucky with women – but then, as the fellow said, the more you practise . . . and no one has striven harder towards perfection than I. But Mrs Hannah Popplewell was a double stroke of good fortune, first because her presence in Harper's Ferry, which afforded me a refuge, was a chance in a thousand, and secondly because she was one of those insatiable ornaments of her sex who would rather gallop than go to church, and just what I needed after a hard night's rebellion against the Commonwealth of Virginia. If her conduct was forward, well, her connubial expectations had been dashed by the recreant

289

Popplewell, and the arrival of Flashy with whiskers rampant must have seemed like the answer to a randy young matron's prayer.

And if you wonder that I succumbed to the brazen bitch's advances, with peril threatening on every side . . . don't. Fear has never damped my ardour yet (as Sharif Sahib's harem, into which I blundered accidental during the battle of Patusan, could tell you), and the contents of that corset, flopping out voluptuously under my very nose, banished all thoughts but one. I buried my face between 'em, nearly crying, and wrenched at the laces with one hand while discarding my britches with the other, which ain't easy when you're suffocating, but love will find a way. Taken unawares, the coy little flirt squeaked in pretended alarm.

"Easy, boy!" giggles she. "The door – gotta shoot the bolt – "

"Leave that to me, ha-ha!" I seized handfuls of rump, kneading away as she struggled playfully, making feeble noises of protest.

"But, honey – you ain't even tol' me yo' name yet . . ."

"Allow me to introduce myself!" I chortled, and with one tremendous heave I hoisted her up, all black and glossy, into the firing position. Her eyes bugged out of her chubby face, and with a silent scream she enveloped my mouth with those enormous lips, heaving against me; I reeled back, muscles creaking, as she surged up and down – my stars, it was like wrestling an elephant – my legs hit the bed, and I collapsed supine beneath that ponderous mass of ebony flesh, wondering whether I'd be crushed or smothered, but resolved to die game. For a moment it was touch and go, for the selfish slut had no thought but her own lustful gratification, but then she remembered to take the weight on her knees and elbows, as a lady should, and settled into a fine raking action that sent the bed jerking across the floor and brought the canopy down on us. I could tell she'd done it before, so I settled to the enjoyable task of holding those gigantic black boobies at a safe distance, letting her have her head, and as we plunged ecstatically past the post I thought, good riddance, Popplewell, she'd have been wasted on you.

It had all been so deuced sudden, flight one moment, fornication the next, that I was glad of the chance to lie and take stock afterwards, listening to the bride's contented lip-smackings and reflecting that J.B. and Joe had more to do than fret over me, and the last place the citizens would think of looking for an absconding raider was the upper floor of their hotel. It wouldn't be safe to play the government agent card yet awhile, though; better by far to lie snug and safe, rogering this prime piece of dusky blubber, until J.B. skipped town, as he soon must, or perish, then wait for night and slip away unobserved . . . or better still, shave off my beard and whiskers, wait until tomorrow if need be, muffle up well, and board a convenient train – perhaps with Mrs Popplewell on my arm to lend colour, so to speak. With the hotel at sixes and sevens they'd never look twice, and she was the sporty kind who'd think it a great lark, provided I continued to give satisfaction in the meantime.

Which I was soon called on to do; it seemed that I had no sooner slipped into a ruined stupor before she was billowing all over me again, slipping her tongue into my ear, and whispering, as she teased away with practised fingers, that I was her sho' nuff honeymoon baby, of all things, an' whenevah she saw a cucumber aftuh this, she'd think o' me, and similar endearments. She'd no notion of leisurely love-making, either; thirty seconds of gentle dalliance and she started behaving like the Empress Theodora run amok, with poor old Flashy fighting for his life, belaboured by balloons of black jelly. Capital fun, mind you, but gruelling, and so the morning wore away, and myself with it.

Meanwhile there was little disturbance from without. Now and then there would be a few shots, but whenever I looked out the state of play seemed unchanged – J.B. and Co. ensconced around the armoury gates, but taking no harm from the occasional sniping, and now and then some of the townies would even approach the railings to confer with them, without result that I could see. It was a damned rum business, when you think of it, a quiet little town being held up by a gang of fanatics to no apparent purpose, the two sides taking pot shots and confabbing by turns, and folk going about their business a stone's throw away. I couldn't fathom J.B. at all; if he didn't move he was done for, but he seemed content to sit and wait, while the precious minutes ticked by.

I gave up at last and bedded down – and had the horrors when I woke to find that Mrs Popplewell was absent and the door ajar, but at that moment I heard her on the landing saying she'd take the tray in herself, 'cos Mistuh Popplewell wuz still abed, plain tuckered out he wuz – this with a lewd giggle for the waiter's benefit – and here she came, fat cheeks wreathed in smiles, bearing vittles and news.

"Such a ruckus down theah, they don' know who's in the place an' who ain't!" says she. "So lean to an' hit that fry, *Mistuh* Popplewell! Got to keep that fine frame o' yours fed, I reckon – come heah, honey, 'n let me nuzzle yuh!" She engulfed me lingeringly. "Say, tho', yo' man Smith, or Brown, whatsisname, got hisself treed, but good, they sayin'. Militia comin' f'm Charles Town, an' sojers, an' ev'yone scared to pieces that the nigguhs'll cut loose an' massacree the white folks, an' raise cain all aroun'! Heah, try this corn bread, dahlin', 'tis succulent . . . an' they talkin' real wild – say they goin' burn this Brown feller alive when they cotch him!" She shuddered between gargantuan mouthfuls. "Ah declare he mus' be crazy! Freein' the nigguhs, whoevah heard the like! Anyway, jus' so long's they don't burn *you* up, big boy . . . mo' coffee?"

She poured, and no Belgravia mama ever did it more elegantly, tipping in the precise amount of cream without a drip, and as I considered her, noting the delicacy with which those enormous fingers handled cups and spoons, the erect posture on the edge of her chair, the assured tilt of the splendid Zulu figurehead with the flaming red curls spilling over her shoulders, I found myself thinking back to my conversation with Joe on the Night Flyer.

"You don't approve of abolitionists, then?"

"Dam' right Ah don't! Runnin' off black trash fieldhan's an' low-life nigguhs – to *freedom*? Think that makes 'em free? They goin' to be slaves a long time yet, whether they got 'mancipation papers or not." She tossed her head. "Yo' frien' Smith – oh, sho', Brown – mus' be a fool to think he can free 'em. No white man can . . . on'y us nigguhs . . . in heah." She tapped her brow. "Like Ah did, long time ago."

"How was that, Hannah?"

"Why, you know how!" She slapped my hand, chuckling. "Soon's Ah saw a white man look at me, ten yeahs back, when Ah's jes' sixteen – not as big's Ah is now, but well-fleshed, y'know, an' when they saw me shakin' as Ah went by . . ." She stood up and took a few steps, swaying with ponderous grace and rolling her eyes. ". . . Ah sez to maself, 'Hannah gal, you totin' yo' fortune aroun' right heah, an' don' make no matter whether you black or white or sky-blue pink, you jes' shake that meat an' you nevah go hungry'." More soberly, she added: "Sho', Ah's a gal – but ev'y nigguh – ev'ybody – got sumpn to take to market, if they got the spunk an' gumption to make the most o' they-selves. You is whut you think you is – an' that's why Ah'm a *lady*."

She had determined to catch a wealthy husband, "but Ah went mad for this coloured gamblin' man in 'Frisco, an' wuz wed an' widowed inside a month. Yeah, Billy shot two fellers in a faro school – one wuz a Chink, so didn't signify, but t'other wuz white *an'* a blacksmith, mighty valuable man, so Billy got hung, lef' me nothin' but his watch and twen'y-two dollahs. Then Ah married Homer, lot older'n me, mulatter gen'leman he wuz, lent money to the coloured folks, nice l'il business, but he up an' died on me in bed." Happy Homer, thinks I, but no wonder. "He lef' me a tol'able sum, but li'l Hannah see the on'y *real* money is *white* money, so Ah set me to cotch some."

She sipped at her cup complacently. "Tuk time, an' a heap o' patience, till Ah snagged Popplewell, owns shares in half the canals in Illinois, bachelor gen'leman, 'gaged me as housekeeper. I see right away he was crazy fo' black meat, wanted me to be his fancy woman, but no suh, Ah sez, you wan' to bed, you got to wed. 'Ah cain't marry a *nigra*!' he hollers. 'Then you can go without,' Ah says." She whooped with mirth, dealing me a playful slap that almost broke my leg.

"My lan', how he went on, a-pleadin' an' entreatin' – an' Ah jes' kept a-shakin' till he wuz fit to boil ovah! 'You mus' be mine!' cries he, nigh weepin'. So Ah says, 'Why, whenevah you please, Mistuh Popplewell, suh – but you got to bid fo' my han' afore you gits the rest o' me.' So he did, las' week, an' we wuz wed in Pittsbu'gh, reg'lar Piskypalian . . . an' he still ain't had the rest o' me." She giggled, admiring her ring with deep content.

"And the little juggins ran away, on the train last night?"

"Greased lightnin' off a shovel," says she cheerfully. "'Ah cain't 'bide violence!' says he, all tremblish. 'We mus' fly, my own, 'fore wuss befalls!' Ah sez, 'You kin fly, Popplewell, but Ah's comf'table right heah.' An' he flew. 'Meet me in Washin'ton, deah creecher, an' heah's a hundred dollahs – do not fail me!' They wuz his partin' words. So Ah'll meet him, in ma own sweet time . . . meet his canal shares, too. But right now . . ." She rose with a fine billowing of her peignoir, put her arms about my neck, and slid her splendid bulk on to my knee ". . . Ah's *real* comf'table."

The unworthy thought crossed my mind that her present misbehaviour rendered her eminently blackmailable where Popplewell was concerned – but it was a purely Pickwickian reflection, you understand. I'd not have dreamed (I'd not have dared) even given the chance, for I'd taken a liking to this hearty black trollop; a true kindred spirit, pleasuring her rump off at a moment's notice – aye, and drumming up breakfast from a kitchen in bedlam, gathering the news, and preparing the way for my departure as "Mr Popplewell" into the bargain. You don't find many like her – and I told her so. "Well, now, s'pose you jes' *show* me," says she, squirming on my lap and licking my lips. So I did, for the third and last time.

For even as we buckled to, the curtain was rising on the final gruesome act at Harper's Ferry. Twelve hours had passed since we'd crossed the Potomac bridge, and all unknown to us the alarm had been spreading since dawn, from village to town to city, clicking along the wire even to the White House. Already militia companies were tramping through the leafy Virginia lanes from Charles Town, and mustering in Frederick and Winchester and Martinsburg, and even eventually in Baltimore. That young beau sabreur, Lieutenant J. E. B. Stuart, who was in Washington trying to hawk his patent swordfrog to the War Department, found himself ordered to ride for Arlington to summon Colonel Robert E. Lee of the 2nd Cavalry (didn't old J.B. attract the big guns, eh?), and within hours the two of 'em were bound for the Ferry in the wake of the U.S. Marines.[51] The steel trap that Douglass had prophesied was closing, while J.B. mooned away his time (waiting for the slaves to rally to him, waiting for the arms to arrive from Owen, waiting because the poor old peasant didn't know what else to do), and Kagi kept sending frantic messages from the rifle works, beseeching him to move, and the citizens of Harper's Ferry lost patience, and began to gather in earnest, and I – well, you know what I was doing, and not a man in Virginia was better employed, and you may tell Mrs Popplewell I said so.

It came as sudden as a thunderclap – a deafening burst of shooting, and I was springing to the window, and all hell was breaking loose between the town houses and the armoury railings with both sides blazing away, and the far bank of the Potomac was alive with armed men in civilian duds, the Charles Town militia, led by a man who knew his business, for he was cutting off J.B.'s line of retreat. From the side window I saw them streaming down towards the Potomac bridge, which was out of sight from where I was, behind the hotel, so I didn't see them storming over the bridge shouting and huzzahing, chasing Watson Brown and Taylor, who fled to the armoury – I saw them run across from the tracks, firing back, and then the militia came into view below the hotel, scores of men who looked like farmers on a rabbit hunt. They spread out along the track beneath my window, and on the open ground, pouring fire at the armoury gates, and I thought, you're done, J.B., for I expected them to rush the railings, but an officer bawled to them to take cover in the Wager House, and I heard him ordering parties to Galt's saloon and the Shenandoah bridge, where Oliver was stationed.

Now it was pandemonium below stairs, and the building shook as about fifty clodhoppers surged in, hollering and crashing among the furniture and firing from the windows. Female shrieks arose, and a stentorian voice ordered all ladies to take refuge on the upper floor: there was a great pattering and squealing on the stairs, and I was in terror that we'd be invaded, but Mrs P. put paid to that by showing herself in our doorway, bold, black, and bedizened – no respectable Southern female was going to share a room with a *nigger*, why, 'tis a scandal, allowing such a creature in civilised lodgings, what *is* the world coming to . . .

Suddenly there was uproar outside, a fusillade of shots, and from the front window I saw young Oliver racing across before the hotel, letting fly with his Colt at pursuing militiamen. He'd been driven from the Shenandoah bridge, and was going like a stag for the armoury gates, with Bill Thompson at his heels, and hard behind them came the old black, Dangerous Newby. Oliver and Thompson won clear, with shots kicking up the puddles around them, but Newby suddenly staggered, his head thrown back, and I saw that a shot had torn his neck horribly open; he stumbled sideways and sprawled on his back in the mud – and that was the first of John Brown's "pet lambs" gone, and as I stared down at the twitching body and the blood welling across the ground, I suddenly remembered him sobbing in a corner at Kennedy Farm, over a letter from his wife, who was still in slavery, hoping that he'd be able to buy her and their children soon, and J.B. setting a hand on his shoulder, saying "They shall be free, Newby, depend upon it," and old Dangerous saying "Ah know it, cap'n; Ah know it."

They didn't let him be. Now that the militia were on hand, and the raiders' number was patently up, all sorts of ragged town heroes came to join in the fun, and in no time they were at the liquor in the Wager House and Galt's place; there was a fine drunken commotion beneath our feet, singing and cheering and guffawing, and great rage being voiced against J.B. and his gang. They were full of bile because

296

Oliver and Thompson had escaped, and soon, when J.B. sent out a hostage with a white flag to hold some parley or other with the militia, half a dozen of the town vermin emerged from the hotel to take out their spite on Newby's corpse, kicking it and dragging it about with cries of there, ye damned nigger, rot in hell an' serve ye right. One barefoot rascal dragged off the dead man's boots, and then Mrs Popplewell, who was with me at the window, cried: "Oh, sweet Jesus!" and turned away, for the rest of them were hurrahing round the corpse, egging on one who knelt and sawed at its head and presently came running to the hotel, bellowing who wanted a couple o' abolitionist souvenirs, hey – and I saw he was flourishing Newby's bloody ears aloft. His mates cheered and clapped him on the back.

That was when the nightmare began. Shooting had broken out again, heavier than ever from the houses and the heights behind the town, and J.B.'s beleaguered party had to abandon the railings and take cover among the armoury sheds. They had no way out now; more militia were arriving, over both bridges, and soon the ground about the hotel and tracks was thick with them, clamouring to git at them dam' nigger-lovers, but 'twas all shouts and no action; either their leaders were concerned for the hostages, or, more likely, had a healthy respect for J.B.'s marksmen, who were holding their fire now except when their tormentors came too close – one idiot on horseback, waving a shotgun, was picked off like a squirrel from a branch, and another, venturing too far down the railroad tracks, was dropped with a single shot.

As I learned later, he was the Mayor of Harper's Ferry, and when the news of his death spread among the people, their rage knew no bounds. What with that and militia-men enflamed with drink, I could see J.B. and Co. being torn limb from limb when the mob finally worked up the nerve to storm the armoury, but in the meantime they were content to plaster the sheds with shot and roar blood-curdling threats.

And then J.B. sent out another white flag. There was a great howl of fury when it appeared in the armoury gateway, but a militia officer bawled to them to hold their fire, for it was borne by one of the hostages, who came marching towards the hotel with young Bill Thompson by his side. The crowd surged out and surrounded them, drowning the hostage's plea to be heard, the flag was torn from him, and Bill Thompson was dragged into the Wager House, battered and kicked, with yells of "Lynch the bastard! No, no, hangin's too good for him – burn the son-of-a-bitch!" The drunken din from beneath was now so deafening that there wasn't a word to be made out, but since they didn't haul Thompson out for execution I guessed he was still alive – for the time being.

You'd have thought J.B. would have learned from that incident, but not he – not long after, another white rag was seen waving in the armoury, the order to cease fire was shouted again, and this time it was Aaron Stevens and Watson Brown who came out, side by side. You bloody fools, thinks I, you're done for, but on they came towards the hotel, Watson stiff as a ramrod, with his head carried high, and big Aaron ploughing along with one hand raised like an Indian in greeting. For a moment it was so still I could hear their boots squelching through the puddles – and then a rifle cracked, and Watson stumbled forward and fell on his hands and knees. A great cheer went up, a volley of shots followed, Stevens seemed to hesitate, and then he came for the Wager House like a bull at a gate, hurling the flag away, and was cut down within twenty paces of the hotel – I absolutely saw his body jerk as the slugs hit him, and then the hostage who had been with Bill Thompson came running out, arms spread wide, turning to put himself between the two shot men and the mob. Another hostage who must have been following Stevens and Watson from the armoury ran forward to join him, and together they dragged Stevens to the Wager House, one of them yelling: "You cowardly scum! Stop it, damn you – cain't ye see the flag?" For a moment the firing stopped, and then it was seen that Watson was crawling on all fours back towards the armoury, and the mob set up a great yell and let fly again. He scrambled up and ran, clutching his stomach, with the bullets churning the dirt around his feet, and went down again, but he still kept crawling and

298

managed to roll to cover behind one of the gate-posts. That sent them wild, and they poured in fire harder than ever.

But what, you ask, was Flashy doing while the tide of battle rolled o'er Harper's Ferry? Crouched shivering at the curtains, that's what, sweating pints at the thought of what those booze-sodden villains would do if they chanced to seek sport abovestairs and discovered that the trembling occupant of the Popplewell chamber was none other than the raider who'd come demanding breakfast . . . I only had to look out at the bloody shreds that had once been Newby, and listen to the hell's chorus from below, to be almost physically sick.

The same thought must have occurred to Mrs Popplewell, for after an age in which we'd barely exchanged a word, I felt her hand on my shoulder, and the jolly black face was grim and set. "Bes' git yo' clo'es on, dearie," says she, and I saw that while I'd been glued to the window and the horrors outside, she'd been attiring herself in a vast gown of dazzling green silk with yellow bows, an enormous hat with a yellow plume, and matching ribbons in her hennaed hair – you can't imagine what she looked like, luckily for you. She even had a rolled umbrella.

"Sumpn's up down yonder," says she. "Ah's goin' to len' an ear." And she tiptoed with elephantine delicacy to the door, a finger raised and an ear to the panels.

"Don't open it!" I yelped. "Christ, if those brutes see you, God knows what they'll do! If they find me here –"

"Git them pants on an' hold yo' noise! They ain't goin' to see nobody!"

She opened the door a crack, and suddenly above the clamour from below we could hear voices – and they didn't soothe me one little bit, for the first words I heard were:

". . . so string the bastards up, I say! Damn it to hell, there's Mayor Beckham layin' dead, an' you want we should be tender o' these dam' Kansas butchers? You an abolitionist yo'self, or whut?"

"I'm a soldier!" snaps another, one of your cold-steel voices. "And these men are prisoners, to be treated as such –"

"Oh, sure, you're a soldier! Goddam Frederick militia, ain't you, comin' in at the tail-end! Well, *Captain*, we tuk these yere *prisoners*, as you call 'em, an' I reckon it's for *us* to say how they tret, ain't that so, boys?"

There was a roar of agreement, and the hairs rose on my neck as I heard Thompson's voice, crying out, but not in appeal – he was shouting something about dying gladly in liberty's cause, but it was drowned in yells of execration.

"Why, you vile white nigger, you! Have him out, boys, I cain't stand to listen to him! Why, gimme that pistol, Jem, I'll finish him myself! Now – you see this gun, you Kansas hawg, you feel it 'gainst yo' head –"

"Put that down!" To my amazement, it was a woman, shrill with anger. "You won't sully this house with murder while I'm here! Put it down, I say! The law will take its course –"

"Law, by thunder – an' who asked you to stick in yore pert nose, missie! This heah's men's work, I reckon, hey, boys?"

"You pull that trigger, my son, and I'll give you men's work!" shouts the captain. "Good for you, Miss Foulkes!⁵² They'll commit no outrage under this roof, I promise you!"

"Won't we, though? Oh, well, now, we wouldn't want t'offend the good lady's feelin's! Would we, men? No, sir, I reckon not! So with yo' kind permission, ma'am, we'll just take the lousy abolitionist *outside*, an' 'tend to him there! Heave him up, boys – an' that other wounded son-of-a-bitch, too!"

"No, no, let him be – he's dyin' nice an' slow as 'tis, with good ole Georgie Chambers's slugs in his guts! Let him suffer, I say –"

"Why, you drunken cur!" cries the captain. "If that man could stand up with a gun in his hand, you'd all jump out the window!"

A storm of yells and curses greeted this, and then I heard Thompson again, wild and high: "God bless you, Aaron Stevens! They may take our lives, but eighty million will rise up to avenge us –" and then Mrs Popplewell closed the door and leaned her back against it, looking solemn.

300

"You was right, honey," says she. "They ain't in no mood to b'lieve you's a gov'ment man."

"Oh, my God! Maybe they won't come up, though!"

"Don' bet on it! They's three or four a-settin' on the stairs this minnit, drinkin' theyselves wicked, an' castin' eyes at the rooms wheah them other shemales is!" She swayed across to the window. "It be dark in an hour or two. You bes' slide out then, git yo'self to one o' they off'cers, or someone'll listen to yuh –"

"Slide out – through that? Christ, woman, every militia-man in America's out there! They'd tear me to pieces! No, no, I must hide – under the bed, or . . . somewhere! In the cupboard – the closet, you stupid slut! Oh, God, too small . . . look, could you throw some of your clothes over me, if I lay down? They'd never think . . . why not, confound you? Dammit, you could hide half Harper's Ferry under that bloody tent you're wearing! Help me, you brainless sow!"

"Is that so? You wuz glad 'nuff to git under it!" snorts she. "My, ain't you the bedtime hero, though? You some kin o' Popplewell's, Ah reckon!"

"And these infernal Yankee pothouses don't have chimneys, even –"

"They got attics!" snaps she, pointing aloft – and there, praise be, was a trap in the ceiling. "If yo' so downright timid –" But I was already on the table, throwing back the trap, and sure enough it opened into a great musty loft which must have extended over the whole building, dim and cluttered with rubbish, just the bolt-hole for a deserving poltroon. "God bless you! Back in a jiff!" cries I, and I'll swear I heard her giggle as I heaved up, lowered the trap, and took stock, treading softly. From the small windows in either gable and the low skylights in the sloping roof I had a capital view all round: north to the armoury, south to Galt's saloon and the Shenandoah bridge, and west to the Bolivar Heights overlooking the town, with the orange ball of the sun sinking in a dirty autumn sky; those distant buildings towards the Shenandoah shore must be the rifle works – was Kagi still there? Closer at hand the arsenal building seemed to be deserted; no sign of Hazlett.

The front of the town was crawling with men keeping up a desultory fire on the armoury, and, weighing up, I could see only one line of retreat for J.B. – through the armoury proper and along the railroad between Bolivar Heights and the Potomac. But even as I looked I saw movement in that direction: the figures of militia, a good hundred of them, skirmishing in to close on the armoury from the rear. So now he was ringed in on all sides; his revolution was dead, and he and his juvenile fanatics with it.

They went piecemeal, did J.B.'s pet lambs, and I saw most of 'em go – already there'd been Newby, Watson, and Stevens, and now, even as I prepared to tiptoe back to the trap, Bill Thompson. There was a commotion behind the hotel, and hastening to the skylight on that side I saw a noisy crowd milling at the mouth of the Potomac bridge tunnel. They were hustling Thompson on to the trestle, and then they stood off from him, levelling their pistols. For a second he was stock-still, hands by his sides, and then they were blasting at him point-blank, and he toppled over out of sight. The whole mob surged forward, shouting curses, and his body must have landed on the bank below, for they kept emptying their pieces downwards, and I found I was jerking with the shots, for it might have been me.

I watched, sick and shuddering, until a fresh burst of firing came from the Shenandoah side, and from the other skylight, which was broken, I saw distant figures surging round the rifle works, and heard guns popping like toys in the distance. With the setting sun in my eyes I couldn't make out much, but a few moments later there was a great haw-hawing and laughter as a group of roughnecks and some militia came hurrying down towards Galt's saloon, shouting that that was another couple o' the bastards settled, one white, one nigger, an' 'twould ha' been three, for there had been another nigger they'd been goin' to lynch, but that cussed sawbones wouldn't allow it, damn him, spoilin' sport thataway – say, but if you boys wantin' some target practice, that abolitionist skunk's still a-layin' there! Sure, got him in the shallows, tryin' to swim for it . . . too much hot lead in him for swimmin', though, haw-haw!

So that was Kagi gone, J.B.'s right arm, who'd sat under that signpost by Chambersburg, twiddling a flower between his fingers. He was the best of 'em, the Switzer – consoling, ain't it, that it's always the good 'uns who stop the shot, while fellows like me slip out from under? Which reminded me that I'd some fair slipping to do yet, if I was to come out intact. It was beginning to grow dark; lights were twinkling in the town, and down below the crowds around the Wager House and Galt's were kindling torches; by the sound of it they were drunker than ever, and bursting with mischief. Rain was pattering on the roof, and I debated whether to wait in that gloomy loft until full dark, and then try to scramble down from one of the windows . . . no, if I didn't break my neck, there'd still be those boozy ruffians between me and safety. Better to return to the room, where Mrs Popplewell was probably still undisturbed, and lie up in comfort until morning, or even longer if need be. If danger threatened I could always take refuge in the loft again.

I tiptoed to the trap . . . and stopped short when I saw a chink of light showing. Of course, with dusk coming she'd lit the lamp. I stooped to raise the trap – and almost fell over in terror, for someone was talking in the room below, and it wasn't Black Beauty, unless her voice had broken in my absence. I crouched quivering like an aspen, as a harsh bass growl came to my ears:

". . . never see a nigger yet that didn't lie truth out o' Dixie! You had him in here, ye black bitch! Hid him up, didn't ye – yeah, yore abolitionist friend! Where'd he go, hey?"

"Don' you call me liar!" It was Mrs Popplewell, no docile darkie she. "Ah's a 'spectable woman, an' no white trash goin' to bust in on me an' gimme his lip! You git out o' heah, all on yuh, leave me be! Ah don't know nothin' 'bout no abolitionist –"

"White trash? Strike me dumb, ye hear that? I've a mind to haul you out an' lash you good –"

"You hold your noise!" It was the captain who'd interceded for Thompson. "See here, my girl – there was a man here. We *know* it. You told the waiter here it was your husband – what's his name, Popplewell? That right?"

"That's it – Popplewell!" The waiter, babbling. "But *he* got on the train went out at dawn – and she brung up breakfuss for two this mornin', like he was still here . . . least, I *think* that's what she said –"

"There, now! You hear him, girl –"

"He's mistook!" Mrs Popplewell was standing firm. "Said no sech thing! An' no man's been in heah! Whut kin' o' female d'ye think Ah am?"

"A lyin' nigra whore, that's what!" bawls the ruffian voice. "If you was alone, what you need *two* breakfasts for?"

"Ah is a large lady," retorts she with dignity, "an' Ah eats hearty."

"Leave that, 'tis by the way!" says the captain impatiently. "Now, see here, girl – how d'ye explain *this*?" And there followed a breathless pause.

What the devil could "this" be? Something damning, obviously – but you'd think a man in my plight could have restrained his curiosity, wouldn't you? After all, it didn't matter to me whether he was presenting his card or baring his buttocks . . . so before you could have said: "Don't, you damfool!" I had my eye to the gap at the edge of the trap, goggling down into the room.

I could see only a portion of it, filled mostly by Mrs Popplewell in the height of fashion, holding her brolly like a club, and two ugly scoundrels with beer-bellies and beards crowding her either side. Of the captain I could see only an outstretched hand – and on it lay my Tranter pistol, which I'd forgotten in my haste.

"Well?" says he. "What o' this?"

"Ma husban' left it, fo' ma purtection!" cries she gamely.

"Did he now? Favours an English firearm, does he? You, waiter – didn't you say the abolitionist who bespoke forty-five breakfasts[53] spoke with a foreign accent – British, perhaps?"

I didn't stay for the answer. If I'd been a man of iron nerve, no doubt I'd have raised the trap, bade them a cheery good-evening, and descended nonchalantly to explain myself to the captain, who was plainly a man of intelligence and

304

sound judgment. And he might have believed me. Again, his raffish companions might have shot me on sight. We cannot tell, for what I absolutely did was to start to my feet in sudden alarm, hit my head a shattering crash on a sloping joist, lose my balance, and step heavily on the trap, which must have been rotten at the hinges, for it gave way with a rending of timber, and down I went into the room like Lucifer descending, the table bursting beneath my weight, Mrs Popplewell screaming, and her interrogators exclaiming in shocked surprise.

The only one who spoke to the point was the waiter, who cried "By cracky, that's him!", and call me hasty if you will, it seemed prudent to remove rather than offer explanations. I was afoot and would have been through the open door in an instant if one of the ruffians hadn't barred the way. I sank my knee in his essentials, blundered into Mrs Popplewell, saw the other thug start towards me and the captain beside him levelling the Tranter, and knew in a split second that there was only one thing for it. Casting gallantry aside, I seized her amidships, swung her off her feet with a herculean effort, and hurled her at them – and I'm here to tell you that a tenth of a ton of well-nourished negress, point-blank and well driven, is a damned effective missile. They went down all three with a shock that rattled the hotel, and I was out and bounding down the passage to the back stairs, missing my footing and going arse over tip to land with a sickening jar beside the kitchen door. The outer door stood open, I heaved myself up and went through it bull-at-a-gate into a torch-lit twilight which seemed to be full of drunken, shouting rascals who stared in astonishment as I raced through them, heedless of direction; behind me a voice cried: "Stop him! Halt, or I fire!" It was the captain – no slouch in pursuit, he – and then came the crack as he let fly with the Tranter. I plunged on, dodging between trees, cannoning into bodies, knocking over a stand of piled rifles, with angry yells and pounding feet behind me, and no notion of where my terrified flight was taking me.

Well, it wouldn't have made much odds if I *had* taken care; all ways led to disaster and death, and mine took me into the open ground between the Wager House and the armoury gates, where I slipped in a puddle and went head-long in the mud. At least in scrambling up I was able to take my bearings, and damned discouraging they were, for every gun in Harper's Ferry seemed to be slinging lead at me – from the railroad tracks to my right, from the town to my left, and from the Wager House at my back. Shots were slapping into the mud around me, militiamen were rushing towards me from the hotel, and the only place that wasn't stiff with ill-wishers, and seemed to offer the ghost of a chance, was the armoury itself. I floundered out of the mire and went bald-headed for the gates.

It was just my confounded luck that my flight took place at the precise moment when those militia whom I'd seen skirmishing towards the rear of the armoury a few minutes earlier, launched their attack through the sheds at the remnants of J.B.'s little force. Even as I was leaving the hotel at speed, they were storming up among the workshops, and J.B. and his boys, assailed from behind, were downing eight of them before being forced to retire into the engine-house just inside the armoury gateway. What with my panic and the uproar around me, I knew nothing of this until I sped screaming through the gates and met the militia coming the other way; ahead of me the avenue between the sheds was alive with roaring ruffians charging towards me in the failing light, orange flames leaping from their muzzles – even as I slithered to a terrified halt, shots were whipping past, and as I turned to fly something like a whiplash seared across my neck, and I knew I'd been hit, oh Jesus, this was death, and I pitched forward in agony, sobbing: "God damn you, Spring, damn you to hell!", clutching at my wound, the warm blood running between my fingers, my ears deafened by the hellish din of rifle fire and battle-cry, torchlight blinding me, and I knew this was the end . . .

"Joshua!" A harsh voice was shouting, close by. "Joshua!" I struggled up on one elbow – and not ten yards before me were the great twin doors of the engine-house, with J.B. himself standing between them, his Sharps smoking in his hands, his scarecrow coat flapping round his lean shanks, his battered hat jammed down on his brows. The door in the left-hand arch was shut, but that on the right was wide, and there was Joe, his face contorted with rage, a Colt in either fist, pumping shots at the advancing militia, and Taylor the Canadian kneeling, his Sharps at his shoulder, and Oliver was waving his rifle: "Come on, Josh – we'll cover you!"

By God, Flashy, you ain't dead yet, I thought, and then I was on my feet, bellowing with fear, staggering towards them. All four were firing now, and from the tail of my eye I saw the militia's advance waver, but they were shooting back, damn them, slugs were buzzing about me, something plucked at the skirt of my coat – missed, you duffer!, but the next one didn't, a hammer blow struck my thigh, numbing my leg, and I went down like a shot rabbit, sprawling in the mud within a few feet of cover and roaring, if I remember rightly, for Jesus to save me. Which was optimism run mad, I admit – but I was dying, remember.

God knows how I crawled the few yards to the engine-house doorway, heaving along on two hands and one knee, plastered with filth, my precious blood leaking in two places, howling my head off – and Taylor was darting forward, hoisting me up and dragging me on. Then everything seemed to be happening terribly slowly, but crystal clear, as is often the case when you're helpless in deadly danger: Taylor's grip loosed, and something warm and wet struck me in the face, and as I fell back he was standing over me, but where his head should have been was a hideous crimson mess, and I cried out in horror, pawing at his blood and brains that had spattered over me. Someone heaved me to my feet; it was J.B., and I remember the earthy cattle smell of his coat as my face pressed against it, Joe's pistol exploding almost in my ear, his shout of "Goddam slavin' bastards!", Oliver firing round the door-post while rifle balls smacked into the timber and brickwork, and the choking reek of powder smoke in my mouth and eyes.

As I clung weeping to J.B. I heard Oliver sing out: "I see him, Paw!", and I can still see the eager grin on the pale, handsome face under the wideawake hat, but as he whipped

307

the Sharps to his shoulder he suddenly staggered, with an odd barking little cough, looking down at the bloody stain spreading on his shirt. He dropped the Sharps and sat down heavily against the door, raising his head in surprise and exclaiming: "Oh, Paw, look!", and that is the last thing I remember before . . . well, I could say something poetic about blackness enfolding me like a shroud, or a dark mist engulfing my senses, but the plain fact is that I fainted from pure funk.

Wounds, believe it or not, can be quite handy, if you know how to make use of them. I speak with authority, having taken over twenty in my time, from my broken thigh at Piper's Fort to the self-inflicted graze which enabled me to collapse artistically during the Boxer Rising (I was seventy-eight at the time, an age at which you can get away with a lot). In between, I've been shot in the back, the breast, the arm, the leg, and the arse, been blown up now and then, flogged, scalped (by my own son, if you please), racked, and roasted, had my shoulder opened by a Chink hatchet, my cheek by a German *schlager*, and my abdomen by a Turkish knitting needle (at least, I believe she was Turkish), and still carry a scorch-mark on my elbow from the hot metal of the cannon from which I was dam' near blown at Gwalior. Not bad going for a thoroughbred coward and decamper, and those are only the ones I remember – there's a small-calibre hole in my left palm, and blessed if I know how I came by *that*. Senility creeping on, I suppose.

The point is that I've made capital out of my dishonourable scars by adhering to one golden rule – Flashy's Sufferance, I call it: always convey, but *never* say, that your injury is a sight worse than it really is. It's elementary, really. In convalescence this ensures sympathy, if you play it properly – the barely perceptible wince, the sharp little intake of breath, the faint smile followed by the quick shake of the head, and never a word of complaint from the dear brave boy – but far more importantly, in the heat of battle it enables you to feign mortal hurt and shirk any further part in the action.

Not that I was faking when I keeled over maiden-like in

309

the engine-house – I was convinced that the Great Peeler had His hand on my collar at last, and only when I came to and recalled that the pandemonium around me was not Hell after all, did I discover that my wounds, while painful, were not fatal, or even serious. My shirt and coat were sticky with blood, but frenzied inspection assured me that this came not from my jugular but from a nasty nick near the shoulder, and my other hurt was quite a curiosity: the slug must have been almost spent, for it was only half-embedded in my leg some way above the knee, like a currant on a cake. I pawed at it, weeping tears of gratitude that it hadn't struck home a few inches nor'-east, and the beastly thing fell out, leaving an ugly hole oozing gore. I subsided, whimpering with anguish and relief, clutching the affected parts and lying petrified as I took in the appalling scene.

For the interior of that engine-house looked and sounded like the Inferno gone wild: the building reverberated to the incessant din of rifle fire, glass was shattering, timber splintering, men were screaming and cursing, and all in half-darkness, for there wasn't a light in the place bar the flashes from the guns, and only torch-glare outside. As I cowered down by the wall, half-choked by smoke and panic, I could just make out the shapes of bodies on the straw at my feet, and beyond them shadowy figures which crouched in the half-open doorway, shooting out, while answering shots crashed into the walls and the long low fire-carts which seemed to fill most of the great brick-built shed: one slug hit a fire-bell with an ear-splitting clang, setting it swinging and pealing. All I could do was lie there, trying to staunch my neck wound with my sleeve, praying that I'd not be hit again – God, of all the cruel strokes of fate, after all my scheming and evasion and taking cover, at the eleventh hour I'd leapt from the fire back into the frying-pan, and now there was nowhere to run, even if I'd been able to.

Only a yard away Jerry Anderson was hacking at the bricks to make a loophole; fragments rained down on me, and when I sang out he dropped down beside me, eyes wild in a blood-streaked face.

"My God, Josh!" cries he. "Are ye done for?"

"Brandy!" croaks I, and he thrust his flask at me. I clutched it, and as he jumped back to his loophole I set my teeth and spilled half the contents on my neck, squawling to wake the dead at the burning agony of it. I clapped the mouth of the flask to my leg wound, writhing and whimpering, and had just enough strength to pour the rest down my throat. I was half-fainting with pain, and I must have swooned again, for the next thing I knew there was a blinding glare before my eyes, the shooting had ceased altogether, and there were voices talking close by. I raised my head and saw that the glare came from a storm-lantern in the doorway, where J.B. seemed to be holding a parley with a couple of civilians, while Joe covered them with his six-guns. The light fell on the faces of the bodies near my feet, and I shrank back horrified as I saw that they were Watson and Oliver, both apparently dead, and beyond them the shattered corpse of Taylor sprawled on the blood-sodden straw. To my right, on the back wall behind the engines, young Ed Coppoc and Emperor Green, the black, had their rifles at the ready through loopholes in the brick, and Jerry Anderson was at his post on the side wall, straddling Oliver's body. Dauphin Thompson, the pretty youth who looked like a girl, stood by the nearer engine, a rifle in his hands – my God, was this all that was left? Six sound men, three corpses, and Flashy playing possum . . . Now one of the civilians was speaking, a tall brisk chap with a trim moustache and goatee – my captain from the Wager House. By George, he got about, though, didn't he?

". . . you can only make it worse!" cries he, pointing to the bodies. "Sakes alive, man, isn't that enough? You're surrounded by hundreds of militia, *and* Colonel Lee's marines! They're under orders from the President of the United States to demand your unconditional surrender, nothing less!" He gestured about him. "Look at this – the end is certain, and resistance can mean only more bloodshed –"

"They know my terms!" rasps J.B. His face was dreadful in the lamp-glare, haggard with hunger and lack of sleep, but his voice was strong. "When all my men, living and dead,

311

have been delivered to me here, with their arms and ammunition – and our horse and harness –"

"Your *horse*?" cries the other in disbelief. "God help us!"

"– then, and only then, I shall retire into Maryland, taking the prisoners with me," continues J.B. calmly. "There I shall release them at a safe distance, and enter into negotiations with the government –"

"You'll not take us into Maryland!" It was old Washington, coming round the back of the engines, and I saw there were half a dozen of the hostages lurking at the far side of the shed.[54] He strode past where I was lying, up to the group in the doorway. "No threat shall compel me from this spot, I'll tell you that!"

They stood eye to eye, the old soldier planted like a rock, J.B. with his head thrown back, rifle in hand, Frederick's sword trailing at his hip. The goatee'd captain stepped between them, hands raised, forcing himself to speak quiet but firm.

"It won't do, Captain Brown. Can't you see, sir, Colonel Lee cannot yield to those terms – the United States cannot!" He took a deep breath. "Your position . . . oh, come, sir, in the name of sense – what do you hope for?"

J.B. turned on him, eyes flashing. "For honourable dealing, according to the usages of war! Would you have me surrender to the creatures who shot down my men like dogs – under a white flag? My own son, sir, dying there of wounds inflicted by those drunken cowards?"

"That was the militia! Colonel Lee is a gallant gentleman and stone-cold sober!" retorts the captain. "Oh, I am sorry for your son . . . but, my God, when men take up arms in treason against their country, they can expect to be shot like dogs! What of the poor souls you've killed this day?" He broke off with a helpless shrug. "Oh, where's the sense of it? I beg of you, sir – see reason, and give up while you can. Colonel Lee will show you every consideration, and in the meantime," he gestured at the bodies, "at least let Doctor Taylor see to your wounded."

J.B. considered a moment, and then nodded to the other civilian, a stout little greybeard with a black bag who signed to Jerry to bring the lantern, and knelt down by Watson, fumbling for his pulse. Even through half-closed eyes in that light I could tell it was the Stars and Stripes for Watson, no error: his face was like wax, and he didn't seem to be breathing. The little sawbones evidently agreed, for he pursed his lips and moved on to Oliver, whose eyes blinked open in the light. He stirred, and gave a little whispered sob.

"Paw . . . shoot me . . . oh, Paw, please, it's awful sore! Let me . . . die . . . please, Paw!"

J.B.'s voiced croaked out of the shadows in an awful parody of reassurance: "Oh, you'll get over it, Noll –", interrupted by a stifled scream from Oliver as the belly-butcher probed at his chest. You mayn't credit it, but I believe I heard the loving paterfamilias mutter something about "dying like a man". Say that to me, you old sod, thinks I, and I'll spit in your eye.

I was reviving, you see, under the spur of self-preservation, and while I was weak as a rat with fear and shock, and hurting like sin, I was by no means *hors de combat*: the feeling had returned to my leg, and the gash in my neck seemed to have stopped bleeding. But the outlook was uncertain, you'll agree. If this parley (one of many in that extraordinary day, in which one side tended the other's wounded between the hostilities) ended with J.B.'s throwing in his hand, all would be well: once he'd been disarmed I could show my true colours and refer them to Messervy. If he wouldn't surrender, I could only keep mum – declaring myself a U.S. agent in the hope that the captain could protect me would be madness: why, the crazy old bastard would probably shoot me on the spot. Then there was the vexed question of where the devil I'd been all day . . . and Joe was lurking in the background . . . On the whole, the closer I appeared to be to death's door, and unable to answer embarrassing questions, the better. So when the poultice-walloper shook his head over Oliver, and glanced towards me, lying there all blood-spattered and pathetic, I was ready with a feeble gesture to keep him at a distance – the last thing I wanted was the little bugger poking at me and exclaiming:

"Why, this fellow's barely scratched! A spoonful of jalop and he'll be fitter than I am!"

I needn't have fretted. Possibly he was fed up peering at abolitionists, for having glanced, he shrugged, and said he'd call again in the morning. (Those were his very words, as though we were in Tooting with the mumps; you may find them in the history books.)

Meanwhile the goatee'd captain had been moving heaven and earth to make J.B. see reason, with as much success as you'd expect. "I knew what we might be called on to undergo when I set my hand to this work," says the stubborn old ragamuffin. "I have weighed the responsibility, and shall not shrink from it."

"And your prisoners?" cries the captain. "If this madness continues, and they pay for it with their lives, you'll take responsibility for that too, will you?"

"I shall take every care of them," replies J.B. "They are in God's hands. So are we all."

The captain could have burst at the sanctimonious smugness of it, but he mastered himself, and stood up tall.

"You are a vain and selfish man," says he. "God forgive you." Then anger got the better of him. "You'll die! To no purpose – you know that?"

"Oh, to some purpose, I believe," says J.B., and laid a hand on his shoulder, as though talking to a child. "Be of good cheer, Captain Sinn. We shall this day light such a candle by God's grace in Virginia as shall never be put out."[55]

This was too much for old Washington, who went purple. "You dare – you dare to use those words!" He spluttered. "Why . . . why, it's a blasphemy! You're a pagan, sir, a brazen forehead –"

"Go behind the engines, colonel," says J.B. "There is no more to be said." The old soldier stood fuming for a moment, then turned on his heel and strode off to the far side, where the other hostages were peeping over the engines, looking scared.

"Come along, doctor," says the captain. "We have done

what we could." He hesitated in the doorway, and turned to J.B. "For the last time, Mr Brown – will you not reconsider?"

J.B. stood silent, staring at the ground, and Sinn and the doctor went out into the darkness.

I'd listened in growing consternation, for there was no doubt what was coming, thanks to the blind stubborn folly (aye, and vanity) of that pig-headed yokel – the besiegers would storm the engine-house, their first ranks would be cut down by the defenders' fire, and when the drunken rabble finally burst in by sheer weight of numbers they'd butcher every last one of us in a fury of spite and vengeance. I'd not have a dog's chance of surrender, or to proclaim myself . . . to them I'd be just another Kansas murderer, to go the way of Thompson and Stevens and Watson – unless in the meantime I could make myself known to old Washington, and take shelter among the hostages when the final charge came home; the Marines would have orders to look out for them and see them safe. But how to put Washington wise, without betraying myself to J.B. . . . ? and even as the thought formed, here came our gallant commander, brushing aside something that Jerry Anderson was saying, ordering him back to his post, and moving purposefully in my direction. He passed his sons' bodies without a glance and loomed above me, and my innards turned over at the sight of that ravaged headstone of a face with its burning eyes; the tangled hair sprouting from under the old hat was dirty white, like his scrub of beard, and when he spoke it was like gravel under a door.

"Can you hear me, Joshua? Are you badly hurt? What became of you?"

I had my answer ready, a red herring that should distract him if anything could, delivered with a weary flicker of the eyelids and a tremulous whisper, to let him see I was at my last gasp.

"Kagi . . ." I muttered. "Kagi . . ."

"What of Kagi?" cries he, stooping over me.

"He's . . . dead, captain," says I, very faint. "Shot . . . at the river . . ."

"And the others? Leary? Copeland?" Those were the two blacks.

"Dead . . . I think . . ." I gave a muted gasp of agony by way of business. "And . . . they killed Thompson, too . . . murdered . . . used his body . . . target practice . . ."

He made a dreadful noise; it was his teeth grating. "So they did with Leeman. The fool ran for the river, and was taken. They put a pistol to his head and . . ." He knelt down by me, and there were tears on the leathery cheeks. "Did you speak with Kagi?"

I ventured a weak shake of the head. "No . . . I tried to . . . no use . . . too many of 'em . . . ah, my leg!" I gave just a touch of feeble thrash, eyes tight shut in anguish.

"Joshua!" The callous ruffian actually gripped me by the shoulder. "What happened? Why did you run from the hotel?"

That was the question, of course, and I'd been cudgelling my wits for an answer – and in a heaven-sent flash it came to me, the perfect excuse that might also be my salvation, if only I played it properly; the one thing that might turn this selfish lunatic from his fatal resolve.

"Kagi . . ." I whispered. "Went to . . . bring Kagi . . . ah, too late!"

"What's that you say?" He was frowning in bewilderment. "You wanted to fetch Kagi? To me, you mean? But why?" Playing for time, while I chose my words, I gave a shivering moan and bit my lip (fighting the agony, you know) and could have cheered when he went on in a puzzled tone: "Joe told me you had deserted . . . I would not believe it! Why, then? Joshua – do you hear me? Speak, man!"

I decided it was time to rally a little, so I forced a brave, wry smile, and when he asked if I was in great pain, I half-raised a palsied hand and let him grip it in his horny fist.

"Not . . . too bad . . . thank'ee," says I. "Loss o' blood . . . and my leg . . . but I'll be . . . at my post . . . presently . . . never fear." Gad, I was game. "Got a gun . . . have you?" I'd no least intention of joining the defence, but it showed the right spirit, and whatever happened I wanted a piece handy. He drew a Colt from his belt and laid it by me, asking again about Kagi, but I was taking my time.

"Ah . . . thank'ee, skipper . . . that's fine. Want to . . . go out . . . fighting, you know." Talk about the last act of Hamlet. "If I must . . ." I opened my eyes wide in gallant appeal. "Must we, captain?"

"What d'ye mean, Joshua?" says he, frowning, and I clenched my teeth as in sudden pain, breathed a silent prayer, and let him have it.

"Why I went for Kagi," I began, gasped, and went on: "I knew . . . you'd fight to a finish. You're like me," I explained, with a ghastly grin. "No surrender, what? Aye . . . but the last thing Kagi said to me . . . at the farm . . . he said: 'At all costs, Josh, you must . . . see the captain safe. He must live, even if . . . we die. He has . . . the voice . . . and it must not be silenced'." I paused, almost at the end of my tether, but determined. "Well . . . when I saw . . . this morning, that if we waited . . . for the slaves, you know . . . we'd be cut off . . . killed, most likely . . . I knew I must bring Kagi to . . . to talk to you . . . make you see that your life was . . . well, too precious to lose." Another pathetic smile. "I knew you wouldn't . . . listen to me. I knew you'd heed Kagi, though . . . you always did . . . made me quite jealous sometimes . . . ne'er mind . . ." I stopped for another useful wince, and any fool could have seen I was gathering my strength for one last noble effort. I gripped his hand. "Listen to Kagi now . . . won't you? Surrender . . . for his sake!" Inspired, I drivelled on. "And for the sake of . . . of all those poor black souls . . . crying for deliverance . . . don't fail them now! Live . . . that the voice may not be silenced! Oh, surrender, now . . . call back that captain . . . and Kagi won't have died in vain . . ."

I sank back, eyes closing, in an exhaustion that wasn't entirely bogus, for I'd given it all I knew. Fine fevered stuff, in my best heroic style – a deathbed variation on the theme I'd used when I talked Wheeler into running up the white flag at Cawnpore two years earlier. Aye, but Wheeler was a level-headed soldier, not an ignorant fanatic, and when I opened my eyes again my heart sank, for the bright eyes were as hard as ever, and his mouth was turned down in a stubborn scowl. He withdrew his hand from mine.

"You too, Joshua," says he. "First Anderson, now you. He hears Captain Sinn talk of treason, so his conscience smites him now; he'll not fire again on his country's flag, he says." Good for you, Jerry; sanity at last. "And Kagi, you tell me . . . and now you." He gave a deep sigh, and went on in a weary voice. "Cannot you see, we are all dead men? If we surrender, we hang, and where is my voice then? And if we surrender, we shall have betrayed our cause – and that I'll not do!"

God, he was dense. "Captain!" I croaked, and in my desperation I forgot I was dying and came up on one elbow to whine at him in earnest. "Don't you see, if we surrender, there's bound to be a trial! You'll be able to speak out then – to tell America, tell the whole world, what . . . what we came here for! The cause, dammit, and the darkies, and everything . . . For God's sake," I yammered, "everyone will hear you, and . . . and be inspired to carry on, but if you die here, why, they'll never know! Don't you understand?"

D'ye know, I doubt if he did, for before I'd done bleating he had turned his glance aside in that brooding, distant way I knew so well; he hadn't even noticed how suddenly I'd come to life. I could have wept, for I wanted to shout in his face: "Listen, you pudding-headed dotard, I'm showing you the finest soap-box your bloody cause could have! You'll speak your piece, and then you'll swing, and good riddance, but they'll have heard you from Hell to Honolulu! (And they did; that's the irony of it.) And I'll be out of here, alive and safe, you selfish hound!" But it would have done no good; I knew that, from the grim dull set of the lined puritan face; he'd fixed what he called his mind, and that was that. He stood up, moving stiffly, and brushed the straw from his ragged britches.

"I have stated my terms," says he, "and I believe them to be honourable. If they will not accept them, for the sake of the prisoners . . ." He paused, frowning, and I wondered did he still have some wild hope that he could bluff his way out – or even that the slaves would rise to his rescue? He was daft enough.

He stood there a moment, a gaunt tattered figure silhouetted by the lamp that still burned near the doorway,[56] the outline of his stark profile like that of some great bird of prey, and looked slowly around the engine-house half in shadow, the light glinting on the metal of the long fire-carts. Maybe he was reviewing what was left of his pet lambs – Joe on guard at the half-open door, Ed Coppoc at the side loophole, the cherubic Dauphin Thompson at the rear wall, Emperor Green stretched half-asleep on the straw, his lips moving in an inaudible mutter, Jerry Anderson dozing with his back to an engine, mouth open and fair hair tousled. Beyond the engines I could hear the hostages stirring on the straw: that, and the occasional uneasy gasp and groan from Oliver, were the only sounds in the big gloomy shed. From the dark outside came the distant sound of singing and laughter from the Wager House and Galt's, and the dull incessant murmur of the surrounding troops.

"No, I'll not go back on my word." It was J.B., calm and quiet now, as though he were talking to himself. "I came to this place of a purpose, to set free the slaves, and until that is done I'll not lay down my arms. I came in no vindictive spirit, seeking no man's blood, but only to liberate those held cruelly in bondage. To that end we have fought, a handful of us against a great multitude. To surrender now would be to deny our cause, and to abandon those we fought for. We have kept the faith with them, and with our fallen comrades, and I'll not break it at the last."

He raised his head and looked about him again, eyes bright and far away, and just the glimmer of a smile on the old face. "It doesn't end here," says he. "It begins."

*　　*　　*

They left us alone all night, and you may well wonder why. There were more than a thousand men ringed about that dingy building by the armoury gates, besieging half a dozen; very well, most of 'em were green militia and drunken louts, but there were near a hundred of America's crack regiment,

319

too, the vaunted Leathernecks from the Halls of Montezuma – why the devil didn't they walk in on our pathetic rabble then and there? I've heard it asked since (at a safe distance) by the usual valiant know-alls, and the answer is because my old chief Robert Lee knew his business, that's why, and wasn't about to waste lives, and risk the hostages, by brawling in the dark when he could wait until daylight – and until the spirits of those in the engine-house were that much lower, and possibly open to reason.

So he waited, canny, imperturbable Lee, and if that long cold night did nothing to weaken the resolve of the idiot-in-chief of our ridiculous garrison, it played havoc with the yellow belly of the chief-of-staff, cowering in his corner in despair. I'm not at my best wounded and in the dark, with corpses at my feet, and not even a ray of hope visible – for I'd quite given up the notion of making myself known to old Washington: I doubted if he'd believe me, he never came within whispering distance anyway, and I didn't dare try to attract his attention, what with J.B. prowling about armed to the teeth, and Joe turning every now and then to view my recumbent form with scowling suspicion.

I'd half-expected him to be at my throat over my desertion at the Wager House, but of course he wasn't. There was nothing he could say or do, however much he mistrusted me; we were both sailing under false colours with J.B., and he couldn't expose me without exposing himself. But I can't pretend to know what was passing in that strange black mind. I knew that from having been a loyal agent of the Kuklos, and devoted to Atropos, he'd apparently found his Road to Damascus in the months at Kennedy Farm, and become a worshipper of J.B. and a fervent enemy of slavery – or at least so he said, and the glimpse I'd had of him during the retreat to the engine-house bore him out, for he'd been fighting like a Ghazi, blasting away and damning the militia. Well, I've known stranger changes of heart, and I'd seen enough of J.B. to know the kind of spell he could cast; Joe might be educated, but he had all the black's deep-seated hatred of the white race, and I guess J.B. had given him a different slant on his slave condition. Again, he may simply

320

have been as mad as a hatter; many people are, you know.

He was certainly in the grip of some kind of brainstorm on that last night in the engine-house. Violent action does that to some folk; faced with death, they lose all sense of habit and ingrained conduct, and their primitive nature, hidden under years of custom and training, comes raging out – why, even I, in extremity, have been moved to belligerence against chaps bigger than I am, and run risks that I go weak to think of afterwards. Mind you, in my case the madness don't last above a split second.

Not with Joe; his derangement was permanent, and it took the oddest form – a growing anger against J.B. If that astonishes you (and it did me) I can only illustrate it by telling you what I heard passing between them in the long watches of that awful night.

I never slept, you see, what with distress of mind and body, and there was nothing to do but lie and quake in the dark – for the lamp burned out after an hour, leaving us in pitch black, so no one moved about much: Old Washington came round to talk with J.B. at one time, but I couldn't hear what they were saying: it wasn't a quarrel though, for their voices never rose. I heard Jerry Anderson and Emperor Green croaking that they'd never understood that what they were doing was treason (a fine time to realise the error of their ways, you may think); Jerry shut up after a while, but the nigger crawled under one of the engines and sobbed his soul out, calling himself a pore blind fool, and railing against J.B. and Douglass who had brought him to this mis'able end, an' he hadn't wanted to do hurt to nobody, or free any niggers, 'cos he was jes' a plain pore nigger hisself, an' oh Lawd ha' mussy on an unhappy sinner.

His cries made a doleful chorus with the groans and pleas of young Oliver, who was delirious most of the time, but would wake now and then with a scream, and his agony was terrible to hear. When he fell silent, J.B. called his name a couple of times, and then I heard him say, "I guess he's dead."

It was after this that Joe pitched in his two penn'orth; I may have dozed, for I was suddenly aware that he was nearby, whispering angrily, and J.B. was snapping back at him: indeed, the first words I heard were J.B. growling to him to keep his place and mind who he was talking to.

"Min' ma place! An' whut place is that, hey?" That was when I realised we had a new Joe on our hands: he'd never have dreamed of taking that tone with J.B. at the farm. "Ah'll tell yuh, John Brown – it's right heah, waitin' to git kilt, when Ah should ha' bin in the hills this minute! That's wheah ma place should ha' been!"

"You forget yourself, Joseph!" J.B. sounded more shocked than angry. "Get to your post, my boy, and no more of this!"

"Ah ain't forgettin' nothin'! You the one that's forgettin' – how we was goin' to free the niggers and make an army in the hills! Wheah is they – all them slaves you was goin' to free, that was goin' to come in to us? You nevah looked near 'em – you didn't *try* to rouse 'em! All you roused wuz hostages – an' that dam' toy sword you wearin'! Call this a rebellion? – gittin' ou'selves caged in heah like dam' runaways in a bottom, gittin' shot down –"

"Hold your tongue!" barks J.B. "You dare raise your voice to me – are you mad? Or in fear of your life –"

"Ain't feared o' nothin'! 'Tis a lie – an' not th'only one you tol', neethah! You say we wuz goin' clear out th'arsenal, an' hightail! Well, you didn't! Jes' set heah, doin' nothin' – an' Stevens tellin' yuh to git out, an' Kagi sendin' messages, an' you di'nt pay no heed, an' they gits theyselves kilt 'cos o' yo' foolin' an' playin' wi' yo' dam' sword'n pistols!" J.B. was making outraged noises, but Joe swept on: "Whyn't you git while we cud? Even that rat Comber had *tole* you we dassn't stay heah! Why, you goddam ole fool, you destroyed us! An' wuss – you *betrayed* us, an' the coloured folks an' all, with yo' fine talk an' promises, an' gittin' us trapped an' all git kilt, 'cos high'n mighty John Brown ain't got the brains of a buzzard! An' didn't *need* to – cud ha' been in the hills right now, rousin' the niggers to tear up you white slavin' bastards if you'd jes' listened –"

The oily double click of a Colt hammer stopped him dead, and I knew J.B. was covering him.

322

"Get to your post, Joe." His voice was firm, but almost gentle. "I might shoot you for mutiny, but you are not in your right mind, so I have not heard you. Now – go!"

There was a long moment in which I held my breath in sudden excitement – for J.B. didn't know what he was dealing with, the blinding speed with which Joe could unlimber and fire . . . suppose he blew the old man to blazes, we might win clear yet, arrange a surrender – no, Joe himself would never allow that, he'd likely try to shoot his way clear . . .

"Go!" says J.B. again, while I strained my eyes uselessly against the darkness – and then there was the shuffle of the straw as Joe turned away and went to the open doorway; I saw his outline for a moment against the night sky glowing faintly with the torches of the besiegers, then he crouched down in the shadow. I could picture the black face contorted with anger, glaring out into the night – who'd have thought it, eh? Joe, of all people, to tell J.B. the truth to his face. Much good it would do now – Oh, lord, why hadn't I lain doggo in the hotel loft instead of barging about like a headless fowl? I might have been snug and warm and larruping Mrs Popplewell this minute. Why hadn't I bolted from the farm, or jumped out of the train to Hagerstown, or dived down an alley in New York? Why, for that matter, had I let myself be lured into that Washington hotel by the designing dwarf Mandeville, and gone like a lustful lamb to the slaughter with Spring's diabolical daughter, or slavered after that dough-faced heifer in Calcutta? That had been less than a year ago, and here I was like a rat in a pit awaiting the terriers . . . and around me the blackness was fading to grey, figures and objects were coming into view in the dim interior of the engine-house, and in the distance a cock was crowing.

There was a stirring in the surrounding host, a whistle blowing, shouts of command, and the clatter of equipment; the militia were standing to. A kettle drum began to beat in a sharp staccato roll followed by the tramp of marching feet; Washington stood up beyond the engines, listening with his grey head to one side, signing to the other hostages to be still. J.B. was already on his feet; he put down his Sharps,

323

carefully examined the cylinder of his pistol, and finally drew Frederick's sword with a slow grating noise that had every head turning towards him.

"Stand to your arms, men," says he. "Be ready for a sudden rush."

I picked up the pistol he'd given me, and checked the loads with trembling fingers. God alone knew what I was going to do with it, but I wanted it ready – God knew what I was going to do about anything, if it came to that . . . wait, and fight back my fear, and hope for some miracle. I eased myself up against the wall, moving my wounded leg. I'd flexed and tested it in the darkness, and knew it would bear my weight; the flesh around the bloody pock caused by the slug was one great black bruise, and it ached abominably, but that mattered less than the stiffness in my joints. Could I run if need be? I hauled myself up by the wall, leaned on the limb, and almost came a cropper – Jesus, I'd be lucky if I could manage a hobble!

I clung to the rough brick for support, the sweat running off me, for all that it was bitter cold. J.B. glanced round and saw me; for a second he seemed puzzled, then he gave me a grim approving nod; faithful to the last, he'd be thinking . . .

"Someone comin', cap'n!" Jerry Anderson was at a loop-hole, shrill with excitement. "Two officers – an' they ain't armed! Oh, cap'n, don't shoot 'em – we don't want to fight no more!"

I was lurching along the wall before the words were well out of his mouth, clinging to the brickwork like a stricken lizard and praying that my leg wouldn't betray me, for the news he'd shouted could mean only one thing – another parley before the storm, and I was going to be in on it, if I had to crawl every inch of the way. Pain stabbed through my knee, and I'd have fallen if I hadn't wrenched Jerry's carbine from his hand and thrust it into the ground as a crutch. It was too short by half, and I tottered there like Long John Silver in drink, roaring for assistance, until Emperor, who'd emerged from under the engine where he'd been weeping, gave me a shoulder. J.B. was already at the doorway, cocking his rifle, motioning Joe to stand aside, when I arrived at a stumbling run, grabbing at the closed side of the door. J.B. shot me a startled look, so I gave him a glaring grin, a hand on the Colt in my waistband, to let him see I was at his side, ready to sell my life dearly; he said nothing, and we both turned our eyes to the crack of the door.

Two men were walking towards us, a tall, black-avised fellow striding like a guardsman, and a smaller chap in the dark-and-light blue of the U.S. Marines. But what took my eye was the dense throng of people watching, hardly more than a long stone's throw away – there were hundreds of 'em, among the armoury sheds and outside the gates on the open ground towards the railroad tracks, militia mostly, but many townsmen, and women and children, too, all spell-bound in a strange silence broken only by the steady tread of the two approaching officers.

They stopped about twenty yards off, conferring, then the

325

Marine turned and marched back, and the big fellow came on alone, more slowly. He wore what looked like a cavalry cloak and uniform cap, an erect soldierly figure, and I was wondering where I'd seen him before when it dawned: he was devilish like *me*. Not a double, perhaps, and lacking a couple of inches of my height, but like enough, what with his handsome head, broad shoulders, and damn-you-m'lad carriage. He walked up to the door, and J.B. shoved out his carbine and demanded his business.

"James Stuart, lieutenant, First Cavalry," says he, in a pleasant Southern voice. "Am I addressing Mr Smith?"

J.B. pushed the door wider, and Stuart surveyed him a moment with keen blue eyes (mine are brown, by the way) before glancing briefly at me, propped panting against the timber and looking like the last survivor of Fort Despair, I don't doubt. He pulled a paper from his breast and offered it to J.B.

"I have a communication from my superiors, Colonel Lee, commanding the troops . . . and Mr Messervy of the Treasury Department," he added, his eyes averted from me – and as I caught his slight emphasis on the second name, and realised what it meant, I almost cried out – he knew who I was, and was letting me know it! Of course, he must have had my description from Messervy himself, and had recognised me under all the blood and filth, the alert resourceful subaltern – I was to form a good opinion of Jeb Stuart in later years, but I never held him in higher esteem than at that moment. For whatever happened now, even if J.B. refused to chuck in the towel and it came to a final storming party, the attackers would be looking out for me, and I'd be immune, and safe, at last . . . Even as Stuart, at J.B.'s request, began to read the letter aloud, I was warily scanning the distant spectators – the militia, the Marines, a group of officers apart, a regimental-looking buffer in civilian duds astride a horse by the trees (Lee himself, as it turned out), and, sure enough, a tall, graceful figure pacing leisurely to and fro by his stirrup: Messervy, all careless elegance at six in the morning.

People were crowding behind us to hear the message –

326

Washington, a couple of other hostages, Jerry, and Joe absolutely breathing down my neck. It was a plain demand for surrender, promising that we'd be held pending orders from President Buchanan, but that if we resisted, Lee couldn't answer for our safety. J.B. listened in grim silence, and if you'd been there, and seen that huge crowd hemming us in, and the militia standing to their arms, and out before them the navy frocks and sky-blue pants and white belts of the Marines drawn up at attention . . . well, you'd have *known* he must give in at last. But damme if he didn't come straight back at Stuart with his own impudent demand that we be allowed to march out unmolested, and given time to get clear away. Stuart said politely that there could be no terms but Lee's – and *still* the stubborn jackass went at him, sounding ever so calm and reasonable, never raising his voice, but keeping his carbine trained on Stuart's midriff and refusing to budge: let us go, or we'd fight to the end.

How long these futile exchanges lasted, I don't know – Jeb said later that it was a long parley – but they became quite heated, with Washington and his friends joining in, begging Stuart to bring Lee in person, Stuart shaking his head, Jerry protesting that he hadn't known it was treason, Joe grunting most alarmingly in my ear, and J.B. prosing away blandly as though he were passing the time of day with a fellow-idler on a street corner. At one point he asked if he and the lieutenant hadn't met before, and Jeb smiled and said, yes, when his cavalry had dispersed J.B.'s riders after some scrimmage on the Santa Fe Trail three years before. "You were Ossawatomie Brown in those days," says he, and J.B. said solemnly that he was glad to see that Jeb was well and prospering in the service.

"You behaved with great good sense on that occasion," says Stuart. "Will you not do the same now, and spare many lives?"

"My life is a small thing," says J.B. "I am not afraid to lose it."

"I dare say not," says Stuart. "It may be forfeit sooner than you think."

"That is all one to me," says J.B.

327

"Well, I'm sorry," says Stuart. "But if you are determined, and there is no more to be said . . ."

There he paused, and all of a sudden there was that electric feeling in the air that comes in moments of crisis. J.B. sensed it, his hand tightened on his carbine stock, and imperceptibly Stuart shifted his weight from his heels to his toes. He hadn't looked at me since that first glance, but now he did, without any expression at all, and then his eyes travelled to the Colt at my waist and back to my face again before returning to J.B., all in a couple of seconds, while J.B. waited for him to finish his sentence, and Stuart waited . . . for me? I could hear Messervy's voice in that Washington office, clear as a bell: "John Brown must die somewhere along the road . . . for the sake of this country, and tens of thousands of American lives, he must not survive for martyrdom . . ."

Stuart glanced at me again – and I've no wish to impute anything to a chivalrous Southern gentleman, but if his look wasn't saying: "Mr Messervy's compliments, and if you'll be good enough to shoot the old bastard on the spot, and roll out of harm's way, he'll be much obliged to you", then I've never seen an unspoken invitation in my life.

He didn't have a hope. Not my style at all – especially not in the immediate presence of a highly unpredictable coloured gentleman who was one of the fastest guns I'd ever seen and had been itching to give me lead poisoning for months. I've often wondered how Joe, in his excited condition, would have reacted to the assassination of his erstwhile hero, but I'd no intention of finding out; I let my right hand fall loose at my side – and what happened next is history.

Stuart's version[57] is a masterpiece of nonchalance: "So soon as I could tear myself away, I left the door and waved my cap." I'd say he tore himself away at the speed of light, sideways like a leaping salmon, but I didn't see him wave because even as he sprang the Marines were charging forward from fifty yards away, bayonets fixed, with the little officer brandishing his sword, and J.B. was letting fly a shot and slamming the door to all in one movement;

unfortunately he closed it on my injured leg, and for several seconds I took no further interest, being blind with agony, and rolling on the floor, in which time he and Joe had jammed the bar into place, Coppoc and young Thompson were blazing away through gaps in the door timbers at the advancing Marines, and Emperor Green burst into tears and tried to hide behind an engine.

It had happened in split seconds, one moment peaceful parley, the next carbines and revolvers booming in the confined space, the hostages diving for cover, Jerry yelling: "No, no, we surrender!", the doors shuddering to the blows of sledge-hammers wielded by the leading Marines, a great roaring and cheering without and shouts of defiance within mingling with the crash of shots and splintering of timbers, black powder smoke filling the engine-house in a stifling cloud – and Flashy scrambling away as fast as his game leg would take him, intent on rounding the engines to take cover among the hostages. I didn't get even halfway.

There was a rending crash behind me, and as I clung to the nearer engine for support I saw that a bottom section of the battered door was caving in: the planks were starting asunder, and through the narrow gaps could be seen glimpses of the attackers. J.B. had stepped away to reload his carbine, Joe had his back to the door, stretching sideways to shoot through a ragged hole in the wood, and suddenly he screamed like a wounded horse and staggered away from the door, clutching his left arm: behind him a bloody bayonet point was jutting through the planks.

"Stand firm, men!" bawls J.B. "Sell your lives dearly!"

He ran to the shattered section of the door, stooping to shove his Sharps through the opening, and firing: either side of him the two boys, Coppoc and Thompson, were shooting through the gaps point-blank at the Marines heaving at the outside of the door. Joe had half-fallen a couple of yards behind J.B.: he came up on one knee, his black face demonically contorted with rage and pain, mouthing curses that were lost in the uproar. J.B. turned and shouted, gesturing to him to come on.

"Courage, Joe! Don't give in now!"

329

I can't explain what followed, though I've had more than half a century to think about it. I can only tell you that Joe let out a terrible anguished cry and levelled his pistol at J.B. The old man was turned away, revolver in one hand and carbine in t'other, shooting through the half-wrecked door, when Joe squeezed the trigger – and his piece misfired. He screamed wordlessly, and I can only think that all the fury he felt at J.B.'s failure – betrayal, I'd heard him call it – had welled up at the last when death was staring him in the face, and he was venting it on the old fellow in a fit of blind anger, as a passionate child will strike out at a parent. That I can accept – what I cannot explain is what happened in the next second, when Joe thumbed back the hammer for a second shot, and I put two bullets in his back.

I can't pretend I was consciously trying to save J.B. Why should I, when I'd no thought for any life but my own, and God knows I owed him nothing? I drew, and fired, as instinctively as you throw up a hand to ward an unexpected blow. Dick Burton, who fancies himself a psychologist, says I gave way to a primitive impulse of race-survival, and killed Joe because he was black and J.B. was white – would I have shot Kagi or Stevens if they'd been in Joe's place, grins clever Dick. Likely not . . . but snooks to you, Burton, I'd not have shot Mrs Popplewell or Ketshwayo, either, because I quite liked them, you see, and Kagi and Stevens, while I detested Joe. So perhaps it comes to this, that deep down, for all the harm and horror he did me, I must have quite liked old J.B. – well enough, at any rate, not to have him shot by that black son-of-a-bitch if I could help it.

Anyway, I settled Joe, and he went down like a riven oak, his pistol exploding into the floor as he fell, and at that moment the bottom of the door gave way with a tremendous rending of timber, and through it like a ferret from its hole came the little Marine officer, flourishing his sword. He plunged straight past J.B., I threw myself aside, and he darted round the engines, yelling to the hostages to stand clear. Washington sang out: "There's old Ossawatomie!" pointing over the engine to J.B., who was standing erect before the doorway, throwing lead for all he was worth as

330

the Marines came bursting and yelling through the shattered wreckage of the door, their bayonets at the present.

I believe he downed two of them, for I saw one reel away clutching his face, with blood running through his fingers, and another pitched headlong at his feet, and then the little officer was on him like a wild-cat, thrusting at his body. J.B. tumbled forward, and as the officer hacked at his head I saw that the blade was bent at right-angles; he hammered away at the old fellow's skull, and all around was screaming, struggling confusion as the Leathernecks came surging in, bayonetting everything in sight. Jerry Anderson was skewered to the floor, shrieking horribly, as he tried to dive beneath an engine, young Thompson was flung bodily against the back wall and pinned, kicking like a beetle, by several blades, someone was bellowing "Quarter, quarter, we surrender!", everywhere were snarling faces, glittering steel, swirling smoke – but never a shot now, for the last of our people was down or overpowered, and the Marines had been ordered not to fire; one of them, a red-faced corporal, glaring like a madman and roaring inarticulately, came lunging out of the press of struggling men, his bayonet driving at me, and as I threw myself back the little officer thrust him aside shouting "Not him! Prisoner!", and I echoed him, bellowing "Not me! I'm a hostage!" The corporal fairly howled with disappointment, but kept his point to my breast as I struggled into the corner, my hands raised, and as I sat there trembling there was a long, bubbling scream from above, and Thompson's body, streaming blood, slid down the wall beside me and collapsed across my legs. He was still alive, for I felt him give a convulsive shudder; then he was still, and as he died, so did the shouting and confusion. The Harper's Ferry raid was over.

I reckon about two minutes had passed since Stuart jumped aside at the doorway, and in that brief terrible scrimmage four men had died, which was fewer than I'd have guessed as I gazed in horror at the shambles. There was blood everywhere, spattering the walls and soaking the straw, and more bodies strewn on the floor than there were men standing up, or so it seemed. A Marine was slumped against the post of the now-open door ahead of me, clasping a hand to his wounded face; another lay still across the threshold. J.B. was lying face down, his white head horribly dabbled, and beside him Joe was on his back, his pistol in his hand. The bodies of Oliver, Watson, and Taylor lay close by, Jerry Anderson was twitching in death beneath the engine, and Thompson, his girl's face slack and ugly under the blond curls, lay lifeless on my legs until the Marine corporal rolled him clear.

The only unwounded raiders seemed to be Emperor Green, who was crouched wailing against the wall (he was the one who'd told Douglass he'd "go wid de ole man", more fool he), and young Ed Coppoc, who was looking pretty cool, considering that four Leathernecks were standing over them with bayonets poised. The officer was shepherding the hostages out through the other door, which had been unbarred, and an almighty cheer went up from the crowds outside as they passed into the open air.

There was a time when I'd have lain shivering from shock after such an ordeal: I might even have wept (from reaction, not grief, you understand) at the carnage around me. But as I sprawled exhausted in that engine-house, watching the Marines making short work of heaving the bodies and wounded away, I felt nothing but a huge blissful weariness and a growing exultation – the nightmare that had begun at the Cape, when I heard Spring's tread on the deck overhead, was surely past and done with now; the frantic days and nights when Crixus and Atropos and the damned Yankee bogies had plunged me into this mad business, the long months of weariness while J.B. mismanaged his preparations, the terror of the raid and this final horror in the engine-house – I was here, safe and whole, with nothing but two paltry scratches that did no more than ache, coated with blood and filth to be sure, but who minds that when you see before your eyes what might have been . . . young, handsome Oliver of the merry laugh; brash, eager Jerry Anderson; poor daft Taylor gone to explore his spirit world; Dauphin Thompson, who had blushed like a maiden if you so much as asked him the time – all being dragged out by

332

the heels to lie in the mud under blankets. Bad luck, lads, but sooner you than me.

J.B. and Watson were still alive, so they carried them away on stretchers; the old man's hair was stiff with dried blood, and one hand dangled from the stretcher like a skinny brown claw. Then they marched out the two prisoners, which left me and the corporal and the late Joe Simmons. I made shift to rise, but the Leatherneck growled to me to stay put, those were his orders. I didn't mind lying there, holding my private little thanksgiving service and listening to the distant murmur of the mob outside, and after a while Marines came at the double, placing lanterns on the engines, shrouding the broken windows and loopholes, heaving the wrecked door into place, and closing it behind the little officer and a tall civilian in a tile hat and frock: Messervy, surveying the ruin impassively, prodding at Joe's corpse with his walking stick, and then picking his way carefully through the bloody straw to where I lay.

He looked down at me, stroking his moustache with a gloved finger, the long-jawed Yankee Corinthian as ever was, and just the sight of him, looking so cool and civilised, cheered me up even further.

"Well, well," says he. "How are you?"

I couldn't be bothered to think of a smart answer, so I said pretty fair. He asked if I was wounded, and when I told him, he sighed, removed his hat and gloves, looked for a place to put them, declined the corporal's offer to hold them, and finally set them down on the engine. Then he stooped to examine my neck and knee.

"Nothing that soap and water won't cure," says he. "Mr Green, would you be good enough to bring them yourself, with bandages, a towel, some spirits, and a Marine cloak and cap." He rose, smoothing his coat, and resumed his hat and gloves.

"Now, I want a Marine guard round this building. No one to be allowed closer than twenty yards. That," he indicated Joe's body, "is to be removed after dark, and buried away from the town, and the burial party are then to forget all about it. This gentleman," he turned to me, "never existed.

You'll not mention him, and if questions are asked by *any-one*, you never heard of him. Is that clear?" Green nodded, looking keen. "Corporal, you understand?"

"What gen'leman are you referrin' to, sir?" asks the Leatherneck, staring to his front. Messervy gave a faint smile.

"I beg your pardon. I should have said *sergeant* . . . shouldn't I, Mr Green?"

"Yes, sir!" beams Green. "I'll see to it."

"Capital. Now, I'll be leaving here presently with some-one in a Marine coat and cap. We are to be ignored, and I trust by that time you will have dispersed any gaping sight-seers. The soap and water now, if you please."

They were all I needed to complete my restoration, and when Green had brought them and left us alone, I sluiced away the filth with a will; I felt as though I was cleansing myself of Harper's Ferry, and John Brown, and the whole disgusting business. The wounds looked clean enough, and when I'd clapped on the dressings Messervy helped me with the bandages, talking to the point, as usual.

"Brown is not only alive, but surprisingly well, and damned talkative – which, as you know, is the last thing we wanted. The old brute must be made of leather. Run through the kidneys, the doctor tells me, and has lost any amount of blood, though you'd not know it to hear him. Conversing like a politician, which I suspect he is." He knotted my neck bandage and stepped back. "Pity you didn't shoot him. 'Twould have saved a few lives today . . . and who knows how many hereafter?"

"Well, mine wouldn't have been one of 'em," says I. "Not with Joe crowding me in that doorway."

"Ah, yes, Joe." He glanced at the body. "Your work, I take it . . . the Marines had orders not to shoot. Settling a score, were you?"

"Accident. He got in the way when I was sighting on Brown." Why shouldn't I get credit by pretending I'd tried to do Messervy's dirty work for him? "Since you were so all-fired eager to have Brown dead, why didn't you get the Marines to do it when they stormed this place? Or have someone shoot him yesterday – hang it, he was walking

334

around town large as life? Why don't you slip something in his dinner now? And don't tell me it ain't your style!"

"Unofficial death warrants have a habit of recoiling," says he coolly. "My countrymen have one great failing – they talk too much."

"Aye – so you shanghai some poor bloody foreigner to do the job! Well, I didn't have the ghost of a chance, until today . . . and I'll tell you, Messervy, I ain't apologising! I served your turn because that damned little squirt Seward put a pistol to my head . . . but why the hell should I murder for you? Tell me that!"

He shrugged, leaning against the engine and stirring the straw with his cane. "It would have been convenient. Now . . . the law must take its course, and God only knows where that will lead. Still, that's not your affair. I guess you did what you could to keep Brown out of Virginia –"

"You're damned right! A pity your own people didn't do as much! I still can't fathom it – you knew what he intended, where he was, who his backers were, what men and money he had – confound it, you knew the very bloody place – here! Why in God's name didn't you stop him?"

"You and I tried," says he. "But we ain't politicians. What did you call us – government ruffians?" He wrinkled his fine nose, and became business-like. "That's neither here nor there. The sooner you're out of this, the better –"

"Hurrah for that! Lord Lyons –"

"He don't want to see you. Yes, there's been a word in his ear, from the very highest quarter – and warm in your praise it has been, too. But he agrees with us that there's no useful purpose to be served by prolonging your presence in this country a moment longer than need be –"

"Sensible chap! When do I leave?"

"You catch the Baltimore train tonight, from the station over the way. It's a train you're probably familiar with," says he drily, "since your friend Brown held it up two nights ago. It is now running normally. At Baltimore, there's a berth already reserved for you on a packet sailing for Liverpool tomorrow. It's paid for, and this –" he handed me an envelope "– is three hundred dollars to cover expenses en route . . . for which I'd like a signed receipt, in the name of Comber, I suggest."

I'll say this for the Americans, they waste no time. Why, by tomorrow night I'd be at sea, with all this horror behind me – a couple of weeks, and I'd be in England! Home, with Elspeth, and my Indian honours thick upon me, and "warm praise" conveyed by diplomatic channels . . . it was too good to be true, and standing there in that beastly blood-stained shed, with the reek of powder smoke and the stench of death, I felt the tears start to my eyes and absolutely had to turn away. Messervy brought me back to earth.

"I've arranged quarters here where you can wait unobserved until the train comes in tonight. Go straight aboard, keep to your cabin until you reach Baltimore, then take a cab directly to the dock and the ship – all your tickets and directions are in the envelope with the money. In the meantime you can shave off your beard, and I'll furnish you with some decent clothes. Keep your collar up and your hat down. No sense in taking risks."

That's a word that always makes me raise an eyebrow; what risk, I asked, and received one of his ironic looks.

"Well, now, I don't suppose you'd want to run into anyone from the Underground Railroad or the Kuklos on the street, would you? Not that you haven't served their turn admirably – John Brown has run his raid, which is what they both wanted, and while Crixus will go into deep mourning when he learns the result, I'd say Atropos will be drinking your health with three times three. Still, better not to renew their acquaintance, don't you think?"

At the mention of their names I'd started like the dear gazelle. I hadn't given them a thought since the raid began, but now . . .

"I'll telegraph to have someone keep an eye open in Baltimore, anyway," he reassured me. "Those Kuklos operators are still in the Tombs, by the way, and if Atropos set other men to watch you . . . what of it?" He shrugged. "He certainly has no reason to wish you harm, after this splendid debacle. He doesn't know about *that* . . ." he pointed his cane at Joe's body ". . . and he never will. No,

336

right now he'll be congratulating himself on five thousand dollars well spent –"

"He can keep it for me!" says I, and meant it. "You're right, though . . . why, he'll think I've done him proud!"

"Which you have," says he drily. "Prouder than you did Crixus, or the U.S. Government. Not that your efforts aren't appreciated." He was peering through a crack in the make-shift door. "I think we might venture out now . . . the citizens seem to have lost interest in the sight of Marines guarding a dilapidated fire-house, though I dare say the souvenir seekers will be stripping it bare shortly. What, you don't care to take a brick as a memento . . . ?"[58]

There were still a number of folk idling beyond the armoury gates, staring hopefully through the railings, but our way led into the armoury proper, where Messervy had commandeered an office, guarded by two beefy civilians in hard hats. One of them brought me an enormous fry from the Wager House, with a jug of coffee – and I smiled to think what the little waiter would have said if he'd known who the customer was. From that I turned inevitably to fond memories of the generous Mrs Popplewell – gad, she'd been an unexpected windfall, splendidly equipped, if you like abundance, which I must say I do after a long abstinence. Resourceful lass, too, finding me a bolt-hole – and loyal, the way she'd answered back those ruffians who'd been threatening her. Aye, she'd served her turn, in more ways than one, bless her black bounties.

There was a cot in the office, but I was too excited to sleep, so I followed Messervy's advice and removed my face furniture, all but the moustache and whiskers, of course. It's a great delight to see your chin again after a hard slog in the field; reminds you that there are finer things in life, like England, and home, and sleeping sound, and strolling down Piccadilly with your hat on three hairs, and women, and drink . . . and Elspeth.

I was grinning at myself in the mirror when Messervy bowled in and told me to put on my cap and coat, double quick, and to muffle up well: he had something to show me. I followed him, wondering, along an alley between the armoury buildings; he stopped at a door and told me to pull my cap well down over my brows.

"Stay close behind me," says he softly, and led the way. There was an open inner door ahead, with men's backs turned to us. Messervy went right up behind them, and I followed, peering over his shoulder. The little room was crowded with people, standing and sitting, all intent on a man lying propped up on a palette against the far wall, and I bit back a gasp: it was J.B.

He'd never been a happy sight, but now he looked like the proceeds of a grave robbery. They'd washed the blood out of his hair and beard, and given him a clean shirt, but his face was gaunt and pallid, tight over the bones, and there were dark stains under the sunken eyes – but they were burning still, with that same grim fire, and his voice was harsh and strong as ever. For he was croaking away on the old line, about how he'd come to free the slaves, and for no other purpose; no one had sent him here but God and J.B. – or the Devil, if that was how they chose to view it – and he could have got clear away, but had been concerned for his hostages (and the fears of their wives and daughters in tears, if you please), and had wanted to reassure anyone who thought he was only there to burn and kill.

Someone cried out that he *had* killed people going quietly about the streets; J.B. replied that he didn't know about that, and had done his best to save lives; he'd been fired on repeatedly without shooting back.

"That's not so!" cries another. "Why, you killed an unarmed man by the tracks – yes, and another one!"

J.B. turned his head with an effort and pointed a talon at the speaker. "See here, my friend, it's useless to contradict your own people who were my prisoners. They will tell you otherwise."

There was a babble of protests and questions, and I saw that two fellows sitting close to him had pencils and note-books – newspaper reporters, if you'll credit it. The rest of them were sober citizens; Lee was there, and a dignified cove who I believe was the Governor, and Jeb Stuart with a face like thunder – and all crying out and badgering away

338

at the old beggar, and him with a hole clear through to his kidneys, and his head cut to bits.

My first thought was, why, you bloody vandals. I don't shock easy, and have no more of the milk of human kindness than you'd put in a cup of tea; I'll taunt and gloat over a fallen foe any day, and put a boot in his ribs if he sasses back – but I'm a brute and a bully. These were your upstanding pillars of society, bursting with Christian piety and love thy neighbour, and here they were, shaking their sanctimonious heads as they harassed and goaded a seemingly dying man – aye, and feasted their eyes on him as though he were a beast in a circus, when you'd have thought that decency (on which I'm an authority, as you know) demanded that he be let alone. They even had the effrontery to argue and hector him, now that he was beat and helpless – I'd have liked to see 'em argue with him eight hours back, when he was standing up with his guns on.

Why, Flashy, you ask, this ain't pity or sentiment, surely? Not a bit of it: don't mistake disgust and contempt for the tormentor with compassion for the victim. I didn't pity J.B. one jot, but I was enraged, at first sight, by those worthy ghouls enjoying the sensation ("Say, don't talk to me about John Brown – why, I sat as close to him as I am to you this minute! Spoke to him, too – an' *told* him, yes, sir!"), and as I watched him, old and stricken and frail, answering so calm and courteous . . . well, I couldn't help thinking: good for you, J.B., that's your sort.

And then it dawned on me that the old bugger was fairly revelling in it. He'd got his audience at last, hadn't he just, the first of that world-wide congregation who would revere his name and sing his song and enshrine him in history forever. I'll swear he knew it – Lee had asked him if he'd like the mob excluded, but J.B. wouldn't hear of it; come one, come all, was his style, so that he could preach to as many as possible. That they were enemies, who'd come to vent their abomination of him and his notions, or to gloat, or just to indulge their curiosity, made it all the better for him; he could answer their harrying and abuse with urbanity and resolution – and that's where the legend was born, believe me, in that shabby little paymaster's office, for in whatever spirit they came, they left in something like awe . . . and admiration. "The gamest man I ever saw," the Governor said, and Jeb Stuart (who was bloody rude to him at the time, I may say) remarked to me years later that without men like J.B. there wouldn't be an America.

You see, like so many legends, it was true. He deserved their respect – and didn't he know how to make the most of it, the vain old show-off? Here were his enemies, the ungodly oppressors of the enslaved, against whom he'd struggled for years, who'd cursed him for a border cutthroat and nothing more – and now they were hanging on his words, recognising him in dead earnest, with wonder and no little fear. Ironic, ain't it? He'd failed . . . and found his triumph. Wounded and doomed, he was a man uplifted, and he laid it off to them with his matchless mixture of deep sincerity and sheer damned humbug.

You can read all three hours of it in the New York papers of the time, and it's an education. I heard only some of the words, but they should be enough to give you the tune, which was truly extraordinary. There he was, wounded in half a dozen places, too weak to stand, fagged out and facing certain death, and talking as easily and pleasantly as though he were in a drawing-room, answering their questions like a kindly old professor dealing with backward students. When a young militia greenhorn scoffed that he couldn't have hoped to achieve anything with just a handful of men, J.B. looked him over, smiled, and said patiently: "Well, perhaps your ideas and mine on military matters would differ materially," and when another demanded that he justify his acts, he sighed, as though explaining something to a dunce for the umpteenth time:

"I don't wish to be offensive, but I think, my friend, that you of the South are guilty of a great wrong against God and humanity. I believe it is perfectly right for anyone to . . . ah, interfere with you so far as to free those you wickedly and wilfully hold in bondage. Please understand, I don't say this insultingly."

He went on to lecture them on the Golden Rule of doing

340

unto others as they would have others do unto them, which for some reason put Jeb Stuart in a bait, for he accused J.B. of not believing in the Bible, and got a pained look and a gentle "Certainly I do", in reproof. Jeb, the ass, came back at him: when someone asked how much he'd paid his followers, and J.B. said, no wages whatever, Jeb cried out piously: "The wages of sin is death!", to which J.B. replied gently:

"I would not have made such a remark to you, if you had been a prisoner and wounded in my hands." He rubbed salt in it by observing that he could have killed Jeb "just as easy as a mosquito".

They tried to make him tell who his Northern backers were, and got nowhere. "Any questions that I can honourably answer, I will," says he, and when they quoted a letter in the papers from a prominent Yankee abolitionist predicting a slave uprising, he even raised a laugh by saying drily that he hadn't had the opportunity of reading the *New York Herald* for the past day or two. More soberly he went on:

"I wish to say that all you people of the South should prepare yourselves for a settlement of the slave question, and the sooner you are prepared, the better. You may dispose of me very easily; I am almost disposed of now, but the question is still to be settled."

Once or twice, I regret to say, he lied. He claimed that he'd been wounded "after I had consented to surrender, for the benefit of others, not for my own". He didn't surrender, ever, not that I heard. He also claimed that he had not impressed any slave against his will – and to my astonishment someone called out, "I know of one negro who wanted to go back", and who should it be but Aaron Stevens, lying on a palette farther along the wall; I had to crane my neck to see him, mighty pale, with a bloody bandage on his chest. Who that negro was I don't know. But J.B.'s biggest stretcher was that he'd done his damnedest not to kill anyone . . . I dare say he meant it, but you've read my account and can judge for yourselves.

When someone called him a fanatic, he bristled up and

said they were the fanatics, not he, at which the Governor weighed into him, telling him his silver head was red with crime, and he'd do well to start thinking of eternity. J.B. put him down in his best style.

"Governor," says he cheerfully, "judging by appearances, I have about fifteen or twenty years start on you in the journey to that eternity of which you so kindly warn me. Fifteen years or fifteen hours – I'm ready to go. The difference between your tenure of life and mine is only a trifle, and I tell you to be prepared. All you who hold slaves have more need to be prepared than I."[59]

*   *   *

"It's going to be worse than I feared," says Messervy, when we were back in my quarters. "Far worse. If only he didn't sound so almighty reasonable . . . and . . . and *saintly*, damn it!" He was more upset than I'd seen him; absolutely tweaked his moustache instead of stroking it. "What did you think of him . . . from an English point of view, I mean?"

What I was thinking was that I was damned glad I'd shot Joe when I did. I'm as sentimental as the next man, you see.

"From an English point of view? Well, they'd not take him in Whites . . . not sure about the Reform, though. Oh, very well, seriously, then – they mayn't put him up in Trafalgar Square in place of Nelson, but it'll be a close-run thing. If you hang him, that is. Put him in a madhouse, and nobody'll notice."

"He's not mad," says Messervy. "I'm not sure he wasn't the sanest man in that room. No, he'll hang. Before the next election, fortunately, or he'd be liable to beat Seward for the Republican nomination. Join me in a drink? My sorrows are in need of submersion." He poured them out. "I ask myself . . . if he talks like that when he's shot full of holes, what will he be like when he's better and standing up in court, with every paper in the country reporting him? We'll be lucky," says he thoughtfully, "if this doesn't lead to war. Well, we must just hope for the best."

I thought he was talking through his hat – one crazy farmer being topped for murder and treason didn't strike me as a reasonable *casus belli*. Which shows how much I knew. But it didn't matter to me, anyway, so I devoted myself to the brandy and contemplation of home while he sat meditating. Finally he gave a little rueful smile, and said reflectively:

"D'ye know, Flashman, sometimes I wish I had Presidential power . . . and the whole U.S. Treasury to draw on, secretly."

I said I'd fancy it rather above half myself, and what had he in mind?

"At this moment? I'll tell you. I'd consider very seriously paying you and Pinkerton a fortune to rescue John Brown from the clutches of the law and spirit him to Canada. 'Twould be an international scandal, I dare say, and a great rattling of sabres, but I've no doubt Buchanan and Palmerston could settle it without too much fuss . . . possibly with the assistance of Prince Albert and our Northern Liberals. Interesting idea, don't you think?"

"Highly diverting. What good would that do?"

"Apart from sparing us a martyr, it would unite North and South as nothing else could. Perfidious Albion meddling in our most sacred private quarrel – even the diehard abolitionists would be up in arms against you."

"You could have him shot trying to escape," says cynical Flashy.

"Too late now," says he, and closed his eyes. "If only he could have stopped a bullet in that engine-house . . . if only that ass Green had been carrying a sabre instead of his toy sword.[60] What we might have been spared . . . well, we can only leave it to the lawyers and politicians and the great American public, now."

We've come to the parting of the trails, J.B.'s and mine – and high time, too, if you ask me. He was to take the high road to the gallows and immortal fame, and I the low road to . . . well, I'll come to that in a moment. First I should tell you briefly, and at second hand, what happened to him in the little time that was left to him, and the momentous effect it had on America and, I dare say, on the world.

My last memory of him is in that paymaster's office, propped up on his mattress, battered but bright-eyed, not two pounds of his stringy old carcase hanging straight, but laying down the law in his best accustomed style, God help him . . . and I suppose I must say God bless him, too, for form's sake. Of all the men of wrath who have disturbed my chequered course, he's about the only one towards whom I feel no ill will, old pest and all that he was. He was decent enough to me, and if he led me through hell and high water . . . well, you might as well blame the lightning or the whirlwind.

I wasn't there to see his departure from the Ferry next day, but he came near to being lynched. There was a great crowd full of drink and fury when they put him on the train to Charles Town; he and Stevens had to be carried through the throng baying for their blood in panic as well as rage, for the wildest rumours were flying – that the raid had been only the prelude to a general invasion, that the slaves were on the brink of rebellion, that a great conspiracy was brewing in the North – it was even reported that a family in a village just a few miles from the Ferry had been massacred, but when Lee went galloping to the scene he found everyone safe in bed, and the slaves tranquil.

344

The fact was that not a single slave had joined in the raid, other than those taken by Stevens from Washington's farm and places nearby, and most of them had slipped off home as soon as they could, or been passive altogether. But the mischief was done: a great thrill of fear ran through the South, Virginia was preparing for war, some places were under martial law, Dixie suspected (quite mistakenly) that it was sitting on a black powder-keg ready to explode, and the storm that broke in the newspapers only added to the hysteria. One of Lee's first acts had been to send Jeb Stuart to the Kennedy Farm, where they found all J.B.'s papers and correspondence, with the names of his Northern supporters, which the brilliant old conspirator had left behind in a carpet bag, and once the Democrats and pro-slavery journals got hold of the names, the fat was in the fire. The "Black Republicans", the Secret Six, and even moderate abolitionists, became the villains of the day, plotting to wreak havoc in the South, and among those who came in for special vilification, and serve him right, was William H. Seward, the cigar-chewing blighter who'd blackmailed me into the business in New York; he was "the arch agitator who is responsible for this insurrection", and for all I know this may have cost him the Presidency.

It did no good for him and other Northerners, including Lincoln, to condemn the raid; all the South could hear was the growing peal of admiration for Brown the champion of liberty, which came even from those who deplored what Brown the raider had done. You can see the South's point of view: he was a murderous old brigand who was out to overthrow them. And you can see the North's: he was a fearless crusader who wanted only to set black men free. Both views were true, and one can't blame the Southerners for believing that he represented the North in its true colours, or the North for believing, as one speaker put it, that whether his acts had been right or wrong, J.B. *himself* was *right*. The truth was that he'd fuelled the passions of the wildest elements on both sides, and convinced even sensible and moderate people that the only answer was disunion or war.[61]

345

His trial, which began only a week after the raid, fulfilled Messervy's glummest fears. Here was the poor old hero, so weak and wounded that he had to be toted into court on a cot, submitting to his fate with Christian patience – in fact, he wasn't as poorly as he looked, and could walk when he had to. And he put on the performance of his life, telling them he'd never asked for quarter, and if they wanted his blood they could have it there and then, without the mockery of a trial. As to his defence, he was "utterly unable to attend to it. My memory don't serve me; my health is insufficient, although improving. I am ready for my fate."

I'll bet there wasn't a dry eye from Cape Cod to Cincinnati.

The trial was a formality, or a farce, if you like. Much was made of the speed with which it took place, but if they'd given him until 1870 it would have made no difference, for there could be no question of his guilt, or the penalty. His lawyers would have had him plead insanity (half his ancestors were barmy, you know), but the old fox wouldn't hear of it – and d'ye know, if I'd been called to testify on the point, I'd have had to back him up. I know that in these pages I've frequently called him mad, and lunatic, and suggested his rightful place was in a padded cell, but that's just Flashy talking; we all say such things without meaning that the object of our censure is seriously deranged. No, he wasn't mad; read his letters, his speeches, the things he said to reporters, and take the word of one who knew him well. A fanatic, yes; a man driven by one burning idea, certainly; a fool in some things, perhaps, but never a madman.

It wasn't a long trial, but seems to have had some interesting features; one of the prosecutors was too drunk to plead, they say, and t'other was the father of one of the men who'd murdered Bill Thompson on the bridge (which I'd have thought made for a nice conflict of interest, but I'm no lawyer). None of that, or the legal wrangling about jurisdiction and delays, was of the least importance. Only one thing mattered, and that was the bearing of the accused – that's what the world remembers, "the brave old border soldier", calm, dignified and unflinching, rising gamely to speak with

346

a chap supporting him either side, lying patiently on his cot as sentence of death was passed, closing his eyes in unconcern and pulling the blankets up beneath his chin. Even the most hard-bitten pro-slavers couldn't but admire "the conscientiousness, the honour, and the supreme bravery of the man". You may imagine what the good ladies of Concord and Boston thought, and the fervour with which they wept and prayed for him.

They made the mistake of giving him a month's grace before he was topped, which meant that all America could picture the gallant lonely old martyr in his cell, worn with struggle but wonderfully cheerful, waiting with quiet courage for the end. It gave the wiser heads time for second thoughts; some suggested that he should be jailed, or put in an asylum, for they knew the revulsion with which his execution would be greeted, not only in America but the world; they knew that his martyrdom would only harden the resolve of the North to carry on his campaign, and the determination of the South to resist. On the other hand, there were those who hoped that his death would hasten the rupture between North and South which they regarded as inevitable.

Messervy's notion of a rescue occurred to others, by the way; there was a plot, but when J.B. heard of it he wanted no part of it.[62] He wanted to die, I'm sure of that, because like the wiser heads he could see clearly what it would lead to. The last note he wrote, on the morning of his execution, put it plain:

> I John Brown am now quite *certain* that the crimes of this *guilty land*: *will* never be purged *away*; but with Blood. I had *as I now think*; *vainly* flattered myself that without *very much* bloodshed; it might be done.

They hanged him outside Charles Town, Virginia, on December the second before a great host of troops, among whom were John Wilkes Booth, who murdered Lincoln six years later, and Stonewall Jackson. He didn't kiss a little black child on his way to the gallows, as the sentimentalists like to believe, but as he rode on his coffin across the meadow he looked around and said: "This is a beautiful country. I never had the pleasure of seeing it before." When they asked if he wanted a signal before they dropped him, he said it didn't matter, but he didn't want to be kept waiting. His admirers, of course, treasure such details, but what struck me peculiar when I read about it, and made me think, yes, that's my old J.B., was that he was hanged in his carpet slippers.

They rang the bells for him in the North, and there was talk of statues and memorials, and such an outpouring of eulogy and grief and noble sentiment as would have done credit to Joan of Arc and Lord Nelson together; I doubt if any man in the history of the United States was more deeply or sincerely mourned – and I ain't forgetting friend Abraham, either. He was even more detested in Dixie than J.B., and he was just a politician, while J.B. was a fighting man and a rebel, a combination which no American can resist. Even in the South they respected him for his courage; I remember the verdict, delivered to me during the Civil War, of a grizzled Alabama veteran, crimson with booze and chewing on his Wheeling tobey:* "Ole Ossawatomie? Well, now, suh, Ah reckon he lived like a skunk – an' died like a lion."

I'm not arguing. You know my views on bravery, and by now you should know 'em on J.B. He was a bit of a crook, and a lot of a humbug, and he put me through the mangle, and there's a case to be made for saying he was the most evil influence ever let loose in North America. Three-quarters of a million is a powerful lot of dead men, to say nothing of wounded and crippled and bereaved. You may say their great war would have happened anyway, but he's bound to bear some of the blame. Maybe he would have thought it a price worth paying for the destruction of slavery – but I say slavery would have ended anyway, without the war and without him.

But that's no business of mine. I came through Harper's

---

* A particularly pungent cigar.

Ferry and the war that followed, so he did me no lasting damage, though he scared the innards out of me, and took a year out of my life. I can tolerate him, at my time of life, and when I hear the grandlings singing the old song, I can look back, if not with pride, at least with a curious satisfaction, as the young faces pass by in memory . . . Kagi, Stevens, Oliver, Watson, Leeman, Cook, Taylor, Ed Coppoc, the Thompsons, dear old Dangerous Newby, and all the other ghosts, white and black, whose features have faded . . . and last of all, the grizzled old Ironside with his eagle face and burning eyes.

No doubt my satisfaction is because I'm still here, and they're all long gone, one way or another. Watson died of his wounds; Coppoc and Green, who'd survived the engine-house fight, were hanged two weeks after J.B., as was Cook, who got himself captured in Maryland, the duffer; Stevens survived the four bullets they took out of him, but was hanged in the spring of '60, with Hazlett, who'd escaped from the Ferry but was caught later; the black who was with him in the arsenal got clear away, and so did the fellows whom J.B. sent back with the wagon to collect arms, and the men who'd been left behind at the farm – Meriam, who'd brought the six hundred dollars, and Tidd, and another of the young men, and Owen Brown. All those who escaped served in the Civil War (two of 'em died in it), except Owen, who lived to a ripe old age.

Like your humble obedient. As I say, I take no pride in my part in Harper's Ferry, and was a damned unwilling actor, but . . . well, I was one of John Brown's pet lambs, after all, and dine out on it regular, and am redeemed (very slightly) in the eyes of such as Miss Prentice and others of the elect, who figure that an old man, however deplorable, must have *some* good in him if he stood at Armageddon and battled for the poor downtrodden darkies. They don't know about Joe, of course.

Which brings me back at last to the point where the trails parted, and I went my separate way from Harper's Ferry, rejoicing, en route to Baltimore and home.

I spent the day resting in the office which Messervy had

made my quarters. He was out and prowling about most of the time, like a good little civil servant, and when we dined together in the evening he told me what he'd seen and heard. I could see he was depressed and agitated, for he frowned at least twice, and stroked his moustache *both* sides; what was disturbing him was that Stuart (as I told you a moment ago) had found all J.B.'s letters at the Kennedy Farm, and the Wager House was agog with rage and alarm at the proof they appeared to contain of diabolical Yankee designs.

"That stupid oaf Wise –" this was the Virginia Governor "– has been reading them aloud to the drunken rabble over yonder, and you may guess the effect. By this time tomorrow half the South will have heard of them, and be convinced that a Northern army is on the march, with the Republican Party in the van, intent on rousing the slaves to butcher their masters and burn every plantation 'tween here and Texas. What immutable law," he went on, "decrees that the obtuser the politician, the higher he will rise? I suppose it takes a peculiar combination of the imbecile, the toady, and the braggart to run for office in the first place. Can't Wise see the harm he's doing . . . or can he, I wonder?"

I looked intelligent, and he explained that Wise was a former secessionist who might be out to make mischief. "He's put them in a rare frenzy, I can tell you. Packs of drunken ruffians are out nigger-hunting this minute, and at least two fools have been arrested who claim to be John Brown raiders. Harper's Ferry will be lucky if it's still standing in the morning. I've put you on an earlier train, by the way – no sense lingering in this madhouse."

So it was about midnight that I wrapped a scarf round my chin, pulled my hat down, and made the short walk to the station with Messervy at my arm and the beefy birds striding ahead. As we passed the engine-house, shuttered and silent, with the Marine sentries on guard, I wondered about Joe, and Messervy must have read my thought, for he remarked: "They buried him down on the river a couple of hours ago. Lord love me, is that ass Wise still at his folly? I believe he won't rest until he has the whole State in an uproar!"

It was like Mafeking Night between the armoury gates

and the station, the Wager House was blazing light at every window and shaking to the uproar within, there were groups of staggering merrymakers everywhere, militiamen and roughnecks, some discharging their pieces in the air, others forming raucous glee-clubs, and in two places thronging round tub-thumpers on makeshift platforms who were working themselves and their listeners into a riotous frenzy; their themes seemed to be the necessity of lynching John Brown, closing ranks against the murderous Yankees, and putting every black in the State under lock and key – or lynching them, too, if they felt like it. Our escort shouldered a way through the torch-lit confusion of milling figures and flushed, yelling faces, to the comparative quiet of the station where the train stood – it had been there half an hour, and Messervy had timed our walk to arrive just as the bell was beginning to clang and the whistle was adding its plaintive wail to the general din.

He didn't shake hands, simply murmured, "Good-bye", with a tap on the arm, and I climbed aboard into the quiet, dim-lit corridor with only a brief glance at the tall figure raising his cane to his hat-brim in nonchalant salute before he turned away. The darkie porter showed me into my cabin – and all of a sudden I was dizzy with tiredness and an overwhelming sense of relief as I sank on to the cot, the train jolted and clanked into motion, and a moment later was booming and rumbling over the trestles of the Potomac bridge across which I'd come running, rifle in hand and heart in mouth, only forty-eight hours before. Now it was behind me, the nightmare which I could hardly believe had ever happened – the rush of action in the dark, the shouted commands, the bearded faces hurrying by, the crack of shots, and the inferno of the engine-house . . . and here I was, safe and sound bar the two smarting wounds in my neck and knee, rattling over the ties out of that awful world, and back to life again.

I couldn't be bothered to undress – I'd no nightshirt, or a blessed stitch except what I was wearing, anyway. Have to do something about that . . . no time to shop in Baltimore, even if I'd been fool enough to venture into the town

. . . borrow some duds when I got aboard the packet, perhaps . . . the devil with it, sufficient unto the day . . . I was content to lie, exhausted, wondering idly if the porter could forage me a bottle of something sensible.

Pat on the thought there was a soft knock on the door, and his beaming black face appeared.

"Yo' podden, suh," says he. "De party in de nex' cabin axes if you kin'ly like to partake o' some refreshment, 'fore you settles to rest." He chuckled, with a knowing look. "Says if yo' sociably inclined, be honnered to make yo' acquaintance over a little glass or two."

I'd seen that look before, in French hotels, and while it was unexpected here it was by no means unwelcome – I wasn't as exhausted as all that. Of course, I might be misreading his expression, and find myself closeted with some boring old buffer who couldn't sleep . . . and Messervy had told me to stay close . . . but what the blazes, it was only next door, and the darkie was positively leering.

"That's most civil of the . . . gentleman?" says I, and he tittered behind his hand in a way that settled my doubts and brought me off the cot, smoothing my hair and glancing in the glass. He effaced himself, and I slipped out and knuckled the timber adjoining. No reply, so I turned the handle and found myself in an empty but well-lit cabin . . . ah, it was one with an alcove bunk, with the curtains drawn. Eureka, thinks I, twitching the curtains aside, and . . .

"Well, hello yo'self, handsome," says Mrs Popplewell.

I stood rooted in astonishment, partly from the shock of seeing her, of all people, when I'd expected some railroad rattler, partly because she was reclining languidly on one elbow like that Continental tart in the painting – you know the one, bare buff except for a ribbon round her neck, and a nigger maid in the background. Mrs Popplewell wasn't wearing even a ribbon; she lay there all black and glossy in the lamplight, smiling a welcome and extending a plump hand, and if I hadn't been so dumfounded I dare say I'd have pressed it to my lips on the spot, if you know what I mean.

"Seen you comin' to the train," says she, in answer to my

352

incoherent inquiry. "Couldn't hardly b'lieve ma eyes! Why, Ah made sure you was gone, in that awful fightin' las' night, an' this mornin'! Nevuh see such doin's – shootin' an' killin'!" She seized my nerveless hand and dragged me into a sitting position beside her. "Well, don' jes' gape like a fish out o' water! Tell me whut happen, an' wheah you bin, and how you come to be heah . . . unless . . ." She grinned hugely and transferred her hand from my wrist to my britches ". . . unless you can think o' suthin' better to do fust . . . oh, my, Ah should think you can!"

She was right, you know. The babble of questions that rose to my lips became a muted howl as she fondled with one hand and hauled me down with the other; I seized hold, marvelling at my luck, and fairly wallowed, partaking of refreshment as the porter had advised, and I must say de party in de nex' cabin was sociably inclined to the point of delirium. It was a wonder the train didn't jump the tracks, and only when she had subsided, moaning, and I had got my breath back, did we resume the conversation, with mutual expressions of bewilderment before all was explained.

Explained on my side, that is, for she brushed aside my demands to know how she had fared with Sinn and the ruffians who had been interrogating her. I'd have thought that my sudden descent from the skylight and my precipitate departure thereafter would have compromised her altogether, but apparently not; she had been able to satisfy Sinn of her innocence, she said, and ten dollars apiece from her purse had been enough for the others.

"They ain't used to black ladies with money – tuk the starch right out o' them," she chuckled. "But that don' matter – Ah's heah, ain't Ah? But how'd you git out o' that scrape – why, honey, Ah nevuh thought to see you 'live again! Now you jes' tell Hannah, 'cos she's dyin' to heah – say, but lemme kiss you fust, you deah big lovin'-machine! Theah, now, you jes' play gentle while you tell me . . . but don' talk too long, will yuh, 'cos we got a deal o' pleasurin' to do 'fore we gits to Baltimo' . . ."

So I spun her, at greater length, the yarn I'd told her on

first acquaintance – that I was in the employ of the U.S. Government, and had enlisted in J.B.'s band as a spy, even to the length of taking part in their raid. All of which was true enough, as was my explanation of why I'd taken refuge with her until such time as it was safe for me to reveal myself to someone in authority.

"You saw what it was like, all the confusion and shooting, with those drunk madmen who'd have killed me on sight . . . it was only after I got away from your room – and I say, I'm awfully sorry I had to mishandle you so roughly –"

"You mishandle me any ole way you like, dahlin'," she purred, toying lazily in a most distracting fashion. "Go on, honey . . . tell me mo' . . . but keep right on mishandlin' . . ."

"Well, I managed to get away, and by great good luck the Marines had arrived, and I was able to make myself known to Colonel Lee –"

"That the fine soldier with the moustache Ah saw this aft'noon? Came to the hotel, with Gov'ner Wise, an' the other people? Say, there was one real fine man theah, big an' han'some, kinda like you, but not neah as lovesome. Made me all shivery, tho', jes' to look at him . . . my, but Ah jes' love men with black beards'n whiskers! Like you best with jes' yo' whiskers, tho' . . . gives me somep'n to bite at!" And she nibbled my chin.

"Yes . . . well, when I'd spoken to Lee, of course, every-thing was all right. You know what happened after that . . . the Marines caught Brown and the others, and that was the end of it. And now, I'm on my way to Baltimore, as you see, to report to my superiors."

"You sure are one lucky man," says she, stroking my whiskers. "An' Ah'm one lucky gal. Why, when Ah saw you comin' to the train, with that tall gen'leman – say, he's a right pretty feller, too. He a friend o' yours?"

"What? Who? Oh, that fellow . . . no, don't know who he is – one of the Governor's people, I think." Why, I don't know, I felt the less I said about Messervy the better. "The handsome man you saw with Colonel Lee, by the way, was probably Lieutenant Stuart. Fancied him, did you? D'ye know what, Hannah, I've a notion you fancy *all* men, don't you?"

"You bet, dahlin'," says she, pushing her tongue into my mouth. "That's mah weakness. But Ah jes' fancy 'em one at a time . . . now, hold on theah . . . you mus' be dry aftuh all that talkin'." She slipped from my grasp and got out to fill two glasses at the buffet. I put mine down at a gulp, while she sipped hers standing. Then she put down her glass, and vibrated her gleaming bulk in the lamplight, looking down at me and hefting her huge poonts in her hands, smiling wickedly at my reaction.

"Ah reckon you 'bout ready now," says she, and, once again, she was right, absolutely.

"Well, now," says she afterwards, "that was whut Ah calls . . . pleasure!" She shivered, sitting astride, and stretched luxuriously, her arms above her head. Then she sighed, regretfully, and removed her massive weight from my creaking thighs, climbing out and donning her peignoir. "Ah'm real sorry 'tis over . . . Shouldn't ha' done it, not once let 'lone twice. But Ah got to tell you, dahlin', you are the screwin'est man Ah ever did see! That's my 'scuse." She sighed again. "Anyway, that was pleasure . . . an' now – business." She sat down carefully on the chair across the cabin, and asked mildly: "What happened to Joe Simmons?"

I gave a start that almost brought the cot loose from its moorings, but I couldn't speak for shock, and she went on:

"You know Joe, now . . . he was with you when you came to the hotel, first time I saw you. Mr La Force's man, who brought you up to Noo Yawk, and then to Concord, and so on after." She fluttered her fingers, and even in my stunned bewilderment I realised that the broad Dixie-nigra voice had modulated into soft Southern tones. "We know he was in that engine-house . . . but he never came out with the others. What happened to him?"

"We?" It was all I could say.

"Sure . . . the Kuklos." The plump pug face beamed in a smile. "Didn't Atropos tell you we'd be watchin' you an' Joe all the way? Sure he did . . . oh, we lost you in Noo Yawk for a spell, when the police took those three fellows

355

who were shadowin' you and Miz Mandeville. Mr La Force was real grieved 'bout her . . . thought she was true to him, never suspected she was operatin' for the gov'ment . . . till you an' she showed up in company with Messervy. You see, we have a man watchin' him, permanent. Those three men of Hermes's, in Noo Yawk, they weren't the only ones we got up there."

I found I was shaking in every limb as I lay there stark on the cot; instinctively I jerked the sheets over myself, and her big lips twitched in a smile.

"Don't do that, sweethea't . . . I jus' love lookin' at you. My, but you are the finest! Now, then . . . tell me 'bout Joe."

"I . . . I don't know what you mean! If he was in the engine-house . . . well, he must have been killed or captured –"

"*If* he was in there? You know he was . . . you were in there your own self. We saw you come out, this mornin', with Messervy."

"You . . . you saw –"

"Not me. One of my boys. I have two of them, they're at the Ferry right now, watchin' the engine-house, waitin' to see what happened to Joe." She was regarding me almost amiably, shaking her head. "But you're all confused, so I'd better tell you. I'm Medusa . . . you know Mr La Force likes to give us those ole names. I've been in these parts all summer, havin' you watched, at the farm an' so forth. Oh, Joe didn't know 'bout that . . . didn't know 'bout *me*, even, bein' a lot lower down in the Kuklos than I am. All he had to do was watch *you*, see you did as Mr La Force desired. You know, the raid." She smiled approvingly. "You did that right well, too . . . didn't you? Leastways, it happened . . . which was what we wanted. Mr La Force'll be right pleased with you. Maybe give you the ten thousand dollars you asked for . . . if you feel like collectin'. Do you?"

She was watching me closely now, as I sat palpitating, too shaken to think, let alone speak. I felt as though I'd been struck by a thunderbolt . . . it was incredible, too much to take in.

"We didn't mind you workin' for the gov'ment . . . or *pretendin'* to work for them, whichever it was. As things were, you didn't have a choice, did you? What did they want you to do, anyway? Stop Brown makin' the raid . . . or help him to make it? Mr La Force couldn't make up his mind 'bout that . . . My belief is . . . oh, well, it don't matter what I believe. The raid went in; *that's* what matters."

She rose from the chair, took my glass, and refilled it.

"You look like you need this, dahlin' . . . go on, drink it down! An' don't look like you saw a ghost – all's well . . . except for Joe. We have to know what happened to him, in that engine-house. He was quite a pet of Mr La Force's, you know . . . he'll be real grieved if anythin' bad's happened to Joe." She swayed ponderously back to her seat. "So there's two questions to answer: what happened to Joe . . . and why didn't he cut loose an' run at the hotel, when you did? When I watched the two of you, from my window, comin' to the hotel yes'day mornin', I thought: clever fellers, they've done their work, an' now the raid's *happened*, they're gettin' away from Brown. You did – an' you know what?" She chuckled, the great body shaking with mirth. "When you came in my door, I thought, how does he know to run to *me*? He can't know who I am, that I'm Medusa, he *can't* know I'm Kuklos . . . and then pretty soon I saw that you didn't, it was just chance brought you to me. An', dahlin'," she broke into laughter, "I never miss such a chance! Oh, that was some mornin's sport we had together! I was so melted, I thought to tell you who I was . . . but then, I'd *seen* Joe go back to Brown – I couldn't understand that. I suspicioned somethin' was wrong, somewhere . . . so I kept quiet. Showed you the way out to the loft, tho', didn't I, when it looked like –"

It don't usually take me long to act, when I'm cornered, but I'd been so shaken that only in the last minute had I summoned my wits sufficiently to move. One ghastly fact had imprinted itself on my mind: she had men watching the engine-house, they'd have seen the Marines bring out Joe's body under cover of darkness and bury it by the river – they'd dig it up for certain, and find two bullets in his back

357

. . . and who'd put them there, then? From all that I'd seen of the Kuklos (especially in the last ten minutes) they were experts; they'd know, or soon find out, that the attackers hadn't fired a single shot . . . they'd report to Atropos that his pet nigger had been shot and buried clandestine by the government, for whom I might or might not have been acting . . . by God, he'd want to get to the bottom of it . . . and he'd not ask as gently as this damned Medusa-Popplewell . . .

All this in a flash through my mind, to one lightning conclusion – instant flight. And she was only one woman . . . I came off the bed in a bound – and stopped dead before the Derringer in her great black hand.

"Oh, dahlin'," says she, "that was foolish. What you got to be fractious for? H'm?" She shook her head, no longer smiling. "Now, then . . . I've asked, an' I'm waitin'. Why did Joe go back to Brown . . . and what happened to him afterwards?"

Well, I could answer the first question, at least. "He went back to Brown because he was betraying you. It's the truth! He . . . he went over to Brown's side . . . I don't know why, but he . . . well, Brown convinced him, at the farm, that the raid would lead to a slave rebellion . . . and that it would succeed, and they'd all win their freedom! Joe believed him, I tell you! He changed sides! He told me so! I swear to God, it's true!"

She didn't move a muscle; the plump black features were without expression. The Derringer stayed trained on my midriff.

"An' what happened in the engine-house?"

"I don't know! I . . . I never saw him, after the attack . . . I don't know, I tell you! Maybe he was killed, or captured –"

"You didn't like him, did you? Fact is, you couldn't 'bide him. So Mr La Force figured . . . he thought it was real amusin'. Figured you an' Joe were rivals for the favours of Miz Mandeville. Were you?" When I didn't reply, she shrugged. "It don't matter. She ain't around any more. Mr La Force can't abide traitors."

"Well, Joe was a traitor! I swear he was!"

"I don't disbelieve you, dahlin'. I wouldn't trust a nigger an inch myself." She sat there, black and placid, as she said it. "Did you kill Joe?"

"No, for God's sake! Why should I?"

"Maybe 'cos you hated him. Maybe for the U.S. Gov'ment. Maybe even 'cos you're tellin' true when you say Joe went over to Brown, an' you killed him out o' loyalty to Mr La Force an' that five thousand dollars he promised you. Honey, I don't *mind*!" She leaned forward, smiling almost wistfully – but the Derringer was steady as a rock. "What's one black buck more or less? If you killed him, fine! It don't matter to Hannah."

"I didn't! I swear to God –"

"Dearest, you don't need to – not to me! It's what you swear to Mr La Force that signifies . . . an' whether he believes you. An' I truly do doubt whether he'll believe Joe betrayed him. You know Joe'n he were boys together? Playmates? Why, he loved that Joe like a brother . . . 'bout the only thing he ever loved, I guess. An' if Joe's dead . . . an' my boys'll find it out, if he is . . . I don't know what Mr La Force'll do." She shook her head sadly. "But if he suspicions that you killed him – an' *I* do, so I guess *he* might . . . well, I jus' hope you can prove you didn't."

I sat like a rabbit before a snake, while she regarded me with pity and concern. Then she smiled again, and reached out to stroke my cheek with her free hand.

"Oh, dahlin', don't look so down! I tell you, it don't matter to me! You can kill every nigger in creation if you've a mind to, far as I'm concerned. You know why?" Her eyes narrowed, and her voice was trembling. "'Cos you pleasured me like I never been pleasured before . . . I didn't *know* there was pleasurin' like that, an' believe me, boy, I made a study! I come over faint, jus' thinkin' 'bout you." She shivered and grimaced. "An' now I got to go back to Popplewell. Oh, sure, there *is* a Popplewell, randy little runt – all I tol' you 'bout him an' my other husbands is true, 'cept I married him two years ago, not two days, an' 'twasn't him, but one o' my white boys, left me at the Wager House." She gave one of her gross chuckles. "Think they'd take a nigger woman there, be her husband never so rich? No – but they'd take the Devil hisself, if the Kuklos is payin' the bill."

She stood up, and to my amazement slipped the Derringer into the bosom of her robe. Then she stooped over me, took my face in her hands, looking soulful, and kissed me with sudden passion, her tongue and lips working feverishly at my mouth and cheeks and eyes and back to my mouth again, before she broke moistly away, breathing hard.

"Oh, Ah got sech a kindness fo' you, Mr Beauchamp Comber, or Mr Tom A'nold, or whatevah yo' name is! Ah don' know, an' Ah don' care! An' Ah got sech a mis'ry when Ah think whut Mr La Force'll do . . ." She shuddered enormously, with a little whimpering sigh – and I thought, now's your time, lad, and thrust my whiskers between her boobies, going brrr! She let out an ecstatic wail, the Derringer clattered to the floor, and I sank clutching fingers into her buttocks and munched away for dear life, for I could see only one way out of this fearful dilemma, to play on her feminine frailty in the only way I know how, but even as I grappled, roaring lustful endearments, she heaved away from me, eyes rolling, and thrust out a mighty hand to hold me at arm's length.

"Oh, dahlin'! Oh, goddamussy!" she gasped, and in her agitation it came out in broad Dixie. "Oh, honey, don' think Ah ain't cravin' you, 'cos Ah is, sumpn cruel! But we ain't got the time, dammit!" She stamped, rattling the cabin, and her eyes were wild. "They's on'y one stop 'tween heah an' Baltimo', an' it comin' up real soon – oh, lordy, dere's de whistle! Don' stand theah!" she panted, seizing my wrist. "You gotta git off, 'cos mah boys at the Ferry'll telegraph ahead when they fin' out whutevah's happened to Joe, an' the Kuklos'll be a-waitin' at Baltimo' . . . an' Ah cain't let 'em take yuh, Ah jes' cain't, 'cos, oh, mah dearie, if anythin' wuz to happen to yuh, Ah b'lieve Ah'd die!"

She surged to the door and wrenched it open, and damned if she wasn't snivelling great tears over her shiny black cheeks.

"So git outa heah, now, will yuh . . . oh, gi' me one las'

360

kiss, do! Now, git yore ass offa this train . . . an' take care, ye heah?"

[*Here the tenth packet of the Flashman Papers ends, at what one must assume is the conclusion of the author's memoir of John Brown and the Harper's Ferry episode. What followed will no doubt appear in a later instalment of Sir Harry's recollections; all that can be said with certainty is that he did not catch the Baltimore packet to Liverpool, since we know from evidence in the eighth packet of the Papers, already published, that six months after his emotional parting from Mrs Popplewell, he was in Hong Kong, without having visited England in the meantime.*]

APPENDIX I:

Flashman and John Brown

Flashman's was not an affectionate nature. That he loved (or at least was enthralled by) his wife, Elspeth, is evident from his memoirs, and now and then his regard for other ladies goes some way beyond the merely physical – usually, one suspects, when he is writing in a mood of brandy-assisted nostalgia. But outside his family – he plainly doted on his great-grandchildren, and felt for his natural son, Frank Standing Bear, a paternal affection which lasted for several days – he seldom finds much to like in people. He betrays an occasional fellow-feeling, at a safe distance, for such rascals as Rudi von Starnberg, and has a half-amiable tolerance of acquaintances whom he has no cause to detest, like his old chief, Colin Campbell, and his Afghan blood-brother, Ilderim Khan. But that, as a rule, is his limit.

Yet he seems to have had a kind of protective affection for John Brown. Underneath the sneers and curses there is a hint of indulgence, an inclination to defend the old nuisance and even to give him a Tuscan cheer, which is not characteristic of Flashman. We may be sure it springs from no kindly or charitable impulse, or the least sympathy with Brown's aims; he found the man and his mission ridiculous, and writes of them with contempt. At the same time, he remembers Brown as "a bloody hard man to dislike", which is a rare tribute. Of course, it may have been a gratifying novelty to Flashman to come across a strong and fearsome autocrat who treated him with some deference and respect; a strong man, moreover, whom he could manipulate, and in whom he detected an appealing streak of humbug. And however lofty his disdain of Brown, there is no doubt that he took a perverse pride in their association: "I was one of John Brown's pet lambs, after all." This is pure Flashman. Throughout his memoirs, he revels in reflected glory, the more so when it is ingloriously undeserved, and when it comes to "dining out", Harper's Ferry plainly ranks with Balaclava and Little Big Horn and Cawnpore. One detects a condescending gratitude to Brown and his ragged commandos for adding another leaf to the Flashman laurels, and a complacent satisfaction that he helped them along the road to immortality.

Whether he liked Brown or not, he has done him justice. The figure who stalks his narrative is the man of the biographies and contemporary accounts, even to his quoted speech, thoughts, manner, appearance, and the small details of everyday. From their first meeting at Concord to the last glimpse of the weary, serene old prisoner lying in the paymaster's office, Flashman's story tallies convincingly with recorded fact, and differs no more from the standard authorities than they do from each other. His record of Brown's travels in the North may be verified in Villard, as may his account of life at the Kennedy Farm, of which Mrs Annie Brown Adams, Brown's daughter, who acted as look-out for the conspirators, has left a lively record.

As invariably happens when there is a multitude of eye-witnesses, there are many discrepancies to be found in accounts of the actual raid on Harper's Ferry. It would have been tedious and confusing to footnote them all, and most of them are trivial: it hardly matters whether John Brown visited the rifle works in person, or at which end of the Potomac bridge the watchmen were posted, or whether Lee was on horseback, or what kind of hat Jeb Stuart wore, or the precise moment when Brown retreated to the engine-house, or the exact place and time of certain incidents. There is no conflict on the main course of events, and here Flashman is in step with other historians.

It was a weird affair, the handful of men invading in the dark, the hold-up and release of the train, the taking of the prisoners, the first haphazard shootings, the bewildered township waking to find itself menaced by terrorists, gunfight

and murder alternating with parleys and demands for breakfast, the militia storming in and taking to drink, the brutal
lynchings and the local doctor tending the invaders'
wounded, the siege of the engine-house, the final call to
surrender, the last bloody mêlée with the Marines, and, most
bizarre of all, the wounded Brown holding court while his
captors bombard him with questions. The whole thing has
elements of a modern hostage drama followed by a television
press conference.

It was a fiasco; the irony is that it need not have been.
Brown, the most incompetent of planners and irresolute of
leaders, gained an initial success of which a commando
leader might be proud – and then did nothing. He could
have stripped the arsenal and been in the hills without losing
a man; that he could have organised a slave rebellion is
highly improbable, but he would have struck a blow to shake
the nation (it was shaken enough, even by his failure). Why
did he delay? Did he cling to the hope that the slaves would
rally to him, as Cook had assured him they would? It is
possible, yet it seems more likely that Flashman's diagnosis
is sound: faced with crisis Brown simply did not know what
to do. His judgment failed him, as his courage never did,
and with that fatal indecision which was his besetting weakness he threw away what little chance he had.

But while Flashman may have read him aright at the
Ferry, and while his whole portrait of Brown is a fair one,
he has probably come no closer than other biographers to
explaining the old abolitionist's strange and complex character. It is not surprising. Brown was not understood in his
own time, and much that has been written about him since
has done more to embellish the legend than to clarify the
nature of the man. He and his cause are emotional subjects,
and the emotions often run to extremes. He has been
described in terms that would become a saint, and vilified
with an intemperance that is self-defeating. The impression
persists in most people's minds of a good and simple soul
on fire with a dream, a fanatical crusader pursuing a splendid
goal with imperfect means, a misguided Quixote whose head
was wrong but whose heart was right. Great men and women

365

have given him the accolade, and who that reads his story can dissent? Kindness, compassion, a burning love of liberty, a gift of inspiring devotion, and matchless courage, he had; if, as has been charged, perhaps not unjustly, he was also devious, foolish, vain, selfish, unscrupulous, and irresolute in crisis, his admirers can say that these are human faults, and far outweighed by the simple nobility of the martyr who died, and died gladly, to make men free. And then there is Pottawatomie.

The question of his sanity cannot be answered now. He was held fit to plead at his trial; rightly, so far as we can tell, but not many laymen would, on the evidence, call him normal or balanced. "Reasoning insanity" is the judgment of one eminent historian, and it will do as well as any other. We cannot know him, but it does not matter. He is part of history and historic legend, and if what he tried to do was not heroic, then the word has no meaning.

APPENDIX II:

The Harper's Ferry Mystery

The most remarkable thing about John Brown's raid is that it was allowed to happen at all. Months beforehand it was known in Washington's corridors of power that he intended to invade Virginia, and that his first target would be Harper's Ferry. At least eighty people in the country, including the Secretary for War and two U.S. Senators, had been told of the plan; how many others had picked up the rumours, or had reason to believe that some great stroke was imminent, it is impossible to say. Yet nothing was done to stop him. No defensive measures were taken.

This should be one of those great historical mysteries that scholars love to debate; when one considers the oceans of ink that have been spilled over Little Big Horn and the Alamo, the comparative neglect of the question: "Why wasn't Brown stopped?" is almost as baffling as the mystery itself.

Brown had invasion in mind as early as 1847, when he described to Frederick Douglass how he would use a small picked band to run off the most restless and daring slaves and wage a guerrilla campaign in the Alleghenies. In late 1854 or early 1855 he proposed a raid on Harper's Ferry to Colonel Daniel Woodruff, a veteran of the War of 1812; Brown's daughter Annie, the sentry of Kennedy Farm, remembered the Ferry being specifically mentioned at the time. Hugh Forbes knew about the plan in some detail in 1857, and revealed it to Senators Wilson and Seward in 1858, at which time the Secret Six also knew of it, and the scheme was postponed. Early in 1859, James Redpath, who had met Brown and was to become his first biographer, published a book dedicated to "John Brown, senior, of Kansas", citing him as a believer in slave insurrection, advocating revolt, and hinting at future "servile and civil wars" – not hard information, but a significant straw in a wind that had been blowing for some time.

Secret intelligence-gathering was fairly makeshift in the U.S. before the Civil War, and it is possible that the government had no substantial knowledge of Brown's intentions before 1859, or, if they had, that they did not take him seriously. The wild schemes of a crazy farmer might well be dismissed as moonshine, although given the growth of abolitionist feeling in the North, and Southern anxiety about slave unrest, it seems odd that no one thought them worthy of any inquiry at all.

But "odd" is not the word for the behaviour of John Floyd, Secretary of War, when he received a detailed and (one would have thought) compelling warning of the raid on August 25, 1859 – seven weeks before it took place. It came in a letter, admittedly anonymous* but obviously the work of a responsible person, who named "Old John Brown" of Kansas, stated that he intended to liberate the slaves of the South by general insurrection, gave particulars of his preparation and armament, identified Harper's Ferry as the point of invasion, and predicted that the slaves would be armed and the blow struck within a few weeks.

Nothing could have been clearer, but Floyd, whom Bruce Catton generously describes as a bumbling incompetent, ignored the letter because, among its wealth of cogent information, it contained one trifling error – the writer stated that Brown had an agent "in an armoury in Maryland". Floyd apparently had not the wit to connect "Old John Brown" of the letter with the notorious John Brown on whose head President Buchanan and the State of Missouri

---

* The writer of the letter was one David Gue, who had learned of the plot from a Quaker named Varney. Many years later Gue claimed that he had written out of no ill will to Brown, but "to protect [him] from the consequences of his own rashness and devotion" by alerting the authorities who, Gue hoped, would deter the raid by setting a guard on the arsenal. Two copies of the letter were sent to Floyd, but only one reached him.

had put a price, but like a good little bureaucrat he knew that there was no armoury in Maryland – that there *was* a large undefended armoury within a stone's throw of Maryland, just across the river in Virginia, did not occur to him. He decided, incredibly, that the rest of the letter must be untrue; according to Sanborn, he did not even bother to read it twice. Explaining himself later to the Mason Committee investigating the raid, Floyd said that he was satisfied that "a scheme of such wickedness and outrage could not be entertained by any citizens of the United States". And the committee decided that no one apart from Brown's gang had "any suspicion of [the raid's] existence or design".

Committees know their own business best, and there is no reason why a senior minister should not be an ill-informed idiot; such things have been known. But even if Floyd was guilty of nothing worse than stupidity and negligence, it is still remarkable that despite all the advance publicity John Brown and his projected raid had received, from the halls of Congress to the Kansas border and from the drawing-rooms of Boston to the saloons of Ohio, no one in Washington took any notice or apparently felt a moment's unease.

To be sure, governments can be uncommonly blind, deaf, and lazy – to which the last survivor of John Brown's band would certainly add: "Aye, especially when they don't *want* to see, hear, or move." There were many in the North, and doubtless some in the South, who wanted the raid to happen; Crixus and Atropos were not alone; but probably only a cynic like Flashman would speculate that there were those in authority who, knowing of the plot and having the power to prevent it, allowed it to go ahead, for their own inscrutable ends. Since there is no evidence to support this view, we can only accept the alternative: that it was just monumental bad luck that no responsible person got wind of the plot, or took it seriously, or bothered to investigate it, or thought it worth posting even a couple of armed sentries on an unguarded arsenal at a time when talk of slave insurrection was in the air, or decided to keep an eye on the most violent and ruthless abolitionist in the country, the butcher of

369

Pottawatomie, who was stumping the sticks and cities preaching the invasion of Virginia . . .

Bad luck indeed, for the upshot was that against all the odds, and in spite of all his follies and hesitations and mismanagement, John Brown was given what he had no right to expect: a clear run at Harper's Ferry.

APPENDIX III:

John Brown's Men

John Brown's knapsack is strapped upon his back,
He's gone to be a soldier in the army of the Lord,
His pet lambs will meet him on the way,
And they'll go marching on.
Glory, glory, hallelujah . . .

John Henry Kagi, 24, killed
Aaron Dwight Stevens, 28, hanged
Owen Brown, 34, escaped
Watson Brown, 24, killed
Oliver Brown, 20, killed
Jeremiah Goldsmith Anderson, 26, killed
John Cook, 29, hanged
Albert Hazlett, 22, hanged
Charles Plummer Tidd, 25, escaped
William Thompson, 26, killed
Dauphin Osgood Thompson, 21, killed
Edwin Coppoc, 24, hanged
Barclay Coppoc, 20, escaped
John Anthony Copeland, 25, hanged
William Leeman, 20, killed
Stewart Taylor, 22, killed
Osborn Perry Anderson, 29, escaped
Dangerfield Newby, 44, killed

371

Lewis Sheridan Leary, 24, killed
Shields Green, 23, hanged
Francis Jackson Meriam, 21, escaped
John Brown, 59, hanged

To which may now be added the names of

Beauchamp Millward Comber, 37, escaped
Joseph Simmons, 23, killed.

Fourteen persons were killed or wounded by the raiders at
Harper's Ferry. No slaves were liberated.

NOTES

NOTES

1. John Arthur (Jack) Johnson (1878–1946), the first black boxer to win the world heavyweight title, was the most unpopular of champions and, in the opinion of the most respected ring historians, the best. He won the title in 1908 by beating Tommy Burns of Canada, having pursued him from America to England and finally to Australia, and lost it in 1915 to Jess Willard of the U.S.A. In the intervening years he was the object of a campaign of race hatred unique in sport; in that colour-conscious age Johnson's arrogance in and out of the ring, his cruelty to opponents, his white wives, his complacent smile showing gold-capped teeth, his skipping bail to Paris to avoid a prison sentence in America (he had violated the Mann Act by taking a woman with whom he was having an affair across a State line), and above all, his undoubted supremacy in a game which had always been a peculiar source of white pride, brought out the very worst in the sporting public. None was more vicious than the novelist Jack London, who had covered Burns's "funeral" as he called it, for the *New York Herald*, and who conducted the notorious "Whip the Nigger" campaign to "remove the golden smile from Johnson's face". He and others persuaded Jim Jeffries, a former champion, to come out of retirement to challenge for the title. The fight took place in Reno, Nevada, in 1910, and so highly charged was the atmosphere beforehand (fatal race riots had followed some of Johnson's previous victories) that Sir Arthur Conan Doyle was invited to act as referee; it was felt, rightly, that no sportsman on earth was so universally respected, or more likely to exert a calming influence. Doyle wanted to accept, but his own campaign against the atrocities in the Belgian Congo was demanding all his attention, and after a week's hesitation he reluctantly declined. In the event, Johnson won easily, there were no disturbances, and the quest for a "White Hope" lasted another five years, until Johnson succumbed (voluntarily, in the opinion of many) to the gigantic but undistinguished Willard.

Flashman's view of Johnson was widely shared; his unquestioned brilliance as a ring mechanic apart, the black champion was not an endearing figure, but it is only fair to quote the opinion of another well-known Victorian, who had the rare distinction of meeting him in the ring and coming out on his feet. Victor McLaglen was an admired British heavyweight long before he became a film actor; he went six rounds to a draw in a "no-decision" bout with Johnson in 1909, and wrote afterwards that the champion "fought like a gentleman", was "undoubtedly the hardest man to hit whom I ever met", and was also "the most charming opponent". (See Terry Leigh-Lye, *In This Corner*, 1963; Nat Fleischer and Sam Andre, *Pictorial History of Boxing*, 1959; M. and M. Hardwick, *The Man Who Was Sherlock Holmes*, 1964; Jack London, in the *New York Herald*, 1908; Victor McLaglen, *Express to Hollywood*, 1934.)   [p. 13]

2. Flashman was born in 1822, so the present memoir was presumably written in 1913, two years before his death.   [p. 14]

3. The famous march, one of many John Brown songs sung in the U.S. Civil War, is said to have originated in "a sarcastic tune which men in a Massachusetts outfit made up as 'a jibe' against one Sergeant John Brown of Boston". If so, it soon became associated with the famous abolitionist; a Union soldier, Private Warren Lee Goss, records that when the 12th Massachusetts Regiment marched down Broadway on July 24, 1861, they sang "the then new and always thrilling lyric, John Brown's Body". Five months later Mrs Julia Ward Howe (1819–1910), the author, reformer, and abolitionist, wrote new words to the old tune; they subsequently appeared in the *Atlantic Monthly* as "The Battle Hymn of the Republic". One tradition (hinted at by Flashman) is that she had been scandalised by the words which she heard soldiers singing; the accepted story is that she and a party of friends were singing patriotic songs, and one of them suggested to her that new verses would be appropriate. (See Stephen B. Oates, *To Purge This Land with Blood*, 1970, quoting Boyd B. Stutler, "John Brown's Body"; Warren Lee Goss, "Going to the Front", in *Battles and Leaders of the Civil War*, vol. 1, ed. R. U. Johnson and C. C. Buel, 1887.)   [p. 17]

4. For evidence that Benjamin Franklin ("Agent No. 72") and his assistant, Edward Bancroft, were working for British Intelligence during their time at the American Embassy in Paris, and passed information to London which resulted in heavy American shipping losses, see Richard Deacon, *A History of British Secret Service*, 1980.   [p. 24]

5. Flashman is habitually vague about dates, and it is impossible to say when he left Calcutta – it may have been late in 1858 or even early in 1859, but he was certainly at the Cape sometime in January or February of the new year. In that case, it seems probable that the stranded wreck was the *Madagascar* (351 tons), which ran ashore off Port Elizabeth on December 3, 1858. (See Marischal Murray, *Ships and South Africa*, 1933.)   [p. 28]

6. The self-destruction of the 'Zoza tribe (more usually spelled Xhosa or Amaxosa) began late in 1856, when the belief arose that spirits of the dead, speaking through the medium of a girl of the tribe, had promised that if all cattle and crops were destroyed, these would be replaced in abundance on a certain day, and the hated white men driven from the land. In obedience to their chief, the Xhosas destroyed their food supplies entirely, and in the famine which

376

followed more than 60,000 are believed to have died. (See sources to Note 9.) [p. 31]

7. In view of recent South African history, and the common belief that 1994 would be the milestone marking the introduction of universal suffrage, it is worth noting that in Cape Colony in the 1850s, under British rule, every man had the vote, regardless of race or colour. The only qualifications were birth in the Colony and a financial condition set so low that many non-whites were enfranchised. Like many progressive features of the old British Empire, it is one that modern revisionists are either unaware of or choose to forget. (See sources to Note 9.) [p. 32]

8. The pollution of the Thames and the anti-smoking campaign were perennial topics; the Act of Parliament removing the disabilities of the Jews had passed in July, 1858, and Lionel de Rothschild had become the first Jewish M.P. [p. 34]

9. Flashman's summary of South African affairs in 1859, if characteristically sketchy, is accurate and perceptive, and his portrait of the Cape Governor is fair; if anything, he gives him more sympathetic treatment than he usually metes out to imperial pro-consuls, a class of whom he tended to take a jaundiced view.

Sir George Grey (1812–98) was that peculiarly Victorian compound of the man of action, scholar, visionary, and maverick. His guiding principles were the welfare and progress of the people he was given to rule, and getting his own way, and he pursued them with an energy and impatience which frequently brought him into conflict with his superiors at home, and eventually brought his career to a premature close, which was his country's loss, for he was one of the best. He left the army when he was twenty-three to explore north-western Australia, an adventure of extreme danger and hardship in which he skirmished with Aborigines, was wounded, lost his supplies, and finally tramped alone into Perth, so altered by suffering that he was unrecognisable. He was twenty-nine when he was appointed Governor of South Australia, and subsequently of New Zealand, where he defeated the Maoris, won their friendship, and established a popular and prosperous administration before being transferred to the Cape in 1854. There he prevented a Kaffir uprising, encouraged settlement, and acquired something rare, if not unique, in South African history – the trust and respect of Britons, Boers, and tribesmen alike. Foreseeing that the peaceful development of the country depended on recognising and balancing the interests of all three (particularly between the Boers and the black tribes) he worked tirelessly to bring about a confederation, won the support of the Boers of the Orange Free State and the British of the Cape, and would have succeeded but for the reluctance of the home government to assume further responsibility and expense in Southern Africa. His persistence caused offence at the Colonial Office ("a dangerous man"), and he was recalled in 1859, a few months after Flashman met him. Palmerston's new administration reinstated him, but his plan of confederation was shelved. In 1861 he was again Governor of New Zealand, fought in the Maori wars (personally leading the attack and capture of their main stronghold), and was making progress towards a settlement between settlers and Maoris when, his highly individual style having given renewed offence in Whitehall, he was recalled. He was only fifty-five. The rest of his life was spent mostly in New Zealand. He left behind a standard work, *Polynesian Mythology*, and splendid libraries at Cape Town and Auckland, but his great achievement was that, whatever his chiefs at home thought, the people of all races and colours whom he governed were invariably sorry to see him go.

A handsome, slightly-built man with a cold eye and a quiet voice, Grey seems to have been quite as assured and impatient of opposition as Flashman found him: an idealist, he had a strong ruthless streak, and his portraits do not suggest a man whom it would be safe to cross. During his final months at the Cape his health was poor, and his marital relations were approaching a crisis – something with which we may be sure Flashman had nothing to do, or he would certainly have told us about it. (See G. M. Theal, *History of South Africa*, vol. 3, "Cape Colony, 1846–60", 1908; James Milne, *Sir George Grey, the Romance of a Pro-consul*, 1899; G. C. Henderson, *Sir George Grey*, 1907; James Collier, *Life and Times of Sir George Grey*, 1909; W. H. S. Bell, *Bygone Days*, reminiscences of pioneer life in Cape Colony from 1856, 1933; J. Noble, *Descriptive Handbook of the Cape Colony*, 1875.) [p. 34]

10. The first ministry of Lord Palmerston, who had sent Flashman on secret service to India shortly before the great mutiny of 1857, had ended in February, 1858, when he was succeeded as Prime Minister by the Earl of Derby. Palmerston regained office in June, 1859, a few months after the meeting of Flashman and Sir George Grey at the Cape. [p. 35]

11. The outdoor swimming pool was an occasional feature of private gardens at the Cape: the Constantia mansion, the first large country house in the Colony, dating from the seventeenth century, had one in its grounds. (See Alys Fane Trotter, *Old Colonial Houses of the Cape of Good Hope*, 1900.) [p. 45]

12. A native of New England, especially a typical seafarer from the coast of Maine, reputed to be unusually tough and reactionary, and supposedly so-called because the region lay east and down-wind of the main American Atlantic ports. The term was also applied to ships. [p. 64]

13. There was no British Embassy in Washington at this time: H.M. Government was represented by a minister, not an ambassador – a diplomatic distinction which Flashman could not be expected to appreciate. [p. 68]

14. If so, it was a slow passage; a clipper would have done it in half the time, given favourable weather, which Flashman's ship does not seem to have had. [p. 69]

15. Captain Robert ("Bully") Waterman was one of the foremost clipper captains of the day, famous for his record-breaking runs in the *Sea Witch* between China and New York, and notorious for the brutal discipline he imposed on his crews. Flashman mentions him twice in earlier packets of the Papers, but there is no evidence that they ever met. [p. 73]

16. There is something of a literary mystery here. The Knitting Swede's hostelry is mentioned in *The Blood Ship*, published some time early in this century by Norman Springer, but I cannot recall whether it was located in Baltimore or not. However, the two bucko mates of *The Blood Ship* were certainly Fitzgibbon and Lynch – the names of the skipper and mate of the vessel which carried Flashman to America. These things can hardly be coincidental. [p. 74]

17. A remark attributed to Senator David R. Atchison of Missouri, when urging on Border Ruffians before the sack of Lawrence, Kansas, headquarters of the Free Staters, on May 21, 1856. [p. 91]

18. Crixus's account and Flashman's interpolations between them provide a rough but balanced biographical summary of John Brown up to the spring of 1859. Whether the famous abolitionist was a *Mayflower* descendant has been disputed, but he certainly came of old American stock. Born in Torrington, Connecticut, on May 9, 1800, he received a rudimentary education and worked at various rural trades with indifferent success; his business ventures ended in failure, and he was usually hard pressed for money. He married twice, and had twenty children. His hatred of slavery, inherited from his father and nourished by his own observations, took an active form when he was still in his twenties, and his home was a station on the Underground Railroad. In 1851, at Springfield, Massachusetts, he organised a black defence group, the League of Gileadites, to resist slave-catchers and prevent fugitives from being returned to the South. It is not certain when he conceived the idea of invading Virginia, but he was talking about it as early as 1847, and in the winter of 1854–5 was discussing a raid on Harper's Ferry and making notes on guerrilla warfare from Stocqueler's *Life of the Duke of Wellington*. At this time several of his sons, imbued with their father's abolitionist zeal, went to Kansas, where the "slave or free territory" issue was coming to a head, and were soon followed by Brown himself, ostensibly to set up in business but in fact to fight on the Free State side. He soon became the most notorious of the Border irregulars, organising a guerrilla band called the Liberty Guards, with himself as captain and four of his sons, Owen, Frederick, Salmon, and John, junior, among his followers, and earning a fearsome reputation as a result of one savage exploit in the summer of 1856.

The Pottawatomie Massacre took place on the night of May 24–25, and arose directly from the destruction of the town of Lawrence (see Note 17 above) and another incident on the following day. On May 22 an anti-slavery orator, Senator Charles Sumner of Massachusetts, denounced the Lawrence attack in the U.S. Senate, and was then assaulted by Representative Preston Brooks of South Carolina, who invaded the chamber and thrashed Sumner, who was seated at his desk, so brutally with his cane that the unfortunate Senator did not recover for two years. Brown, who had been too late to defend Lawrence, and was in a fury because the citizens had not put up a fight, was already contemplating retaliation against the pro-slavers when news of "Bully Brooks's" outrage reached him on May 23. At this, according to his son Salmon, the old man "went crazy – crazy!", and on being urged to use caution, cried: "Caution, caution, sir, I am eternally tired of hearing that word caution! It is nothing but the word for cowardice," and set off to strike back at "the barbarians". This consisted of descending on three houses along the Pottawatomie Creek, first murdering a pro-slavery man named Doyle and two of his sons, then another named Wilkinson, and finally one Sherman. The killings were carried out with the utmost brutality, the men being forced from their beds and, despite the pleas of wives and the presence of children, hustled out into the dark and literally hacked to pieces with sabres; fingers, hands, and arms were severed and skulls split. Owen and Salmon Brown killed the three Doyles, and Brown's son-in-law, Henry Thompson, and a man named Theodore Weiner, murdered the two other men. Brown himself does not seem to have struck a blow, although he probably fired a single shot into the corpse of the oldest Doyle. Later, when his son Jason taxed him with the killings, Brown said: "I did not do it, but I approved of it". Nor did he ever deny responsibility, and only once offered anything like an excuse for the crime: according to an old Kansas settler, Brown claimed that the five had been planning to kill him. "I was satisfied that each of them had committed murder in his heart . . . and I felt justified in having them killed." This is doubtful, and even Brown's most admiring biographers are at a loss when confronted with Pottawatomie; one suggests that he was in a trance, another refers to the murders as "executions", but none can offer an acceptable explanation, let alone a defence. At the time, Crixus's view of the affair was shared by many in the North, who believed that Brown was justified by necessity, and that his terrorist tactics and subsequent skirmishing against the pro-slavery forces were of critical importance in the Kansas struggle. Certainly Pottawatomie did nothing to lessen support for Brown among Northern liberals; some might condemn it, but others, especially the group known as the Secret Six (see Note 32), gave him moral and financial assistance, and the great mass of abolitionists regarded him as a champion. He continued to operate against the pro-slavery forces with some success before being driven from his base at Ossawatomie in a battle in which his son Frederick was killed. For almost three years thereafter Brown divided his time between campaigning for the abolitionist cause in the East, and preparing in the field for his projected invasion of Virginia.

There are many biographies of Brown, and they cover the closing years of his life in detail, drawing on a wealth of contemporary

380

sources. Indeed, there is almost an embarrassment of information; one writer, Villard, has even been able to compile a daily calendar of his life from mid-1855 to his death in December 1859. Most of the early biographies, including those by Sanborn and Redpath, who knew Brown personally, are friendly: one, by Peebles Wilson, is a raging denunciation. Of special interest is the autobiographical sketch written by Brown in 1857, which is the best source for his early life, and is quoted in full in Villard. (See O. G. Villard, *John Brown*, 1910 (the fullest account); Franklin B. Sanborn, *The Life and Letters of John Brown*, 1885 (Sanborn was a friend and leading supporter): James Redpath, *The Public Life of Captain John Brown*, 1860 (Redpath was a newspaperman who met Brown in the field); H. Peebles Wilson, *John Brown, Soldier of Fortune*, 1913; Barrie Stavis, *John Brown, the Sword and the Word*, 1870; Oates; R. D. Webb, *Life and Letters of Captain John Brown*, 1861; Louis Ruchames (ed.) *A John Brown Reader*, 1959; Allan Keller, *Thunder at Harper's Ferry*, 1958.) [p. 92]

19. Hugh Forbes, the British adventurer whom Brown hired as an instructor and military advisor at $100 a month, shared certain characteristics with Flashman; he was tall, handsome, soldierly, plausible, and probably something of a confidence man. He was born about 1812, had been a silk merchant in Italy, claimed to have fought under Garibaldi, and styled himself "Colonel", but when Brown met him in New York in 1857 he was eking a bare living as a fencing-master, translator and occasional journalist. In Brown's employ he worked on a manual of guerrilla tactics and produced a pamphlet apparently designed to lure U.S. soldiers to the abolitionist cause, but his chief talent was for absorbing money to support his family whom he described as starving in Paris. Eventually he and Brown fell out over alleged arrears of pay and, perhaps more seriously, the Harper's Ferry project: Forbes was convinced that an attempt to rouse the slaves for a guerrilla campaign must fail, and proposed instead a series of "stampedes" in which small parties of slaves would be run off from properties close to the North-South border, thus eventually making slave-holding impossible in the region, and forcing the "slave frontier" gradually southwards. It was at least a feasible plan, but Brown rejected it. Forbes then began writing to Brown's leading supporters, from many of whom he had begged money, hinting that unless further payments were made he would divulge the invasion plan, a threat which he carried out in the spring of 1858, when he accosted two Republican Senators, Seward and Wilson, on the floor of the Senate, and told them what was planned. The Senators, both devoted abolitionists, seem to have kept the information to themselves, but warned Brown's supporters, and the project was postponed. (See Villard; Sanborn.) [p. 94]

20. The marble frontage, and later clues in Flashman's narrative, suggest that the hotel was Brown's, at the junction of Pennsylvania Avenue and Sixth Street. It was much patronised by Southerners. (See Margaret Leech, *Reveille in Washington*, 1942.) [p. 110]

381

21. The Parcae, or Fates, of classical mythology were Clotho, Lachesis, and Atropos, the arbiters of birth, life, and death. The dandy's little joke lay in suggesting that they should have called themselves Eumenides ("the good-natured ones"), the name ironically applied by the Greeks to the Furies. The white hoods and the name "Kuklos" are strongly reminiscent of the infamous Ku Klux Klan, founded by Confederate ex-officers in Tennessee after the Civil War; originally a social and literary club, it became an anti-negro terrorist organisation which flourished intermittently into modern times. It certainly owed its name to the Greek *kuklos*, a circle (not, as the fanciful theory has it, to the triple click of a rifle being cocked), but there is no evidence either of its existence before 1866, or to suggest that it had its origins in the kind of Southern intelligence network which Atropos described to Flashman. The identities of "Clotho" and "Lachesis" cannot even be guessed at. [p. 122]

22. Telemaque ("Denmark") Vesey and Nat Turner led the two most notable slave revolts, in 1822 and 1831 respectively. Vesey, a mulatto who had bought his freedom with lottery winnings, organised a plot to take Charleston, but was betrayed by a slave out of affection for his owner, and went to the gallows with more than thirty black comrades; several whites who were implicated in the plot were imprisoned. Nat Turner, a black lay preacher who was inspired by the Bible to believe himself the chosen deliverer of his people, led a rebellion of some seventy slaves at Southampton, Virginia, in which more than fifty whites and twice as many blacks died; Turner himself was executed. How many other smaller outbreaks took place it is impossible to say; no doubt some went unrecorded. Unrest was certainly more widespread than Southerners cared to admit; the contention that slaves were happy or resigned concealed a genuine fear which was reflected in strict laws against black assembly and education, patrols, curfews, and the kind of savage treatment dealt out to a band of about seventy Maryland runaways who were executed or sold down the river in 1845. Rumours spread of a general slave conspiracy in the years before the Civil War, a by-product perhaps of Southern fears of the growing abolitionist feeling in the North, for they seem to have been unfounded. [p. 129]

23. If Flashman and Annette had a table for two, as he seems to suggest, they were singularly favoured, since most American hotels of the period favoured the common table – "the comfort of a quiet table to yourself . . . is quite unknown", complained a British traveller of the period. "The living [dining arrangements] at these hotels is profuse to a degree, but, generally speaking, most disagreeable: first, because the meal is devoured with a rapidity which a pack of fox-hounds, after a week's fast, might in vain attempt to rival; and secondly, because it is impossible to serve up dinners for hundreds, without nine-tenths thereof being cold." (See Henry A. Murray, *Lands of the Slave and the Free*, 1855.) [p. 140]

24. Stephen A. Douglas (1813–61), leader of the Democrats in the North,

382

was a portly, dynamic figure known to admirers as the "Little Giant" and to enemies as the "Dropsied Dwarf" (he was only five feet tall), and best remembered for the debates in which he successfully defended his seat as Senator for Illinois against Lincoln in 1858. Douglas was to the fore in the slavery question; his first wife was the daughter of a slave-holder, but Douglas himself was a champion of "popular sovereignty", holding that it was up to the residents to decide whether a state should be slave or free, and his declaration that any territory could exclude slavery irrespective of the Supreme Court's ruling cost him the support of many Southern Democrats. The party split before the Presidential election of 1860, with the Deep South States breaking away, and although Douglas was nominated as one of the candidates against Lincoln, he was heavily beaten. His second wife, Adele, was a noted beauty and leader of Washington society in the years before the Civil War. [p. 140]

25. The cynic was Anthony Trollope, who gave this unflattering view of New York in his *North America*, 1862. [p. 151]

26. Flashman's impressions of New York are echoed by other British travellers of the mid-nineteenth century, as well as by American writers. Like them, he was struck by the size and up-to-date appointments of the hotels, with their hundreds of apartments, half-hour laundry services, no-smoking areas for ladies, dining-rooms which seemed to foreshadow mass-production, peanut shells, cigar fumes, and continual clamour and bustle which many European visitors, used to smaller and cosier establishments, found trying. Nor is he alone in his admiration of the city's women, and the freedom and independence which they enjoyed (and asserted) compared to their European sisters; Trollope had the same experience of paying ladies' fares on the omnibuses, and James Silk Buckingham, an English observer of the previous decade, enthused at some length about their beauty ("almost uniformly good-looking . . . slender and of good symmetry . . . a more than usual degree of feminine delicacy . . . a greater number of pretty forms and faces than [in England] . . . dressed more in the extreme of fashion . . ."). He also noted the deference shown to them by American men, and their dependence on it. A contemporary of Flashman's, G. Ellington, devoted a long book to the city's women of every class and kind, from the society set of Fifth and Madison Avenues to the fallen angels of the House of the Good Shepherd; he is a mine of information on fashions, parties, amusements, social behaviour (and misbehaviour), shopping, menus, and polite trivia, as well as on the female underworld – the "cruisers" of Broadway, the down-town cigar-store girls, the all-women gambling and billiard halls, and the drug scene. From him we learn of the popularity among society ladies and their imitators of powdered hands, the Grecian bend, dancing "the German", blonde hair, and exaggerated high heels; he knows the price of everything from Murray Hill boarding-school fees to the going rate paid by white slavers for "recruits", and presumably is a reliable guide to what was "done" –

going to Saratoga and the White Mountains in summer – and what was "not done" – being seen anywhere south of 14th Street. Among other commentators, Theodore Roosevelt is critical of '50s New York (which he was not old enough to remember personally), deploring its vulgarity, devotion to money, and slavish copying of Paris fashion, and is interesting on the "swamping" of "native American stock" (Dutch-Anglo-Scots-German) by Irish immigration, the growth of Roman Catholicism, the New York mob's tendency to riot, the corruption of local politics, and the attempt by its Democrat mayor to align the city with the South in the Civil War by seceding from the Union and establishing the commonwealth of "Tri-Insula" (the three islands of Manhattan, Long, and Staten). The Hon. Henry Murray, whose strictures on public dining arrangements are mentioned in Note 23, is an entertaining source of domestic detail – barbers' shops, hotel security, Bibles in bedrooms, and bridal suites ("the want of delicacy that suggested the idea is only equalled by the want of taste with which it is carried out . . . a matrimonial couch, hung with white silk curtains, and blazing with a bright jet of gas from each bed-post!"). Alexander McKay is worth reading on Anglo-American attitudes in general, and American sensitivity to British opinion in particular: his reporting of conversations is first-class. (See Murray; Trollope; James Silk Buckingham, *America*, 1841; G. Ellington, *The Women of New York*, 1869; Theodore Roosevelt, *New York*, 1895; Alexander McKay, *The Western World*, 1850.)   [p. 153]

27. The enamelling studio, in which ladies had their faces, shoulders, and busts coated with a mixture of arsenic and white lead, was the forerunner of the modern beauty salon. To judge from advertisements of the time, the range of cosmetics, treatments, and appliances for enhancing the female face and figure was almost as extensive as it is now; Flashman's description is accurate, and the prices he quotes tally with those of one of the Broadway studios. What the effect of an application designed to last for a full year must have been can only be imagined. (See Ellington.)   [p. 160]

28. Allan Pinkerton (1819–84), the most famous of all private detectives and founder of the agency which bears his name, was born in Glasgow, the son of a police sergeant. He trained as a cooper, and became an enthusiastic member of the Chartist movement for workers' rights, taking part in the Glasgow spinners' strike and in the attempt to free a Chartist leader from Monmouth Castle, Newport, in 1839, when shots were exchanged between rioters and police. It was about this time that Flashman was engaged in training militia at Paisley, and was briefly involved in a disturbance at a mill belonging to his future father-in-law, John Morrison (see *Flashman*). Subsequently Pinkerton's Chartist activities took him into hiding to avoid arrest, and in 1842 he emigrated to Chicago. He worked as a cooper at Dundee, Illinois, but crime prevention was evidently in his blood, and after running down a counterfeiting gang he was appointed deputy sheriff of Kane County, and later of Cook County, Chicago. Here he organ-

ised his detective agency in 1852–3, and had considerable success against railway and express company thieves. He foiled an assassination attempt against President-elect Lincoln in 1861, and in the Civil War became effective head of the U.S. secret service, but while he was an efficient spy-catcher – he broke the Confederate espionage ring operated in Washington by the glamorous Rose Greenhow (see also Note 43) – he was less successful as a gatherer of military intelligence, and his over-estimation of Confederate strength in the peninsular campaign contributed to a Union reverse. He was eventually replaced, but his agency continued to flourish; one of its principal successes, ironically enough, was against a working-class movement, the Molly Maguires, who terrorised Pennsylvania coalfields for more than twenty years before being penetrated by a Pinkerton agent.

Almost from his arrival in America Pinkerton had been a dedicated abolitionist and Underground Railroad agent. His house in Chicago was used as a "station" on the escape route to Canada, and after John Brown's Missouri raid of December, 1858, in which eleven slaves were rescued, Pinkerton met them at Chicago, provided them with a railroad car and $500 which he raised at a meeting by personally taking round the hat, and saw them, "rejoicing at the safety of the Union Jack", across the Canadian border.

Physically he was as Flashman describes him – dour, tough, small but burly, and of nondescript appearance; in his best-known picture, taken during a meeting with Lincoln, he looks like a discontented tramp with a conspicuously clean collar.

George McWatters, of the New York Metropolitan Police, was another Scot, born probably in Kilmarnock about 1814, and brought up in Ulster. He emigrated to the U.S. in the mid-1840s, studied law and collected debts in Philadelphia, took part (unsuccessfully) in the California gold rush, and settled in New York as a theatrical agent, his principal client being Flashman's old paramour, Lola Montez. In 1858 he joined the New York police, and recorded his twelve years' service in a wonderfully self-admiring autobiography which is nonetheless a mine of curious information about the New York underworld of his day. (See J. D. Horan and H. Swiggett, *The Pinkerton Story*, 1952; Allan Pinkerton, *Thirty Years a Detective*, 1884; Mrs Rose Greenhow, *My Imprisonment, and the First Year of Abolition Rule at Washington*, 1863; George S. McWatters, *Knots Untied, or Ways and By-ways in the Hidden Life of American Detectives*, 1873.) [p. 166]

29. Flashman's reaction to the hamburger is what one would have expected. He would not know it by that name; the expression "Hamburg steak" does not seem to have come into use until later in the century. [p. 170]

30. For once we are able to assign a definite date to an incident in the Flashman Papers. Senator Seward, the Republican leader, sailed from New York for Europe on May 7, 1859, on the ocean steamer *Ariel*,

receiving a tumultuous send-off from two Republican committees and three hundred well-wishers "with shouts and music, bells and whistles, dipping ensigns, waving hats, hands, and handkerchiefs". (Frederic Bancroft, *The Life of William H. Seward*, 1900; G. G. Van Deusen, *William Henry Seward*, 1967.) [p. 177]

31. William Henry Seward (1801–72), who had been a school-teacher and lawyer before embarking on a political career, was an implacable enemy of slavery. As Governor of New York he had refused to move against those who rescued slaves, passed laws to hinder the recapture of runaways, and in a memorable speech in 1858 coined the phrase "irrepressible conflict", which "means that the U.S. must and will, sooner or later, become either entirely a slave-holding or entirely a free-labour nation". His nomination as Republican candidate in the 1860 Presidential election was widely taken for granted, and when he visited Europe in 1859 he was received with the attention due to a President-elect: as he had forecast to Flashman, he met the Queen, Lord Palmerston (who had just become Prime Minister for the second time), the Foreign Secretary Lord John Russell, Gladstone, Lord Macaulay, and many other prominent figures. When the Republicans met in Chicago in the following year Seward was still firm favourite, but although he won the first two ballots he was defeated on the third by the comparatively unknown Abraham Lincoln, the "prairie lawyer" as Seward called him. He became Lincoln's Secretary of State and rendered vital service to his country in the Trent Affair of 1861, when the seizure by an American warship of a British vessel carrying Confederate diplomats to Europe caused a crisis which might well have led to war. Three things helped to a peaceful solution: the breakdown of the transatlantic cable made hasty communication impossible; Prince Albert and the Queen moderated the tone of the British Government's demand for the release with apologies of the diplomats, and Seward performed the apparently impossible by climbing down without losing face.

It was a turning-point in American history, for if the U.S. had refused to yield, and war had followed, she could not have hoped to fight Britain and the Confederacy together; the Civil War would have been lost and Southern independence assured. Yet yielding would have outraged the American public, which was jubilant at Britain's discomfiture, and might have weakened Lincoln's government to the point where it could no longer save the Union. That Britain was for once entirely in the right, naturally made the problem no easier. Seward solved it with a reply to the British demand which was a masterpiece of flannel, confused the question brilliantly (he even contended that the diplomats' persons were contraband), managed to suggest that America had won the argument, and concluded by saying that the diplomats would be "cheerfully liberated". He heaped coals of fire on the lion's head by granting free passage across American soil to the British expeditionary force which had been sent to Canada in anticipation of war with the U.S., but had been forced to put in at an American port because the St Lawrence was ice-bound. Seward's other claim to fame is as the purchaser of Alaska in 1867.

Flashman paints a fair picture of the shrewd, egotistical little states-man of whom it was said, justly or not, that he never spoke from conviction. His passion for cigars, and for informal behaviour (one observer described it as "lawless") is well attested; in private he was genial, given to cursing, and to kicking off his shoes. He could not be described as an Anglophile, yet he obviously took entirely for granted what came to be called the "special relationship"; references to the natural "sympathy and affection" between the "European and American branches of the British race" are to be found in his speeches and letters. (See Bancroft, Van Deusen, and S. E. Morison, *Oxford History of the American People*, vol. 2, 1965. William Howard Russell describes an interview with Seward in *My Diary North and South*, 1862.)   [p. 184]

32. The Secret Six were *Dr Samuel Howe*, a devoted freedom fighter who had served in the Greek army against the Turks and aided the Poles against the Russians before becoming a pioneer in the education of the deaf and blind; *Gerrit Smith*, philanthropist, reformer, and Congressman who had run for the governorship of New York; *Theodore Parker*, a leading theological scholar and a tireless and influential abolitionist; *George Stearns*, a Boston businessman who, with Smith, was Brown's principal source of funds; *Thomas Higginson*, a fiery clergyman who became colonel of the first black regiment during the Civil War; and *Franklin Sanborn*, schoolmaster, poet, and author, who was Brown's biographer and most devoted supporter. (See Villard; Oates; Sanborn.)   [p. 188]

33. "Young Stearns", the twelve-year-old son of George L. Stearns, one of the Secret Six, had given all his pocket money to John Brown two years earlier, to help the anti-slavery cause. In return, Brown wrote the boy a remarkable letter, his famous "Autobiography", in which he describes his childhood in picturesque detail mingled with sound moral advice. The "Autobiography", addressed to "My Dear Young Friend" and dated Red Rock, Iowa, 15th July, 1857, was much admired by Brown's supporters as evidence of his warm human quali-ties, but excited the scorn of Brown's fiercest critic, Peebles Wilson, who found it "valuable as an exhibit of his scheming to finance [his] operations". No doubt Brown knew it would impress young Stearns's parents, on whom he depended for funds, but that is not to say that he was being insincere, or was unmoved by the boy's gift. Any-way, it is a fascinating document; simple, homely, naive perhaps, eccentrically punctuated, and quite beautifully written. One would have to be a hardened cynic to be altogether untouched by it, and if, as Wilson suggests, it was written for sordid motives, then Brown, in addition to being a fine English stylist, carried hypocrisy into the realms of high art. (See Peebles Wilson; Villard; Sanborn.)   [p. 206]

34. There are two words to describe John Brown's appearance: grim and formidable. Even allowing for the fact that photography of the time required the sitter to hold his pose for some seconds, which often resulted in a fixed stare, the face that looks out of his pictures is a daunting one; the long Anglo-Saxon head, prominent nose and ears, wide mouth set like a trap, stern certainty of expression, and above all, the level implacable eyes ("piercing blue-grey, flashing with energy or drooping and hooded like an eagle") bring to mind immediately words like Ironside, Yankee, Puritan, and Covenanter. It is, if not handsome (as most of his sons were), an extremely fine face, and it is easy to understand the spell that he seems to have cast over his followers and supporters; equally easy, too, to see why he was called a fanatic. The most impressive portraits show him clean-shaven: the early photograph, taken when he was in his mid-forties, one hand raised in pledge while the other holds the white flag; the imposing Boston portrait of 1858, by J. J. Hawes; the daguerreotype of 1857, in which he looks drawn and tired – quite the least convincing is the full-bearded painting by N. B. Onthank, based on a photo taken in the month when Flashman met him; by the time of his famous raid Brown had trimmed his beard short. Although only five feet nine inches in height, he looked taller, despite the stoop of his later years; he walked slowly, had a deep, metallic voice, normally wore a "serious and patient" expression, and had a fine head of dark brown hair sprinkled with grey. [p. 207]

35. This promise of Brown's explains what would otherwise have been an insoluble mystery: why, in the highly detailed records of the Harper's Ferry raid, and in all the correspondence of John Brown and his associates, is there no mention of "Comber" and Joe Simmons? Plainly, Brown kept his word – as did those American agents and officers who were well aware of the presence in Brown's band, and at the Ferry, of these two additional raiders. [p. 207]

36. Brown visited London in 1849 on a wool-marketing venture which proved a costly failure. He travelled to Yorkshire, and spoke highly of English farming, stone-masonry, and roast beef, but thought the horses inferior to those of the U.S. He had time for a brief trip to the Continent, where he visited Paris, Hamburg, Brussels, and the field of Waterloo. The "poodle hair" story is to be found in his biographies. [p. 210]

37. Undoubtedly Mrs Julia Ward Howe, who two years later became famous as the author of "The Battle Hymn of the Republic". (See Note 3.) [p. 213]

38. This grim joke of Brown's was obviously one he enjoyed repeating; it occurs in a different context in his biographies, as do many of the remarks which Flashman reports from their first meeting at Sanborn's house. Artemus Ward's description of Brown appeared in the *Cleveland Plain Dealer* of March 22, 1859. [p. 215]

39. From the martial hymn, "Lift Up Your Heads, Ye Gates of Brass", by James Montgomery (1771–1854). [p. 216]

388

40. Jerry (Jeremiah Goldsmith) Anderson echoed his words to Flashman in a letter of July 5, 1859: "Their cries for help go out to the universe daily and hourly . . . there are a few who dare to answer this call . . . in a manner that will make this land of liberty and equality shake to the centre." [p. 217]

41. The speaker may have been Henry David Thoreau, the celebrated American writer, who makes the comparison in his "Plea for Captain John Brown" (*A Yankee in Canada*, 1866). Thoreau first met Brown in 1857, and became an immediate admirer, writing of his "rare common sense . . . a man of ideas and principles" and "his pent-up fire". He also coined the description quoted earlier by Flashman: "A volcano with an ordinary chimney flue". [p. 223]

42. The first of Brown's anecdotes is to be found in his own "Autobiography", the second in Villard. [p. 225]

43. It is remarkable that Flashman never mentions "the Senator" by name, and it is possible that he never knew it, but this was Henry Wilson of Massachusetts. The physical description fits, and Senator Wilson described his meeting with Brown at the Bird Club (an abolitionist group who dined regularly at a Boston hotel) when he testified before the Senate Investigating (Mason) Committee after the Harper's Ferry tragedy; his account echoes Flashman's. Whether the warning note reached him or not is unimportant; the date apart, it merely confirmed what he knew already, for he was one of the Republican Senators (Seward being the other) to whom Forbes had disclosed the plot a year earlier. Wilson was a fervent abolitionist, a former farm labourer and shoemaker who became chairman of the Senate Military Affairs Committee during the Civil War. He was one of many leading politicians (President Buchanan and Seward were others) who came under the spell of the magnetic Mrs Greenhow, the Washington hostess who was also a highly successful Confederate spy. When she was arrested by Pinkerton, love-letters signed "H" were found among her papers, but hand-writing experts decided that they were not Wilson's, which in view of his official position was just as well. (See Leech.) [p. 227]

44. Flashman is slightly misquoting Sir Francis Drake's famous dispatch to Walsingham: "There must be a beginning of any great matter, but the continuing unto the end until it be thoroughly finished yields the true glory." [p. 234]

45. Newby's Christian name was Dangerfield, but he may have been known jokingly as "Dangerous". The average age of Brown's followers was twenty-five; only two of them were over thirty, and this has led some commentators into the error of underrating them. In fact, they were a formidable party (in spite of Flashman's occasional disparagements) with no lack of experience of irregular warfare, and the standard of their weapon handling and marksmanship appears to have been high. The ironical nickname "pet lambs", which occurs in "John Brown's Body", speaks for itself. (For a full list of Brown's band, see Appendix III.) [p. 245]

46. Frederick Douglass (1817–95) was born in Maryland, the son of a white father and a Negro-Indian mother. He escaped from slavery in 1838, worked as a stevedore and handyman, and became a lecturer for the Massachusetts Anti-Slavery Society; his success as a speaker and journalist, combined with his fine presence and polished manners, gave rise to the suggestion that he had never been a slave at all, but he refuted this by publishing a detailed autobiography. He was frequently assaulted by pro-slavery supporters, for he went out of his way to fight segregation, and was also in danger from slave-catchers, but purchased his freedom in 1846 with funds raised on a visit to Britain. He published an abolitionist newspaper, *The North Star*, campaigned for women's suffrage, was active in black recruiting during the Civil War, and held the post of marshal of the District of Columbia before becoming U.S. Minister to Haiti. As Flashman says, he was the most famous black man in America; as a campaigner for his people he was to the nineteenth century what Martin Luther King was to the twentieth. [p. 250]

47. The "mutiny", Brown's resignation as leader, and his re-election, took place more or less as Flashman describes. Villard says that "twice at least" there was almost a "revolt" against the plan. Watson Brown's letters to his wife at this time give an interesting indication of the feeling at Kennedy Farm; in them he describes the suicide of a local slave whose wife had been sold, and the murders of five other slaves, and says: "I cannot come home as long as such things are done here," but it seems plain that, like some of his companions, he regarded Harper's Ferry as a death-trap. [p. 257]

48. Francis Meriam, the son of an abolitionist family, had made previous attempts to join Brown, but he was a frail, unbalanced youth, and according to Owen Brown his only qualification was his hatred of slavery. In September, 1859, he heard from a black freedman in Boston, Lewis Hayden, that Brown was short of money, and resolved to contribute part of a recent inheritance to the cause; he arrived at Harper's Ferry on the day before the raid, and was brought to the farm – by Kagi, according to Flashman, by one of Brown's sons, according to Villard. [p. 259]

49. If Flashman's map of Harper's Ferry is primitive and incomplete, it should be remembered that he was drawing it more than half a century later, and relying entirely on his memory of only a small part of the town, observed mostly at night and in a state of some alarm. It was a curious-looking place that he saw in 1859, half-village, half-armoury, standing on its peninsula surrounded by heights, and enclosed along its river banks by the tracks of two railways, the Winchester & Potomac and the Baltimore & Ohio, which ran on trestles and stone embankments designed to prevent flooding; six years later it had been reduced to ruin by nine major Civil War actions fought in the vicinity, and with the old landmarks gone it is not surprising that most historians of the Brown raid have confined themselves to written descriptions, or that Flashman's rough sketch leaves much to be desired.

For example, in the area marked "Town", where he has shown a bare right angle of shops and houses, there were many more buildings behind, as there were between the arsenal and the rifle works; there were also some minor buildings between the Wager House and the armoury railings, close to the tracks, and beside Galt's saloon on the Shenandoah shore. He has forgotten that the arsenal and the large building adjoining (formerly an arsenal, then a storehouse) were within a railed enclosure, and has erred in showing the Shenandoah bridge farther downstream than it actually was. But despite these flaws, his map is accurate enough in its essentials – the relative positions of the Wager House, the armoury gates and engine-house, the arsenal, Galt's saloon, the railway lines, and the forked covered bridge across the Potomac – as I have been able to verify by comparison with the U.S. Government Printing Office maps of 1859, made available to me through the kindness of Jeff Bowers and Kyle McGrogan of the Harpers Ferry National Historical Park. (See GPO publications, "John Brown's Raid" and Harpers Ferry pamphlets of 1981 and 1993; *Frank Leslie's Illustrated Newspaper*, October 29, 1859; Dave Gilbert, *A Walker's Guide to Harper's Ferry*, and photographs and illustrations in Villard and others.) [p. 268]

50. "Old soldier" was a natural mistake on Flashman's part. Colonel Lewis Washington, great-grandnephew of George Washington, behaved with soldierly courage throughout the Harper's Ferry raid, but in fact he held his military title as an aide to the Governor of Virginia. (See Keller.) [p. 281]

51. It was a strange chance that brought two of America's great military heroes together at a time when both were still virtually unknown. Robert Edward Lee (1807–70), a lieutenant-colonel of cavalry with a sound but unremarkable record as a military engineer and superintendent of West Point Military Academy, happened to be in Washington on leave from Texas in October, 1859; James Ewell Brown Stuart (1833–64), a subaltern who had invented a patent device for attaching a sabre to a belt, was waiting in the hope of showing it to the Secretary for War when news came of the Harper's Ferry crisis and he was abruptly despatched to summon Lee to the White House. When Lee was sent to deal with Brown's raid, Stuart accompanied him as aide – a curious beginning to a famous association. Only a few years later, Lee, as commander-in-chief of the Confederate armies, was being hailed by many as the greatest captain since Wellington, a reputation which his surrender to Grant at Appomattox did nothing to diminish, and "Jeb" Stuart's skill and daring had made him the outstanding cavalry general of the U.S. Civil War; Lee called him "the eyes of the army". (See Captain Robert E. Lee, *Recollections and Letters of General Robert E. Lee*, 1904, and works cited in Note 57.)

Flashman, who served on both sides in the Civil War, as a Confederate staff colonel and as a major in the Union forces, with whom he won the Congressional Medal of Honor (mysteries which will no doubt be explained when the relevant packet of his Papers comes to light), seems to have known both men well. That he rode with Stuart is already established (see his interview with President Grant in *Flashman and the Redskins*). He refers to Lee as "my old chief" in the present volume, and in an earlier one (*Flashman*) recalls a conversation which suggests that they were more than official acquaintances. [p. 295]

52. The young woman who intervened on Thompson's behalf was Miss Christina Fouke (not "Foulkes"), sister of the Wager House's proprietor. In a letter to the *St Louis Republican* she explained that she wanted to see the law take its course, and to prevent any outrage in the hotel. [p. 300]

53. Although Flashman did not know it, his order for breakfasts for the raiders and hostages had been filled by the hotel, not without reluctance. The dishes were carried to the armoury by waiters, but Brown, Washington, and another hostage ate nothing, apparently suspecting that the food might have been poisoned. [p. 304]

54. In fact there were eleven hostages in the engine-house, chosen by Brown as being the most important of the thirty-odd whom he had taken prisoner. The remainder were left in the watch-room, which was attached to the engine-house but had no communicating door. [p. 312]

55. In view of Brown's religious upbringing, it is not surprising that he was familiar with the famous last words of Bishop Hugh Latimer, burned at the stake in 1555: "Be of good comfort, Master Ridley, and play the man. We shall this day light such a candle by God's grace in England as shall never be put out." [p. 314]

56. Flashman's memory must be playing him false here. There may have been a lantern in the engine-house during the parley with Captain Sinn, but Brown would hardly have left it burning afterwards to assist the besieging marksmen. Whatever illumination there was probably came from the engine-house stove. [p. 319]

57. J. E. B. Stuart described the parley at the engine-house door in a letter to his mother, and seems to make it clear that this was his only interview with Brown. However, Captain Dangerfield, clerk of the armoury, who was one of the hostages in the engine-house, and gave a detailed account of his experiences to the *Century Magazine*, states that Stuart made an earlier visit to the engine-house during the night with a demand for surrender, and said that he would return at dawn for a reply. Dangerfield's recollections are so convincing – he talked at length with Brown during the night, and gives a vivid description of the fighting and final storming of the engine-house – that it is difficult to know what to make of this discrepancy, unless Dangerfield confused Stuart with Captain Sinn, who as we know called on Brown to surrender during the night. (Sanborn; H. B. McClellan, *Life and Campaigns of J. E. B. Stuart*, 1885; John W. Thomason, *Jeb Stuart*, 1930.) [p. 328]

58. Messervy was right. There was some trade in Harper's Ferry

souvenirs, including fakes of the pikes with which Brown had intended to arm the slaves. [p. 337]

59. "There have been few more dramatic scenes in American history," wrote O. G. Villard of the extraordinary interview with John Brown which took place only a few hours after his capture. It was recorded by a reporter from the *New York Herald*, and the essentials are given in Sanborn. What must strike anyone who reads it is Brown's complete composure and alertness throughout; considering his wounded condition, it was a remarkable performance. Once or twice he gives a sharp retort to an aggressive question, but for the rest he is unfailingly courteous, measured, and even good-humoured. The impression he made on his interrogators was profound, and the report of Governor Wise of Virginia is particularly significant in view of the controversy about Brown's sanity:

> They are mistaken who take Brown to be a madman. He is a bundle of the best nerves I ever saw . . . a man of clear head, of courage, fortitude and simple ingenuousness. He is cool, collected, and indomitable.

Flashman's brief version of the interview corresponds with the *Herald* report, but he differs on small points from *Harper's Weekly*, which says that Brown's hair "was a mass of clotted gore" and that "his speech was frequently interrupted by deep groans, reminding me of the agonised growl of a ferocious beast." [p. 342]

60. Because the Marines had been ordered to wear full dress, Lieutenant Green was carrying only a light ceremonial sword. This almost certainly prevented his killing Brown in the engine-house. [p. 343]

61. Political reaction to the raid was predictable. Stephen Douglas spoke for the Democrats when he called it the inevitable result of Republican policy. The Republican leaders denounced it and disclaimed all responsibility, but could not deny their sympathy with Brown's cause, if not with his methods. Lincoln thought it right that he should hang "even though he agreed with us in thinking slavery wrong. That cannot excuse violence, bloodshed and treason". Seward condemned the raid as a criminal act of sedition and treason, but could pity the raiders "because they acted under delirium". Neither statement did anything to mollify a South furious at the discovery that wealthy and influential Northerners like the Secret Six and others had been Brown's paymasters. For their part, three of the Six took prompt evasive action: Sanborn decamped to Canada, but soon returned and was briefly arrested; Dr Howe and George Stearns followed him and stayed away until after Brown's execution. Of the other three, Theodore Parker was dying in Europe; Thomas Higginson, the most militant of the Six, stayed put and tried, with Sanborn, to organise Brown's escape (see Note 62); Gerrit Smith went temporarily mad and spent six weeks in an asylum. Of all Brown's supporters, Frederick Douglass had most to fear; within hours of the raid a warrant was out for his arrest on charges of murder, treason, and inciting

slave revolt, and he fled to Canada on the day after the raid, and subsequently to Britain. [p. 345]

62. Plotting to rescue Brown began within a few days of his capture. A group who included two of the Six, Higginson and Sanborn, commissioned one of Brown's defence counsel to investigate the possibility of an escape, but Brown himself refused to be party to any such attempt. Allan Pinkerton may also have considered the possibility of a jail-break; his biographer quotes him as follows: "Had it not been for the excessive watchfulness [of Brown's captors] . . . the pages of American history would never have been stained with the record of his execution." [p. 347]